# TARGET: KREE

An explosion rocked the building. Tony Stark grabbed for a chair to brace himself.

Jennifer Walters – She Hulk – moved to assume a defensive position, back-to-back with him. "What's going on?" she asked.

"Something on the roof, from the sound of it." Tony touched his earpiece. "F.R.I.D.A.Y.?"

Ms Marvel ran to the window and looked outside. "I can see energy flashing, down on the pier," she said. "And people. Maybe three or four..."

"F.R.I.D.A.Y., talk to me." Another explosion. "What are we facing? Galactus, the Wrecker? Black Order, maybe?"

"No, boss. I'm afraid it's..."

A shadow fell over the building. Suddenly, Tony knew. His heart sank in his chest plate. No, he thought, anything but that. Don't let it be them. Don't let it be...

"...the Guardians of the Galaxy."

ALSO AVAILABLE

# MARVEL
# CRISIS PROTOCOL

# TARGET: KREE

## STUART MOORE

ACONYTE

FOR MARVEL PUBLISHING

VP Production & Special Projects: Jeff Youngquist
Associate Editor, Special Projects: Caitlin O'Connell
Manager, Licensed Publishing: Jeremy West
VP, Licensed Publishing: Sven Larsen
SVP Print, Sales & Marketing: David Gabriel
Editor in Chief: C B Cebulski

Special Thanks to Tom Brevoort

First published by Aconyte Books in 2021

ISBN 978 1 83908 070 8

Ebook ISBN 978 1 83908 071 5

Cover art by Xteve Abanto

Distributed in North America by Simon & Schuster Inc, New York, USA
Printed in the United States of America
9 8 7 6 5 4 3 2 1

**ACONYTE BOOKS**
*An imprint of Asmodee Entertainment Ltd*
Mercury House, Shipstones Business Centre
North Gate, Nottingham NG7 7FN, UK
*aconytebooks.com // twitter.com/aconytebooks*

# PART ONE

## MISSION CREEP

# CHAPTER 1

The ground shook beneath Gamora's feet. Kree people screamed and scrambled, rushing past her in a massive wave, dodging the falling mining equipment and collapsing structures of the poverty-stricken settlement. Wind whipped through the swirling sky, a slate-gray vortex that swept across the land, threatening to wipe away all life.

The world is ending, Gamora thought. Again.

A fissure opened up, a great crack in the ground that spread from the edge of the spaceport all the way back to the main dome of the Kree settlement. A tall plasteel-jointed oil derrick quivered, toppled, and fell – straight toward a small girl, no more than four years old, who stood frozen in fright.

Gamora, the deadliest woman in the galaxy, felt her heart skip. She lunged for the girl and whipped her out of the way before the derrick crashed to the ground. The girl screamed as Gamora held her close, tumbling and rolling while the earth convulsed in a new series of tremors.

The girl struggled in her arms. "It's OK," Gamora said. "I know. I know how it feels." She thought of her father's face, the last time she'd seen him – her real father, just before the Badoon invaders blasted his head open. With each passing year, she had a little more trouble remembering that face.

"I won't let this happen," she said, releasing the girl. "Not to you. Not to your world, too."

But a tiny voice inside told her: *you can't stop this.*

"Go," she said. "Run to the ships. There's still time!"

The girl stared at Gamora in shock. Then she turned toward the spaceport, the only point of departure from the planet Praeterus: a vast open field with a warehouse-style hangar building in the center. A horde of Kree were converging on the port – most of them on foot, a few riding broken-down, sputtering skycycles. They'd already ripped down the fence surrounding the port.

Still the girl didn't move. Gamora was about to yell at her when a thick brown vine came snaking through the air, wrapped itself around the girl's waist, and lifted her up off the ground. The vine deposited her back down a few feet closer to the spaceport and tapped her lightly on the back. "I am Groot!"

The girl's head whipped around, her eyes widening at the sight of the fifteen-foot-tall sentient tree urging her forward. Then she turned and ran for the spaceport.

Despite the grim situation, Gamora laughed. "That's one way to motivate her," she said.

Groot nodded, scattering a few leaves into the air.

Gamora turned to survey the situation. This settlement was the largest on Praeterus with three barracks buildings surrounding a huge central dome. The dome had originally been built of plasteel and stone, and reinforced over the years as extra rooms and equipment were added to it. It towered over the settlement, an ugly monument to half-measures and neglect.

The outer chambers of the dome, Gamora knew, housed assembly lines for guns, bombs, and any other munitions the

Kree Empire desired. But at the center of the structure, a massive power tap reached down to the core of the planet. Ever since the Kree had settled here, that tap had provided energy for all of Praeterus. Now it might spell the planet's doom.

A group of Kree rushed by, jostling Gamora and Groot. Most of them, she noticed, were pink-skinned, with a few blue faces mixed in. They carried patched-up kit bags and wore faded olive and off-white uniforms or solid green jumpsuits. A far cry from the gleaming battle-suits of the proud Kree army.

The ground cracked and shook, toppling the smaller oil and geothermal derricks surrounding the main dome. Even the rushing air felt stale and humid – Praeterus lacked the weather control machinery of the core Kree worlds. Everything on this planet was ugly, utilitarian, designed for one purpose only: to serve the greater Kree Empire.

"I am Groot," Groot said, pointing a long finger-branch toward the spaceport. In the middle of the field, Drax the Destroyer stood halfway up the steps of a starship gantry, ushering the locals up the walkway into the first of the evacuation ships.

"Yeah," Gamora said, and took off at a sprint, following Groot toward the spaceport. But her heart sank as she surveyed the scene ahead. Three ships – no, four – stood pointed toward the stars, clustered together in the vast empty field. Light transports, she realized, and one bashed-up luxury liner well past its active-duty date. No heavy cruisers, no Plenum-class longships. Not even an ore miner with a large cargo bay.

That, above all else, told Gamora how little the Kree Empire valued the people of Praeterus.

As they reached the first ship, Drax unsheathed one of his deadly knives and swung it in the air. "THIS VESSEL IS FULL!" he cried.

The Kree let out a collective cry of fear. They pressed forward, swarming the gantry stairwell, as the ship's hatch slid shut. Gamora could see more Kree pressed tight inside the viewports, looking out with fear and regret at the people they were leaving behind.

"I said this vessel is at capacity!" In a single motion, Drax kicked the gantry free of the ship and leaped gracefully to the ground. The ship began to rumble as its engines coughed to life. Thick smoke billowed from its base.

The horde on the ground rippled back, startled. They looked around frantically, then scattered in different directions. Gamora ran up to join Drax, watching with Groot as the Kree converged in groups on each of the remaining three ships.

Drax sheathed his knives. "These people," he said, "are not behaving rationally."

"I can see why," Gamora replied. "Those ships can each carry, what? Sixty people? Seventy, max?"

"You underestimate my abilities," Drax said stiffly. "I was able to load seventy-four into that vessel. I could have fit more, had they been smaller in size. Or more easily stackable."

Gamora shook her head. More and more Kree were swarming past the munitions plant into the spaceport. Some of them rode single-tread tractorcars, the kind used in the more remote, rural regions of this world.

"There must be eighty thousand people on this planet," she whispered.

Groot said nothing. At length, Drax let out a low rumble. "I sense the vile hand of *Thanos* in this," he muttered.

"Thanos is dead," Gamora snapped, tapping a comm-button on her shoulder. "Peter? How's it going up there?"

There was a burst of static.

"Peter!" she repeated. "Any good news for us?"

More static, and then the filtered voice of Peter Quill, Star-Lord, came over the comm. "Hey Gam," he said. "I assume you're asking whether we've figured out a way to stop this planet from, uh…"

"Exploding, Quill." That was Rocket's voice. "The word is exploding."

"Yes!" Gamora yelled. "That is exactly what I'm asking. Are you getting anywhere? Is there any chance we can save these people?"

"We're working on it," Quill said.

The tone of his voice was not encouraging.

"Gam? Groot, Drax?" Quill said. "You know we're monitoring you from orbit–"

"We are aware of this," Drax said.

"Yeah, well. You might want to step away from the space vessel that is preparing to lift off."

The ground shook again as the fully loaded Kree ship flared to full power. A blast of smoke hit Gamora. She coughed, blinked, and dropped to the ground. Groot's branch-arm reached for her, but she slapped it away.

"I'm fine," she said, then dissolved into another coughing fit.

The roar of engines filled the air. When the smoke cleared, she saw the Kree vessel climbing toward the unnaturally gray sky. The ship wobbled, moving a bit slowly for a light transport. Seventy-four people was a heavy load for a vessel that size.

"I expect they will reach escape velocity," Drax said, shading his eyes against the rocket-glare. "I am reasonably sure of it. Somewhat sure."

"I am Groot!" Groot called.

They turned to see him pointing at the next vessel, which stood parked on the field near the hangar building. The Kree swarmed over it, up and down the gantry, pouring in through the open hatch. This transport had seen better days. Its hull was pocked with battle-scars and old meteor impacts.

"We had better attend to this," Drax said. "Gamora, will you assist me?"

She started to reply, then a flash of light caught her eye, and she turned back toward the center of the settlement. Something odd was happening to the central dome. A strange glow seemed to emanate from its upper half, an almost fiery luminescence.

"Your frighteningly manic demeanor," Drax continued, "would be of assistance in ensuring an orderly evacuation."

She ignored him. Kree ran past her, dodging fallen geothermal taps and piles of discarded equipment. But now an actual flame burned atop the dome, rising up from it without actually seeming to touch or damage its patched, uneven surface. The overall effect was of a candle being burned – but not, obviously, a normal candle.

"Gamora?"

She whirled around again, eyeing the spaceport. Groot was already on his way toward the grounded ship. More Kree poured onto the field, lugging their packs, desperately seeking refuge aboard the remaining ships. Gamora counted at least a dozen ragged and frightened children among them, clutching their parents' hands.

"Be with you in a minute, Drax," she said, and took off at a sprint toward the dome.

As she charged into the oncoming Kree mob, she remembered the words she'd said to the little girl: *I won't let this happen.* Keeping that vow looked more and more unlikely, as the planet literally crumbled beneath her feet.

But if there was any chance at all, she had to try.

# CHAPTER 2

"What do you know?" Peter Quill said. "They achieved escape velocity."

The small screen set into the dashboard showed a blurry, flickering image of the Kree evacuation ship climbing up out of the atmosphere. Above the screen, a pair of fuzzy dice dangled in front of the ship's main viewport, which opened onto star-flecked space. Quill smiled at the dice, as he always did, and reached up to give them a little nudge.

Behind him, in the rear of the cockpit, Rocket stood grumbling, his little raccoon hands scrabbling and scratching around a hologram that stood taller than him. The only word Quill could make out was "flark" – Rocket's favorite curse – muttered several times in succession.

A shower of sparks from the dashboard made Quill jump. He let out a saltier, Terran equivalent of "flark" and frantically tamped out a few flames. Then he noticed the screen had gone dark. He thumped it hard – most of the instruments on the Guardians' ship responded only to hard thumps – and it came to life again.

But now the screen showed an aerial view of the Kree planet.

Thick emerald-burgundy forest surrounded the settlement, with small towns and individual farms scattered beyond. Quill could just barely make out a flow of Kree bodies, like ants, converging on the dome and the spaceport beyond. Even from this distance, it was obvious the Kree would never all fit into the remaining ships.

"Man," he said aloud, "the Empire does *not* care about this planet."

He twisted a control, zooming in on the dome. Its plasteel surface was pockmarked, weather-beaten and glowing. Whatever was going on, whatever chain reaction threatened the integrity of the planet Praeterus, it was definitely centered in that structure.

Quill straightened in his chair. Time to be the commander, he told himself. The Guardians were a good crew, but sometimes they needed discipline. They needed a good kick in the butt.

They needed Star-Lord.

"We're running out of time, people!" he said, thumbing the commlink open. "Give me options!"

Silence. Even Rocket, still studying that hologram, ignored him.

"There are no bad ideas!" Quill added.

The sound of a deep throat-clearing came over the comm. "In that case," Drax said, "I have a suggestion."

"Go! Yes!" Quill replied.

"If these people were not alive," Drax said, "I could more easily pack and transport them off the planet."

Quill sat for a moment, stunned. "You want to kill the people before you save them?" he asked.

"It would allow the ships to carry more."

He looked over at Rocket, who just shrugged.

"As you know," Drax continued, "I possess two extremely sharp knives. They are ideally designed for–"

"OK!" Quill said. "There's *one* bad idea!"

"Oh," Drax said. He sounded vaguely hurt.

A low, snarling chuckle made Quill turn in his chair. "That's what you get for askin'," Rocket said, smirking.

"I didn't hear you make any useful suggestions." Quill jumped out of his seat and stalked toward the anthropomorphic raccoon. "Man, I hate these pro bono jobs. 'Help, help, my planet's exploding!' The Kree Empire better cough up some kind of reward for us saving their people's lives."

"Yeah, that'll happen," Rocket replied. "'Cause they're the giving kind."

Quill moved to look over the raccoonoid's shoulder. The hologram showed overlapping wavefronts of energy, rising in a waterspout formation from a schematic of Praeterus's central dome. Strands of light flickered and wove in and out, growing thicker and stronger with every second.

"You figure this out yet?" Quill asked.

Rocket reached out with a metal pointer, touching a schematic of machinery at the center of the dome. "This is the main power tap," he said, "which the Kree use, in less catastrophic times, to pull as much power as possible from the core of the planet."

"Uh-huh..."

"And this..." Rocket swept his pointer up to indicate the pulsing energy lines, "...is an exponentially multiplying gamma curve. Whatever's causin' this chain reaction, it's centered right there."

Quill peered at the image. "So the tap is what's making the planet go..." He pulled back and mimed an explosion with his hands.

"I ain't a geological engineer. But I don't see how." Rocket's eyes followed the energy as it flowed up from the tap. "That tap powers the Kree settlement, but it's not nearly strong enough to destabilize the planet's core. There's gotta be something else at work here, something that's messing with the laws of thermodynamics pretty badly."

Quill frowned. "Is the Kree government doing this deliberately? Maybe as a test of some weapon or something?"

"Dude, the Kree are homicidal warmongers who'd slit your cat's throat as soon as look at you. But even they don't go around blowin' up their own planets." Rocket shrugged. "Usually."

"Don't you have…" Quill gestured in the air. "I dunno, maybe, a big gun that could stop it?"

"A gun?"

"Yeah, you know. A gun! You always got a lot of… of guns?"

"A gun. Yeah." Rocket turned back to the holo. "Why didn't I think of that? A gamma explosion strong enough to take out a solar system – just fire a flarking gun at it. ARE YOU AN IDIOT?"

"Now you're just being… no bad ideas, remember?"

Quill turned away, his eyes wide. Focus, he thought. You're Star-Lord. You've got to *be* Star-Lord. Your people, the inhabitants of that poor planet… they're all depending on you.

"You know what our problem is?" he asked.

Rocket gestured at the energy strands, which looked thicker and angrier than ever. "Impending planetary extinction?" he offered.

"Mission creep."

The raccoonoid's eyes narrowed. "What did you call me?"

"What? No no – not you. *Mission* creep."

"I don't have to take that." Rocket flung his metal pointer to the floor with a sharp clang. "I might not be the prettiest creature in this sector. I know I ain't the Deadliest Woman in the Galaxy or Mister Muscles with the sharp scary knives. But nobody calls me a creep. Not even you."

"Dude! It's an Earth term." Quill crouched down before the hologram, placing himself at Rocket's level. "A Terran term. It means we're trying to do too many things at once. Stop the explosion *and* evacuate the planet. We're dividing our efforts."

"Huh. You know, that actually makes sense." Rocket stared at Quill as if the Earthman had done something totally unexpected, like sprouting wings or breathing underwater.

Quill pointed at the hologram. "How long do we have?"

"I ain't no physicist either. But I'd say minutes. Half hour at most."

"Which means…"

"Yeah. Stopping the explosion probably ain't gonna happen."

"Then we've gotta concentrate on the evacuation." He slapped the comm button on his collar. "Gam, listen. We're running out of time. Just get as many of those people off-planet as you can and get out of there. We're coming to pick you up."

Silence.

"Gam? Gamora?" He crossed back to the dashboard and began flipping switches. "She's not answering."

He turned to the small viewscreen. Out on the spaceport, a second evacuation ship prepared to take off, dark smoke rumbling all around it. The tide of refugees formed two streams, one heading toward each of the remaining evac ships. There were so many refugees, Quill could barely see the ground.

"Gam?" he repeated. He couldn't make her out in the tide of green and white uniforms. "Agh! I can't find her."

"Is that all you want?" Rocket brushed past him, reaching for the copilot's controls. "I planted a camera on her before the mission started."

"You planted a ..."

"Just a sec." As Rocket fiddled with the controls, the small screen blurred to static. "Interference from all this gamma schmutz ..."

"Did you ..." Quill frowned. "Did you plant a camera on *me*?"

"That's, you know, that's a real good question. Hey, I got one for you. Why do people ask things when they know they won't like the answer?"

Quill peered at the screen. Shapes began to take form... people, running...

Rocket held up both freakishly human-like hands in triumph. "Voy-lay!"

"For the eightieth time, it's pronounced '*wah-lah*'..."

The screen shifted again, resolving into Gamora's point of view. Hordes of Kree, rushing past in a panic. A huge chunk of mining equipment crashed to the ground, shaking the image.

"It looks like she's running..." He frowned. "Against the stream of Kree. Away from the spaceport."

"Yeah. And look what she's running toward."

The image tipped up, revealing the pockmarked dome at the center of the settlement. It glowed brighter than before, towering four stories high above the chaos.

"The dome. The power tap." Quill hissed in a breath. "She's gonna try and stop the reaction."

"I never bet against that lady." Rocket made a matching hiss, eerily similar in pitch to Quill's. "But I don't think a sword is gonna do any better than a gun here."

The dome loomed larger as Gamora drew close to its tall,

central entrance. A few panicked Kree slipped out the door, lugging travel bags over their shoulders.

"Mission creep," Quill whispered.

"That creep is gonna get her killed." Rocket strapped himself in. "We gotta get down there."

"Roger," Quill agreed. He reached up, gave the fuzzy dice a good slap, and flicked a built-in cassette player to life. "Let's hit it." Thruster rockets roared to life; gravity compensators kicked in hard. And as the little ship tipped its nose down, speeding into the atmosphere, the falsetto tones of Journey's *Greatest Hits* filled the cockpit like a battle anthem.

# CHAPTER 3

Gamora ripped the heavy plasteel door off the dome with one savage yank. The old rusty hinges snapped like twigs – another sign that the Kree had neglected Praeterus for a long time.

Peter's voice was chattering in her ear. Something about a pickup, about running out of time. She slapped her comm, switching it off.

Inside, a long corridor with moss-colored stone walls stretched straight ahead, ending in another plasteel security door. Lockers lined the walls, many of them left open, abandoned. The workers had fled this facility in a hurry.

Gamora tensed and started forward, just as a robot dropped down from the ceiling, blocking her way.

"HALT," it said.

She snarled, studying the thing. It was a miniature Sentry, the standard Kree design with thick limbs, reinforced torso armor, and a headpiece that bizarrely resembled a mushroom. Battle Sentries towered twenty, sometimes thirty feet high; this model was human-sized, intended only for light guard work.

"ONLY – KREE – ALLOWED IN – THIS FACILITY," the robot said. "COMMENCING – ID SCAN."

A large blinking light on its chest began to strobe from red to green and back again. Gamora rolled her eyes and placed a hand on her sword.

"SCANNING," the robot continued. "WHEN WE ARE – FINISHED   WOULD YOU BE WILLING TO TAKE A – SHORT SURVEY ON MY – PERFORMANCE?"

She was considering several choice replies when the robot's chest-light settled down to a deep, glowing red. "SCAN – FAILURE. ANALYSIS: ALIEN – MOST LIKELY SKRULL. PLEASE – REMAIN STILL WHILE – SECURITY FORCES ARE *AWWWWWK.*"

Her sword slashed into the robot's stomach, knocking the thing backward in a shower of sparks. It sputtered, said something that might have been "SKRULL TRICKEREEEEEY," and then fell to the floor, shattering its eye-lens on the bare stone. Gamora stabbed it a few more times for good measure. Its limbs spasmed, then went still.

"Don't call me a Skrull," she said.

She walked past it, beginning to holster her sword. Then she stopped and looked down. The light on the Sentry's chest was blinking again, red-green green-red.

She crouched down, raised her sword, and sliced into the robot's chest. Then she sawed the sword up and down in an even, rectangular pattern around the blinking light. When the mechanism came loose, she reached down, yanked the Kree detector free, and held it up to the dim light.

"Rocket's birthday is coming up," she said, and tucked the thing into her pack.

She didn't really know when Rocket's birthday was. No one did; he'd been created in a laboratory. But he loved gadgets, especially stolen ones.

She continued down the corridor, staying quiet and alert for further security measures. But the facility seemed deserted. She forced open a door and found herself in a longer, narrower corridor, with no doors or windows along its walls. Up ahead, she could see yet another door – and this one was glowing slightly.

A tremor struck, shaking the hard stone beneath her feet. She picked up speed, sprinting toward the glowing door. Her path was taking her to the center of the dome, which doubled as a munitions factory and power plant. According to Rocket's scans, the source of the planet's instability could be found there.

But what, she wondered, was really happening? Was someone deliberately trying to blow up this sad, hopeless planet on the edge of Kree space? Or was it all just some terrible, random accident?

She thought of the little girl up on the surface. Where was that girl now? Safely aboard one of the evacuation ships, or trampled beneath the boots of her fellow Kree? For that matter, were the ships even spaceworthy? Were they leaving now, engines straining to clear the atmosphere of this doomed world? Or had they already sputtered, failed, and caught fire on the launch pads?

As she reached the glowing door, a wave of despair washed over her, a feeling of utter helplessness. As if this mission, this crisis, were so far beyond her abilities, there was no point in going on.

But Gamora had learned, at the lash of Thanos, to keep fighting until all hope was gone. So she wrenched open the door and stopped short at the sight beyond.

She entered a high-ceilinged chamber filled with machines. Matter replicators and huge computers led to creaky conveyor belts, only a few of them still in motion. Partially assembled laser rifles and photon cannons were everywhere, stacked haphazardly in piles and stuffed into crates. The curve of the domed roof could be seen above, arcing down at an angle.

This was the main assembly line for the munitions factory. The place where the Kree of Praeterus had sweated and toiled, while their merciless rulers sat a thousand light-years away drinking wine from the skulls of conquered peoples.

And a few of those workers – a few Praeterans – were still here.

They turned toward Gamora, regarding her with dull, resigned expressions. A middle-aged woman in a wheelchair, seated at a conveyor-belt control panel. An old man on crutches, bracing himself against a crate of rifles. A blue man with three prosthetic limbs – one of the few blue-skinned Kree she'd seen on Praeterus.

"What…" Gamora paused, shaking her head. "What are you all still doing here?"

The wheelchair-bound woman clucked her tongue and pressed a control button. The conveyor belt wheezed briefly to life, depositing a single proton rifle in a hopper basket.

"Where's there to go?" she asked.

"After the war," the blue man said, "I came here. Wanted to retire, just be with my family." He sighed. "But they never let you retire."

"The Empire took everything from us," the woman said. "Soon it will take our lives."

"Unless…" the old man hobbled his way toward Gamora, hope lighting up his eyes. "Did they send you? The Empire?"

Gamora grimaced, avoiding the man's gaze. Beyond the conveyor belts, past rows of machinery, the far wall was glowing. The source of the reaction, whatever it was, lay on the other side of that wall, in the very center of the dome.

She started to answer the man, but the words caught in her throat as she noticed a fourth Kree. A young woman with withered arms and legs sat in a permanent chair-station. A hundred or more glowing cables stretched from implants in her dull green helmet into the surrounding computers. Her eyes flicked from side to side, wholly focused on the glowing screen before her.

She doesn't even know I'm here, Gamora realized. All these people – they're veterans. Casualties of the Kree-Skrull War, of a thousand other campaigns their Empire has waged. Cannon fodder, living shells spent on the battlefield and dumped here to die.

They're already dead, she thought. Whatever happens to this world, their lives ended long ago.

She felt a stab of pity, followed by a rush of anger and regret. These were pointless emotions. If she'd learned anything in life since her escape from Thanos, it was to keep moving forward.

With an obvious effort, the old man staggered up to her and placed a hand on her shoulder. "Are you here to save us?" he asked.

On the far wall, the glow pulsed brighter.

"No," she said, and pushed him gently aside.

She sprinted toward the far wall – dodging machinery, leaping over heaps of weapons. The eyes of the Kree workers followed her, but she ignored them. There was no time to comfort these people, no time for mercy. Any possible salvation for them lay beyond that wall.

The wall was thick wood, reinforced with plasteel crossbars. Energy seeped through the seams, leaking out from the chamber beyond. Gamora scanned for a door, but there was no way through. Just a ladder leading up to a high, dark alcove.

She leaped up and grabbed hold of the ladder. As she climbed, spiderlike, three rungs at a time, she thought of the Kree rulers a hundred star-systems away. They live for war, she mused; they made that decision a long time ago. Did *I* make a decision, to become... this? To be an assassin, or a Guardian of the Galaxy?

She couldn't remember.

The ladder ended at a narrow metal catwalk. She scrambled up onto it and stared down into Hell.

The catwalk looked down on a complex of machinery. She recognized a few standard-issue power accumulators, the type used in sublight engines on older starships. At the center, she knew, was the power tap leading down into the planet's core. But that equipment was lost in the blinding light that filled the chamber, radiating up and out like a star.

She shielded her eyes, squinting into the light. Thick liquid spurted up in geysers, wrenched from the molten core of Praeterus, flashing into view at the edge of the glow and evaporating in the unimaginable heat of the chamber. As she watched, that glow seemed to transform into a living flame, an unnatural fire consuming everything in its path. A fire that would soon reduce this world to ash and dust.

And at its center, barely visible within the white-hot brilliance, she could just barely make out a human figure. It raised its arms to summon the power, drawing the energies into its small, frail form.

Heat and radiation burned into Gamora, raising a hot rage inside her. Who was this? How dare they take the lives of so many people, so quickly, so thoughtlessly? What dark power commanded them, what monstrous master?

And what power had brought Gamora here, at this exact moment, to bear witness to this horror?

It didn't matter, she realized. She was what she was: a Guardian. She might not be able to stop this force, whatever it was. She would probably perish here, with the remaining citizens of Praeterus. With people who, like her, had never had the luxury to choose their fates.

But she had to try.

The energy surged brighter, obscuring the figure within, shaking the catwalk beneath Gamora's feet. She tensed and scrambled up onto the railing. She reached down to her waist and drew her sword, feeling its hard, comforting hasp in her clenched fist.

Then she let out a cry and jumped.

The fire, the radiation, stabbed into her like a thousand tiny knives. The figure turned to look up in surprise – and as it did, the rage burned again within Gamora. It's *their* rage, she realized, not mine. A hatred that could snuff out the stars; could reduce worlds, whole galaxies, even universes to smoldering embers.

Gamora landed in a crouch, shielding her eyes from the blinding glow. She raised her sword, knowing it was useless, that even the deadliest woman in the galaxy was no match for this elemental power.

The figure turned to face her, and for just a moment she saw its face.

But before she could strike, the unearthly fire washed over her one last time and she screamed in agony. As her mind shut down, she saw her father again, and winced at the look on his face as he prepared to die. Then that face exploded into atoms, and Gamora saw nothing at all.

# CHAPTER 4

Winds howled and roared. Tectonic plates shifted and clashed, ripping open fissures across the planet's surface. Long-dormant volcanoes roared to life, covering land and sea alike with the blood-lava of a dying world.

The planet called Praeterus had only minutes left to live.

A hundred miles above, the Guardians' ship screamed downward. Peter Quill peered forward, studying the planet through the front viewport. From this altitude, he could make out the small, primitive towns surrounding the munitions installation – clusters of tents, small wooden buildings. A sea of people flowed out of them, toward the spaceport miles away. The remaining Kree of Praeterus: eighty thousand souls, all dressed in simple beige and green garb, hoping against hope that they might secure one of the precious seats on the evacuation ships.

"Those poor bastards," Quill hissed. He frowned, reached up, and clicked the music off. "Hold on. What's Gam doing?"

On the screen, the Guardian's body cam showed a bright glow with a human figure at the center of it. The figure's features were obscured, but it wavered and wobbled with Gamora's every move.

Rocket unstrapped himself and leaned over to look. "I ain't sure…"

"She's looking down on that glowy thing, whatever it is. Right?"

"I think so." Rocket frowned. "She was climbin' a ladder before."

"Now it looks like she's leaning over… oh. Oh no. Don't do it, Gam."

"Oh, man. She's gonna jump!"

"I can see that!" Quill yelled. "I can see she's gonna jump!"

"Don't get excited." The raccoonoid cocked his head. "Hey, whadda you think are her chances of survival?"

"Not… not good."

"No, I mean numerically. You wanna put some money on it?"

Before Quill could come up with a suitably horrified response, the ship screeched and shuddered to a stop in midair. Rocket tumbled back into his chair.

"What was that?" Quill asked.

"Ah." Rocket consulted some instruments. "We just hit the Kármán Line."

"What? What the hell is that?"

"The Kármán Line! You know, suborbital altitude? The place where satellites spin and dreams are made? The ship auto-stopped when we got to sixty miles up."

"I don't… Why do I care about…" Quill trailed off as, on the little screen, Gamora's bodycam flashed pure white and went blank. For a moment, he couldn't breathe. No, he thought. Gam…!

"You see that?" he yelled, turning to address Rocket directly. "Get us moving! We gotta get down there!"

"Dude." Rocket looked at him like he was an idiot. "You don't want to go below the Kármán Line."

"*Why not?*"

"'Cause it's the Kármán Line! It's like an unwritten rule." Rocket gestured out the viewport. From this height, glowing cracks could be seen spreading across the planet's surface. "The Kármán Line, right? When a planet is gaspin' its last, about to blow moon-sized chunks of dirt and water into space, you never go below the Kármán Line!"

"I will give you ten thousand credits to stop saying KÁRMÁN LINE–"

"Human?" a voice said over the comms. "Laboratory-bred raccoon? Can you hear me?"

Rocket rolled his eyes. "Hey, Drax."

"I wish to inform you that this planet may be becoming unstable."

Quill stared out the window. Storm clouds were swirling, making it harder to see the ground. He could just see two escape ships still standing in the spaceport. As he watched, the ground split open beside one of the barracks buildings, swallowing a group of screaming refugees.

"Unstable," he repeated, keeping his voice flat. "Copy that."

"Valuable intel," Rocket added.

"Yes," Drax replied, "and I believe the sinister mind of *Thanos* is behind it all."

Rocket laughed. "Thanos is dead, you musclehead."

Quill panned the screen image over to the munitions dome, still standing in a tangle of human and mechanical wreckage. Fissures fanned out all around the dome, but it glowed brighter than ever, its light piercing the cloud cover.

There, Quill thought. That's where Gamora went.

He stood up, thumbing a button on his neck. His faceplate snapped down over his head, telescopic night-vision goggles covering his eyes. He pulled his element gun free of its holster, twirling it once on his finger.

"You're goin' down there?" Rocket asked.

"Yup." Quill turned and strode toward the airlock. "It's better'n arguing with you about the Carlin Line."

"That's Kárm… ah, never mind. Hey, Quill?"

"Yeah?"

"Go get our girl."

Quill turned, shot Rocket a semi-ironic salute, and opened the airlock hatch. Thirty seconds of decompression later, he shot out of the ship into a dust-clouded sky. Here in the lower ionosphere, the air was thin but raging; torrential winds buffeted him back and forth. He turned downward and blasted his jets, arrowing toward the planet below.

The clouds closed in, obscuring his view. He sent out a radar ping, but no airborne objects appeared on his optic display. No flying Sentries, no omnicannons. The Kree hadn't even cared enough about Praeterus to leave a suborbital dronecam behind.

The clouds parted, giving him a clear view of the scene below. In the spaceport, Groot had formed a thickly woven vine-fence, walling off one of the rescue ships from the approaching Kree horde. The ship smoked and rumbled, its engines warming up for takeoff. The Kree clawed at the Groot-barrier, climbing desperately, struggling to reach the ship. Drax sat on Groot's elongated shoulders, swatting people down as they reached the top.

Quill clicked his comms on to passive mode.

"Retreat!" Drax yelled to the crowd. "This vessel is full. Your certain doom will not be averted by this action!"

Good old Drax – no bedside manner to speak of. The horde retreated, looked around, and took off running toward the last remaining ship, a distinctive model with luxury-style fins that had been in fashion a few centuries ago.

And all around, hundreds… no, thousands more Kree were flowing into the settlement to join the refugees. Quill grimaced. At best, eighty or ninety people might fit on that last evac ship. And that was *if* they didn't trample it, hyperdrive engines and all, under their panicked rampage.

He shook his head and veered toward the dome. It glowed like an incandescent bulb, stone and plasteel crackling and rippling. Something, some massive source of heat and radiation, was bubbling up from inside, rising inexorably to the surface.

And Gamora was trapped in there with it.

He swung around the dome in a circle and whipped out his element gun. The weapon, unique in all the universe, could project energy in any of the four basic elements. Fire, earth, air…

…or water.

An ice-cold stream shot forth, sizzling and spattering against the top of the dome. A thin plasteel plate, patched between the original stones, let out a high whine and cracked wide open. Quill grinned and let out a whoop of triumph. "Thermodynamics," he screamed. "Thermodynamics, BAY-BEE!"

Bracing himself, he held up his arms before him and flew down into the dome. Fire rose up all around him, heat and radiation at levels he'd never seen before. A creeping sensation stole up his neck, a primal fear of some kind. This wasn't a normal fire – not even the searing heat of a planet's molten core. There was something else at work here, something distinctly unnatural.

He dropped down into a large open chamber, forcing his fear away. Red-glowing shards of molten machinery – power absorption rigs and small computers – littered the floor. And in the center of it all, the fire raged. An inferno so bright that, even with his protective goggles, he had to shield his eyes.

Was Gamora here? He could barely see anything. He raised his gun and swept it around in a wide arc, firing short bursts of air to force the flames away. There – on the far side of the room – a slim blur of green and violet, lying on the floor.

"Gam!"

She wasn't moving. Heart racing, he arced through the air in a quick leap, narrowly avoiding the glowing fire rising up from the core tap. He crouched down next to her, wincing at the third-degree burns blistering her arms and shoulders. Her sword lay chipped and cracked on the floor.

"Gam," he said, touching her cheek. "Oh Gam, don't die. Please don't be dead."

Her eyes snapped open. She rolled aside, almost too fast to see. Before he knew what was happening, she was propped up on one elbow with her sword in her other hand, the tip of the blade touching his neck just below the Adam's apple.

He smiled, eyeing the sword blade nervously and blinking away tears. "Y'rrg gglive," he managed.

She shook her head, coming fully awake for the first time. "Peter," she said.

He raised a finger cautiously and nudged the blade away from his throat. Gamora hissed instinctively, and Quill felt a moment of doubt. Even after all this time – the tender moments they'd shared, the battles they'd fought together – he still wasn't sure how she felt about him. The adopted daughter of Thanos didn't give her heart away easily.

She winced. "Can't feel... left leg."

"It's OK," he replied. "I got you."

"Peter..." She waved an arm toward the glowing energies, wincing with the effort. "Evil... inside. It... it burns..."

"Burns? Yeah, that's for sure!" He lifted her gently by the waist, taking her limp form in his arms. "Take it easy – I'll get you back to the ship. Maybe you could holster that blade? It's crazy sharp."

"Ship." She shook her head; she seemed dazed. "Ship…"

"It's hovering up around the Kármán Li… you know, never mind that. Just go limp, let me take you."

"Last time someone said that to me…" She smiled, grimacing in pain. "I sliced his gut open."

"I get that! But cutting me wouldn't be in your best interest right now, would it?"

The energy flared, grazing Quill's side. He winced, hefting Gamora in his arms, and took off into the air. He skirted the blinding energy, hugging the top of the dome as he zigzagged toward the hole.

"Hang on!" he said.

They shot through the gap and into the air. Behind them, the fiery energy surged up, flaring high enough to singe Quill's boots as he climbed into the sky. Gamora slowed him down, but only slightly.

"Oh, Peter," she said, staring down. "All those people."

He turned briefly to look. The sea of people had become an ocean, desperate souls trampling each other in a final march through the settlement. They climbed over fallen equipment, knocked down tents in their haste. All desperate to reach the spaceport, the one final ship that couldn't possibly hold them all.

"I know," he said.

The ground looked like it had been shredded by a giant cheese grater. Glowing fissures leaked energy, seeping out from the planet's core. A rusty oil derrick toppled and fell into a crevice, disappearing from sight.

"I tried," Gamora gasped. "Couldn't save them."

"I know." Quill climbed higher, keeping a tight grip on her. "I know you did."

Beneath them, the dome let out a groan and crumbled inward. The blinding energy glow flared up into the air. Quill caught a quick glimpse of Drax and Groot, trying desperately to maintain order as they hustled people onto the final ship. Screams of help, of panic, rose up and vanished in the air.

"Empire… took everything," Gamora said. "Took everything from them."

"We can't save them," Quill said. "I'm sorry."

To his surprise – shock, even – Gamora rested her head on his shoulder. She'd never done that before. He moved his arm around her shoulder and turned his attention to the sky above.

She's right, he thought. We've failed. We can't save them. That failure would weigh on all of them in the weeks to come: Groot, Rocket, Quill, even Drax. But he knew that, under her tough exterior, Gamora would take it hardest of all.

"I'm so sorry," he said.

# CHAPTER 5

"ATTENTION PINK AND OCCASIONALLY BLUE HUMANOIDS! I AM KNOWN AS DRAX THE DESTROYER. CONTRARY TO MY NAME, I HAVE BEEN SENT TO THIS HEAP OF RAPIDLY CRUMBLING ROCK AND WATER TO SAVE YOUR LIVES. IT IS IMPERATIVE THAT YOU LISTEN TO ME, BECAUSE–

"NO! NO NO NO, YOU CANNOT DO THAT! STAY OFF THE GANTRY WHILE I SPEAK! THIS IS IMPORTANT. YES, I AM TALKING TO YOU, GUY WITH MOHAWK HAIRCUT!

"AS I SAY, MY ADMITTEDLY OFFPUTTING FRIENDS AND I HAVE COME TO THIS WORLD TO SAVE YOUR LIVES. HOWEVER, BY NOW YOU MUST REALIZE THIS IS IMPOSSIBLE. THERE ARE FAR TOO MANY OF YOU AND TOO FEW BERTHS LEFT ON THIS FINAL EVACUATION VESSEL. WHICH, I ADMIT, IS A MOST UNLIKELY RESCUE SHIP. I BELIEVE IT BELONGED TO A RETIRED SHI'AR ADMIRAL, WHO USED IT FOR PLEASURE JAUNTS TO WITNESS THE EXPLOSION OF SUPERNOVAS. LIKE MANY DENEBIAN LUXURY YACHTS, IT SPORTS OSTENTATIOUS FINS THAT, TO MY EYE, RUIN THE LINE OF THE HULL.

"WHAT? YES, THE SHI'AR DO TREAT THEIR RETIRED MILITARY FAR BETTER THAN YOUR EMPIRE DOES. THAT IS BUT ONE OF

35

MANY INJUSTICES WHICH I AM POWERLESS TO CORRECT. AS MY CAPTAIN WOULD SAY, IT IS 'ABOVE MY PAY GRADE.'

"PLEASE STAY IN LINE! YOU MUST BOARD THE SHIP IN AN ORDERLY MANNER AND ALLOW MY FRIEND, THE DISQUIETINGLY AMBULATORY TREE, TO USHER YOU TO YOUR ASSIGNED SEATS. DO NOT LOOK AT ME THAT WAY, MISSY. I HAVE TWO VERY LARGE KNIVES AND I AM WELL TRAINED IN THEIR USE.

"TO CONTINUE: ONCE AGAIN, THE GREAT PROBABILITY IS THAT THIS WORLD IS DOOMED AND MOST OF YOU ALONG WITH IT. ANOTHER OF MY FRIENDS, A DISTURBINGLY HOMICIDAL GREEN WOMAN, HAS BEEN TRYING TO SOLVE THAT PROBLEM. HOWEVER, I JUST WITNESSED HER LIMP FORM BEING HOISTED UP INTO THE SKY BY THE AFOREMENTIONED CAPTAIN. SO I ASSUME ALL HOPE IS NOW LOST.

"HEY! THAT IS NO REASON TO PANIC! WELL, ACTUALLY, I SUPPOSE IT IS. BUT I ORDER YOU NOT TO PANIC ANYWAY! KNIVES, REMEMBER?

"NO NO NO – DO NOT CROWD THE GANTRY. LIKE EVERYTHING ELSE ON THIS PLANET, IT IS OLD AND WEAK AND BEGINNING TO BUCKLE IN THE WINDY DEATH-THROES OF THIS WORLD. ONLY THREE PEOPLE ON THE GANTRY AT A TIME, AND PLEASE PRACTICE SOCIAL DISTANCING. THREE PEOPLE AT A TIME. *THREE PEOPLE–*"

Drax whirled as a group of young Kree men, in faded green jumpsuits, leaped for the ship all at once. When they landed on the gantry, its rusty framework creaked and groaned. One of the men, the "Guy with Mohawk", turned, smirked, and pointed his elbow down at Drax – a Kree gesture of unparalleled rudeness and disrespect.

"Groot!" Drax called.

Groot stuck his head out of the ship's hatch just as the gantry supports snapped, sending the Kree already in the boarding line tumbling toward the ground. Groot rolled his eyes and shot out four limbs at once, extending them to several times their normal length, and snatched the Kree out of the air.

The ground shook again, filling the air with an apocalyptic rumbling noise. Drax turned to see the dome in the center of the settlement crack open in a paroxysm of fire. Energy shot out of it into the air, like a fountain of coruscating light.

The Kree let out a cry of panic and surged toward the ship, moving like a single organism. They screamed, held up babies, begged for salvation. Drax waved his battle-knives in the air, but the crowd ignored him. They surrounded the former luxury craft, massing around its base – but with the gantry collapsed, there was no way to reach the elevated hatch.

"STEP BACK!" DRAX HOWLED, "YOU CANNOT ALL FIT ON THE SHIP. THERE IS ONLY ROOM FOR ... UH ..."

Groot stuck his head inside the ship, then turned to look down at Drax. He shrugged helplessly and held up a single twig-finger. Then, grimacing, he held up two.

"THERE IS ONLY ROOM FOR—"

"For us, sonny. At least, there better be."

Drax cast his gaze down, raising his knives. An old man in a formal uniform stood before him, holding a tiny old Kree woman's hand. They both carried travel bags. Unlike the majority of Kree filling the spaceport, these two had deep blue skin.

"I do not understand," Drax said, lowering his voice. "There are only two spaces left on the evacuation ship. They belong to me and my arboreal friend."

"Is that what your daddy taught you?" the old man demanded, his withered chin set. "Cut and run, save your own butt? Leave others to die?"

"I do not remember what my daddy taught me. My memories were wiped and altered by Kronos, who recreated me as a weapon against the Mad Titan Thanos." Drax paused and looked up as a chunk of debris from the dome flew by overhead. "Thanos," he rumbled. "His stink is all over this."

The old woman frowned at her husband. "I thought Thanos was dead."

All around them, the masses of people milled and shouted, struggling to board the ship. The old man ignored them, jabbing a finger into Drax's bare chest. "Listen here, tattoo boy. I don't care about myself–"

"In my experience," Drax said, "people who say that generally care a great deal about themselves."

"–but my beloved Ann-ya here has had a rough life. I promised to protect her five decades ago, and that's what I'm gonna do. Our two grandkids already got on the last ship, but we got lost in the crowd." He paused, out of breath. "So what do you say? You gonna be a hero, or a chicken-man?"

Drax stared at the man for a moment. The wind grew stronger, the rumbling of the planet's crust louder.

Groot yelled something that was lost in the wind. It was probably either "I am Groot" or "These idiots are about to knock the ship over."

Drax let out a lusty burst of laughter, startling the two elderly Kree. As they took a step back, he reached out and grabbed the old man by the arm.

"You," Drax growled, "are far smaller than I."

The old man swallowed and nodded.

"And you–" Drax turned to glare at the old woman, "–are smaller still."

She looked up defiantly, saying nothing.

"Your combined weight approximates my own," Drax continued. "Perhaps exceeds it slightly."

"Are, uh…" The old man peered up at Drax. "Are you gonna kill us?"

Drax laughed again, a bone-chilling sound. Then he reached out, picked up the old man, and hurled him into the air. At the hatch of the luxury liner, a startled Groot turned just in time to catch the man, swing him around, and hurl him inside the ship.

"You next, tiny Kree lady," Drax said. He reached out his arms.

The old woman hesitated. Her eyes, set deep within wrinkled blue skin, looked at him with something that might have been either gratitude or resentment. Maybe a touch of both.

"Thank you," she said. "Thank you for *whoaaaahh!*"

Then she too was flying through the air, her travel bag flailing in the wind. Groot caught her and placed her down on the narrow gantry platform outside the hatch. Then he stopped, hesitated, and looked down at Drax.

"I am…?" Groot asked, gesturing toward the ship.

Drax grimaced at him. "Go."

"But I am—"

"I said go!" Then he smiled sadly. "It has been an honor to know you…"

For the record, his parting words were "…ambulatory vegetable of the tiny vocabulary." But they were drowned out by the roar of the one-time luxury liner's engines surging to life. Those engines, Drax noticed with disdain, were louder than the other ships' had been. Retired Shi'ar admirals were notorious showoffs.

Groot cast a sad glance down at Drax, then slammed the hatch shut. The ship smoked, rumbled, and began to rise. As it lifted off the ground, Groot stretched out his arms and legs, wrapping his body across the outside hull. Branches stretched out and wove together, snaking around the ship's fins, forming a tight latticework to fasten Groot's organic form tightly around the entire vessel.

Drax watched as the ship rose, struggling under the weight of several dozen refugees, and climbed toward the raging clouds. How noble of Groot, he thought, to take his chances outside the ship, rather than deprive a single Kree of a spot inside.

"Good luck, ambulatory vegetable," he said.

Drax stood for a moment, a calm eye in the center of the storm. Huge chunks of the planet flaked off, flying into the air. Pulse cannons, computers, entire houses rolled in the wind like half-ton tumbleweeds.

The remaining Kree stood staring up at the departing ship. With the last hope of rescue gone, all their fury and panic seemed to ebb away. A few of them milled around, kicking stones and struggling to talk over the wind. One latecomer screamed onto the scene on a rickety skycycle, tumbling off it as a chunk of the main dome grazed his front wheel.

Drax did not fear death. He'd already experienced it once, and it shadowed him every moment of his life, ever since his resurrection at the hands of the Titan Kronos. Would it be different this time, he wondered? Would it be sad, violent, painful? Would it be… funny, maybe?

"Hey dude?"

He turned. The young Kree with the Mohawk stood nervously before him, backed up by his crew.

"Just wanted to say," Mohawk continued, "that was pretty cool. Giving up your space to the old folks."

"Thank you." Drax puffed out his sizable chest. "I endeavor in all things to provide a good example to others."

One of the other young Kree, a clean-shaven man with a light blue complexion, stepped forward. "We've, uh, got a stash of gah'jar root tucked away in the hangar," he said. "Thought you might want to come ingest it with us."

"Since we're all gonna die anyway," Mohawk added.

The earth broke open, a dark mix of ash and superheated water sizzling out to cover the ground. The Kree backed away; Mohawk yelped as Drax yanked him off his feet and deposited him down, a safe distance away.

"Thanks!" Mohawk said, blinking nervously. "So, uh, what do you say?"

Drax glared at him. "I do not know what 'gah'jar root' is," he rumbled, "but I suspect it to be both unhealthy and contrary to the laws of most civilized planets."

"Well, yeah," Mohawk said. The others shrugged in agreement.

Drax glanced across the spaceport at the large, utilitarian hangar. Amazingly, the building was still standing. For now.

"Oh, why not," he said.

# CHAPTER 6

The last of the tectonic plates shattered. The remaining atmosphere of Praeterus flailed in a final planetary-scale gasp before escaping into space, where it would freeze into hard tiny chunks. Heat, seismograph readings, gamma radiation levels – all of them were... well, they were...

"They're useless," Rocket muttered, "because they're all off the flarkin' scale!"

His tiny nimble hands swiped across the touchscreen, summoning another hologram. This one showed a flickering radar image of the settlement, with the shattered dome in its center. But the spaceport was a blur of pixels. He couldn't tell whether or not the last ship had made it off the surface. Too much E/M interference to get a clean scan.

"Groot," he said to the screen. "Buddy. Where are you?"

The ship lurched, flung upward by another rush of escaping atmosphere. Rocket scrambled up onto the dashboard, hopping from one foot to another to keep his balance. He peered out the front viewport, but all he could see was a swirl of ash and clouds.

A strangled noise made him whirl around. In the back of the

cockpit, Quill lay flat out on the floor – with Gamora's sword pressed to his neck.

"Seriously?" Quill croaked. "Again?"

Gamora's eyes were like steel. "What. Did. You. Ask me?" she demanded.

"I asked if you wanted that bandage changed!"

"Oh." She looked down at the wrapping on her leg. "That's not a hostile act, then."

"Uh, no!"

She sheathed her sword.

"You two are a riot," Rocket snickered.

"Don't you have something important to do?" Quill asked. "Like keeping us from being vaporized in the death-throes of a planet?"

"You should have heard yourself, down there," Rocket continued. "'Oh Gam, don't die. Please, please don't be dead.' Get a room, why don't you."

"I knew it!" Quill cried. "I *knew* you had a camera on me!"

Gamora leaped to her feet and stalked to the pilot's chair. Rocket gulped in panic, holding up his strangely humanlike hands in a gesture of surrender. "Easy, Gam. You wouldn't stab the pilot, would you?"

"I haven't lost my mind, Rocket." She glared at Quill, who followed her cautiously. "Just tell this one to stop sneaking up on me."

"Tell him yourself! Next time you're..." Rocket closed his eyes and made an exaggerated smooching noise.

Before she could react, Quill placed himself, rather deliberately, between the two of them. He raised both his hands in two-fingered peace signs, a gesture that invariably made Rocket want to throttle him.

Then Quill turned to stare out the front port. He squinted in that irritating way humans had of squinting, when they wanted you to think they were smart.

"I tried that, genius," Rocket said, gesturing at the sky. "Visibility is effectively zero."

He pushed the stick, causing the ship to nose downward. Quill half-fell against the console, then slumped back into his chair.

Gamora grabbed Rocket's shoulder. Her fingers were badly burned, but that didn't seem to have affected her grip. "What are you doing?" she asked.

"Are you..." Quill strapped himself in, checked the altitude gauge. "Are you actually bringing us *closer* to the exploding planet?"

"Yes," Rocket said.

"Oh. Just checking."

Gamora tightened her grip. "And exactly *why* have you initiated this utterly suicidal course of–"

A deafening crunch cut her off. Rocket braced himself as the little ship made a full 360-degree flip in the thinning air. He and Quill were strapped in; Gamora wasn't so lucky. She flew up into the air and landed on her bad leg, grunting in pain.

"Sorry." Outside the front port, Rocket caught a glimpse of a huge mass of dirt hurtling off into space. "I think a chunk of exploding planet just hit us."

"Compensators are kicking in," Quill reported. "But hey, Gam's right. Seems like flying *away* from exploding planet chunks might be a better plan than driving *into* them. Besides–"

"I can't pick up the last escape ship," Rocket said. "I don't know if they made it off the surface or not."

"So you're worried about Groot and Drax," Gamora said, climbing to her feet again.

"Drax! Yeah, him too. I keep forgetting about that guy."

"OK," Quill said, "but what about–"

"What about all this debris? What about the gamma radiation? What about the *flarking volcanoes tearing the planet apart?* I know, I know. Whoa! There goes a small mountain. That was close."

"Yeah, but what about–"

"I know! I'm endangering all our lives." Sweat dripped into Rocket's eyes as he gripped the control stick, steering into the storm. "But we can't just leave 'em behind. They'd do the same for us. If there's a chance they're out in this somewhere, we gotta try an' oh wait you're smirking. I can see you out the corner of my eye, with that big dumb human smirk plastered all over your pasty hairless face. This isn't what you're concerned about at all, is it. Is it?"

Quill just kept smirking.

"Oh, flark," Rocket spat. "Oh, just say it."

"What about…"

"Come on, spit it out. You look like you're gonna pop."

"What about the KÁRMÁN LINE?!"

Quill doubled over with laughter, clapping his hands together in delight. Rocket freed one tiny hand from the controls just long enough to punch him on the shoulder.

Gamora stared at them as if they were insane.

"He…" Quill turned to Gamora, pointing at Rocket with uncontrolled laughter. "He wouldn't stop talking about the Kár… the KÁRMÁN…" He dissolved into hysterics again.

Rocket ignored him. The screen was bright with static. He ran his fingers over each sensor control in sequence, then pounded the panel in frustration. This close to the radiation source, the ship's instruments were useless.

A thick cloud of ash closed in over the front viewport, then cleared all at once. Quill placed both hands on the dash and leaned forward. "I can almost see the ground!" he exclaimed. "Well, what's left of it. That big hangar building is the only thing standing."

"Forget the building!" Rocket said. "Any sign of the ship?"

"It's not on the ground ... oh wait ..."

Rocket glanced up just as a spray of superheated water hissed onto the front viewport. The hull's sealing held firm, keeping the water outside – but Quill and Rocket both flinched anyway.

Gamora rolled her eyes. "My brave space pilots."

"I was distracted," Rocket offered. "Quill, did you see it? Before the, you know, steam bath hit. Did you see the ship?"

"I'm not sure." Quill studied the viewport, which had been badly fogged over by the water. "I saw something, flying up toward us."

"Like what?" Gamora asked.

"Yeah," Rocket said. "Was it a taco-restaurant-severed-from-its-foundations sort of something, or a rescue-ship-with-our-pals-in-it sort of something?"

"I didn't get a good look." Quill frowned. "I think it was covered with vines."

"Vines?" Rocket turned as a shrill beeping rose from the console. "Huh, looks like proximity sensors are online. I thought they'd been knocked out."

"Proximity sensors?" Gamora said. "That means something's about to–"

The ship lurched hard, jarring sideways in the thin air. Something sliced up past them in the viewport and vanished quickly from view. Then a loud *thump* shook the upper hull, forcing the ship downward. Rocket struggled with the controls, managing to arrest their plunge just as an uprooted Kree barracks building tumbled up past them.

"What…" Quill looked upward in dread. "What was that?"

Several smaller *thumps*, from above. "Is it me," Rocket said, "or is something, uh…"

"Crawling on top of the hull?" Gamora pulled out her sword. "Sure sounds that way."

All three of them went silent, listening as the *thumps* continued. Their eyes followed the path of the sound as it moved across the top of the ship, heading toward the front.

Rocket watched in alarm as Quill pulled out his blaster. "I hope," Rocket began, "that you are not planning to blast through our hull to take out an invading enemy."

"I'm with the rodent, Peter." Another hunk of the planet's surface flew past. "I've grown fond of breathing."

The ship hit an unexpected pocket of calm air, an eye in the storm of the dying planet. As the *thumps* approached the front of the ship, Rocket locked the controls to stationkeeping and leaned forward, watching the viewport along with Quill and Gamora.

A tree branch flapped over the top of the ship, coming into view at the edge of the viewport. As the three Guardians watched, it shaped itself into a fist and rapped gently on the outside window. *NOK NOK NOK.*

Rocket's heart leapt. "Groot?"

*NOK NOK NOK!*

The tree-man's face lurched into view. He looked like he'd been through a hurricane. His branches were mostly bare, his few remaining leaves ruffled by the rising winds. He grimaced, gesturing frantically.

Quill laughed. "He jumped. He jumped from the rescue ship!"

Rocket felt tears of relief rising to his eyes. He wiped them away savagely and turned back to the controls.

"Get him!" he barked. "Get him in here."

As Quill and Gamora rushed to the airlock, Rocket crept back up on the dash, staring out the viewport. On the planet below, a mile-wide fissure gaped across the surface of the main settlement. The munitions dome collapsed and tumbled down into the hole, glowing with a radiance that would soon consume this world.

Rocket scrambled back to his chair, flipping switches. "Is he inside?" he asked.

He felt a familiar leafy touch on his shoulder. "I am Gr– "

"Got it! Good to have you back, buddy." The ship lurched again. "Now strap in, folks. The planet's crust is breakin' up – which means the last of Praeterus's atmosphere is about to wheeze out into space, like a ham actor givin' his final performance. And like it or not, we're goin' with it."

# CHAPTER 7

Once they cleared the atmosphere, the ship stopped shaking. They retreated to a safe distance, observing in eerie calm as the planet cracked, shuddered, and split into a thousand pieces.

Gamora forced herself to watch every second of it. The tremors, the fierce eruption of gamma radiation. The chunks of dirt, ice, and quick-frozen lava spewing out from the planet's core. The first few rescue ships, flitting into view at quick intervals before flashing away into hyperspace.

Once again, she remembered the vow she'd made to the little Kree girl: *I won't let this happen.* She clenched her fists, wincing in pain. The burns on her hands were already healing, but still they chafed and itched. That only made her squeeze harder. She wanted to feel that pain. She wanted to hurt.

*I deserve it,* she thought. *I failed.*

At the pilot's console, Quill and Rocket were grilling Groot about events on the ground. Rocket had set the ship on autopilot, maintaining a fixed position several thousand klicks from the planetary reaction.

"He wasn't on the last ship?" Peter asked.

Groot shook his head sadly.

"Are you absolutely sure?" Rocket gestured dramatically. "I mean, you know Drax. Maybe he slipped aboard, unnoticed, all stealthy-like without anybody seeing… YEEEAAAAAAAH, you're right. He's toast."

"I am Groot," Groot agreed.

"Drax. Ahhh, Drax." Quill leaned his hands on the dash, watching as another of the evac ships loomed into view. "How many did we save?"

Groot lifted a leafy hand and began to count on his fingers. "I. Am. Groot. I am Groot? Groot."

"Three hundred and seven," Quill repeated. "Out of eighty thousand."

Outside the viewport, the last evac ship flashed bright as it vanished into hyperspace.

"And we still don't even know why this happened," Rocket grumbled. "Was it some weapon? A terrorist attack? A stupid, pointless accident?"

"It was no accident," Gamora said.

They all turned in surprise as she approached. "Inside the dome," she said, "There was… something. Someone."

Quill blinked. "Really?"

"Didja get an ID?" Rocket asked. "Was it male, female? Human, or something more pleasing to the eye?"

"Human," she said, ignoring the insult. "Or humanoid, at least. I don't remember much – the radiation was just too much – but I *felt* something. An ancient hatred, a… a hunger for conquest. A need so overwhelming, it couldn't be contained within the bounds of one universe."

She looked up. They were all staring at her.

"Whoa," Quill said.

"That's your reaction? 'Whoa'?" She placed her hands on her

hips. "Faced with possibly the greatest evil in all of known space, you say 'Whoa'?"

"Um," Quill replied. "'Yikes'?"

"Well, whoever it was, they're prob'ly dead." Rocket gestured outside at a severed continental shelf drifting by. "Nobody could have survived that."

"You're wrong. They survived."

Again, the stares. "I am Groot?" Groot asked.

"I don't know how I know," she replied. "I just do. I felt that malevolent presence, up close and personal. And somehow I know: it's still out there."

"If that's the case," Quill said, "it might already be looking for more planets to suck dry. We gotta find it."

"I dunno." Rocket turned away. "Isn't this more of a job for somebody like the Nova Corps? Or Supremor's goons? Or the Shi'ar, maybe! I feel like the Imperial Guard hasn't had a win lately."

"Right, yeah," Quill agreed. "When I said *we* gotta stop it, I meant the big universal we. Not, you know—"

"—you and me, we. Yeah, agreed."

"So we're on the same page."

"Absolutely—"

"Aren't you forgetting something?" Gamora's voice chilled the air in the room.

"P- Probably," Quill acknowledged.

"That thing killed eighty thousand people," she hissed. "Including our friend."

"I *am* Groot," Groot agreed.

"Drax," Gamora continued. "He must be avenged."

Groot nodded. Rocket let out a long sigh, and finally Quill smiled a grim smile. "So we're Avengers now."

"I don't think it works that way, dude," Rocket said.

A high-pitched beeping rose up from the control panel. Rocket studied the console and let out a short curse. "It's one of the evac ships," he said. "A distress call… well, sort of. They're saying they've managed to engage hyperspace engines, but they got no place to go."

"I'm not surprised," Gamora said. "The Kree don't care what happens to these people."

"Yeah, but what are we supposed to do about it? Haven't we done enough for them? Except for the part where we let all their friends and neighbors get killed, I mean."

"Actually," Quill said, "I might have an idea. Let me make a call."

"And then," Gamora said firmly, "we get on the trail of our planet-killer." She pulled out a jagged metal object and tossed it to Rocket. "This might help."

He caught the device, pressed a button, and laughed in delight as a red light lit up. "A Kree detector! Where'd you get it?"

"I cut it out of the chest of a robot."

"As one does." Rocket held the detector up to the light. "Thanks, kid."

"Happy birthday."

She turned away, shivering at the memory of that consciousness – the savage, evil mind at the heart of the gamma reaction. A living *need* that had consumed everything within its reach, and now hungered for more.

Quill leaned over Rocket's station as the raccoonoid activated the comms system. Outside, pieces of the planet wafted by, water frozen like winter lakes on thick chunks of crumbling soil.

"Gamma levels dropping," Rocket said.

"You know," Quill said, "I was just kidding about that Avengers business."

"Suuuuure, fanboy." Rocket smirked. "Sure you were."

OMNI-WAVE MESSAGE
SECURE PROTOCOL
DELIVERY SPEED: INSTANTANEOUS (PRIORITY ONE)

FROM:   CAROL DANVERS, OMNIWAVE ID "CAPTAIN MARVEL"
8TH SECTOR, DENOBIAN GALAXY

TO:      ANTHONY STARK, OMNIWAVE ID "IRON MAN"
EARTH

HEY TONES – HOPE THINGS ARE COPACETIC. HEY TO YOU TOO, PEPPER, IF YOU'RE SCREENING THIS. HOPE THE BIG DOPE ISN'T DRIVING YOU TOO NUTS.

I'M UP TO MY SASH IN TROUBLE OUT HERE. EGO THE LIVING SOIL SAMPLE HAS PICKED A FIGHT WITH A BUNCH OF CELESTIALS, AND I'VE GOTTA STOP THEM FROM TRAMPLING A DOZEN CIVILIZED WORLDS IN THEIR COSMIC TESTOSTERONE SPAT. YOU KNOW, THE USUAL. ANYWAY, I JUST GOT A MESSAGE ABOUT SOMETHING AND I CAN'T HANDLE IT MYSELF, BUT I THOUGHT YOU MIGHT BE ABLE TO HELP. DETAILS ARE ATTACHED.

GOTTA GO – SOME GLOWING DUDE WITH THE INSECURE NAME "GODHEAD" JUST WHIPPED UP A VORTEX RIGHT ON EGO'S EQUATOR. OUCH! ANYWAY, TAKE A LOOK AT THIS AND SEE WHAT YOU THINK. IF YOU FEEL LIKE BEING A REAL HERO FOR A CHANGE, THAT IS. HA! JUST KIDDING. BUT NOT REALLY.

YRS FOR BETTER AVENGING,
       CAROL

SIX MONTHS LATER

# PART TWO

## LOST IN THE FIRE

# CHAPTER 8

"This is how we're supposed to spend our Friday afternoon?" Zoe leaned back against the bleachers, let out an exaggerated yawn, and rolled her eyes back in her head. "In the *gym*?"

Kamala Khan laughed. She studied the gym floor, watching as the kids filed in. A burst of laughter made her turn and look behind; a group of meathead jocks had already claimed the back row of the bleachers, talking loudly in their school jackets.

"I have to agree," said Nakia. "I can think of many more useful things I could be doing right now."

"I can think of many more *fun* things," Zoe snorted.

Kamala turned toward her two friends, who couldn't have been more different from each other. Zoe Zimmer was a snarky, popular girl who'd been born in France. Nakia Bahadir, who came from a strict Turkish family, practiced her Muslim faith as rigorously as she pursued her studies. When the two girls had first met in high school, they despised each other on sight.

But recently, they'd become almost inseparable. Which proved, Kamala thought, that no matter how well you thought you knew people, they could always surprise you.

"Hey," Zoe said, nudging Kamala. "Check out the new kid."

Kamala turned again to look. On the far side of the bleachers, near the back, a young man in a beige jumpsuit sat alone, his expression grim and distant. He took a bite from a packet in his hand, something that looked almost like combat rations. The meatheads sat behind the kid, pointing and laughing at his clothes.

"Poor kid," Zoe continued. "Another fashion casualty. Remember Stewart, last year?"

"He's not like Stewart," Kamala said.

More students tromped in, filling up the spaces in the bleachers. Kamala studied the new kid. He had a strange intensity about him, and she could see his taut muscles even through that unfortunate jumpsuit. But no, this guy wasn't quite like Stewart. Or like Thierry, the bullies' target the year before.

This kid had bright blue skin.

"Hey, Kam," Zoe said, laughing. "You like that action? Take a picture."

"Shut up," Kamala replied, turning away.

"He's cute! For a dude, I mean." Clearly Zoe wasn't going to let this go. "And he looks loooonely."

"I'd be careful with that boy," Nakia said. "He was blocking my locker earlier, and when I asked him to move, he gave me a very hostile look."

"Hey guys!" Bruno Carrelli plopped down onto the bleacher site just behind them. "Fun times, huh? I miss anything?"

"No," Nakia said.

Zoe smirked. "Kamala likes the blue dude."

Bruno's whole face seemed to slump, as if all the air had been drained out of him. He looked away.

"Zoe!" Kamala cried. She turned to explain. "Bruno…"

She trailed off. Bruno was her best friend, but just last week they'd shared a kiss – and now, suddenly, things were complicated. She wasn't sure how he felt about him anymore, and he seemed pretty confused too.

The bleachers were almost full now, and a rumble of restless Friday-afternoon conversation filled the air. But nobody had sat down within six feet of the blue kid, who glared straight ahead, munching on his food packet. It was like he had some invisible force field around him.

"I suppose he's... wiry," Bruno said. "But hey, anybody would look cut in a jumpsuit like that."

Kamala laughed, allowing Bruno the weak joke. Their eyes met and he gave her a grateful smile.

Zoe just snorted and spread her arms back along the bleachers. "Almost showtime," she said. "Hey, it's getting pretty full in here. Think we could sneak out?"

"No," Nakia replied.

"Come on. We're not gonna learn anything anyway."

"We are not skipping out. Not after last week."

Kamala smiled. Last Friday, her friends had covered for her while she slipped out of school. "Sorry, guys."

"Hey, proud to help," Bruno said. "What was that thing rampaging down Grove Street? A dragon?"

"Yeti," Kamala said. "I think."

When Kamala had read the emergency phone alert about the yeti – or whatever it was – she knew she had to stop it. So she'd enlisted the help of her friends, the only three people alive who knew her secret. They'd all been late to trig class, but only Kamala wound up with actual detention.

Still, Zoe, Nakia, and Bruno had risked severe disciplinary action in order to help her. She hated putting her friends through that. But ever since she'd become Ms Marvel, Kamala Khan had gotten used to making those choices.

"Here comes the principal," Bruno said, pointing down at the gym floor.

"That's not the principal," Zoe said ominously.

A scowling Black woman steered her wheelchair up to the edge of the bleachers. Ms Norris, the physics teacher, looked up at the assembled students and shook her head.

"Hello everyone," she said – with a lack of enthusiasm, Kamala thought, that was actually impressive in its intensity. "Settle down now and listen. I said settle down!"

The room went quiet.

"That's better. Now, as you know, this is a career session for juniors and seniors. Anybody who isn't a junior or senior, get your butt out of here. Now."

A few small kids looked around sheepishly, then got up and scurried away. The meatheads watched them go, snickering and muttering "Losers."

"OK," Ms Norris continued. "Now, we were supposed to have a career counselor come in today, but she seems to have cancelled. And since Principal Stanton also seems to have better things to do on a Friday afternoon, it looks like you're stuck with me."

"First time I have respected Principal Stanton," Nakia whispered. Kamala stifled a laugh.

"So." Ms Norris reached into a bag and pulled out a thick sheaf of paper. Adjusting her glasses, she began to read stiffly. "'What is a career? You may think it's just a job. But it's much more than that. Anyone can get a job…'"

Kamala's attention strayed back to the new kid. The jocks were smirking, inching closer to him. They were up to something.

"His family just moved to Jersey City," Zoe whispered, pointing at the kid. "I hear their old home was lost in a fire or something."

"'Hard work is the foundation of success,'" Ms Norris read aloud. "'If you believe in yourself and keep your nose to the grindstone, you can accomplish miracles.'"

"Grindstone?" Bruno leaned down to whisper in Kamala's ear. "This is making my brain hurt."

Kamala turned to smile at him. "I don't even think Ms Norris believes it."

"Kamala?"

She whipped her head around. Down on the floor, the teacher had swiveled to face her directly.

"Uh, yes, Ms Norris?"

"I was asking where you saw yourself in five years."

"In, uh, what now?"

Ms Norris glared, peering up over her glasses into the bleachers. "Since you have so much to say, I thought you might like to be the first to answer that question."

Kamala froze, her mind suddenly blank. The whole room was staring at her. She thought of that day, down on the docks, when the Terrigen mist had swirled over her, imbuing her with strange, alien-based powers. Of the yeti, stomping and kicking its way down Grove Street. And of another time, just two weeks ago, when Tony Stark – Iron Man himself – had approached her after a battle in Manhattan, offering her a trial membership in the Avengers.

"I, uh, haven't thought about it," she said. "I've been a little busy lately."

"Oh, Kam," Bruno whispered.

"Wrong answer," Nakia added.

"Busy?" Ms Norris's voice rose in volume. "Well, I suggest you start making time. High school won't last forever."

"Feels like it will," Zoe whispered. Nakia let out a snort of laughter, then went very quiet.

Ms Norris turned and rolled her wheelchair away, dismissing Kamala with a look. "Anyone here have a more substantial answer? Someone who cares about their future, maybe?"

A few hands went up. One of the jocks, a grinning pretty boy named Russell, reached out and pointed at the blue kid. "Ask him!"

"I know better than to ask *you*," the teacher snapped back. Then she turned, considering Coles Academic High's first extraterrestrial student. "Mister, uh…" Ms Norris paused and scrolled through something on her tablet. "…Holler, is it?"

The blue kid looked up at her, snorted, and tossed his empty food packet aside. "Halla-ar," he said.

"Halla-ar," Ms Norris said. "First of all, welcome to our school."

Halla-ar said nothing.

"Would you like to take a crack at the question?" she continued. "Where do you see yourself – that is, what do you want to do with your life?"

The boy grimaced. "I do not know how to answer that," he said, in an accent Kamala couldn't identify. "My people are rarely given the opportunity to choose."

"Your people?" Russell called out. "The Smurfs?"

Laughter rippled through the room. As Ms Norris's sharp voice cut through the laughter, Russell reached down and punched Halla-ar on the arm. It was a playful jab, not hard enough to hurt. But the new kid's eyes went feral and, without warning, he leaped across the empty space. Before anyone knew what had happened, he had Russell pinned down against the long bench, hand clamped down on the jock's throat.

Everyone froze. Gasps filled the gym. Across the surrounding rows, kids sprang to their feet. The jocks clustered together, eyeing their friend with concern – but, Kamala noticed, none of them moved to help him.

"Stop!" Ms Norris said.

Halla-ar didn't reply. He stayed perfectly still, crouched over Russell, holding the other boy by the throat.

Kamala rose to her feet. The new kid clearly had combat skills; was he dangerous? She felt a tingling in her limbs. Her hand started to expand in size, but she willed it back to normal. This wasn't a crisis *yet*, and she wasn't ready to reveal her secret identity to the whole school. Not if the situation could still be resolved peacefully.

"Hey," she said. "Let him go, huh?"

Halla-ar didn't look up. The jock let out a strangled noise.

"He's just a meathead," she continued. "Not worth a week's detention."

Halla-ar gritted his teeth, staring at the helpless jock. "You ask what I would do with my life?" he repeated.

"For God's sake, stop!" Ms Norris called out.

Russell let out another noise. His eyes rolled up, his head went limp. Blast it, Kamala thought, this isn't working. The school security guard was probably on his way, but that might take too long. She tensed herself for action.

"Like the rest of my people," Halla-ar yelled, "I would like to *not* work like a dog for Tony Stark!"

In one smooth motion he released Russell, whirled, and leaped off the bleachers. By the time Kamala registered what had happened, Halla-ar had sprinted across the gym floor and disappeared out the door.

The room erupted into chaos. People rose to their feet, talking in alarmed voices, pointing at the door and snapping pictures. The jocks converged on their coughing, gasping friend and forced a water bottle into his mouth. Russell waved them away angrily. Down on the floor, Ms Norris tried to restore order.

Kamala stood up, her mind racing. Tony Stark? she thought. *That* Tony Stark?

"Whoa," Bruno said, laying a hand on her shoulder. "What a psycho!"

Maybe, she thought. And yet... Russell *had* touched the kid first...

"Guys," she said, gathering Zoe and Nakia together with Bruno. "Cover me? I gotta make an exit."

"Got it," Zoe said. She nudged a girl out of the way and took up position between Kamala and Ms Norris. Not that the teacher was watching them. She had her hands full trying to quiet down the crowd.

Nakia stood up next to Zoe. Bruno hesitated, frowning at Kamala. "You're going after him," he said.

She gave him a pained smile. "I have to."

Shaking his head, Bruno joined her other friends, forming a circle around her. "Be careful," he said, in a voice that sounded like it meant, "You'll be sorry."

When she was sufficiently hidden from view, Kamala concentrated and began to shrink. Normally, Kamala used her powers to "embiggen" – expand the size of one or more limbs, or sometimes her whole body. This was the opposite, a process that allowed her to slip between the boards of the bleachers and drop to the floor below.

She scurried to the wall and headed for the door, unnoticed at only five inches tall. *Sorry, Bruno,* she thought; *I'll make this up to you.* But there was something weird going on here, something that might just wind up being Avengers business. And Kamala had a strange feeling that only she could put all the pieces together.

# CHAPTER 9

"Father?"

Gamora craned her neck, struggling to see. Her father sat on a rock, turned away, staring into the mist. She couldn't make out his face.

"Father, say something. Please."

She knew she was dreaming; she'd had this dream before. In times of crisis, her subconscious always dragged up the memory of her true father. As if his shadow, her lost anchor, held all her answers.

"Father, something's happening." She trembled. "Something has been set in motion, something very bad. Peter and the others – they're worried about planets blowing up. That's horrible enough, but I'm afraid it's even bigger than that."

The father-shade muttered something, but she couldn't make it out.

"What?" She peered at him urgently. "Tell me, Father. Tell me what to do!"

His figure wavered, shimmering in the haze. Panic rose inside her. Was his memory, the part of him that guided and helped her, fading away? Was he finally, absolutely, leaving her?

"No," she said. "No, tell me! You have to tell me!"

He muttered something again. This time she could almost hear it.

"What?" Panic surged, turned to rage. "Tell me. Tell me!"

The figure began to turn. This was different too. She struggled, held in place by some unknown dream-force. Desperate to see him.

"You know," he rumbled.

A bolt of shock ran through her. That was not her father's voice. As she watched in horror, the figure grew thicker, taller. By the time it was facing her directly, the face had become a map of chiseled stone, blank white eyes glimmering over a cruel smile.

"You know," Thanos repeated.

Thanos. The Mad Titan, scourge of the entire universe. His genocidal schemes had only been thwarted by an assemblage of heroes from seven galaxies. And Gamora had been a part of those schemes. From the day Thanos took her in, an orphan girl from a decimated race, he had trained her as a weapon in his insane master plan.

She'd rebelled, helped turn the tide against her adoptive father. But she still bore the scars of that upbringing, the brutal discipline he'd delivered with cold joy. The combat training, the endless sessions that she endured until her bones ached and her muscles screamed in agony. Always striving, but never good enough. Not for him.

Thanos began to glow, pure white light shining from those soulless eyes. The light spread out to cover him, bathing his figure in a familiar radiance. Soon she could barely see him; he shrank to a thick, squat shadow inside the blinding glow. A shadow that continued to shrink, growing smaller.

With a shock, Gamora realized what was happening. She was back in the dome, on Praeterus, staring into the blazing glow of the gamma reaction. Once again she peered into the fire, struggling to make out the tiny figure at the heart of that unimaginable energy. Its evil, she sensed, was the equal of Thanos himself.

It wasn't Thanos, though. She knew that much. And yet, as the light seared her eyes, she heard once again the Mad Titan's voice:

"It's inside you."

She forced herself to look closer. Her corneas burned, her nerves seemed to dissolve into ash. But now she could see. She could almost see it–

She felt a hand on her shoulder. Suddenly she could move again. Her limbs flexed, her hand grasped her sword and swung it around. The world flashed bright, then went dark…

…and then she was in her bunk, on the ship, crouched on all fours with the sword pressed down on Peter Quill's throat.

*"Again?"* he croaked.

"Peter." She reared back, tossing the sword aside. "I told you to *stop sneaking up on me!"*

"You were asleep!" He rubbed his throat. "And mumbling some pretty weird stuff, I might add."

"I saw." She stared at him, eyes wide. "Peter, I saw it. Saw them."

"Them? Them who?"

"The assassin. The planet-killer." She squeezed her eyes shut, trying to recall the image. "When I was in the dome… before you arrived. I saw the killer's face."

"Really?" He sat up on the bed, reached out for her, then thought better of it. "Why didn't you say so before?"

"I didn't remember. The shock… the radiation… but I remember now."

"You saw the killer." A dark look crossed his face. "The monster that murdered Drax."

"Yeah."

"Well? What did they look like?"

"I can't…" She shook her head, looked away. "It's gone again."

"Oh." He looked down, clearly disappointed.

"I saw it." She slammed a fist down on the bedside table. "I saw that face! If I came across it again, I'd know. I would remember."

"Well, maybe you're about to get that shot." He smiled, puffing out his chest with pride. "You remember that organlegger back on Chandilar? The one with the bad breath and the—"

"—and the unusual assortment of limbs. Yes?"

"Well, he gave Rocket a tip that wound up paying off big. Something about genetic enhancements made to a Skrull agent, specifically to get him through Kree security screenings."

"A Skrull." She stared at him. "That's our killer?"

"No, no, the Skrull was just a middleman. Looks like he smuggled in some Shi'ar explosive wingtips to a Kree starpost, just fifteen light-years away from Praeterus. Delivered them to a Phalanx Technarch who incorporated them into her—"

"A Technarch! So that's the killer—"

"No no no! The Technarch was a dead end. But this is where it gets interesting. The wingtips turned up on a K'Lanti customs scan way the hell across the galaxy—"

"Peter!" She took hold of his cheeks and turned his head to face her. "What are you trying to tell me?"

"The, uh, the killer seems to be Kree." He looked hurt. "And Rocket just picked up their trail. I thought you might like to see."

"I would." She was already up, pulling on her battlesuit and fastening her belt. As she started toward the door, Quill followed, grumbling.

"It was a really good story," he muttered.

"I'm sure it was."

"I mean, if you let me tell the whole thing! Otherwise, it kind of falls apart around the end of the second act…"

She ignored him, pushing through a narrow corridor lined with survival gear. She slammed a hand down on the hatch button, squeezed through the opening before it was fully open, and stared around the cockpit. Rocket sat in the pilot's seat, hands clasped behind his head, steering with his feet. Groot had spread his limbs out over a pile of equipment lockers and was rummaging through three of them at once.

But it was the sight through the viewport that made Gamora's heart sink. A blue-white orb, floating in space, soft clouds swirling across its familiar surface.

"Earth," she spat. "Ugh."

"Yep. Earth." Rocket turned, smirking as he twisted a dial with his toes. "I'm keepin' us just out of sight of their dumb satellites."

"Ugh?" Peter asked. "Why ugh? What's wrong with Earth?"

"Everything." Gamora moved closer to the viewport. "For one thing, it's too close to Titan for my taste."

"Not much left of Titan since Thanos got done with it," Rocket observed.

"Exactly." She gestured at the viewport. "Also, everyone from Earth is an idiot."

"Ow!" Peter said. "Right to my face?"

"Hey Groot!" Rocket called. "You find the whatsit yet? The dingus?"

Groot muttered something I-Am-Grootish, then smiled. He pulled a small device out of a locker and stretched out a long branch-arm to deliver it to Rocket.

"The Kree detector," Gamora said.

"Yep! And since that Chitauri intel we got made it very clear that our planet-killer is Kree–"

"Chitauri?"

Quill shrugged haughtily. "*Someone* didn't want to hear the story."

"Ahem!" Rocket clicked the detector on. "As I was saying... if the Kree scum that killed Drax is hidin' out on Earth, this should lead us right to 'em."

A light winked green on the detector. BLEEP.

With a whoop of triumph, Rocket turned back to the viewport. "We're comin' up on... whaddya call that big brown landmass? Shaped like a toilet?"

"North America," Quill growled.

"Right. Someplace in there... up-north-ish, near the flusher..."

BLEEP BLEEP

"Oh! Looks like our planet-killer's got a pal. Or an accomplice, or–"

BLEEP BLEEP BLEEP

Quill and Gamora exchanged glances.

"Maybe, uh..." Rocket glared at the detector. "Maybe we're dealin' with a small *family* of planet-killers. Or a coven. Perhaps a literary salon."

Gamora stared at him. "A salon?"

BLEEP BLEEP BLEEP BLEEP BLEEP BLEEP BLEEP BLEEP BLEEP BLEEP BLEEP BLEEP BLEEP BLEEP BLEEP BLEEP BLEEP BLEEP BLEEP BLEEP BLEEP BLEEP BLEEP BLEEP BLEEP BLEEP BLEEP BLEEP BLEEP BLEEP BLEEP BLEEP BLEEP BLEEP BLEEP BLEEP BLEEP BLEEP BLEEP BLEEP BLEEP BLEEP

"I am Groot," Groot observed.

Rocket held the detector out at arm's length, watching as the light blinked green, over and over again. He looked disappointed, as if his beloved pet had just soiled the rug.

"This, uh…" He shrugged. "This might be a little trickier than I thought."

# CHAPTER 10

By the time Kamala found the new kid, he was sprinting out the main door of the school – remarkably fast, she thought. She started after him, then thought better of it. She ducked into the bathroom and changed into costume, then crept past the main office and out the door unnoticed.

If this *did* turn out to be Avengers business, she'd better handle it as an Avenger. As Ms Marvel.

She caught up with Halla-ar a few blocks away, in the empty playground section of a public park. He stood rigid, facing away from her, toward a set of unused swings and a fenced-off area intended for toddlers. His eyes were closed; he hadn't heard her approach.

She crept through the gate and into the park, studying him. Halla-ar had sharp cheekbones and a trim form – attractive, she had to admit. But what was he doing? Resting? Meditating?

"Hey," she said. "Mountain pose, right?"

His eyes snapped open. He spun around, incredibly fast, and dropped into a crouch, hands thrust out like blades.

"Whoa, whoa!" Kamala stepped back, holding up her hands. "Quick reflexes you got there."

His eyes, filled with suspicion, burned into hers. "I have been trained as a weapon," he said. "Who are you?"

"Ms, uh, Ms Marvel," she said, feeling suddenly awkward. "My friends and contacts back at the school sent me. They were worried about you."

"Your friends." He paused, frowning. "One of them tried to talk to me, back there."

"Kamala? Yeah, she's got a soft spot for outsiders." She shrugged. "Me too, I guess."

She took a step closer, and he backed up. "Easy, easy!" she said. "I'm not gonna touch you. You don't like to be touched, do you? That's cool, that's fine. I've got friends like that."

"Where I come from, a touch is usually a prelude to an attack."

"I get that. I've been in a few brawls myself."

He straightened up, lowering his hands. They stood silently for a moment, facing each other. Then he turned without a word and stalked away, toward the gate.

He was leaving. In a few seconds, he'd be out that gate and out of her life. An outsider on this world, a kid who'd probably never had a decent break. A kid, she knew, who could use a friend.

"You're Kree, aren't you?" she asked.

That stopped him. He turned and gave her a questioning look.

"I had a Kree costume for a while," she said. "It was pretty cool, but it got a little too… assertive. Not everybody bonds with a Stormranger Nanosuit, I guess."

"Stormranger. An ancient elite order of the Kree," he said. "I had an ancestor who held that rank."

"Then we have something to talk about," she said. "Come on."

She led him to a pair of old wooden swings hanging from a rusty frame. "This park is overdue a revamp," she explained. "Watch out you don't get tetanus."

"I don't understand most of those words," he said.

She smiled, settling into a swing. He mimicked her movements, frowning as he grabbed hold of the chains. When she kicked off, he nodded and did the same. He studied her moves, experimenting with his legs and arms as he began to swing faster.

It's soothing him, she realized. Giving him something to focus on. Something other than being in a strange school that hasn't exactly been welcoming, so far.

"I thought you were going to attack me back there," she said. "You've got some moves."

"Those?" He snorted. "Simple opening defenses. I learned them when I was five."

"Five? Really?"

"I've been training most of my life." He kicked off again. "I was selected for Officer Academy training, on Hala. The first in my family."

"Hala," Kamala repeated. "That's the Kree homeworld."

"I was named after Hala. My family saved up everything they could to send me – I was supposed to leave in three months." He sighed. "It was their greatest dream."

"Wait a minute. Saved up?" Kamala frowned. "I thought the Blue Kree were the ruling caste. Don't you get, I don't know, special treatment?"

"You sound like my friends back home. The... the Kree meatheads." He dug his heels into the dirt, coming to sudden halt. "Not all Blue Kree are wealthy or important. My family have always been laborers."

"I'm sorry."

"I was used to that sort of ignorance on Praeterus. I didn't expect to find it here."

"Sorry. I'm really sorry, I didn't know." She smiled sadly. "I guess people kind of suck everywhere, sometimes."

She looked away, feeling terrible. I really jumped to conclusions there, she thought.

He started swinging again, a slower, easy motion. "You did not know," he acknowledged.

"Praeterus," she said hesitantly. "That's your home?"

"It was." He moved faster now, his kicks growing agitated. "Until it was destroyed."

"The whole *planet?*"

He didn't answer. Kamala studied him as he swung, seeing the pain in his eyes. She remembered Zoe's words: *lost in a fire.*

"My whole world," he said finally. "Along with all my family's savings."

"So no trip to Hala." She grimaced. "No Officer Academy training."

"My sister worked so hard." She could feel his anger, like a dark fog in the air. "And now we have nothing. Now we are exiled to this cruel, noisy world."

"Yeah, about that… Halla-ar, right?" He didn't answer, so she pressed on. "Don't take this the wrong way, but why *are* you here? Why pick Earth to settle on? It's a big galaxy."

"Galaxies," he corrected.

"If you say so. It's all just space to me."

The ghost of a smile tickled at his lips, then quickly vanished.

"We did not choose Earth. After the destruction of Praeterus, my people had nowhere to go." He let out a long sigh. "And the Kree rulers had other matters on their minds."

"Rulers usually do," she said.

"Our ships hopped from world to world, but were met with hostility and force at every stop. As our food and fuel grew low, we became desperate. Then, like a gift from the heavens, we received an offer to come to Earth. The work would be hard, we were told, but we would be treated fairly and given good housing." He shook his head. "And we accepted. Because even in the Kree Galaxy, everyone trusts the word of *Tony Stark*."

Kamala jumped. The way he spat out Stark's name, it sounded like a curse.

"We should have known," Halla-ar continued. "When you are weak and have nothing, that is when the predators strike. When you are poor, the system contrives to work you to death, to take what little you own and leave you to die penniless."

"That doesn't sound like Tony," she blurted.

Halla-ar went rigid. He leaped out of the swing and whirled to face her.

"You know Tony Stark?" he demanded.

"I... Yeah." She stood up slowly. "He's a good man. I mean, he's kind of a clueless rich guy, and he can be pretty full of himself. But he tries." She grimaced. "He asked me to join the Avengers."

She shuddered, struck by the pain in Halla-ar's eyes. Was it possible? Tony Stark was a billionaire, after all. Rich people often made their money by exploiting... someone. And Kamala had friends, even relatives, who'd been taken advantage of upon first arriving in this country.

"So," Halla-ar said, "you are allied with him." His whole manner had turned cold now. "Did Stark send you here? To find me?"

"No! I mean, I don't know him that well." She looked away. "But... well, he's a hero too."

"I should have known. I was a fool to trust you – to trust anyone on this foul planet."

"I'll prove it to you. You can trust me."

He frowned. "How?"

"Meet me here, tomorrow morning. We'll take this Tony Stark business right to the top." She stared into his eyes. "And if it's true – if there's any truth to this at all – we'll get to the bottom of it. I promise."

"You would do that?" He looked back at her, startled. "For me? For someone you just met?"

"You bet." She smiled. "After all, there's got to be some perks to being an Avenger."

# CHAPTER 11

Night fell over a desolate stretch of Tenth Avenue on the west side of Manhattan, in what had once been called the Meatpacking District. Office lights went dark, loading-dock doors scrolled down and snapped shut. And a strange neon sign flickered to life: a dusty glass tube twisted into a shape that might have meant something in Russian. Or maybe not.

Below the sign, a few steps had once led down to a long-abandoned subway station. Now those steps ran into a concrete blockade plastered with ancient band posters and faded warning signs. A dead end – except for the thin, inconspicuous wooden door off to the right side of the blockade. And inside that door stood a dusty, windowless tavern with a peculiar name: Staryymir.

A short bar ran down one side of the room, stocked with a surprisingly large assortment of exotic liqueurs. A few high tables filled the rest of the crowded space. The bartender, a lanky middle-aged man with a Russian accent, stood behind the bar, adjusting the antenna of a television that probably dated back to the Gorbachev era.

Staryymir had quite a history. But Kir-ra of the Kree didn't care about that. All she cared about was that it was open during the day, and that it was dark.

A Kree man named Budda-lo sat across from her at a high table, complaining. "…can't do those sixteen-hour shifts anymore," he was saying. "My back is killing me."

"Mmm," Kir-ra said, looking away. She lifted her glass to the light, took a long drink of vodka… and felt nothing. Earth alcohol, she thought. No bite to it. None at all.

"It's the assembly line." Budda-lo rolled his shoulders, wincing. "It's so bad for my neck."

"Yes," Kir-ra said, her voice flat. "You said that four times on the subway trip."

A trip, she thought, that I would have preferred to take alone.

"Did I?" He leaned over the table and stared into her eyes. "Aw, I'm sorry."

Budda-lo seemed a little desperate, a little lonely, and a good deal drunker than she was. She swirled her vodka, thinking: at least it's working for someone.

He launched into a new litany of complaints. Kir-ra ignored him, looking around for help. But there was no one else in the bar except the bartender, who sat staring at a cheap streaming sitcom called *It's the Door, Mommy*.

Kir-ra shook her head. I'll never understand this planet, she thought.

Budda-lo's chatter was intolerable. He'd been a nuisance ever since the munitions plant on Praeterus, when he'd been assigned to the station next to hers. Normally she would have just told him to go away, but after back-to-back shifts at the Stark complex, she was exhausted. So she'd allowed him to follow her here, to the only sanctuary she'd found on this miserable world.

"…haven't seen you in the barracks lately," he said.

"That place is dangerous." She took another gulp of vodka. "My little brother, my grandparents... I had to get them out of there."

"Where? Where do you go at night, anyway?"

"I found alternate housing. In... what do they call it..." She lifted an arm and waved vaguely in the direction of the Hudson River. "Jer-Zee?"

That led to a new round of questions. She tuned them out, half-closing her eyes and forcing herself to take short regular breaths: in, out, in out. Her awareness expanded outward. She could hear the bartender's breathing, the low murmur of the TV. Felt the subway tremble. Heard the honk and screech of traffic a block away on West Street. She tasted the filthy tide of the Hudson, rushing to the sea.

She shivered and took another drink. Still nothing; just a dull ache where the relief should be. She glanced at the door, wondering if Budda-lo would actually try to follow her onto the PATH train, all the way to Jer-Zee.

The door creaked open and a handsome young Earthman stepped into the bar. No, not stepped... *strutted* was a better word. He wore jeans and a sweatshirt, one of those garments the Terrans called a hoodie, with the hood down loose around his shoulders. As he walked past the table, his gaze met Kir-ra's for a moment, and a strange light flashed in his dark eyes.

Budda-lo cleared his throat. "You know," he said, "as bad as all this is... at least we got to experience the awe, the majesty of space travel."

She almost laughed. Really? she thought.

The Earthman crossed to the bar. The bartender nodded, and the man greeted him with a short "Hey, Feliks." They fell into a low-voiced conversation. Kir-ra couldn't make out the words.

Budda-lo continued, undeterred. "The roar of rockets, the view of our world from the endless void. Don't you think it was all kind of…" He paused for effect. "I don't know. Beautiful?"

"I think it was kind of like watching everyone and everything you know get blown to atoms," she said.

The Earthman turned at that. An approving smile teased at the corners of his lips. There was something coiled about him, something almost… Kree. As if he'd been born to violence and expected, even welcomed it.

She felt a surge of attraction for this man, a sudden burst of longing. All at once she realized: I'm very lonely. I was lonely long before I came to this cold rock in space.

Budda-lo glared at the Earthman, who met his gaze without flinching. When he turned back to Kir-ra, his whole manner had changed.

"You think you're so special," Budda-lo said, raising his voice. "Don't you?"

Kir-ra tensed. At the bar, the Earthman slid easily off his stool. The bartender's eyes flitted from one of them to the other.

"All that training," Budda-lo sneered. "You were gonna be a *soldier*. Gonna get offworld, leave us poor grunts behind working on the assembly line. Maybe think about us once in a while, shake your head at the poor wage slaves you grew up with. Right?"

She said nothing. His words didn't sting, didn't hurt at all. The only thing on her mind was getting rid of him, as quickly and painlessly as possible.

"Well, guess what?" He leaned toward her, practically spitting the words. "You're not gonna be a soldier. You're not gonna leave us behind. You're just another sorry little Kree, and you're gonna work till you drop for *Tony Stark,* just like the rest of us."

The Earthman took a step closer.

"I tried," Budda-lo continued. The alcohol seemed to have hit him all at once; his voice quavered. "I have tried to be nice to you. Why can't you just..."

He touched her shoulder – and her training kicked in. Before Budda-lo could say another word, he was flying over the table. The bartender stepped back and the Earthman snatched his drink out of the way, just in time. Budda-lo slammed into the bar with a sharp crack and a howl of pain.

Kir-ra stared at him, breathing hard. "How's your back now?" she asked.

Budda-lo wiped blood off his lip. He scrambled off the bar, avoiding the amused looks of the bartender and the Earthman. He clattered up against a chair, then circled around the high table where Kir-ra sat. She hadn't even gotten off her stool.

When he reached the door, he turned to glare back at her. "You're nothing special," he spat. "You're gonna die here, just like us. Die like the loser you are."

He tried to slam the door on his way out. But it just swung shut without a sound, sealing off the bar again from the outside world.

The Earthman stood up and started toward her. "This place used to attract a better class of people," he said.

She was shaking, she realized. Budda-lo's taunts had meant nothing – until he'd talked about dying here. She had already given up on becoming a soldier; the Kree-Skrull War was long over. But the thought of being stuck on this miserable world for the rest of her life... exploited by the wealthiest of its cruel, venal oligarchs...

"Here." The Earthman handed her a glass filled with a dark brown liquid. "I got Feliks to pull out the good stuff. He saves it for his best customers."

The bartender didn't answer. He sat engrossed in another cheap show, a children's horror series called *Dark Mummy*.

Kir-ra accepted the drink with a polite grimace. She wanted nothing to do with Earth, with its manipulative denizens and their sick games. But there was something about this man, something that drew her in.

And the drink *was* good. It went down smooth, filling her throat with a deep warm fire. The world spun around for a moment; she gasped, drawing the stale air of the bar into her lungs.

When she looked up, the Earthman was seated across from her. Had she invited him to join her? She couldn't remember.

"Nice move," he said, raising his hand to trace the path Budda-lo had taken through the air. "You're pretty lean for a barroom brawler."

She gave him a wary look. Was he making fun of her? He smiled and gestured at her drink. She considered for a moment, then took another gulp.

"What was that technique?" he asked. "Aikido?"

"It's called Sen-Zha," she said.

"Sen-Zha. Not a fighting tradition I've heard of. It involves turning your opponent's strength against them, doesn't it?"

She shrugged.

"You don't look like a fighter." He paused, then hurriedly added, "I mean, you look like you're meant for, well. Higher things."

She closed her eyes. Once again, she felt the evil, the oppressive force that had followed her to this planet. "There are no higher things," she said.

"You're wrong," he whispered.

She was conscious of the silence, the stale air. The only sound came from the TV behind the bar, a low-volume chatter of distant voices.

"That wasn't some random encounter," the Earthman said. "You know that guy."

She nodded. "We work together."

"Office romance! An old story." He straightened up, smirking a little. "I prefer self-employment. Fewer complications."

"Must be nice to have a choice."

"Let's see." He straightened up, studying her. "You're adept at a fighting technique whose name does not derive from any known language. Also – and I admit this is the bigger clue – we don't see a lot of blue girls on the West Side. You're not from around here, are you?"

She took another drink. This man was puzzling, alluring, and infuriatingly full of himself. And this, she knew, was the crucial moment. She could either trust him, or put down the drink and walk out.

"Have you heard of the Kree-Skrull War?" she asked.

"They did a special about it, on one of the streaming channels." He frowned. "Big space battle, right?"

"That's one way to put it. The Kree-Skrull War raged on for years... two mighty stellar empires, neither willing to yield to the other. In the end, it claimed the lives of over five billion people. Including both of my parents."

"I'm sorry," he said. "I'm an orphan too."

"Don't be sorry. They were warriors, proud soldiers in the service of Kree supremacy. They died in battle, serving the purpose for which they were trained."

"And you?" he asked.

"Same deal." She let out a sigh. The alcohol was definitely hitting her now. "Or at least, that was the plan. Praeterus, my homeworld... there aren't a lot of opportunities for advancement. Weren't. Being a soldier was pretty much the only way to get offworld."

"So you, what? Trained?"

"Oh yes." She looked away, remembering. "I wanted to pursue officer training, like my mother and my brother. But like you said, I'm not built like a fighter. My teachers said I might want to consider *dance*." She let out a cold laugh. "To the Kree, that's an insult."

"Not patrons of the arts, your people?"

"You'd be surprised. There's more appreciation than you'd think."

"I meant no offense. Did you want to be a dancer?"

"What? I don't know. On Praeterus, you just don't make your living that way. I come from a long line of... I mean, there have always been soldiers in our family. It was expected." Again, she sighed. "For my little brother, too."

He nodded, gesturing for her to continue.

"Anyway. After my parents were gone, I had to take care of the family, so I just kept working in the plant. Ten hours a day, sometimes twelve or sixteen. Munitions – the only real business on Praeterus. Then, at night, I studied combat. The teacher suggested Sen-Zha. It's a technique used by third-level Kree battalions, designed to allow less physically strong soldiers to fight effectively. It teaches you to tune your senses, to send your awareness out into the world. You take in every bit of information about your opponent and their surroundings, so you can pinpoint their weaknesses and defeat them."

"I'd say the training paid off."

"It might have, except for two things. One, the war ended."

"The soldier's dilemma," he said. "What to do in peacetime?"

"Well, I knew the answer to that one," she snapped. "Keep working in the munitions plant. But that wasn't an option after the planet exploded."

His eyes went wide. "Really?"

"Yeah."

"The planet... exploded? What happened? Was it the Skulls?"

"*Skrulls* – no, I don't think so. Nobody knows, really. One day, life was just the usual mind-numbing drudgery, and then the next... KA-BOOMMM."

"I'm so sorry. But you escaped?"

"A few hundred of us. Out of eighty thousand." She shook her head. "So many lives lost... and then we got this offer. Come to Earth... a *pilot work program*, they said. You'll be welcome, trained and treated well."

"But it hasn't worked out that way."

"Ha! Same lies, different planet. Work the assembly line for long hours, terrible pay. Dirty, cramped barracks with half a dozen people crammed into one room. The work quotas are inhuman... even worse than back home. We all had to sign employment contracts making it impossible to quit. And even if we did, who else would hire..."

"...aliens," he finished.

She smiled wryly and took another sip. Slow down, she told herself. You're talking too much.

"It's almost funny," she said. "Back on Praeterus, I worked full shifts at the munitions plant and studied combat techniques every spare minute. And there was my brother to take care of – he was supposed to go to Officer Academy! And my grandparents, and... I don't think I ever got more than three hours' sleep in a night. I used to pray to leave that place, get on a ship and speed away and never, ever come back."

"Well, you did get away." He paused. "How does it feel?"

She looked at him for a long moment.

"It's the same," she said.

"Look," he said, smiling a warm smile. "Earth is rough. I've had to fight for everything I ever got, and believe me that ain't much. But it's easier if you got friends."

"I have friends," she said, feeling suddenly defensive. "A group of us banded together, even hired a lawyer. But I don't think that's going to…"

She trailed off, feeling a cold lump of panic form in her stomach. "I shouldn't be talking to you," she whispered, rising to her feet. "Who are you? Do you work for him? For Stark?"

The Earthman's eyes grew cold. He stood up, glaring as if she'd just delivered a mortal insult.

"I do *not* work for Anthony Stark," he rasped.

"OK." She blinked, feeling foolish. "Sorry. I'm… I'm so tired. This is my first day off in weeks."

He smiled again. "Of course."

"It's just… I can't afford trouble. I just want to be left alone, to take care of…" She shook her head. "I should get home."

"To your brother," he said.

"And my grandparents. In the evacuation, we… I thought we'd lost them…"

Again, she told herself: stop talking! She hurried toward the door, grabbed hold of the handle–

"Hey, dancer?"

She stopped, turned. The Earthman stood by the table, smiling at her.

"Stop by again," he said. "Feliks and I'll be waiting."

The bartender didn't look up. He'd clicked over to another show, a telenovela called *Dear Marsha*.

She nodded, flashed the man a sad smile, and turned away. Then she pulled open the door and stepped out into the night.

The man watched her go, standing rigid until she was gone. Then, slowly, he reached up to pull the hood up over his head. The smile on his face turned cold, little fires glowing in his eyes.

"She's here, Master," he said.

The bartender raised an eyebrow, but didn't respond. He fiddled with the TV, searching for a new program.

"Yes," the hooded man continued. "Oh, yes indeed. I think I'm going to enjoy this."

# CHAPTER 12

Tony Stark, chairman and CEO of Stark Enterprises and part-time Invincible Iron Man, had a headache. In fact, he had a lot of headaches. F.R.I.D.A.Y., his digital assistant, was reading off a pretty good list of them through the implant in his ear.

"...earnings down in the west coast office. Stock took a slight dip yesterday; not enough to panic over, but a bad leading indicator. In spandex-related news, S.H.I.E.L.D. sent over some intel regarding A.I.M. activity on a private Pacific island... I have updated the Avengers casefile accordingly."

Tony sighed and tried to smile, focusing on his second headache: Jen, the lawyer sitting across from him. She was reading off a list of... something. Labor problems, maybe?

"...unsanitary conditions," Jen said. "Workers forced to sleep in barracks not designed as permanent living quarters. Doors locked from outside after dark, effectively holding them prisoner at severe safety risk."

F.R.I.D.A.Y.: "...in possible acquisitions news, chip manufacturer Zendor has come on the market. They've made some breakthroughs in RFID that might complement our own."

Jen: "...lack of transportation. The workers who do not live on-site must either park a great distance away, or take multiple buses in order to access the facility..."

Tony tuned them both out and swiveled his desk chair, turning to gaze out the window. His third-floor office looked down on the old Stark shipyard, a disused pier jutting out into Long Island Sound. On that pier, his father had supervised the outfitting of battleships, military copters, even nuclear subs. It had been abandoned years ago in favor of the new factories and experimental labs located elsewhere in the complex.

He squinted, taking in the discolored wood of the pier, the dark supports vanishing down into the water. Most of the structures had been razed long ago, but a small shack still stood right in the middle of the pier, its roof tiled with multiple patches applied over the years. As a boy, Tony had hidden in that shack every chance he got – watching the ships come in, the workers load and unload weapons of war. He even had a nickname for it: Shackie.

No one had used Shackie for decades. But he'd never allowed it to be torn down.

A wave of emotion washed over him, a strong sensation that took him a minute to pin down. Nostalgia, yes, but mixed with a strange, helpless exhaustion. This was the original Stark Enterprises facility, the place where his father had amassed the family fortune. Tony rarely came here anymore, preferring to conduct his business from the Manhattan and Malibu offices.

But with Pepper Potts gone, his duties had multiplied. Along with those headaches.

"...lease is up on the west coast nuclear facility." F.R.I.D.A.Y.'s voice was designed to be soothing, but it wasn't having that effect today. "I'm preparing a list of possible alternatives, though the contamination risks involved in a move should definitely be considered..."

"...implicit threat of starvation," the lawyer said. "Long-term 'trial' pay rates far below the legal minimum, forcing the workers to incur dangerous levels of overtime..."

"...code violations in Manhattan," F.R.I.D.A.Y. continued. "It's the building's fault, not ours, but we'll probably have to free up some funds to help them modernize. Oh, and this just in from S.H.I.E.L.D.: a prison escape. It's the Melter–"

"The *Melter*?" Tony snapped. "How could a clown like the *Melter* escape from a secure government–"

The desk in front of him split in half with a loud CRACK, knocking his chair off its casters. He tumbled to the ground and rolled to a crouch, instinctively calling the first piece of his armor to him. Nanomachines responded to the call, flitting through the air to form a gauntlet on his outstretched hand. He looked up–

The lawyer stood over the broken desk, shaking a dark green fist. Jennifer Walters – She-Hulk – glared down at him, dark hair framing her furious emerald features. Her Cartier business suit wasn't quite as expensive as his, but close.

"Are you even listening to me?" Jen asked.

"F.R.I.D.A.Y.," he said. "Pause all feeds."

"Pausing. Would you like–"

"Silent mode."

Jen stepped over the desk and waved the list of grievances at him. "I said, are you listening?"

"I am. Now."

She grimaced, reached out a hand, and helped him to his feet. With a mental command he dismissed the armor, not even watching as the iron glove on his hand dissolved back up into the air.

"Sorry about your desk," she said.

"I probably had it coming." He straightened, ran a hand through his hair, and forced a smile onto his face. "So what is all this? Who's hired you again?"

"Read it for yourself."

He took the paper, yanked his chair upright, and sat down. "'Class action... non-native...'" He looked up. "This is the Kree? This is about that program?"

"Yes."

"Carol – Captain Marvel – she set this up. She *implored* me to set this up. Their planet blew up, they had nowhere to go, so we invited them here. To Earth."

"That doesn't give you the right to exploit them."

"I am not exploiting them!"

"They say differently." Jen sat back down in her chair, crossing her long green legs and staring at him over the splintered remains of his desk. "And they've hired me to resolve the matter."

"Hired you?"

"Well, it's pro bono." She leaned forward. "These are serious charges, Tony. Take a look at this employment contract."

He accepted the new paper. "'Mandatory terms of...' This is ridiculous. This isn't Stark boilerplate... I would never make people sign something like this."

"Well, someone in your company did. I have scans of one hundred seventy-three fully executed contracts, all identical."

"Jen." He lowered the paper. "Should I have a lawyer here too?"

"The next meeting, you will."

"'Punishing work quotas,'" he read. "'Threats of dismissal in the event they join labor unions. Inhuman working conditions.' Well, some of them might *be* Inhumans–"

"That should read 'inhumane'. I haven't proofread this yet." She snatched the papers back. "In fact, I'm committing a questionable act by bringing it to you on an informal basis, before I file it."

"I appreciate that. I'm not too proud to play the Avengers card." He looked up, serious now. "But I swear to you, Jen – this can't be happening. I would never allow it."

"I believe you." Her green eyes bored into his. "So who did?"

"I… well… When Carol dumped this project in my lap… at a terrible time, by the way. She's as bad as Thor – those big-picture cosmic types never worry about who's going to have to work out the details. The legal hoops, the immigration and tax paperwork involved in employing nonterrestrials–"

"Tony!"

"Right, right, yeah. Well, I did what I always do when something new and impossibly complicated lands on my desk. I handed it to Pepper."

"This doesn't look like her signature," Jen said, squinting at the contract. "Can we talk to her, figure out who *she* delegated it to?"

"Talk to Ms Potts," Tony repeated. "Ah. That might be tricky."

"Why? Oh, is she on the west coast?" Jen looked at her expensive watch and laughed. "Tony, I can wait till she gets up–"

"I don't know where she is."

He turned away and walked to the wall, pausing under a grim portrait of his father, munitions industrialist Howard Stark. He ran a hand across the expensive carved frame, the faded wood-grain paneling along the wall. Everything in this office dated back to his father's time; he'd never replaced any of it.

"Pepper needed a break," he said.

Jen cleared her throat. "From, uh–"

"From all of it." He turned, grimacing. "She's gone on an

extended cruise, to get her head together. And I don't… I can't even spare the time to figure out where *we* stand, her and me, because with her gone my workload has quadrupled. My attention's split in a million directions. In programming terms, it's like having to do everything yourself – the conceptual work and the coding and the debugging, too – it's too much. I can't get my breath, Jen."

He paused, eyes wide. Get a grip on yourself, he thought. You're shaking.

Jen frowned at him for a moment. Then she nodded and gestured to his chair. He took a last look at his father's visage, glaring down from the wall like some nineteenth-century railroad magnate. Then he crossed back to his shattered desk and sat down.

"Look," she said, "I get the whole work/life dilemma. I spent so many years focusing on my career, I barely had a personal life at all." She spread her green arms wide. "And then the whole gamma-ray business…"

"Yeah," he replied. "A double life sure doesn't make things easier."

"I just kept climbing that corporate ladder," she continued. "Then, one day I woke up to find myself in a high-paying job, with perks I never dreamed I'd have. And all it made me was…"

He looked down at the remains of the desk. "Angry?"

"Angry," she agreed. "So I decided I had to identify the problem and deal with it. I realized I didn't like myself much, not anymore. I didn't like taking money from rich scum, being paid to protect them from people who couldn't afford to fight back."

"Um. Ouch."

She gave him an apologetic smile. "Sorry."

He smiled back. "So you quit."

"I quit. Hung out my shingle and started cultivating a different kind of client." She leaned way forward, over the broken desk, looking into his eyes. "Which brings me here to you, on this fine Saturday morning."

"Jen." He edged his chair forward, meeting her above the wreckage. "I swear, I don't know–"

"I know, I know. I guess I'm trying to say, I understand." She let out a deep sigh. "It's not easy. Any of it."

He nodded.

"Let's just identify the problem," she said, standing up and moving to the window. "The Kree all work at this location. Is that correct?"

"As far as I know." He frowned; suddenly she sounded like a lawyer again. "Most of them were hired to assemble aeronautics components and special-order equipment. In the factory complex, right next door."

"Then it should be a simple matter to inspect that complex and evaluate the conditions. Right?"

He found himself hesitating. He'd known Jen Walters for years, fought alongside her against the Starbrand, the Masters of Evil, even the godlike Celestials. And he really did appreciate her bringing this problem directly to him. In doing so, she was straining her relationship with her clients, maybe even putting her license at risk.

But even so, a part of him bristled at her suggestion. Who was she to come into his place of business – the company his father had built – and make demands? To insist on an inspection of Stark Enterprises' facilities?

Couldn't she just trust him to sort it out?

"Tony?" Jen prompted.

"Mister Stark?"

"F.R.I.D.A.Y.," he snapped, "I said silent–"

"Yes sir," the voice in his ear said. "But I've detected two unidentified figures in the stairwell, approaching this level."

"Tony," Jen repeated, more firmly. "Is there a problem?"

"Maybe." He turned to face the door. "Someone's coming."

# CHAPTER 13

In an instant Jen was at his side, her fists clenched. "I take it you weren't expecting visitors," she said.

"If I was, they'd have clearance to take the elevator. Which they don't."

He felt strangely calm. Jen was clearly angry about the Kree problem, angry enough to smash office furniture. And yet, when faced with a possible threat, she hadn't hesitated to join forces with him. That was good to know.

"Besides," he added, "no one's working here on Saturday."

"Except the Kree," Jen said.

"Can you let that go for *one second*?"

He reached out a hand. On a table across the room, a swarm of metal components rose into the air, forming the rough outline of an Iron Man costume. Not yet, he thought. Just keep it ready.

"Boss," F.R.I.D.A.Y. said, "They're here."

The door clicked open. Jen stepped forward. Tony glanced back at the hovering costume and summoned a single glove, which wafted over to fasten itself silently on his outstretched hand.

A tall, muscular kid ran into the room. He had blue skin and wore a dirty beige jumpsuit. He couldn't have been more than sixteen.

Tony lowered the gauntlet, frowning "Hey, buddy." He held out his ungloved hand. "You're, uh, Kree, right?"

The kid said nothing. Just stood in the doorway, studying the two Avengers with defiant but wary eyes. Tony had a sudden flash of memory: himself as an angry teenager, visiting this very office. The look in this kid's eyes was familiar.

Jen turned to Tony, raising an eyebrow. "Should I add child labor to the charges?"

He sighed. "*One* second. Just one–"

"Halla-ar! Halla-ar, wait up!"

At the sound of the newcomer's voice, Tony relaxed instantly. "It's OK," he said to Jen. "You can stand down."

"Halla-ar!" A giant-sized leg appeared in the doorway, followed by the normal-sized body of Kamala Khan no, Ms Marvel, to be precise. She stopped short, took in the sight of the kid standing quietly, then furrowed her brow, retracting her leg to its normal length. She turned to Tony with a sheepish smile. "Uh, hi, Mister Stark. Tony."

"Ms Marvel," he said. "How's it going? And, more to the point: who's your friend?"

The Kree kid crept up beside Ms Marvel, his every movement tense and wary. He touched her arm and pointed at the wreckage of Tony's desk. She took it in, blinked, then turned to glare up at Jennifer Walters.

"Tony," Ms Marvel said, "are you under attack?"

"What? No no no! Well, not physically." He stepped forward, between Jen and Ms Marvel. "This is Jennifer Walters. She's not a villain, she's a lawyer."

"Also a Hulk," Jen growled.

"Easy, Jen. This is K... uh, this is our young Ms Marvel. She's an Avenger too, a new recruit."

He winced. He'd almost blurted out Kamala's real name. Like Spider-Man, Ms Marvel kept her true identity a closely guarded secret. Tony could barely remember what that had been like, back in the day.

Ms Marvel frowned. "If you're not under attack, what happened to your desk?"

"Oh, the, uh, desk?" Tony shook his head, embarrassed. "We had a killer end-of-week party in here yesterday. Clowns, balloon animals, the whole nine. Still cleaning up."

"Can't trust those clowns," Jen added, deadpan.

Ms Marvel raised an eyebrow. "You know I'm not five, right?"

Tony paused, his eyes drawn to the Kree teenager – Halla-ar, Ms Marvel had called him. The kid hadn't moved, but his eyes bored into Tony with an uncomfortable intensity.

"What are you two kids doing here?" Tony asked.

"I tried calling you," Ms Marvel said. "A lot of times. But I couldn't get through."

Tony cocked his head. "F.R.I.D.A.Y.?"

"You put me in silent mode," the AI said. It sounded a bit sulky.

"Sorry about that." He grimaced at Ms Marvel. "I am totally overloaded here. What is it?"

"Well..." She hesitated. "I, uh... I needed to talk to you. About, um..."

"The exploitation of my people," the Kree kid said.

"Right. Yes. That." Tony shook his head, feeling overwhelmed. "I assure you, I take this problem seriously. Increasingly seriously. In fact, that's why Ms Walters is here."

Ms Marvel frowned at Tony. "You mean it's true?"

"I don't know!"

Jen was watching him carefully. Ms Marvel's eyes were wide behind her mask. Halla-ar just turned away in disgust.

"Look," Tony continued, "the first I heard of these accusations was literally forty minutes ago. Everything about them is totally, one hundred percent contrary to the ethos by which I run my business. If there is a problem, I promise you I will handle it."

"Um, excuse me for saying this, Mister Stark." Ms Marvel smiled nervously. "But you sound a little defensive."

"What's the matter, Tony?" Jen asked. "Little people ganging up on the poor misunderstood billionaire?"

"Have you seen this one in action?" Tony gestured at Ms Marvel. "Believe me, she's no 'little people.'"

"Enough!"

They all turned as Halla-ar reached up, grabbed hold of the frame holding Howard Stark's portrait, and yanked it free of the wall. He lifted it into the air and hurled it straight at Tony, who leapt out of the way. The portrait crashed to the floor in an explosion of glass and splinters.

"Halla-ar!" Ms Marvel reached for him, growing as she moved. Her body expanded to twice its normal size.

"See what I mean?" Tony asked. "Not so little."

Halla-ar backed up toward the door, dropping into a combat-ready crouch. "Coming here," he growled, "was a mistake."

A repulsor-ray charge glowed red on the palm of Tony's glove. He glanced at Jen, who cleared her throat. "Kid," she said, "I should probably mention–"

Halla-ar ignored her. "You brought me here," he said, glaring at Ms Marvel. "To this exploiter, this rich man's place of power. So you could grovel and apologize and play up to him for favors."

"That's not true," Ms Marvel said.

"My people, my sister – they work themselves to death,"

Halla-ar spat. "To support *his* lifestyle. While he rules over them like a feudal lord, with his money and his paintings and his fancy rich lawyer–"

"Uh, kid?" Jen interrupted. "Point of order. I'm *your* lawyer, not his."

Halla-ar paused, blinking. "You are the woman my sister and the others hired?"

"Well, 'hired' usually implies money changing hands. But yeah."

"Jennifer is also an Avenger," Tony said. "She and I were discussing this problem when you two decided to break and enter the office of a man with nuclear-powered lasers in his gloves. In fact, we were just about to investigate the matter."

Jen raised an eyebrow at him. "We?"

A flood of shame washed over him as he remembered his defensiveness earlier – the way he'd reacted to her suggestion that they inspect the factory together. That, he realized, was the way his father would have reacted. The arrogance of a cold, autocratic man, accustomed to unquestioned loyalty from everyone around him.

"Yeah," he said, looking up sheepishly at Jen. "We."

He crouched down and flipped over the painting, brushing splinters of wood off onto the floor. The canvas was torn in several places. A shard of glass jutted out of Howard Stark's dark, glaring eye.

Love you, Dad, he thought. But I don't want to be you.

"I apologize for the damage," Halla-ar said. Ms Marvel shrank back to normal size, eyeing him carefully.

"Forget it, kid." Tony lifted up the painting, gazed at the torn face of his father, and tossed it on top of the cracked desk. "This place is overdue an upgrade."

An explosion rocked the building. Tony grabbed for a chair to brace himself.

Jen moved to assume a defensive position, back-to-back with him. "What's going on?" she asked.

"Something on the roof, from the sound of it." Tony touched his earpiece. "F.R.I.D.A.Y.?"

Ms Marvel ran to the window and looked outside. "I can see energy flashing, down on the pier," she said. "And people. Maybe three or four…"

"F.R.I.D.A.Y., talk to me." Another explosion. "What are we facing? Galactus, the Wrecker? Black Order, maybe?"

"No, boss. I'm afraid it's…"

A shadow fell over the building. Suddenly, Tony knew. His heart sank in his chest plate. No, he thought, anything but that. Don't let it be them. Don't let it be…

"…the Guardians of the Galaxy."

# PART THREE

## TILL PROVEN GUILTY

# CHAPTER 14

"OK, it's definitely the Guardians," Tony said. "That's their idiot-in-chief down there on the ground, Peter Porcupine or something. Looks like he's picked a fight with some workers... yes, kid. You don't have to raise your hand."

"Sorry, just one question." Kamala smiled, feeling a bit silly. "Who are the Guardians of the Galaxy?"

"Ah!" Tony turned away from the window. He wore his full uniform now, the gleaming red and gold armor of Iron Man, with his face exposed. "That's a long story."

"Are they villains? What do they want?"

"They're not bad guys. They're just mercenaries, and I don't trust mercenaries. Also, they're very stupid."

Jennifer Walters leaned down to mock-whisper in Kamala's ear. "He thinks everyone's stupid."

Kamala laughed a little too loud. As Iron Man, Tony Stark commanded the most advanced battlesuit on Earth. His repulsors could channel three thousand kilowatts of power, his uni-beam nearly three times that. His boot-jets were miracles of miniaturization, and his servo-joints were as nearly frictionless as twenty-first century technology allowed.

But to Kamala, Jen was twice as cool. Imagine being as strong as the Hulk, and a lawyer too! And that suit she wore wasn't just expensive, it fit her perfectly. Jen seemed incredibly confident, too, like she knew exactly how cool she was. Like she'd never doubted it for a second.

Unflappable, Kamala thought. That's the word. She's unflappable.

The building shook again. Tony cocked his head, listening to a voice in his helmet. Then he jetted up into the air and arced over the wreckage of his desk, past the tattered canvas that had been his father's portrait, to land in front of Jen and Kamala.

"The Guardians," he said. "That janky spaceship of theirs is hovering directly over this building. You two want to check it out? I'll handle the imbecile on the ground."

"Got it," Jen said, turning toward the door.

"Wait a minute," Kamala said. "What about Halla-ar?"

The young Kree stood against the wall, eyeing them all suspiciously. Even me, Kamala thought. Was he right? Had it been a mistake to bring him here?

"Right." Tony willed his helmet to close, hiding his eyes. "Get down to ground level, Kree kid. Find a place to hunker down and stay put. And stop looking at me like that. I hate it when people look at me like that."

Halla-ar stood his ground, glaring.

"Hey." Kamala approached him. "It's OK."

"Tony, I've never met the Guardians," Jen said. "How many are there?"

"Well," Tony said, "let's see. There's the sword-woman, Gamora, and … oh, I dunno. Anywhere from two to five – maybe more." He spread his arms, took to the air, and jetted over the desk-wreckage. "I'm calling in the guns, just in case. Backup."

He reached down to open the window. It didn't budge. He swore and pulled harder; nothing. "Aw, Dad," he muttered. "Really?"

Kamala stifled a giggle.

Tony sighed, reached out a glowing hand, and blasted the windowpane to pieces. Kamala jumped, startled. Jen just shook her head.

Tony paused, turned, and surveyed the wreckage of his office. "Yeah," he muttered, "definitely time for an upgrade." Then he lifted off and flew out the window, not looking back.

"We're up, kid," Jen said, starting for the door. "Let's go."

"Coming!"

Kamala turned to Halla-ar. Reluctantly, he took her hand and followed them out the door. As soon as they stepped into the hall, the entire building shook again.

"We've gotta get to the roof," Jen said. "Stairwell?"

Kamala pointed, leading the way. She took huge strides, stretching and retracting her legs. They rounded a corner and came to a fire door that had been wrenched off its hinges.

Jen looked at her, impressed. "You did this?"

Kamala cocked her head at Halla-ar. "Kree combat training," she explained.

Jen was already inside the stairwell, heading up. "Come on!"

"One sec." She turned to Halla-ar – who stood in the doorway, not moving. "Just go home, OK? We got this."

"My sister works in this facility," Halla-ar said. "I must find her, make sure she's safe."

"Oh. I get that." Kamala frowned. "Just be careful, OK?"

"I do not trust any of this." Halla-ar looked away. "You have only the word of Tony Stark that these Guardians are your enemies. What if they are here to *help* my people?"

"Then I'll take their depositions and add 'em to the court filing," Jen said. "Ms Marvel, let's go!"

Kamala took Halla-ar's hand again. He frowned, nodded, and leaned in close. "I will be careful," he said. "Don't worry about me."

Before she could blink, he was down the stairs and out of sight.

She cast a quick, worried glance after him, then began climbing the stairs. Jen had a big head start, so Kamala stretched her legs and vaulted up an entire level to catch up.

"Your boyfriend's a little suspicious, huh?" Jennifer shrugged off her suit-jacket, revealing a sleek purple-white costume beneath.

Kamala dodged the flying jacket, turning to watch as it fluttered down the stairwell. "He's not my boyfriend." A thunderous boom rang out, shaking the stairwell. She reached for the railing to steady herself. Jen just kept on running, her muscular green legs pounding on the metal stairs.

"Halla-ar told me about the Kree planet blowing up," Kamala said. "And about the working conditions here. That's a real thing?"

"It's real, and it's a problem," Jennifer said. "That's why I signed on with them. But there's stuff that doesn't add up."

"You believe Tony?"

"I believe he doesn't know what's going on. Wouldn't be the first time." Jen sighed. "But it's more than that. Their planet didn't just wear out and explode all by itself... Someone detonated it, deliberately. From what I hear, it might have been one of the Kree."

"Where..." Kamala struggled to keep up. "Where did you hear that? Is there a galactic TMZ or something?"

"Nope. Heard it from the Kree themselves. Some of them suspect the planet-killer might be here, hiding among the refugees."

"Here? Are you sure?"

"Nope. That's why I used the word *suspect*." Jen shrugged. "Innocent till proven guilty."

Kamala frowned. An alien planet-killer was a disturbing enough idea, but an alien planet-killer here on *Earth*? That was terrifying.

"Powers, Avenger," Jen said sharply. "What can you do?"

"Uh, they call it morphogenetics. My mass sort of travels through time, connecting different versions of—"

"The short version, please. We're almost out of stairs."

"I can make parts of me bigger or smaller. Or all of me! I heal pretty fast, too."

"That's useful," Jen replied. "Mostly I just punch stuff."

The stairs ended at a thick wooden door with a sign reading NO ADMITTANCE TO ROOF. Jennifer stopped, smiled at the thick padlock on the handle, and motioned Kamala back. Then she clenched her fist, reared back, and let fly a punch that chattered the door to splinters.

Kamala grinned. So cool.

She stuck her head out the door – just as a bright red beam of light shot down from above. Jen jumped back, shielding Kamala with her arm. The beam sizzled hot as it struck the roof, filling the air with a rich burning smell. The roof was pockmarked with blast craters, hot smoking depressions where something had melted the weathered tar of its surface.

A roar of sound washed over them. Cautiously, Jen stepped outside. Kamala followed, turning to look up…

A spaceship hovered in place, not more than twenty feet above. It was about the size of a military helicopter and shaped like a bird of prey, with sharp wings jutting out from both sides of its compact body. Jets pulsed along the lower hull, buffeting Jen and Kamala with blasts of hot air.

"That's the... janky spaceship?" Kamala asked.

The ship began to move, rumbling through the air. In a few seconds it would be out of reach, headed inland toward the newer, high-tech sections of the Stark Enterprises complex.

Jen sprinted after it. "Come on!"

Kamala felt a stab of fear. No, she realized, it wasn't exactly fear, more like insecurity. Jennifer Walters – the She-Hulk – she'd done this a thousand times, fought alongside the Avengers against unimaginable cosmic threats. Can I keep up with her? Kamala wondered. Am I actually ready for this?

Jennifer reached the edge of the roof and, without the slightest hesitation, leaped off. Hands reaching, scrabbling, she grabbed hold of the spaceship's wing and pulled herself up onto its hull.

Kamala steeled herself, gritting her teeth. There was no time for doubts; like Jen had said, she was an Avenger now. She ran forward, covering the roof in three long strides, taking care to avoid the burned craters in the tar. Then she stretched out her arms toward the fleeing ship, hissed in a breath, and jumped.

# CHAPTER 15

Tony Stark paused in midair, just outside his shattered office window. The pier lay below, strewn with girders and cinderblocks, separated from the mainland by an old chainlink fence. Peter Quill – Star-Lord of the Guardians of the Galaxy – hovered a few inches above the pier's surface, arguing with a trio of workers in faded green jumpsuits.

Kree, Tony thought. The workers must be Kree...

"F.R.I.D.A.Y.," he subvocalized. "Who did Ms Potts place in charge of the Kree program?"

"No details available," the voice said. "That information seems to have been deleted from the main server."

"Well, *that's* not suspicious or anything."

He frowned. He didn't know quite where he and Pepper stood. That was a puzzle for another day. But she would never have deleted or hidden sensitive information, any more than she would have hired vulnerable workers under punitive contracts. Not Pepper. Which meant that something *else* was wrong inside Stark Enterprises.

"Track it down, OK?" he asked. "At least find out which office they're working out of."

Down on the pier, Quill whipped out his element gun and started shouting. He wore his usual stupid cowboy suit, but no faceplate. He seemed angry.

"Data tracking will take a few minutes," F.R.I.D.A.Y. said. "There are some odd glitches in the system."

"That's OK," Tony replied. "I think I'm about to be busy."

He sent a silent command, ordering his armor to amplify the volume of Quill's voice. "…when somebody blew up the whole frickin' planet," the Guardian said, pointing at one of the Kree. "Maybe it was you?"

The Kree, a short muscular man with a crewcut, responded with a string of untranslatable obscenities. He seemed angry, but not intimidated.

Quill reached forward and grabbed the man by his shirt, hoisting him into the air. "I got some intel from a Jovian on Xandar," he snarled. "He said the planet-killer was a Kree with a scar."

The man looked puzzled, even in the air. "I don't have a scar."

"Well, I think he said scar. Might have been an ascot."

"I don't have one of those either." The Kree cocked his head. "Are you stupid?"

The other two Kree laughed. They looked like tough dock workers, the Kree equivalent of the working men who'd once hauled heavy equipment during wartime. Tony could almost see the scarred battleships parked alongside this very pier, majestic in their tarnished grandeur. How long ago had they stopped coming? He couldn't remember.

Quill pivoted in midair, pointed his element gun straight down, and fired. A blast of air shot out, blowing a hole in the splintered wood.

Tony turned and shot down toward the pier. By the time he

stopped, a few feet above, Quill was dangling the crewcutted Kree over the hole. The man looked down at the roiling water.

"Know what that is, smart guy?" Quill shook the man. "That's the Long Island Sound. You don't wanna go for a swim in that sewer, I can tell you."

"Actually," Tony said, "Sound's pretty clean."

Quill whipped his head up, pointing the element gun shakily in the air.

"Now, you want to play Jack Bauer with some poor alien…" Tony jetted sideways, still hovering in the air. "I'd threaten them with the Hudson next time. Much sludgier."

"Iron Man," Quill growled. Then, astonishingly, a smile spread across his face. "Iron Man! Been a while. What are you doing here?"

Tony raised an eyebrow and gestured inland. Quill squinted across a disused area just past the pier, overgrown with yellow grass. As he focused on the tall factory complex to the left, he mouthed the word spelled out in eight foot letters on the building's side: STARK.

"Oh yeah! Stark!" Quill looked sheepish. "Forgot where I was."

The Kree in Quill's grip shook his head. One of the other Kree let out a hiss of disgust. "Stark?" he growled. "The oppressor himself?"

"Come to watch us get shaken down?" another Kree asked, balling up his fists. "Maybe hand out a few eighteen-hour shifts?"

Jen was right, Tony thought. Something is definitely wrong in Kree-town.

"Eighteen-hour…" Quill's eyes narrowed. "You running some kind of sweatshop here, Stark?"

"Quill." Tony fought to control the impatience in his voice. "Let the man go, OK?"

"Not till I find out if he's the Kree with a scar. Or maybe it's a scalpel."

"Do your worst, Earthers," the Kree hissed.

Quill shook the man. "That's half-Earther to you!"

One problem at a time, Tony thought. Idiot first, Kree second. He reached out, selected a low repulsor setting, and fired a blast just below Quill's hovering feet. The bolt seared the surface of the pier; Quill tumbled out of the air, landing face-up with a groan. The Kree jumped free and ran to join his friends.

Before the Guardian could recover, Tony jetted over and landed with a thump, planting one foot on either side of Quill's body. "Listen, D'Artagnan," Tony hissed. "I don't know what kind of bounty you're chasing, but this is not going to produce the result you want."

"Boss Stark," Quill snarled. "Just another rich guy…" He raised the element gun and fired.

A tidal wave of water slammed into Tony, flinging him up into the air. He flailed, momentarily blinded, and came down hard, skidding across the length of the pier. He dug metal fingers into the surface, grabbing for the wooden posts along the side – slowing his progress until he jolted to a stop, his back slamming up against some barrier.

He turned to look. It was Shackie, the shack he'd hidden in as a kid. Its windows had been boarded up, the wooden door padlocked. The wall had a brand-new Iron-Man-shaped dent in it. He sighed in annoyance, tinged with a certain level of fatalism. Encounters with the Guardians usually turned violent sooner or later.

"Stay down, Stark." Quill stalked toward him, gun held high. "What's wrong with you, anyway? I'm just trying to mete out some interstellar justice here."

"Mete? Did you just say mete?"

"It's a word!"

Tony struggled to his feet, limbs aching. On paper, Quill's gun was no match for the Iron Man armor; it channeled a tiny fraction of the energy at Tony's command. But there was a weird, primal power to the Guardian's weapon. It packed a punch that couldn't be explained in strict engineering terms.

"What do you really want, Quill?" he asked. "There a reward out for this planet-killer, by any chance?"

"No! Well yeah, actually. But that's not the main reasAAAAAGGH!"

Quill swerved, almost dodging the twenty-foot girder Tony had hurled at him. Almost, but not quite. The half-ton of metal grazed his side, knocking him off balance. "Buckle up, Bill Gates," he hissed. He dropped to a crouch and began throwing cinderblocks, one after the other.

Tony dodged, jetting straight up into the air – with Quill right on his tail. One of the concrete blocks crashed into Shackie, punching a hole in the wall.

"Quill!" he called. "This is, like, not normal behavior. Are you on drugs or something? Space drugs?"

Quill snorted. "I wish!"

He lunged, reaching for Tony's feet. Tony flexed his leg and let out a sharp blast from his boot jets, knocking Quill off balance. But Quill fired as he tumbled away, sending out a spray of rocky earth-soil. Stones pelted Tony's helmet, blocking his vision. He maneuvered himself lower, using radar to zero in on the pier.

The workers turned to watch Tony land, glaring at him with undisguised hatred. A few more Kree had joined them, all wearing those vaguely alien-looking jumpsuits. "Listen," he said, spreading his arms. "I swear to you I know nothing about your difficult working conditions. When this is over–"

Fire engulfed him, setting off a swarm of alarms inside his helmet. He turned to see Quill swooping down, flame pouring out of that bizarre gun.

Stupid, Tony thought, activating foam nozzles to suppress the flame. I got distracted, waited a moment too long – gave him just enough time to recover. All this stress, all these distractions – I am *definitely* off my game–

Then he saw the girder in Quill's hand. "Batter up!" Quill called.

With a deafening *clang*, Tony shot backward through the air. He flew over the hole in the pier, past the glaring Kree workers. He craned his head around to see his path, and his heart sank. No, he thought. Not Shackie–

The weathered wall splintered under the first impact, barely slowing him down. He glimpsed the dusty crates inside the shack, the little improvised desk he'd hidden under as a child, as they sped by beneath. When he struck the second wall, crashing through it like a missile, the little shack buckled and crumbled.

He had no time to register the loss. He blasted his boot-jets, slowing his flight, and tumbled over the barrier at the end of the pier, splashing down into the water in a hiss of steam. Then he flailed beneath the surface, fuming. Suckered by that space idiot, he thought. Maybe I should just stay down here. Less humiliating.

"Boss," F.R.I.D.A.Y. said in his ear, "I have secured the information you wanted–"

"Bad timing, F.R.I.D.A.Y."

Enough, he thought. Time to straighten up, deal with this once and for all. This was Stark Enterprises, a highly respected research and development facility. Who did that cut-rate space cowboy think he was?

Tony flexed his armor, swimming upward. Checked the readouts, one by one, watching with satisfaction as his power levels rose. He fired up both repulsors and activated the uni-beam in his chest. By the time he cleaved the surface, he was glowing like a star.

"Should have stayed on Uranus, loser," he hissed.

The first repulsor blast slammed into Quill's chest, knocking the wind out of him. The second one blew him off his feet. Then the uni-beam glowed bright, channeling all the power of the arc reactor at the core of the Iron Man armor. With a pure white flash, the beam plowed into the Guardian, sending him tumbling and skidding the length of the pier.

The Kree broke and ran, scrambling toward shore. Quill shot past them, then let out a cry as he slammed up against the chainlink fence, tearing it loose from the ground at the base of the pier.

Tony jetted down, landed easily, and started walking toward land. Quill was down, unmoving. Tony read shallow breathing, a slow heartbeat. The Guardian was alive, but definitely unconscious.

Tony turned his attention to the factory complex, the high windowless building dotted with loading docks and fire escapes. Now, he thought. Now to find out what's going on here. Time to root out the cancer in my father's house–

He barely saw the streak of green, heard the icy battle-cry ring out. And then Gamora was upon him. She kicked out expertly, knocking him off balance, and jabbed a hard flat hand into his chest. As he fell backward, he fired off one repulsor, then the other. The first beam grazed her arm; the second one missed her completely.

He landed flat on his back, sending a painful jolt up his spine.

As he rolled up to a crouch, he saw the long, sharp sword in her hands. She brought it down at the edge of his chestplate, then dug in hard.

NO! he thought.

The arc reactor sparked and whined as she pried off its cover, twisting the sword like a crowbar. He reached up and grabbed for the blade, but she was too fast. As the reactor cover snapped free, she raised her sword in the air.

Off my game, he thought. Too many distractions – and in this game, just one distraction could be his last.

Gamora hesitated, staring at him with steel in her eyes. "You asked what we want," she said. "That's simple: to find the animal that killed our friend."

She brought down the sword, stabbing it into the arc reactor in a shower of sparks. Pain lanced through him as his heart convulsed; his world collapsed into an all-pervading haze of pain. And then he passed out.

# CHAPTER 16

A familiar tingle came over Kamala, the sign of her power activating. It felt like a sudden growth spurt powered by electromagnetic force; as if parts of her were changing, evolving, becoming something new.

She extended her body as far as she could, reaching for the fleeing spaceship. With a final thrust of her arm, she grabbed hold of a small protrusion on the bottom. It felt hot and rough to the touch. She winced, struggling to hang on. For the first time she wondered: why doesn't this costume have gloves?

Jen took hold of her arm and pulled her up. The spaceship lurched, and for a moment Kamala flailed in the air. Jen lifted her, as if she weighed nothing, and deposited her on the spaceship's wing.

Wind whipped through her hair; her sash rippled wildly in the air. They were moving inland, toward the gleaming towers and low circular structures of the Stark high-tech energy research sector. That was staffed entirely by humans, Halla-ar had told her, and she noticed now that the area looked deserted. Apparently only the Kree had to work on Saturday.

"You OK?" Jen yelled, over the rush of air and the roar of the engines.

Kamala smiled and nodded.

"Good. Follow me."

Jen crept up to the front of the wing, reaching for handholds and picking her way across the surface. When she leapt up to the main body of the ship, Kamala tensed, stretched out her arms, and followed.

The cockpit formed the raptor-ship's "head" – a semi-detached compartment with viewport windows on all sides, allowing the pilot to see in almost every direction. "Stay on the roof – away from the viewports!" Jen called. "We don't want them to know we're here!"

"Got it!"

Kamala followed Jen onto the opaque roof, extending and retracting her arms and legs to keep from falling off. Her foot came down hard and she winced, afraid she'd given their presence away. But the sound was lost in the thunder of the engines.

Jen moved like a cat, every step perfectly chosen. So cool, Kamala thought. Totally unflappable.

The ship tipped sharply to the side. Kamala tumbled for a moment, then grabbed hold of the roof. She caught a quick glimpse of an airplane hangar below. The pier was out of sight, hidden behind that tall factory building.

"I think they know we're here!" she said, pulling herself back up.

Jen hadn't moved; she was holding onto a gunport near the front of the roof. She shot Kamala a worried look. Kamala made a hasty thumbs-up gesture and then grabbed the roof with both hands as the ship lurched again.

A dark grimace came over Jen's face. She snarled, crouched down, and took hold of the front lip of the roof with both hands. Then she reared back and pulled, letting out a howl of fury.

A shiver ran up Kamala's spine. For the first time, she could really see the Hulk that lived inside Jennifer Walters.

The ship tilted again, but Jen paid no attention. She just held on, fingers straining, pulling back with all her strength. A loud crunching noise filled the air, penetrating the rush of wind and the roar of engines. Bolts cracked, plasteel fixtures snapped, viewport seals popped free…

Slowly but steadily, Jen peeled back the roof like a sardine-can lid.

Kamala stumbled up behind her, stretching her arms to keep hold of the roof supports. The unseen pilot was really shaking the ship now – definitely trying to throw them off. Jen squeezed her eyes shut and tugged one final time, snapping a huge chunk of roof free. As it tumbled off into the air, Kamala leaned forward to peer inside.

"Uh…" she began. "Is it normal for a spaceship to have a forest inside it?"

Thick vines reached up and grabbed hold of her arms, her torso. Jen's eyes snapped open in surprise as the vines seized her too, pulling her toward the opening. Before the two Avengers could react, they were flung one way, then the other, and then slammed down on the floor of the cockpit compartment.

"Uhh!" Kamala cried.

The vines thickened into branches, holding her tight. She caught sight of a figure sitting in the pilot's seat, a small humanoid creature with matted, tangled fur. Then the branches dragged her across the jagged floor to the back of the cockpit, into a thick jungle of floor-to-ceiling tree trunks.

Jen struggled. The branches tossed her up and she landed, with a loud *THUD*, on a crash couch. She sprang back up to her feet, but the branches kept hold of her wrists and ankles.

Kamala shook her head, dazed. Wind rushed all around, swirling in from the hole in the roof. Vines and branches coiled and whipped in the confined space, penning the two Avengers into a small alcove between two seats at the back of the cockpit. The vegetation was all linked together, like some crazy plumbing system made of… well, trees.

An ovoid face with dark eyes began to form in the nearest tree trunk. It jutted forward, wooden features twisting in curiosity as it studied the two women.

"I am Groot?" it asked.

Jennifer grunted, flexed, and snapped the wooden bonds holding one arm. Her fist flew forward, catching "Groot" straight in the nose – or where its nose should have been, anyway. As the creature cried out, the entire forest trembled in anger.

"Keep it down, kids," the pilot called. "Don't make me come back there!"

Jennifer pulled one leg free, lurching forward toward the angry Groot-face. Kamala struggled, but the branches tightened around her. *There's no way to grow my way out of this,* she thought. *I'll have to shrink instead…*

Then she felt a prickling on her arm. She turned to see sharp thorns, piercing her costume, just beginning to break the skin. A vine on her leg had sprouted dangerous-looking sucker protrusions, holding her firmly in place. That meant shrinking was out of the question, too. If the thorns didn't rip her apart, the suckers would tear her to pieces.

Jen kicked at a branch, knocking herself off balance – her

other leg was still restrained by Groot's many limbs. The tree-thing stretched forward and head-butted her, snarling, "I am Groot!" As Jen fell back, dazed, a fresh crop of thick branches snaked toward her, grabbing her tight.

"Just hold these spaceship vandals still for a sec, Groot," the pilot said. "I'm puttin' us on autopilot."

The branches tugged gently at Kamala, nudging her down into a crash seat. In the chair next to her, Jen squirmed and struggled in vain. The tree trunks began to thin and retract, clearing the space between the Avengers and the pilot. Groot eyed them coldly as his trunk-head glided to the side.

The pilot – who, yes, was covered with fur – rose to his feet. He snapped a small device free of the control panel and turned to face them, studying them with ratlike eyes. Then he strode toward them, pausing to wince at the gaping hole in the roof.

"Too bad Quill's not here," he said. "He always wanted a convertible."

"Are you a raccoon?" Kamala blurted.

The creature stopped to glare at her. "You ain't makin' this better," he growled.

Jennifer Walters grunted, struggling. "Let me go!"

The raccoon, or whatever it was, ignored her. "The real question," he said to Kamala, "is what *you* are." He held up his device, which looked vaguely like a large DVD remote, and aimed it straight at her head.

Kamala tensed, eyes wide.

"No!" Jen cried.

Groot, who had shrunk down to a single body with a couple dozen protruding branches, nudged the pilot-creature on the shoulder. "I am Groot," he pointed out.

The pilot glanced at his friend, puzzled, then looked down at the device in his hand. "What? Oh…" Then, smirking, he raised the device, pointed it straight at Jen, and pressed a button.

A light turned deep red on the front of the "remote." Jen blinked in surprise.

"You – hahaha!" the pilot said. "You thought this was a… a gun or somethin'? Hahahahaha!"

Groot looked disapproving. "I am Groot."

"It was too funny." He turned to Kamala. "Wasn't that funny?" Kamala just glared at him.

"Nobody gets my sense of humor." The creature flipped the device around in his hand. "This, sweetheart, is a simple Kree life-signs detector. It's what brought us to this Jersey factory-outlet of a planet in the first place–"

"This is *not* New Jersey," Kamala snapped.

"New, old, whatever." The creature gestured at the device, indicating the red light. "Point is, this dingus says you people ain't Kree. Though I'm gettin' a slightly funny reading off *you*."

He glared at Kamala again. It's my powers, she realized; they're Kree-based. She opened her mouth to explain, then thought better of it. The raccoon didn't look ready to sit still for a long explanation.

"I am Groot," Groot said.

"Huh, that's true," the raccoon said. "They could be *workin'* with the Kree."

"She's their lawyer," Kamala said, and immediately regretted it.

"I am Groot!"

"Right?" the pilot said, turning to Jen. "'Aha', indeed!"

"I will kill you," Jen hissed.

"Ah, objection, counselor!" The pilot ran a very humanlike hand through his thick head-fur. "Hostile. Intimidating the witness, or whatnot."

Jennifer breathed slowly, regularly, in and out. She's calming herself, Kamala realized. Considering what to do next. Trying to regain her unflappability. Unflappableness? Unflappabosity?

"Listen, guys," Kamala began. "I think we got off on the wrong foot here. My name's Ms Marvel... what's yours?"

"I am Groot," Groot said.

"Yeah," his friend agreed.

Kamala and Jen just stared at them.

"Rocket," the pilot said. "He said my name is Rocket."

"Rocket," Kamala repeated. "OK. So why are you hunting the Kree?"

"We ain't hunting all of 'em. Just one."

"I am Groot."

"Yeah, maybe more than one."

Jen cleared her throat. "You may not realize this," she said, "but the Kree have been treated very poorly on Earth."

Rocket shrugged. "I been treated poorly all my life. You don't see me runnin' around blowing up planets."

"What about the heat rays you were shooting at the office complex?" Kamala asked.

"Huh? Oh, that? That was just me blowin' off steam. I had this quantum force generator installed a couple months ago, but Quill won't let me use it. For once he ain't around to stop me." He grinned. "I call it the Big Burn Beam."

"I am Groot."

"Yeah, fair point. It is gratuitous."

"The Kree," Jennifer said, "have engaged my services to improve conditions at Stark Enterprises. Among other things, they have been deprived of medical care and locked in their barracks at night."

Groot and Rocket exchanged glances. For the first time,

they seemed uncertain. Jen had her "forceful" voice on; once again, she sounded like a lawyer. Kamala felt a weird impulse to solemnly swear something.

"Whatever the truth of these accusations," Jen continued, "it's fair to say that the Kree have a lot to deal with right now. So why are you harassing them? What are you actually looking for?"

Groot's eyes narrowed. He nudged Rocket aside, shuffling his arboreal head over to glare directly into Jen's eyes. Several dozen branches still protruded from his body, holding Jen and Kamala tight in their chairs.

"I am Groot," he growled. "*Groot.*"

"He says we're huntin' a planet-killer," Rocket hissed. "A planet-killer that also murdered our friend."

Kamala felt a sudden stab of doubt. Were the Kree, she wondered, as innocent as they seemed? She liked Halla-ar, but there was no denying that he could be… violent. What was he really capable of?

Jennifer stared into Groot's grim wooden features. "I'm sorry about your friend," she said. "But you have to know that the Avengers won't let you terrorize innocent people."

"The Avengers?" Rocket laughed. "Is that still a thing?"

"*I* won't let you."

With those words, Jennifer flexed all four arms and legs, striking out in four directions at once. The Groot-branches holding her cracked and snapped – all except the vines holding her left leg.

"I am Groot!"

"Yeah, got that already," Jennifer snarled. She reached down, grabbed the vine holding her leg, and yanked hard. Groot's heavy tree-body lurched forward, tumbled off balance, and crashed to the floor.

Kamala felt her own restraints loosen as Groot turned his full attention to Jen. She reached up, carefully plucked the thorns from the arms of her costume, and pulled herself free.

"Now listen!" Jen yelled. "First, let's just land this ship and–"

"Ms Walters!" Kamala cried.

She gestured toward the pilot's chair, where Rocket stood aiming a very large weapon at them.

"I got a better idea," Rocket said, watching as Groot climbed to his… well, to his roots. "First, let's find the guy that killed my pal Drax and fry 'im to death slowly in a pit of hot grease. Then we can do whatever thing you were going to say."

Jen and Kamala exchanged looks. Then, slowly, they began to advance on Rocket.

Rocket sighed. "And in case you had any doubts," he said, "this one *is* a gun."

He fired. Kamala tried to dodge, but a blast of energy slammed into her. Quick images flashed before her eyes: Jen turning to her in alarm, Groot turning to attack Jen, Rocket fiddling with the controls–

The floor lurched again. Kamala flailed midair as the ship continued to tilt, twisting all the way upside-down. She fell, almost in slow motion, toward the hole in the roof, catching a glimpse of patchy grass and a pitted tar road whipping past.

"No!" Jen cried, reaching out for her. Kamala stretched her arm out as far as she could, but the pull of gravity was too strong. Her fingers grazed against Jen's for an instant, and then she plummeted through the hole, back out into open air.

# CHAPTER 17

Gamora stood over her fallen foe, tossing Iron Man's chest-covering up and down in one hand. Know your enemy, she thought. That's how she'd beaten him – by studying his armor, his weaponry, his fighting techniques. Once she'd figured out his weakness, it was a simple matter to turn it against him without fatally wounding him.

But the victory, she knew, was a hollow one. Stark lay unmoving on the pier, but he was not the Guardians' true prey. That entity still hid in the shadows, unknown and unseen.

I don't know the enemy at all, she realized.

Quill staggered up to her, favoring one leg. His hair was matted to one side, and his element gun had a dent in it. When he saw Stark lying still, his face fell.

"Did you … Did you kill him?" he asked.

"Peter. Give me some credit." She shot him a deadly side-eye glance. "I don't always go for the main artery."

"Oh, right. Good." He winced as he tried to smile. "That's really good to hear. You might not know it, but I'm kind of a fan of his."

"You may have mentioned that once or twice," she replied. "Anyway, he should be out for a while."

"I had him, you know. Couple more minutes, he'd have been begging for mercy."

She looked from Peter down to the fallen Iron Man, and then at the chest-plate in her hand. With a casual swing, she tossed it into the ocean.

"You, uh, kind of took your time helpin' out," Quill said.

"I think it's important for you to hone your skills."

Quill recoiled at that. Gamora had to force herself not to laugh. Peter looked cute with his ruffled hair, torn uniform, and a fresh cut above his left eye. But somehow she could never resist jabbing at him when he was down.

Maybe it was the Thanos in her. That was a disturbing notion.

She turned and led Quill back toward the mainland, leaving Stark sprawled out on the pier. "I take it you weren't able to learn anything about the planet-killer?" she asked.

"Nah." Quill picked a big splinter out of his jacket. "If those Kree workers know anything, they ain't talking."

"Maybe you didn't ask forcefully enough."

"Hey..." He spread his arms in a helpless motion.

Suddenly she felt bad. "Sorry." She moved in closer and touched his arm. "It's just that I saw the planet-killer. I saw its face, but I still can't remember it. I've tried meditation techniques, self-hypnosis, even that mind-scanner Rocket stole from Arago-7. And it's just a void."

"I get it." He wrapped his arm around her. "We all want to find the scum that killed Drax."

"I know. I know, but it's different. For me, I mean."

She unwrapped his arm and wandered away, looking out over the water.

"I was trained as a weapon," she said softly. "Thanos... he never allowed me to connect with anyone, to care for anything. Never let me feel anything at all, except a constant simmering anger."

"That's over now," he said. "Thanos is gone. We're your family now."

"And I'm grateful. But *family* isn't the same thing as *purpose*." She whirled toward him, feeling a sudden need to explain herself. "For the first time since Thanos died, I have that: a purpose. A righteous place to put my anger – all the pent-up rage I was filled with, every second of my childhood. I will find the killer of Praeterus, of Drax the Destroyer, and I will rip out their heart with my bare hands. As they die slowly before my eyes, I will know a satisfaction, a peace, that I've never known before."

"You realize you're talking crazy." Quill stood watching her, eyes wide. "I like it."

She laughed despite herself, and punched him hard enough to leave a bruise. Then he laughed too, and their foreheads touched.

"We should check in with Rocket," Quill said. "Maybe he's got something."

Gamora peered up past the factory complex and over to the building that held Tony Stark's office. "I can't see the ship."

The sound of ripping metal brought her attention down to Earth. At the landward edge of the pier, a pack of Kree were tearing down the remaining squares of security fence, striding onto the pier like an invading army. Gamora tensed, recognizing the Kree with a crewcut – the man Peter had tried, unsuccessfully, to intimidate. He looked angry, his jaw set, eyes glaring.

But it was the woman at the front of the group who stood out. She was tall and lean, with fierce eyes, and her skin was bright blue. She strode forward, arms held stiff at her sides.

"Which of you Terran freaks threatened to kill Jer-ra?" she demanded, gesturing at the man with the crewcut.

Gamora let out a short laugh. Quill's eyes flicked nervously from her to the blue Kree, and then he stepped forward.

"That, uh, that was me," he said, smiling sheepishly at the crewcutted man. "I'm sorry, dude. I don't actually think you're a planet-killer. And I was *really* out of line with that ascot business–"

Gamora barely saw the blue woman's hand move, but all at once Quill was laid out on the floor of the pier, rubbing his nose. The woman reached into a back holster, fury in her eyes, and pulled out a long metal rod. When she pressed a stud, its entire surface lit up with electric charge.

"You don't want him," Gamora snarled. "You want me."

The blue woman turned slowly. She cast her eyes calmly up and down Gamora, pausing to study the long sword in the Guardian's hand.

"Kir-ra," the crewcutted man said, touching the blue woman's arm. "Be careful."

"You ordered this man to attack my people?" Kir-ra asked.

Gamora gestured dismissively down at Quill. "He only does what I tell him."

"That's, uh..." Quill spat blood, struggling to rise. "That's not the org chart I signed off on..."

Gamora ignored him. She recognized the anger, the pent-up resentment in Kir-ra's eyes. There's only one way this goes, she thought. Only one path forward.

So she charged, sword flashing. The other Kree backed away, giving the combatants room. Gamora lifted the sword above her head and brought it down as she neared her opponent. Kir-ra leaned back calmly, raised her electrified combat rod to meet the thrust–

–then lowered it in an instant and jabbed upward with her other hand, grabbing Gamora's arm. The surprise move catapulted

Gamora up into the air, flipping her uncontrollably over Kir-ra's body. The rest of the Kree scattered, watching as Gamora tumbled over the half-collapsed fence onto the mainland. A jagged wire caught on her shoulder, tearing her uniform.

She landed in a crouch in the long grass. This patch of land was neglected, overgrown with weeds and littered with old cinderblocks and jagged stones. Gamora cursed herself for underestimating Kir-ra; she wouldn't make that mistake again.

Out on the pier, Quill was rising to his feet. Gamora waved him back angrily, watching as Kir-ra strode calmly over the fence to meet her. That electrified rod was raised again, and the other Kree flanked her like a regiment backing up its commander.

Gamora let out a whoop and charged again, swinging her sword in a wide arc. This time the two weapons met in a clash of sparks. Energy crackled from Kir-ra's rod into Gamora's longsword, sending pain lancing through the Guardian's body. She screamed and pulled away.

Kir-ra advanced, holding up her weapon. "You're not from Earth," she said. "Why do you serve Tony Stark? Why do you help in the oppression of my people?"

"Stark?" Gamora frowned. "I don't serve–"

Kir-ra screamed as a halo of flame engulfed her. Peter Quill hovered just above, a steady stream of fire blazing from his element gun. Kir-ra gritted her teeth, loosed a bolt of electricity from her rod, and knocked him out of the sky.

As Kir-ra batted the flames away, Gamora saw her chance. She crouched down and grabbed hold of a broken half-cinderblock. With all her strength, she reared back and hurled it through the air. Kir-ra was patting out the fire, the last flames dying on her jumpsuit, when the concrete block struck her on the forehead. She cried out and tumbled to the ground, the rod-weapon slipping out of her hands. It struck a rock, sparked once, and went dark.

The other Kree were huddled, but Gamora couldn't worry about them now. She leapt through the air, landed on top of Kir-ra, and pinned her to the ground.

Kir-ra bucked, kicking up with her knees, trying to throw Gamora off. But she lacked Gamora's raw strength. Her face was scalded, her clothes torn, and Gamora could see the rage in her eyes.

"I'm not who you think I am," Gamora hissed, "but I don't have time to make you see that." She brought her fist down hard on Kir-ra's nose. Kir-ra groaned in pain. Her blood racing, Gamora raised her arm to strike again—

—and stopped. All at once she could sense something dark and terrible and familiar.

"You," she said, staring down at the bloody woman. "Are you the one?"

"The…" Kir-ra coughed. "The what?"

Gamora stared at the blue face, the high sharp cheekbones and dark eyes. For a moment she was back in the dome, on Praeterus, face to face with the killer of worlds. That face… the face she'd tried in vain to recall, all these months…

Was this her? The killer of worlds?

"Why did you do it?" She stared into those eyes. "Why did you kill all those people?"

"You're… insane."

"Why did you murder my friend?"

"Gam?"

Quill. He stepped up and, to Gamora's surprise, grabbed Kir-ra up by the collar. He pulled her to her feet, whipped her around, and slammed her against the only square of security fence still standing.

The three remaining Kree approached, murmuring. One spoke urgently into a cell phone. Without looking, Quill swung his arm back and sprayed them with a high-pressure water stream, his gun flashing in a continuous motion. They cried out in protest and backed away.

Peter pressed Kir-ra against the fence, his face grim. He seemed furious, almost possessed. Gamora had only seen him like this a few times before.

"This is her?" he hissed. "The planet-killer? You're *sure?*"

Gamora hesitated. The image in her mind... even after all this time, it still wasn't clear. "No," she said.

Kir-ra shook her head, dazed and bloody. Gamora felt a moment of doubt, even pity. She stared into Kir-ra's eyes, searching for... what? She didn't know.

"There's something...." She paused. "Something *clinging* to her."

Again, she felt the stink of that entity, the stench of almost unfathomable evil. And with it the rage, the righteous anger that had given her life a new purpose. If she could wipe out that evil – kill it dead, with a single terrible blow – maybe that would make up for all the lives lost, the atrocities committed. Maybe then she could be at peace.

But if she killed the wrong person... then the cycle would continue. Over and over again.

Quill held Kir-ra firm. "Well?" he asked.

"It's not her," Gamora said. "She's not the one."

Quill eased his grip, and Kir-ra squirmed free. The Kree leaned against the fence for support, coughing and clutching her stomach.

"But she's been in contact with it. With the killer." Gamora cast her eyes out over the Stark office building, the factory complex, and the low storage buildings beyond. So many windowless structures… so many places to hide.

"It's here," she said. "On Earth, in this place. Somewhere."

"You're sure?" Quill asked.

"Yes."

Quill hesitated. He glanced at Jer-ra and the other Kree; they stood at a distance now, glaring as they wrung water from their wet clothes.

"Then go," he said. "Find 'em."

"You sure?"

"Yeah. I got things here."

Gamora smiled. Peter was a screwup and a mass of insecurities, but he was right: they were family. When it came down to it, she trusted him. That was a good feeling.

She turned toward Kir-ra. The Kree woman had edged over to the fencepost, wiping blood from her nose. Gamora tensed, lunged, and punched her hard in the face. Kir-ra cried out and fell to the grass.

Gamora turned to Quill, whose eyes were wide with surprise. "Keep honing," she said, and took off at a run for the factory.

Quill watched her go, smiling. Gamora was a ball of rage and an unpredictable force, but she was family. He trusted her to find the killer – if that entity really was here on Earth, and not a thousand light-years away. Or already dead, lost with so many others in the destruction of Praeterus.

A rustling in the grass made him look down. The Kree woman, Kir-ra, scrambled to her feet, pausing to shoot him a murderous glare. Then she took off at a run toward the mainland, where her friends stood watching with wary eyes.

Quill felt a sudden spasm of guilt. "Hey," he called. "Hey, I'm sorry about–"

Cold metal slammed into his head from behind. He cried out in pain and dropped to the grass, then tumbled into a crouch.

Iron Man hovered just above, both gauntlets glowing red-hot. Stark's helmet covered his face; his chestplate was exposed, but it shone with the full power of the armor's uni-beam.

"One chance, Quill." Stark's voice sounded especially threatening, as if he'd turned up the volume on that suit. "Hand me that gun right now, and let's discuss this like mildly evolved apes."

Quill saw stars and not the kind visible from a hyperspace-equipped scoutship. "Suckered me," he gasped.

"Give it up, cowboy," Stark continued, "and leave those people alone. I already fought the tough Guardian today, and brother, you ain't her."

Quill clenched his fists, shaking his head to clear it. Blasted Stark! he thought. Puffed-up rich kid, with his fancy Avengers credentials. He had no idea what it was like to earn an honest living… to hunt down bounty on an alien world, just so you could buy your next meal…

In the distance, he could hear the Kree laughing.

"I'm takin' you down, Stark," he hissed, "and I don't mean the poster I used to have on my wall!"

As soon as the words were out of his mouth, he winced in embarrassment. Then, before Stark could react, he raised his element gun and fired.

# CHAPTER 18

The little spaceship veered erratically through the air. It slid past a row of sleek low offices, then banked up and around the aircraft hangars, whose dark wide roofs concealed an array of secret aerial prototypes. Then it took a hard left at the edge of the complex, swinging its way back toward the tall factory building manned by the Kree.

On the outside hull, Kamala Khan – Ms Marvel – hung on by her fingertips. Every dip, every lurch threatened to break her grip, hurling her to the ground below.

She gritted her teeth, trying not to look down. She'd tried several times to claw her way back in through the hole in the roof, but that furry pilot Rocket seemed to be doing his best to throw her off. Or maybe he was just distracted. Judging by the thumping and yowling coming from inside the ship, Jennifer Walters was giving the Guardians hell.

Like the She-Hulk she is, Kamala thought. Like an Avenger. And here I am, frozen out of the action, barely managing not to fall to my death!

Once again she wondered: am I in over my head? Should I even *be* here? Surely Jen would rather be risking her life alongside

Thor or Wonder Man. Or her cousin, Bruce Banner. The Hulk might have a bad temper, but he was the best fighter on the Avengers' roster.

She risked a glance down. A field of dark grass swung by, dizzyingly fast, followed by an access road. A small bus terminal came into view, but no buses were parked there on the weekend.

She might survive a freefall drop from this height. Maybe. But the way the ship was whipping around, she'd be flung out like a rock from a slingshot. And the factory was coming up fast: a weathered gray façade, taller than the surrounding buildings, with thick loading-dock doors on each level connected by fire-escape-style metal stairways. The wall itself was solid stone.

And the ship was heading straight for it.

She looked away, feeling sick. Wind whipped past her face; her fingers slipped a bit, and she let out a little noise as she grabbed the hull tighter.

Then she spotted something. There, in a little grassy alcove between the factory and a low, windowless building… something was happening. A small group of Kree, maybe a dozen, stood in a circle, watching two people sparring. One of them she recognized immediately: Halla-ar. He had no weapon, but he moved very fast, leaping and lunging to avoid his opponent…

… a slim green woman brandishing a long sword. That, Kamala realized, must be the Guardian Tony had described. What was her name? Gamora!

The Kree were talking among themselves; Halla-ar and Gamora shouted at each other. But Kamala couldn't make out any words over the roar of the ship's engines. What were they saying? Why were the Guardians attacking Halla-ar anyway?

Grimacing, she turned and started picking her way toward the underside of the ship. The flight had evened out; the jolts came less frequently now. But the ship was still too high for her to jump off – and too low to clear the factory, which loomed dead ahead.

The lower hull was studded with hatches. One of them gaped partway open, with a piece of wheeled landing gear sticking out at a weird angle. Huh, she thought, this *is* a janky spaceship! But maybe that could work to her advantage.

Moving cautiously, trying not to look down, she hooked her legs around the landing gear's axle. The ship had slowed, but there still wasn't much time. Gritting her teeth, she tested the axle for stability and let go with her hands. She felt a moment of panic as her arms swung free, her head pointed down.

Then she stretched.

A few of the Kree noticed the girl with the elongated legs, dangling from a spaceship up above. One of them, a young guy with a Mohawk haircut, pointed at her, speaking in a language she didn't understand.

Gamora noticed too. When she turned to look up, Halla-ar seized the moment. He jabbed out with both rigid hands and caught her once, twice, in the throat. She gasped, coughed, and dropped back in a crouch.

But the Guardian didn't fall. She raised her sword and turned to face Halla-ar directly. Kamala strained to hear, stretching her neck closer to the ground.

"It's on you too," Gamora said to Halla-ar. "The evil. The evil that destroyed a…"

The ship veered sharply upward, pulling Kamala away from the ground. The sound of fighting from the cockpit drowned out the voices below. Jen was still at it, battling Rocket and the tree-man.

Kamala frowned. The ship was rising, moving up in order to clear the factory; at this rate, it would be past that building and out over the pier in less than a minute. If she was going to do something to help Halla-ar, it would have to be soon.

She looked down again. The Kree raised their fists, urging the fighters on; but they didn't seem to be defending Halla-ar – one of their own – against his attacker. Why, she wondered, weren't the Kree helping him? Were they just bored and enjoying the fight? Or... Halla-ar had mentioned that some of his own people held a prejudice against the blue Kree. Did they hate him that much?

There was another possibility – one she still didn't want to think about. "The evil," Gamora had said. Halla-ar had certainly shown he was capable of violence, both at school and in Tony Stark's office. He'd grabbed that kid Russell by the throat and choked him without hesitation, without mercy.

If I hadn't stopped him, Kamala thought, he might have killed Russell. A kid who did nothing but punch him on the arm.

She'd given Halla-ar the benefit of the doubt. Because people at school were cruel to him; because he looked different from them. He seemed to need a friend, and she wanted to be that friend.

But *someone* had destroyed his planet. Someone had deliberately set all this in motion. The Guardians believed that, and the Kree seemed to believe it too.

Could it be an angry teenage boy? A boy who hated his homeworld and almost everyone on it?

The ship was still rising; the combatants became small figures below. Gamora lunged, pressing Halla-ar up against the factory wall. The other Kree closed in, cheering for one side or the other.

No, Kamala thought, I can't abandon him. I can't let some green lady slice off his head! No matter what he's done, no matter what he might be.

I wouldn't be much of a friend if I did. Or an Avenger, either.

She shifted, loosening her grip on the axle assembly. Gritting her teeth, she stretched her entire body... eight feet, then ten... reaching toward the ground below. Wind whipped against her; her torso rippled back and forth. As the factory drew near and the ship turned to rise above its roof, she opened her eyes wide and let go.

# CHAPTER 19

Stark swooped and lunged through the air like a living weapon, firing off repulsor rays from one hand, then the other. Quill danced and leaped along the pier, dodging the beams, struggling to get a bead on his airborne foe.

Kir-ra sat up against the fence, watching the two men fight. She twirled the cold rod idly in one hand; she'd only managed to bring a few of the weapons with her on the evac ship. Now this one was totaled, completely wrecked. Another piece of her past, gone forever.

Jer-ra, the crewcutted Kree worker, approached, holding out a rag. "You want to clean up?" he asked, indicating her nose.

"No," she said, waving him out of the way. "I like the blood."

"Thanks. For fighting for us."

She nodded absently. He shrugged and started back toward the other Kree, who stood on the mainland, in front of the factory building.

A trio of repulsor rays blasted into the pier, throwing up shards of wood all around Quill. With a swipe of his hand, he clicked his faceplate down and took to the air. Stark just leaned back in midair, arms folded, watching him approach – then swatted out hard, knocking the Guardian across the sky.

Stupid men, Kir-ra thought. I should let them fight; I should let them destroy themselves. Stark had lured her people to this planet and then cruelly abused them. Quill had pursued the Kree, seeking vengeance for… something. One was an oligarch, the other a lawless bounty hunter.

If they were to kill each other, then maybe… maybe her people could be free…

Before Quill could recover, Stark blasted him again. Quill let out a huffing noise and flailed, then started to drop. "Aw, no," he said, looking down. "Not the Long Island Sound!"

"I told you," Stark replied, "it's clean as a baby's bottom."

"I ain't going swimming in that either!"

Mere inches above the water, Quill whipped his gun out and fired – straight down. A burst of air shot out, then another, slowing his momentum. Kir-ra could feel the fury in him, even with his face hidden.

"Say your prayers, Richie Rich," he hissed.

If Stark had a reply, he never got it out. Quill flew right into him, grabbing hold of those metal shoulders with a *clang* and a loud scrape. He swung the gun around, aiming it straight at the exposed arc reactor on Stark's chest.

Stark sighed, reached out, and grabbed Quill's gun arm. They struggled, locked together, neither one giving an inch. Kir-ra watched them grapple, reaching out to probe with Sen-Zha training. Stark seemed to have the upper hand; certainly, his weapons were more potent. But that power source on his chest was still exposed, glowing brighter now, and she could sense that he was more vulnerable than he seemed. His body temperature was elevated, his heart pounding fast.

And yet he'd jumped back into battle as soon as he could,

distracting the cowboy's attention from... well, from her and her people. Why? Maybe the two men held an old grudge against each other. Maybe Stark just wanted to protect his property, the Kree servants he'd worked so hard to bring to Earth.

Or maybe, just maybe, he was trying to do the right thing.

Slowly but steadily, Stark forced Quill's gun barrel up between the two men's faces. "Fascinating piece of hardware," he said. "You call it an element gun, right?"

Quill winced. Stark held on tight; his boot-jets kept the two of them hovering in place. He raised his other hand and unleashed a pinpoint beam from a device in the thumb. It sizzled against the gun's barrel, glowing white at the point of contact.

"Huh," Stark continued. "It's designed to reshape matter at the basic building-block level, but it's limited to four or five configurations. You should really get an expansion pack."

"Wh- What are you doing?"

"Just a little product review. Oh, you mean this?" He glanced at the beam emanating from his thumb. "It's an atomic force microscope. Comes in handy when I need to get down to the nano level."

Quill struggled, shifting the gun in his hand. But Stark held his wrist tight.

"Here's the fun part," Stark said. "If I can hack into this thing's firmware, I can alter its basic programming."

"M- My gun has programming?"

"Yeah it does!" Stark deactivated his microscope beam. Then, keeping careful hold of Quill's arm, he swung the gun so it pointed away. "Try it now."

Quill frowned and squirmed, but he couldn't break Stark's grip. Reluctantly, half closing one eye, he tightened his finger on the trigger.

A clod of dirt squeezed its way out of the barrel and fell to the water with a dull splash. Then a few drops of water. A little flame flickered up, and a puff of air extinguished the flame with a humiliating flatulent noise.

"What..." Quill shook the gun at Stark. "What did you do to my gun?"

"Locked it into a diagnostic mode," Stark said. "You know, like when you order an inkjet to print out a few basic patterns?"

"You turned it into a fart gun!"

"That's just a humorous side-effect."

Quill kicked out, enraged, and broke Stark's grip. The Guardian aimed his gun and fired off two more flatulent bursts.

Stark laughed. "Better trademark that fart gun, Quill. Before I get my lawyers on it."

Quill kept firing. Water burbled out, then fire – and this time he got lucky. The flames licked up against Stark's chest reactor, raising sparks. Stark clutched at his chest and began to fall.

"Ha!" Quill cried, thrusting his gloved fist into the reactor. Electricity crackled up the Guardian's arm. He howled, arching his back in pain. Stark grabbed hold of him and together they tumbled down, landing with a crash that shook the whole pier.

Enough, Kir-ra thought. She tossed her rod-weapon aside and strode out onto the pier. She could hear Jer-ra and the others behind her, urging her to stay back. But she kept moving, toward the two costumed men rolling around in close combat.

She turned and called to Jer-ra: "Wait for my signal!"

And then she was running, sprinting at full speed out across the pier. The two men had risen to their knees, grappling again. Stark shot repulsors wildly, while Quill jabbed his gloved hand into that arc reactor again and again, raising sparks.

They didn't even notice her approach. She circled them, dancing, until Quill turned his back to her, and then she lunged. Grabbing hold of his arm from behind, she twisted him up and away from Stark, onto his feet. His face was covered, but she could hear the yelp of surprise as she lifted him briefly into the air – he was heavier than he looked! – and slammed him face-down into the pier.

Quill retracted his faceplate, blinking in surprise. He scrabbled backward and crabwalked away, gasping for breath.

Stark was on his knees, holding a hand over his damaged chest reactor. She crossed to him and, taking hold of his cold metal arm, pulled him to his feet.

"Thanks," he said, his voice filtered by that imposing helmet. "You, uh, you know who I am?"

"I know," she said.

Quill waited at the tip of the pier, crouched down in a defensive position with his back to the water. In the other direction, the Kree workers waited at the fence. Kir-ra lifted her arm and made a brief hand motion to them.

"That your backup?" Stark asked.

"Yes," she said. "I just told them to advance, but slowly."

Quill rose to his feet. He let out an angry snarl and charged.

"Tell 'em to shield their eyes," Stark said. "You too."

She blinked. "I don't have a hand signal for that."

"Oh. Well–"

"Shield your eyes!" she yelled.

The Kree paused in their advance, raising their hands to their faces.

Quill stopped short too, a puzzled look on his exposed face. "What?" he said.

She squeezed her own eyes shut just as Stark let off a blinding flash of light from his armor. She heard Quill cry out in pain. When she opened her eyes, he was standing, dazed and blinded, just a few feet away.

"Well," Stark began, "not *everyone* would have fallen for that, but..."

Kir-ra leaped, somersaulting toward the disoriented Quill. She paused, perfectly motionless, standing on her hands – as still as a tree. Then she reached out with both legs and grabbed him around the waist in a scissor-grip.

"Uh!" she cried. He *was* heavy!

She cast her senses outward, mapping the entire area in an instant. Stark stood *here*; the edge of the pier was *there*. And Jor-ra's crew was on the move... veering left, toward the broken shack, giving Stark a wide berth...

With a grunt, she bent her arms, lifted Quill between her legs, and tossed him into the air. Still blinded, he cried out and landed in the waiting arms of Jor-ra and the others.

"Hey guys," Quill said, "what do you... Hey! Give me my gun back!"

"The fart gun?" Jer-ra asked.

Kir-ra tumbled back onto her feet and dropped into a crouch. Stark had retracted his helmet and stood right next to her, a serious look on his face.

"I owe you," he said.

"I will hold you to that," she replied.

He raised an eyebrow at the hard edge in her voice. Then he nodded.

"Guys," Quill said, "I really don't want to hurt you. Just let go of me–"

"Quill!" Stark called, advancing toward the Kree. "Don't you think you've done enough damage?"

Quill looked up. The Kree held him now, though Kir-ra knew he was powerful enough to break free. But when he heard Stark's words, he seemed to slump down, defeated, as if all the air had gone out of him.

"Maybe," he said.

Stark reached out a hand. Quill accepted it, and the Kree let him go. "Sorry," he said to them. "I might have, well, overreacted." He grimaced at Kir-ra. "Sorry, ma'am." She gave him a noncommittal nod, stepping back to join the other Kree.

They all turned to survey the battle scene. Girders lay strewn everywhere; the pier itself was pocked with holes. One of the water supports had buckled, creating a dangerous drop-off at one corner of the pier.

"Let's all…" Tony Stark grimaced. "Let's just take a minute, huh?"

# CHAPTER 20

Tony sat on a cinderblock, consulting his toolbox. It hovered in midair, the shelves piled with tools, nanometers, and assorted circuitry. He selected a quantum screwdriver and touched it gently to his arc reactor.

"Easy," he told himself. "One wrong twist, and this will go *quite* badly..."

He felt the familiar jump in his heart, a skipped beat, as the reactor re-engaged. Tony no longer required the arc reactor to power his heart, but the two were permanently linked. That, above all else, had convinced him some time ago that he would always be Iron Man, like it or not.

He pulled down his helmet with a mental command. The heads-up display showed a rising power level: five percent... six... eight...

"F.R.I.D.A.Y.," he subvocalized, "any word from Jen and Ms Marvel?"

"No communications," the voice replied, "and no response to my pings. I do have an update on your Kree work program inquiry."

"Put a pin in that, but remind me later. What about that backup I called for?"

"Arrival is imminent. Meanwhile, there seems to be a commotion out behind the factory building, near the bus station. Oh, and the Melter is still at large."

"Oh, no. Dire news for ice cream fans everywhere–"

"Dude?"

Tony willed his helmet to open. Peter Quill stood there fidgeting, a sheepish look on his face. "Sorry about your, you know," he said, jerking a thumb toward the edge of the pier. "Shack."

Tony stared past him to the pile of tin and lumber that had once been Shackie. At the edge of the pier, Kir-ra stood alone, facing the water, her body perfectly still. Tony craned his neck around and scanned the neglected grassy field, then looked up. He winced at the sight of his shattered office window, a tiny jagged gap in a huge white facade.

"Don't sweat it, Quill," he said. "Some things belong in the past."

He waved a hand, sending the toolbox wafting back up toward his office. Then he reached down and picked up his reactor cover, newly recovered from the water. He shook off the last drops, picked off a tangled strand of seaweed, and snapped the cover back on his chest.

"You, uh, you good?" Quill asked.

"It'll take me a few minutes to recharge."

"I get it. Not enough power, right?"

"Actually, too much. The reboot has to be gradual, otherwise … Quill, what are you doing here? What do you want, anyway?"

The Guardian frowned. "Well, I kinda wanted to apologize–"

"Where is your ship? For that matter, where's your girlfriend?"

"I, uh, I wouldn't call her that exactly. We're still figuring out–"

"Quill! Buddy! Can you just focus here, for one minute? For

me?" Tony felt another headache coming on. "You followed a trail to Earth looking for some animal, mineral, or vegetable that you believe blew up the planet Praeterus. Thus setting in motion events that will no doubt leave me remembered as the greatest sweatshop owner in history. Do I have all that right?"

"Pretty much." Quill pulled up a cinderblock and sat down. "My ship ducked down behind the sweatshop – uh, the big factory building there – about the time you and me started our..." He grinned, shadowboxing for a second. "But I'm sure Rocket and Groot can handle themselves."

"I'll check it out in a few." Tony pulled down the HUD for a second and noted the power level: thirty-two percent. "And then we'll have to figure out about the Kree."

"But like I was saying, Stark," Quill persisted, "I really want to say I'm sorry. We got so ragey about our dead pal, we just slammed down onto your turf hard. I should have at least called first! Even if you are the greatest labor villain since–"

"Quill, you got stuff to do, right? Space stuff? Important space stuff, maybe?"

"Huh? Oh, yeah." Quill pulled out a handheld device. "Guess I should call the ship, check out the, the sitch."

"Yeah, you do that. That's what you do in space, right? Hailing frequencies, whatever."

Tony stood up and started toward the edge of the pier. Quill called out another apology, but Tony ignored him.

Kir-ra was staring out over the fog-draped sound. He came up behind her, weighing various opening remarks, but she spoke first.

"Can you ever see the land?" She didn't turn to look at him. "On the other side?"

"Sometimes," he said. "On a clear day."

She bowed her head. "I can't imagine one of those."

"Ah, we're talking in metaphor. Good, I like to keep track."

He studied her sharp blue face. Was that a hint of a smile?

"Your friends sure lit out of here fast," he said. "Where are they now?"

"Hiding." She gave him a hard look. "Do you blame them?"

"You're not hiding. You're one tough lady."

She shook her head and turned back toward the water. "I'm scared out of my mind," she said, almost inaudibly. "Every second of my life."

"Listen." He turned to address her directly. "My armor will take approximately six minutes to become flightworthy again. After that, my second move will be to inspect this complex thoroughly and get to the bottom of these working conditions. I would love for you to accompany me."

"Your second move?" She frowned. "What's the first?"

"Ah." He gestured toward Quill, who was shaking his comm device in frustration. "That would be to make sure Peter Porcupine and his pals are grounded for a while."

"I am more concerned with his female companion." She clenched her fists. "We'll meet again, she and I."

"That's part of the, uh, grounding I mentioned. But one vendetta at a time." He turned back to her, serious. "I realize I'm not your favorite person right now–"

"You lured my people here on false pretenses! You treat them like animals, starve their children–"

"I had no knowledge of that – and like I told you, I'll get to the bottom of it. Whatever is happening here, I swear it ends today. No matter what."

She turned toward him, dark eyes searching. He had a strange feeling she was probing him somehow, her senses reaching out.

Even in his armor, on the grounds of his own company, he felt oddly vulnerable.

"I'm asking you to trust me," he said in a low voice. "Innocent until proven guilty, right?"

Her eyes went wide, almost in wonder. "What a strange notion," she whispered.

"Stark! Hey, Stark?" Quill called.

Tony turned, already rolling his eyes, then immediately snapped to attention. Above a low structure at the edge of the complex, the Guardians' ship had just swung into view around the edge of the factory. It dipped and wove in an erratic path, as if the pilot had completely lost control.

Kir-ra and Tony met Quill in the middle of the pier. "I can't reach 'em," the Guardian said. "I gotta go see what's going on."

Tony had a feeling he knew what was going on: Jennifer Walters and Kamala Khan. "Right behind you ..." He checked his armor display again: forty-eight percent. "... in, uh, about three minutes."

Above, the raptor-like ship swerved sharply, narrowly missing the outer wall of the factory. "Can't wait," Quill said, snapping down his faceplate.

"Quill!" Tony cried. The Guardian paused. "Just ... try to keep the peace, OK?"

"You got it." Quill gave him a thumbs-up. "Boss." He launched himself into the air.

Kir-ra frowned at Tony. "Does that inspire confidence?"

"Not in the least."

"Look," she said, pointing out over the water. "What's that?"

A sleek Avengers quinjet, shaped like an arrowhead with an aerodynamic fin on top, swooped down out of the clouds. It circled above the complex once, then swung down to intercept the erratic flight path of the Guardians' vessel.

"Backup," Tony said.

Quill had seen the newcomer, too. He paused in midair, then dived back down toward the ground. He looked grim, as if he had an unpleasant task to accomplish. He landed on the pier and advanced toward Tony and Kir-ra, drawing his gun from its holster.

Kir-ra tensed. But Tony touched her arm with a metal hand and waited for the Guardian to approach. Above, the two ships wobbled and dodged in the sky.

Quill spoke a few words. Kir-ra leaned forward, not hearing. Tony did hear the words, but he made Quill repeat them anyway. "I said..." Quill held out his weapon. "Could you un-fart my gun, please?"

# CHAPTER 21

Groot and the green woman were really going at it. The tree-man had sprouted dozens of new shoots, circling them around to enclose her in a web of vegetation. The woman kicked and punched, cracking branches, severing vines.

Despite the danger, Rocket was impressed. She's like a female Hulk, he thought. A real Her-Hulk! He decided to call her that.

He shifted the wave-pulse cannon in his hands, struggling to aim. But Her-Hulk was moving too fast, and Groot's branches kept getting in the way. He couldn't get off a decent shot.

He sighed. He'd only gotten to fire the cannon, his new toy, once! It was another weapon, like the Big Burn Beam, that Quill didn't like him to use inside the ship. Probably because one stray shot through the reactor housing could light up the cockpit like a cheap barbecue grill. Rocket didn't tend to worry about those things. He believed this gave him an advantage in tense situations, where an opponent might tend toward caution, weakness, or petty self-preservation.

The ship veered upward, sending Groot and Her-Hulk sliding across the floor. Rocket stumbled, swore, and lost hold of his beloved cannon. It flew up, straight toward the hole in the ceiling.

He scrambled in a panic and managed to snatch it out of the air, just in time.

A shrill beeping sound from the control console. He turned to see that tall factory building looming in the front viewport. High doors and windowless walls, straight ahead and coming up fast. The thrusters whined, struggling to lift the little ship, but it wasn't going to be enough. The autopilot, like most people Rocket knew, was too cautious, too weak-willed.

So he sat down, grinned, and cracked his knuckles in anticipation. "Hang on!" he yelled and yanked the stick back.

The ship tipped hard, the back wall tilting down to become the floor. Groot collapsed into a crash couch. The green woman slammed her butt against the "floor" , swearing profusely.

"You, uh, prob'ly ain't gonna be happy to hear this, Her-Hulk," Rocket said. "But I think that last maneuver dislodged your little girl-pal, outside. She can fly, right?"

He cast a quick glance back just as the Hulk-woman rose, fists clenched, and started climbing *up the floor* toward him. "Land this thing *now*!" she cried.

Groot lashed out at her with a fresh growth of branches. Rocket kept his fists clenched around the stick, ignoring the constant din of grunts and crashes. A Groot-vine whipped past his peripheral vision, then vanished back again into the rear of the cabin. He glanced back and saw a whirlwind of branches, leaves, and emerald arms and legs.

"Whole lot of green going on back there," he muttered.

The little ship climbed straight up; the view through the front port turned to cloudy sky. Rocket checked the altitude readings, craning his neck forward as the top floor of the factory dropped down past them. When the roof came into view, he eased the stick back and allowed the ship to level out.

"You two killed each other yet?" he asked, slipping out of his chair. He turned to see the Her-Hulk climbing, dazed, to her feet—

—but Groot stood rigid, eyes wide, staring past Rocket. A branch-arm shot out from his body, bark flaking off as he jabbed a finger straight at the viewport. "I AM GROOT!"

Rocket whirled back around. In the front viewport, a small airship screamed out of the clouds, dropping down to intercept their course. It was about the same size as the Guardians' ship, but newer, its hull plated in sleek silver and chrome. He recognized the design at once; he'd seen its type during the Thanos war.

"Oh, no. A quinjet?" He leaped for the controls. "Kill me now."

The new ship feinted to the left, then edged back toward its prey. It rose up at the last minute, forcing Rocket to dip down close to the factory roof. He fumed, thinking: flarking Avengers. Trying to force me to land?

A comms button on the dashboard began to blink, but Rocket ignored it. He didn't feel like talking. He felt like doing something stupid.

"Screw caution," he muttered. "Screw weakness, too!"

Self-preservation just sort of slipped his mind.

When the newcomer passed overhead, Rocket made his move. He pulled back on the stick as hard as he could, throwing all his admittedly scant weight into the action. The engines whined in protest as the little ship tilted on its tail and shot, once again, straight up.

Groot and the Her-Hulk crept up behind him, their battle forgotten. Groot's eyes were dark and solid; the woman's were green. But both of them stared at him in shock, disbelief, and appalled fascination.

"What are you doing?" Her-Hulk said.

Rocket leaned forward, grinning, staring at the quinjet looming in the viewport. "Creating a masterpie–"

The impact almost knocked him out of his seat. Her-Hulk tumbled to the floor and rolled, end over end, toward the back of the cockpit. Groot shot out roots to clutch at the deckplates, shielding his eyes with a sudden sprout of leaves as the viewport shattered into a thousand pieces.

Rocket rose to his feet, balancing on the back of the pilot's chair, which now sat at a ninety-degree angle. He stared straight up, through the hole where the viewport had been. The cockpit had buried itself inside the belly of the newcomer, creating a mass of twisting, sparking metal. Outside, fuel leaked from a burst cable; some sort of gas hissed from a conduit in the quinjet, newly exposed to air.

He grinned. The ships were locked together now, fused in midair. The Guardians' vessel hung loose from the underside of the quinjet, like a fishing lure on a line.

Groot eyed the wreckage outside, then stumbled for balance as the ships lurched sideways. A grinding noise filled the air, along with a strange whine caused by the two ships' engines straining to move – probably in different directions.

Scrabbling at the controls, Rocket managed to activate the gravity compensators. His stomach lurched as the cabin swiveled upright, the deck dropping back to its usual orientation. Normally he wouldn't use artificial grav in a planetary situation, but given the… he started to giggle… given the *gravity* of the situation…

Groot stepped forward, extending one branch cautiously. He cocked his head at Rocket and said "I am…?" in a tone you might use to inquire whether a patient on suicide watch has had a disturbing mental episode.

Rocket burst out laughing. He knew he shouldn't be – laughing, that is – but he couldn't help it. He lived for moments like this, moments when sheer, mindless destruction blocked out the essential hopelessness of existence. And the best part... he struggled for breath, pointing at the mess in the viewport... the best, the very best part was...

"We're blind!" he cried. "Can't even see where we're..." He dissolved in another, even greater fit of laughter.

Her-Hulk stomped up, fists clenched, and glared at him. Her uniform was torn, her skin pocked with cuts from a thousand thorns. Rocket looked to Groot for help, but Groot averted his gaze. Uh-oh, Rocket thought. I've done it now. This time, he might let her smash me into paste.

But Her-Hulk just stopped, looming over him, her expression more weary than angry. She shook her head and said, in a quiet, resigned voice, "There's just no helping you, is there?"

The ships lurched again. Rocket squinted out the viewport, looking past the mangled and sparking controls. Something was happening "outside", in the other ship. A torn metal hatch creaked open, falling loose from its hinges, and a colorful round shield with a star in the center pushed its way through.

"Oh great," Rocket said, "*this* guy."

Captain America climbed out of the hatch, shield raised before him. His eyes narrowed in concern as he peered in through the bent framework of the Guardians' viewport. A loose cable sparked in front of him; he brushed it aside with his shield. Then he leaped, crossing the gap between ships to land inside, on the dashboard. His eyes scanned the cockpit.

"She-Hulk," he said. "We're your backup."

"*She*-Hulk," Rocket echoed. "Yeah. That works better."

The green woman rose to her feet, eyeing the two Guardians.

Cap dropped to the floor, favoring the arm that held his shield. His other arm, Rocket noticed, was in a sling.

"My backup," She-Hulk repeated. "Yeah, got that. Also, ouch." She pressed a hand against her arm, where the thorn-wounds were bleeding.

A small woman in black leather, with striking red hair, tumbled in gracefully through the broken viewport. She landed in a crouch next to Captain America and raised one arm, electric power crackling on a wrist-mounted cylinder.

"Which one of you idiots just rammed our quinjet?" the Black Widow asked.

Rocket leaned back against the wall and looked at his feet, avoiding the Widow's glare. Groot let out a casual whistle, but he snaked a vine-finger around to point at his partner from above. Rocket started to protest, then thought: what's the point? So he looked up, shrugged, said "Guilty," and grinned a grin that, to be honest, wasn't half as charming as he thought it was.

# CHAPTER 22

Captain America surveyed the scene. The cockpit looked like a greenhouse that had just exploded. Shoots, leaves, discarded branches lay everywhere, sticking out of crash couches and jutting up from between the deckplates. Rocket and Groot, both of whom he knew from previous battles, stood sheepishly next to She-Hulk, who looked very, very tired.

Above, a jagged hole in the roof revealed the bottom edge of the quinjet and a tiny slice of sky. "Your work?" he asked, raising an eyebrow at Jennifer Walters.

"I got tired of knocking." She moved toward him, gesturing casually back at the Guardians. "You know these cosmic bumper-car drivers?"

"We've fought alongside them," Cap said, staring at Rocket. "They're well-meaning, but..."

"Erratic," the Black Widow said.

"Hey, Natasha," Jen said, eyeing the Widow. "Still working outside the law?"

"Jen." Natasha returned her gaze. "You still pedantically enforcing it?"

Cap grimaced as Natasha turned away. Those two, he reflected, had never seen eye to eye. Different methods, different life experiences. Different paths to justice.

"What happened to you?" Jennifer gestured at the cast on his arm. "Nazis occupy Europe again?"

"Just one Nazi: the Red Skull. And it was Pittsburgh." He smiled. "I guess you could say I suffered damage as a result of an enemy effect. But I like to think I gained power, equal to the amount of damage I incurred."

Jen stared at him blankly.

"I've been teaching him tabletop gaming," Natasha explained.

Cap shrugged. "I'm fine. Really."

He kept his voice even. But the truth was: the close-quarters battle with the Red Skull, in an abandoned steel refinery, had left him badly shaken. The Skull had come very close to killing him this time.

"You look a little rough yourself," he said, indicating Jen's torn costume.

She turned a nasty smile on Groot. "I'm not used to fighting vegetables."

"I am Groot," he warned.

The floor lurched again: a loud *crunch* sounded from the Avengers' ship. "Quinjet's propulsion is shot," Natasha explained, moving toward the Guardians' pilot console. "These *svolochs* took out our entire guidance system."

Cap frowned. "Then what's keeping us in the air?"

"It's called neogravitic repulsion," Rocket said, crossing toward the front of the cabin. "You're welcome."

"You want me to *thank* you? For crippling our ship, putting all our lives in danger?" Cap watched him in disbelief. "Also, would you please put that weapon down?"

"Altitude is about one hundred thirty feet and dropping gradually as we circle around. We'll have to navigate from here …" Natasha's eyes narrowed as she scanned the console. "Where are the viewscreens? Do you even have viewscreens?"

"So let me get this straight." Cap eyed the hole in the roof. "We have one ship that can't fly, and one that's completely blind?"

"Stop. Stop it!" Rocket said, stifling a laugh. "You'll get me started again."

"Who designed this board, anyway?" Natasha threw up her hands. "The controls are labelled 'GIMME THREE STEPS' and 'GET UP OFF THAT THING.'"

"What's so confusing? And yes, of course there are screens! Lemme show you–"

Cap whipped out his shield, blocking the raccoonoid's path. "Don't touch those controls."

Rocket shook his head, dazed. "But the scary Russian lady said–"

"Suppose you explain what you're doing here first." He crouched down to Rocket's level. "Tony Stark's message said you were threatening innocent workers."

"Kree workers," Rocket snarled. "One of 'em might not be so innocent. Your pal Stark could be harboring a fugitive that murdered an entire planet."

Cap looked up at Jennifer. "What's he talking about?"

Jen shrugged. "Someone blew up the planet those Kree came from. The Guardians seem to have followed some kind of trail–"

"Hey!" Rocket protested. "If you can't trust intel from a drunk Ergon in an ice bar, what in this galaxy can you trust?"

"They think the killer is here," Jen said. "Among the Kree."

"If that's true…" Cap frowned. "Tony wouldn't be *harboring* them. I'll alert him, we'll look into this together."

"I am Groot," Groot offered. He lumbered closer, eyeing the confrontation between Cap and Rocket.

"He's right," Rocket agreed. "Even your own teammates ain't sure what Stark's up to."

"What?" Cap felt lost. "Jen?"

"I..." She hesitated. "I'm representing some of the Kree, against... well, against Tony. There are questions about the conditions at this installation."

"A pressing legal matter, I'm sure." Natasha struggled with the controls. "Certainly more important than *keeping us from falling out of the sky!*"

"Questions about..." Cap turned back to Rocket. "Hold it. You said team*mates*, plural?"

"She came here with a little one. Maybe fourteen years old. Or sixty? I can't tell with you humans."

"Ms Marvel!" Jen exclaimed. "She was thrown out of the–"

The ship lurched forward. Cap winced as his wounded arm struck the back of a chair.

Rocket ducked under Cap's shield and scurried toward the controls. Cap dropped the shield, reached down, and grabbed him up off the floor. "I said stay away from that!"

"Let go of me!" Rocket howled. He squirmed, frantic, like a trapped animal. His panic, his anger seemed to fill the air.

"I am GROOT!"

Groot lunged, branches shooting out of his body. Still holding the raccoonoid, Cap reached for his shield with his other hand – then swore as a stab of pain ran up his bad arm. He released Rocket and, in one swift movement, grabbed up his shield and launched it through the air. It sliced through four... no, five Groot-branches, then ricocheted off the inner hull.

Rocket raised his cannon-gun, aiming it straight at Cap's face.

Cap chopped up with his good elbow, knocking Rocket's gun arm off balance. The shot blasted through the air, ringing off the ceiling plates with a loud clang, as the recoil knocked Rocket off his feet.

The shield struck another wall, then a third, its speed barely slowing at all. It took out another clutch of Groot-limbs before Cap snatched it out of the air.

The room exploded in chaos. Jennifer ripped a spare oxygen tank off the wall and hurled it at Rocket, who scurried out of the way – almost. The tank hit him a glancing blow on the head, enraging him further. Jen was already on the move, wading into the thicket of Groot vines, punching and kicking.

Cap whipped his shield up and around, slicing through branches as quickly as they came at him. Rocket backed away, waving his cannon wildly.

Natasha was swearing in Russian at the controls. Groot reached for her with a fresh volley of branches; she turned and, electricity crackling on her wrist, fried them with a high-powered blast.

One of Rocket's shots went wild, sizzling into the control panel. Natasha leaped away as a shower of sparks erupted. The ship groaned, tilted backward and then forward again.

Natasha moved to Cap's side, kicking and firing her widow's sting at the forest of Groot-limbs surrounding them. "So much for the wonders of 'neogravitic repulsion,'" she said.

Cap flung his shield again, severing a fresh growth of Groot stems. The disk struck one wall, then rebounded from the ceiling just inches from the massive gap in the roof. A blank metal face appeared in the hole, flinching away from the impact.

"WHOA!" Peter Quill exclaimed. "What the hell?"

"Great," Natasha said. "It's *Captain* Svoloch."

"Can we give him a different rank, please?" Cap asked.

Quill dropped down through the hole, retracting his faceplate. He looked around calmly, as if the sight of a shape-changing tree-man and a sentient raccoon mixing it up with the superhuman locals was an everyday occurrence. On this ship, maybe it was.

"Has somebody been using the Big Butt Beam?" he asked.

"That's Big *Burn* Beam!" Rocket cried.

"Whatever. Not cool." Quill ducked low to avoid Groot's whipping vines, stumbling once as the floor shook, and approached Cap. "Hey man," he said pleasantly. "You know this ship is falling out of the sky?"

Cap grimaced, sighed again, and punched him in the face. Quill went down.

"Cover me a minute," Cap said to Natasha.

She nodded, dodging Rocket's blasts and Groot's flailing vines. "Nothing better than fighting in a glorified lifeboat."

Cap ducked down behind a crash chair. Rocket was still firing that gun, dislodging pieces of equipment from what remained of the ceiling. Natasha joined Jen, her stinger blazing, blasting and ripping at Groot's rapidly multiplying branches.

"Tony," Cap hissed, touching the receiver on his ear. "Tony, where the hell are you?"

# CHAPTER 23

"Patience, Cap," Tony Stark replied. "I'm on my way."

He arrowed upward, searching the sky for the quinjet. Below, more Kree had emerged from the factory. They milled around, staring at the destruction on the pier. A few of them gazed up at him with cold, hostile eyes.

"Well, you better make it quick."

Cap's voice sounded tense. Tony poured on a bit more power and felt his boot-jets kick in protest. He checked the power level: sixty-eight percent. Barely enough.

He passed the upper levels of the factory, glancing down at a long low structure on his left. It was completely windowless, with a corrugated-metal façade and a faded red, white, and blue American flag painted on its side. In his father's day, the building had been a munitions dump, a storage and testing facility for government-commissioned weaponry. Now…?

"F.R.I.D.A.Y.," he subvocalized, "what purpose does that eyesore serve?"

"It's listed as Employee Support Services," the voice replied. "No details available."

"'No details.' I'm getting tired of that phrase." He frowned. "Detecting elevated heat signatures inside the place. Nothing nuclear, just..."

He cleared the roof of the factory, looked up, and immediately forgot the mystery of the faded-flag building. The reason for Cap's call was clear: the Avengers' quinjet wobbled dangerously, sputtering and leaking fuel. The Guardians' battered little ship hung beneath, its "head" literally embedded in the quinjet's sparking belly.

"Steve? Oh, Steven Grant Rogers?" Tony called. "Mother is not going to be pleased with your driving."

A grunt and a thud came over the comm line. *Great*, Tony thought. *Those space delinquents have started another rumble.*

"Hang tight, Cap," he said, jetting up toward the ships. "Let me see if I can wrench the two ships apart."

"No!" That was Natasha's voice. "Tony, the quinjet is completely inoperative. On its own, it'll drop like a rock."

Tony grimaced. The two ships lurched and sputtered, moving one way, tilting, then veering away again. On the ground, little groups of Kree gathered, pointing up at the aerial chaos.

"I'll have to try and push you out to sea," he said. "Much less chance of bystanders there, plus the inevitable touchdown should be a bit less fatal."

No answer. Just more grunting, and the sound of something hard hitting metal.

"Is Quill causing trouble again? You've got Jen and Ms Marvel with you, right?"

"She-Hulk is with us." Cap sounded out of breath. "Ms Marvel seems to have... fallen overboard."

Guilt stabbed through Tony. He screeched to a halt below the fused ship and initiated a fast scan of the ground. *Kamala,* he thought. *Kid, don't be dead!* She wanted so much to be an Avenger… *What have I done?*

"There," F.R.I.D.A.Y. said. "The inland corner, between the factory and, errr, 'Employee Services.'"

He looked down, zooming in on the ground. Relief flooded through him, followed immediately by a renewed sense of alarm.

"Good news and bad news," he said. "Ms Marvel is alive."

"What's the bad news?" Cap asked.

"I think she's fighting Gamora."

The ships let out a terrible wrenching noise. Tony ducked, jetted away, and grimaced. The factory roof was less than thirty feet below.

"Gamora's a trained killer," Cap said.

"I can't go down there right now," Tony said. "If your little hybrid-ship experiment falls out of the sky-"

"I'll help Ms Marvel," Cap said. "You just do what you do."

"Roger that."

The ships were drifting away from the factory, circling down toward the mysterious warehouse building. Tony checked his power level: seventy-one percent. Still a little low…

Reaching out to steady himself in the air, he jetted in a horizontal line away from the ships. When he cleared the factory roof, he executed a hard U-turn. Boot-jets flared white as he shot straight toward the rear of the quinjet. The Guardians' ship wobbled beneath, holding both ships aloft with whatever power was still active in its engines.

"Ouch," Tony said, preemptively.

He slammed into the quinjet with a loud *clang*. Pain shot through his arm and shoulder; alarms rang in his helmet. His power level reading fluctuated wildly now, flickering on and off.

He pressed his shoulder against the fuselage, pushing, willing his boot-jets to full power. The quinjet's rocket tubes gaped wide just below him, empty and cold. If the jet's engine had been working, those rockets would have fried him alive.

"Come on," he said. "Come on!"

Slowly, with a whine of protesting engines, the ships began to move. Back toward the roof, heading in the direction of the pier and the water beyond.

Tony risked a glance down. Kamala's Ms Marvel suit was a blur of red and blue from this distance, as she leaped and stretched and changed shape. The blue kid, Halla-ar, was down there with her, along with a whole lot more Kree. They seemed to be holding their own against Gamora, but not by much.

A wrenching noise distracted him. He looked up from the ground to see a familiar costumed figure climbing out of a hole in the Guardians' roof, onto the vessel's protruding top fin. Cap looked up at him, smiled, and…

No, Tony thought. No, you corny bastard. You're not gonna do it.

Cap saluted.

Then Steve Rogers, the living legend of World War II, turned toward the ground, flexed his legs, and without the slightest hesitation jumped off into the open air.

Tony shook his head, frowned, and leaned his shoulder against the quinjet. His power level was dropping again: forty-five percent. This wasn't going to be easy.

*I'll help Ms Marvel,* Cap had said. I hope so, Tony thought. Because I've got to keep a ton and a half of mangled machinery from slamming into, let's say, the experimental nuclear reactor on the other side of this complex. Or, more likely: falling straight down on top of the Kree, the very people we're trying to help.

He gritted his teeth and pushed harder.

# CHAPTER 24

Gamora swept her sword in a wide arc, letting out a Zen-Whoberi battle cry. The girl jumped back, startled. She was a joke, that girl, a brightly costumed novice with powers she barely knew how to use. Not worth a minute of Gamora's time.

The boy, Halla-ar, was the real threat. He'd clearly had combat training, and the fury in his eyes brought out the fire in her own. That fury, she thought, might be the rage of an orphan who'd seen his world burn. Or it could be something far more dangerous.

The Kree watched from a safe distance. One group sat on a factory loading dock, cheering Gamora on. Another group, clustered near the building with the flag painted on it, was rooting for Halla-ar. A tall crewcutted man yelled "Come on, kid! Take the outworlder down!"

Gamora shook her head. Was this just a game to them? Did they even care that there might be a world-killer in their midst?

Surprisingly, the girl recovered first. She formed her hand into the shape of a hammer – really? A hammer? – and charged.

Gamora stood her ground, held her sword high, and swung it around with lightning speed. The flat of the blade struck the

Earth girl on the cheek, just below that ridiculous eye-mask, with a dull clang that filled the air. Not quite hard enough to break the skin, or to crack her skull. But close.

The girl cried out in pain and flew through the air. The Kree spectators gasped. When she struck the ground, a handsome Kree man with light blue skin grabbed hold of her, pulling her away through the low grass.

Halla-ar cast a quick, worried glance down at his fallen friend. Then he turned his eyes back to Gamora, fists raised in a defensive posture. Despite herself, she was impressed. Good warrior, she thought. Don't allow sentiment to distract you from the battle.

"Why?" he asked. "Why are you doing this?"

Gamora sheathed her sword. She studied his high cheekbones, the curve of his chin. If only she could remember... the face inside the dome, back on that doomed planet...

"Is it you?" she asked. "Did you do it?"

"Do what?"

She stalled for time, matching Halla-ar's movements – maintaining the distance between them. The face in the fire, the visage she'd seen on Praeterus, still eluded her. This boy – it *might* have been him. But once again, she just wasn't sure.

"The blue woman," she said. "Kir-ra. She wasn't the killer, but she knew the killer."

"Kir-ra?" The kid looked puzzled. "My sister?"

"Sister..." She jabbed out, forcing the boy back. "Yes – oh yes, that makes sense. It *is* you."

"What?" he cried. *"What's me?"*

Gamora edged closer. Yes, she thought. That's why she'd felt the evil on Kir-ra, back at the pier. It had come from this boy, from her brother. Maybe Kir-ra had even protected him, brought him to Earth, all unknowing. Never suspecting that his angry, youthful façade concealed...

"A planet-killer," she hissed.

His eyes went wide. "A what?"

Doubt stabbed at her, making her hesitate. What if she was wrong? What if this was an innocent boy, forced by horrible circumstances to grow up too soon?

She forced herself to think, blocking out the cheers and jibes of the Kree onlookers. In her mind, once again, she saw the face of the little Kree girl. The girl she'd made a promise to, a promise she'd failed to keep. Had that girl survived the destruction of Praeterus? Or was she just another casualty, like so many others?

The memory of that girl – of all the murdered children – made Gamora's blood boil. And Drax, her friend and comrade; his face too loomed in her mind, feeding her rage. Lips twisting into a snarl, she lunged toward Halla-ar–

–then jerked to the side, just an instant too late. A pair of steel-reinforced boots slammed down on her head, knocking her off her feet. Pain lanced through her skull; she tumbled sideways and dropped to the ground.

From the corner of her eye, she saw a blur of red and blue fall from the sky. Captain America landed in an easy crouch, rose to face her, and raised his shield.

"One warning, Gamora," he said. "Stand down."

She rose to her feet, taking in the positions of her enemies. Halla-ar stood behind her, keeping his distance for now. The Kree were clumped in groups, watching. A few of them had crouched down against that odd building with the faded flag design, where they tended to the unconscious Earth girl.

And something was happening above. The ship? She couldn't look. She didn't dare take her eyes off the enemy.

"Stay out of this, Captain," she snarled. "You have no idea why I'm here."

"Your friends told me you're hunting a killer." He gestured at Halla-ar. "I don't think it's this boy. And I know it's not Ms Marvel, the girl you swatted like a fly a minute ago."

"It's on him," she said. "The evil that snuffed out a world." She took a step forward, eyeing him. "Aren't you supposed to be the Avengers? Doesn't Praeterus deserve vengeance?"

"Avengers, yes. Not child-killers."

He shifted, grimacing, keeping his shield up before his body. She raised an eyebrow, noticing the cast on his concealed arm. She reached for her sword.

"You're not quite… whole, Captain," she said.

"Stay *back*."

And then she was within range, swinging her sword. He ducked, kicked out, and knocked the legs out from under her. As she stumbled, he brought that blasted shield up hard, right into her clasped hands. She cried out in pain as the sword flew free, flying up into the air.

Halla-ar moved in. She whirled to face him, thinking: catch *me* by surprise, boy? She aimed a jab straight at his face, but he avoided it easily. She kicked out, catching his flank, but he danced away, blunting the impact.

Captain America charged in hard, landing a punch on her stomach. She gasped and stumbled back, but managed to grab his shoulder and spin him around – slamming him shield-first into the surprised Kree boy.

"Gamora," Cap gasped, tumbling back to his feet. "You don't understand. Your ship…"

She ignored him; she couldn't afford to fall for his diversions. She jabbed and kicked, keeping both enemies at bay. The fight strayed toward the tall factory building, scattering the group of Kree spectators – Gamora's cheering section – away from the loading dock.

"We ought to get Horse out here," a young Kree said. "He loves a good fight!"

Gamora had been trained in Kree fighting moves, but Halla-ar knew a few she'd never seen before, including a rapid-fire uppercut barrage that caught her by surprise. She ducked away and kicked him in the stomach, using a Strontian muscle contraction technique to sharpen her toe into a rock-hard tip. He covered his retreat with a series of jabs, but as soon as he was out of range, he stumbled and fell to the ground.

Cap's technique was more conventional, but no less effective. He alternately jabbed out with that shield and kicked or punched, almost in a predictable rhythm: shield-kick, shield-jab, shield-shield-kick-again. He was favoring one side, but it didn't seem to slow him down. Time after time she tried to get behind the shield, to grab at his wounded arm. But he protected himself well.

Slowly, one step at a time, Captain America forced her up against the wall of the factory. Gamora struggled, but he kept his shield – that shield, that cursed shield! – between them, using its curved surface to press her against the cold stone.

"Now," Cap said, "are you willing to listen to reason?"

She looked out over the lip of the shield. Saw Halla-ar, a few feet away – and something else, too. A shadow dropping out of the sky…

"Not yet," she said.

A puzzled look crossed Cap's face and then the ground exploded in a barrage of force beams. As he flew up into the air, shield flailing, a small figure in an aero-rig descended, a sneer plastered across its hirsute face.

"Sorry, flag guy," Rocket said. "But we got a planet-killer to catch."

Captain America's shield clattered down to Earth a moment before its owner did. As Gamora picked herself up, she thought with satisfaction: that toy won't save your smug carcass this time, Earthman.

# CHAPTER 25

"Dude? Terran kid, you OK?"

Kamala's eyes flew open. A trio of faces looked down at her with concern. A young guy with a Mohawk, a middle-aged woman with hard eyes, and another young man with a kind smile on his pale blue face.

"Kree," she said. "You're all Kree."

"It ain't a crime." Mohawk gave her a crooked smile. "Most places, anyway."

They helped her to a sitting position. The rippled metal of that strange building felt cold against her back. "How long was I out?" she asked.

"Couple minutes," Mohawk said. "Don't worry, we didn't take your mask off."

She tried to stand, but stopped as a stabbing pain went shooting through her head. *I probably have a concussion*, she realized. She sat back against the wall, studying the building. It was low, two stories high at most, with a faded American flag painted across its outer wall. It had no windows or doors, on this side at least. The Kree stood clustered against it, watching her. Did they live inside the building? Were they all employees of Tony Stark?

Never mind that, she scolded herself. Halla-ar. Where was Halla-ar?

"Oh man," the blue Kree said. "I think your friends are in for it."

The wall behind her rattled as a series of blasts rang out. Kamala leaned forward and peered toward the factory. Out in the open, not far away, Captain America knelt in a crouch, shaking off the effects of the blasts. Captain America? she thought. Was he here before?

Gamora eyed Cap, her sword drawn. Above her – hovering in the air, wearing a flying harness and carrying an all-too-familiar, smoking weapon – was...

"Rocket," Kamala sighed.

Cap rolled to his feet, raising his shield. Rocket's cannon-blast struck it at close range, forcing him to his knees.

"You – lunatic!" Cap gasped. "Who's driving – ship?"

"Ha! I dunno," Rocket replied, taking aim again. "But Quill's always tellin' me what a hotshot pilot he is..."

The rest of his comment was drowned out by another blast. Again, Cap's shield took the impact, but the barrage was forcing him back toward the outer wall of the factory.

"Oh, dude!" Mohawk Kree grabbed his friend and pointed. "Poor Halla-ar."

Kamala tore her eyes away from the Cap/Rocket skirmish, her heart sinking as she turned toward Gamora. The green woman had turned her attention away from Cap, toward her true prey. She strode steadily, eyes blazing with fury, toward Halla-ar who lay dazed on the ground.

"No," Kamala said. "Oh no."

Halla-ar leaped up, but Gamora clenched both fists together and swatted him down again. He fell on his back, and by the time he could blink her sword was pointed at his throat. He stared up, eyes wide, keeping very still.

Hang on, Kamala thought. Hang on, new kid! She squeezed her eyes shut, shaking her head to clear it. Just another few seconds...

"Rocket?" Gamora called, her voice unnaturally calm.

The raccoonoid had Cap backed up against the factory wall. Cap raised his shield – just a fraction of a second too late. Rocket's cannon-blast hit him in the chest, and he went down. Rocket arced around in midair and steered his flying rig toward Gamora.

Mohawk stared at Halla-ar. "They're gonna kill him."

"No," Kamala said again. "I can... I can save him..."

She gritted her teeth and willed herself to grow, to become giant-sized. She rose to her feet – and stumbled as the pain shot through her. With a grunt, she collapsed to the ground.

"You better stay down for a while," the middle-aged woman said to her.

"No," she replied. "I've got... healing powers..."

She forced herself up, struggling to see. Gamora's sword was still at Halla-ar's throat. Rocket hovered in the air, his gun pointed at the kid's head.

"No way you can take on those two," Mohawk said.

"Yes, I can," Kamala gasped. "I can! But I need a diversion."

"Hey," the blue Kree said to his friend. "What about Horse?"

"Yeah!" Mohawk turned to her. "We got this friend called Horse. He does six shifts in a row on the line, no complaints, and he's one hell of a fighter. He once took on eight guys by himself."

"Great!" she said. "Where is he?"

"Factory, probably. Like I said, he always takes extra shifts."

"Get him out here, OK? I've got work to do."

She clenched her fists, concentrating. Gamora was yelling something at Halla-ar, but Kamala couldn't worry about that now. She blocked out that voice, the protests of her new Kree friends, and the roar of Rocket's flying rig. Most of all, she had to ignore the pain in her head, which grew steadily worse as she activated her power.

Slowly, excruciatingly, she shrank herself down to four inches in height. She waved up at the astonished Kree, turned away, and started off.

The grass extended up over her head; with an effort, she enlarged her hands slightly to clear herself a path. It would take time and effort to reach Halla-ar this way. But with luck, the two Guardians wouldn't notice a tiny girl moving toward them, hidden in the grass.

Gamora stared down at Halla-ar, gritting her teeth. "No more games, boy," she said. "Tell me what I want to know."

Halla-ar gasped, raising himself up on his hands and knees. Hang on, friend! Kamala thought, struggling toward him. Just a few more minutes–

A pounding shook the ground beneath her tiny feet. She looked up; to her left, Captain America had recovered and was sprinting toward the Guardians. Relief flooded through her. With Cap helping, maybe she could save –

"Get away from my brother!"

Cap whirled around. A tall, lean blue woman leaped through the air behind him, brandishing a long metal rod. Lightning crackled on its tip, sputtered out momentarily, then flared back to life.

"Who– " Cap raised his shield, intercepting the arc of the woman's power-rod. Electricity crackled along the shield's surface; its insulated handle protected him from the bulk of the charge, but he arched his back in pain.

"You don't understand," he said. "I'm not – trying to hurt–"

Kamala shook her head. Her skull was pounding; she felt like all the breath had left her body. She'd told the Kree a half-truth: she did indeed have an accelerated healing ability. But it only worked if she gave it time – if she stopped using her power. At the rate she was exerting herself, her concussion would grow worse, very quickly.

But there was no time to stop. Cap was distracted now, busy with this newcomer, the blue Kree woman with formidable fighting skills. *Brother,* she'd said. Was this the sister Halla-ar had mentioned? Kir-ra – that was her name…

Kamala took off at a run, heading straight for Halla-ar and the Guardians. I'm still too weak, she thought – I can't take on both of them myself. Where's that distraction, guys?

Halla-ar was clutching his stomach now, coughing blood. Rocket circled above, watching in alarm "Gam," he said, "you know no one loves intimidating children more than yours truly. But are you sure this kid is–"

"Just keep that cannon trained on him."

A few yards away, Captain America and Kir-ra were engaged in close-quarters sparring. The Kree woman kicked and danced, then feinted back. Cap boxed and lunged forward; his techniques were more direct, more aggressive.

"I don't want to hurt you!" he said, jabbing out at her arm. She cried out as her electric rod went flying into the grass.

"In my short time here," she gasped, "I've learned not to believe that of any Earthman."

Kir-ra lunged, and he raised his shield easily to block her hand. But she shifted her weight, reached behind the shield, and grabbed his wounded arm. Then she *twisted.*

Cap howled in pain. Instinctively he slammed the shield directly into her face, pushing with all his strength. She let out a scream, a shriek of hurt, pain, and betrayal. Then she staggered back into the grass, clutching her bleeding nose.

Kamala drew close to the Guardians. Gamora crouched low, pinning Halla-ar down with her knees, positioning her eyes inches above his. There was rage in the Guardian's eyes, but something else, too. Desperation, Kamala thought; a lifetime of hurt that could not be contained.

"Why did you do it?" Gamora demanded.

Halla-ar spat in her face.

Gamora reared back, howling in rage. As she wiped the spittle away, Halla-ar turned his head to the side, squinting through the grass. His eyes widened as he spotted Kamala approaching, still at reduced size. He shook his head urgently and mouthed the word *no*.

She ignored him, thinking: no distraction, no Captain America to the rescue. And a headache the size of Newark, just to make things extra fun.

*Let's do this.*

She willed herself to grow, shooting up out of the grass. One hand formed itself into a mace; the other, a baseball bat. Gamora turned in alarm, raising her sword. Rocket swung around in the air, waving that deadly gun in her direction.

The pain was excruciating, but Kamala ignored it. She continued to grow, six feet tall, eight, then ten. She concentrated, expanding her legs, arms, weapon-hands even further. There was no way she could handle the two Guardians, especially in this condition. But if she could distract them for a minute, maybe two – then Halla-ar could escape from–

"Ok, who wants a butt-kicking?"

The voice, which sounded surprisingly friendly, belonged to a tall, muscular worker standing on the factory loading dock. He wore a beige Kree jumpsuit, like so many of the Praeteran refugees. But this was no Kree. This man had deep green skin adorned with an array of ritual tattoos.

Everyone stopped. Captain America frowned. Kir-ra shook loose of him, snarling angrily. Kamala paused at giant size, swaying with dizziness.

Over by the metal building, Mohawk Kree and his friends grinned, pointing at the newcomer. "Horse!" one of them called.

"I SAID," Horse called, "WHO AM I MEANT TO FIGHT? AND CAN WE HURRY THIS UP?" He held up a pair of machine parts. "I HAVE MANY MORE WIDGETS TO ATTACH TO DOOHICKEYS TODAY."

OK, Kamala thought, so this is the distraction! Better late than...

But wait. Rocket and Gamora seemed distracted, all right, but not the way she'd expected. They were staring with open mouths at "Horse". Rocket steered his rig through the air in slow circles. Gamora picked her way through the grass as if she were hunting a ghost.

"Drax?" Rocket whispered.

Kamala had never heard the name Drax the Destroyer – and if she had, she couldn't have known the significance of this moment. But she saw the tears in Rocket's eyes, the way he gripped his aero-rig tighter as he flew over to meet "Horse" . Gamora seemed smaller, more human than before. She ran to the tattooed man, who reached out thick arms and enveloped both Guardians in a bear hug.

Kamala shrank down to human size, willing her hands back to their usual shapes. Pain flashed through her head, painting the world in a speckled haze. She shook it off, searching for Halla-ar. Where was he? Was he safe?

She spotted two blue figures running away. Kir-ra wrapped her arm around her brother, urging him along. Halla-ar cast a quick glance back, and once again Kamala's eyes met his. Then his sister steered him around the corner of the factory, and they were gone.

Kamala felt a weird sense of loss, of unfinished business. Did Halla-ar understand that she'd tried to help him? Was he safe now, or would the Guardians keep hunting him? Would she ever see him again, or would his sister hide him away for the rest of his life?

She tottered and swooned, struggling to stay conscious. She caught a quick glimpse of Mohawk Kree and his friends, moving toward her in concern. And then she passed out again.

She couldn't have been out for more than a minute this time. She woke up among the Kree, who had moved her to the elevated surface of the factory loading dock. She smiled and shook off their concerns, then hopped down and walked over to talk to Captain America.

The pain in her head had subsided to a dull throb. Cap intercepted her, reaching out to grasp her shoulder like she was, well, a fellow soldier or something. He said some nice things about her fighting ability, her courage... something about doing the name Avenger proud. But she was still so hazy, all she could do was smile in return.

"Halla-ar," she managed to say. "He's gone."

"He's safe. Thanks to you."

Cap gestured toward the far end of the low building, along the metal wall with the faded flag pattern on it. Rocket and Gamora stood on the grass with the man they called Drax. Rocket had discarded his aerial gear, and was listening intently as Drax told his story.

"He's another Guardian," Cap explained. "They thought he was dead. When they found him, all the fight – the anger – seemed to drain right out of them."

Kamala nodded, understanding.

"I just compared notes with them," Cap continued. "There really does seem to be a planet-killer on the loose. I agreed to help them find it, as long as they stop assaulting random children and immigrants–"

A grinding noise filled the air. Kamala looked up to see the Guardian and Avenger ships, still fused together, circling around in the sky. She'd almost forgotten about them.

"Tony?" Cap touched his earpiece. "Tony, can you hear me?"

The Guardians noticed too. They pointed in alarm, watching as the ships began to shake and quiver. Above the dangling Guardians vessel, the crimson and gold figure of Iron Man swung into view, his metal gauntlets pressed against the quinjet's rear engines.

"What..." Kamala turned to Cap in alarm. "What's he doing?"

# CHAPTER 26

The cockpit shook with a jolt that rattled Quill's bones – and left him oddly curious. Over the years, Peter Quill had become somewhat of a connoisseur of spaceship disasters. Colliding with a moon: that was a specific, spine-jarring impact. The effect of a Skrull beta ray was different, more of an extended, teeth-grinding vibration. And then there was the skin-tingling sensation of a Shi'ar teleporter.

This didn't feel like any of those things. Hence his curiosity: what *was* it?

He shook his head, stunned. The jolt, whatever it was, had interrupted the seemingly endless battle between Groot and She-Hulk. She stood bracing herself against the back bulkhead, blinking in confusion, while the tree-man retracted a dozen or so branches back into his body.

"Romanoff? Oh, Natasha Romanoff?" Quill started toward the front of the compartment, stumbling over discarded vines. "What did you just do to my ship?"

She didn't answer. Her nimble hands were a blur on the console.

"Romanoff?" He touched her shoulder and immediately

regretted it. She didn't turn around, but her arm whipped back, electricity flashing from the stinger on her wrist. He scurried back, holding up his hands in surrender.

"I used your power core to jumpstart the quinjet's auxiliary engine stack." Her voice was perfectly calm, as if she hadn't just threatened to shoot forty thousand volts into his body. "Where's your plasma feeder, anyway?"

"It's the button marked 'KISS YOU ALL OVER.'"

Her whole body seemed to deflate, slumping forward over the console. He could feel the contempt rising from her.

"Tony?" she said at length, into the console. "Did it work?"

"Yes and no." Tony Stark's voice sounded tired. "Yes, the engines fired. No, that did not dislodge the two ships from each other."

She let out a string of Russian curses.

"By the way," Tony added, "give me a little warning next time? You almost fried my boots off."

"Yeah," Quill said. "Give me some warning next time, too!"

"Well…" Jennifer Walters approached, eyeing Quill cautiously. "I guess this answers the age-old question: what happens when a pack of hotheaded clowns drop out of the sky and start shaking down poor people who just might, maybe, in said clowns' fevered imagination, be planet-killers?"

"In defense of my particular clown car, being a planet-killer? Kind of a severe deal." Quill peered over the Widow's shoulder, taking care to keep his distance this time. "Wait, why are you locking the controls?"

She leaped out of her chair, startling him. "I'm going back to the quinjet. See if I can force it out of this…" She looked helplessly all around, then gestured at the control console. "Stick's all yours, *Svoloch.*"

"It's Quill! Peter Quill. But, uh, you know that..."

She was already up and climbing through the hole where the viewport had been. In a second she was gone, vanished into the mass of tangled metal jutting from the quinjet's undercarriage.

"Ooooh-kay." Quill sat down and cracked his knuckles. "Back in con-*trol*. Back at the *helm*."

"Ow," Jen said quietly, picking at her fingers. "Always hated splinters."

Groot came up next to her, waving a branch in protest. "I am Groot."

She shrugged. "Whatever."

"Tasha?" Stark's voice said, from the console. "You still there?"

"She's, uh, she's gone back to your ship," Quill said. "This is Star-Lord."

"Who? Oh, yeah, awesome... Listen, Quill, I've got a problem out here. The ships are still fused together, and your altitude is dropping."

The front viewport was still blocked, so Quill reached over and pulled up a small viewscreen. Jen and Groot moved to join him. They seemed like old friends now, their battle forgotten. Maybe, Quill thought, being trapped in a plummeting spaceship could bring people together. That was a sweet idea, actually. He could almost imagine it on a greeting card.

Groot grunted at the screen, which showed a haze of static. Quill thumped it with one hand, and an image flickered into view: a grassy field with an access road running through it.

"I am Groot?"

"Yup, that's too clear a shot," Quill said. "We are *way* too low. Stark, you're gonna stop this, right? That's why you're out there?"

"Yeaaahhhh... I don't think I've got enough power."

"I am Groot?"

"Very funny," Quill replied. "No, I do not have a button marked 'STAYIN' ALIVE.'"

"Natasha?" Jen said. "Maybe she can get the quinjet moving."

"Maybe. But if not..."

He leaned into the controls, flipping a series of analog switches. A low hum rose up, all through the cabin.

"What are you doing?" Jen asked.

"What I have to do. What only Star-Lord can do."

He reached over, cued up a song, and smiled. He was in his element now: a hopeless crisis, a plummeting spaceship, dozens of innocent lives hanging in the balance. Peter Quill had never felt happier in his life.

The speakers sang with Deep Purple.

"I'm gonna fire up the Big Butt Beam," he said.

"F.R.I.D.A.Y.," Tony said, "give me an update on our heading?"

"Moving inland again," the voice replied.

He grunted, running his gauntlets across the mangled metal on the underside of the quinjet. He'd barely managed to scurry down here in time when Tasha had fired up the engines. But he was having trouble keeping a decent grip. The Guardians had really done a job on the quinjet – and that battered ship of theirs hung down, just below him, still fused to the Avengers' ship.

"Well, at least we're not headed for Connecticut," Tony gasped. "And Manhattan's a good fifty miles away–"

"Sixty-three miles," FRIDAY said.

"Sixty-three. Thank you. How far to the nearest town? From here, I mean?"

"Ah. That would be only four miles."

Well, *that* wasn't good. At this rate, the quivering vessels could cover that distance in less than five minutes. The last thing he needed was for an extraterrestrial junker and an official Avengers quinjet to crash down together onto some Long Island train station.

Cap's voice crackled in his ear again, asking for a situation report. *Sorry, soldier – no time to talk.* He toggled that channel to silence, called up a schematic of the two ships, and ran a quick simulation. If he were to twist the quinjet at an angle of… no, no good; the image spun out of control, smashing into the ground. Two more simulations led to similar, disastrous results. He grunted, punched the ship's hull in frustration, and tried one more time.

"Jackpot," he said. "Maybe."

"Maybe," F.R.I.D.A.Y. agreed. The AI's voice sounded even less sure than his own.

Calculating the angle, he leaned against the quinjet, aimed his legs carefully, and fired off both boot-jets. The metal bent, pressing hard against his shoulder with a dull groaning noise. He winced, shook off the pain, and boosted his attitude jets to full power.

The quinjet began to twist on its side, veering back toward the pier. The Guardians' ship let out a metallic whine, but remained lodged in the jet's underside.

"Come on, guys," he said through gritted teeth. "Please?"

The pressure increased; the ships continued to turn. The Employee Services building loomed close, with the taller factory off to the left. Ahead lay the pier – and the water. If he could just reach the water…

He checked his power level: fifty-three percent. That was bad; it was dropping fast. The armor hadn't had time to fully repair itself.

*And neither have I,* he realized. Like he'd said to Jen, he couldn't seem to catch his breath. It was all too much: the duties of an Avenger, his responsibilities as head of Stark Enterprises, the sad mess he'd made of his life with Pepper, the problem with the Kree, whatever that was! And now these interstellar morons, playing demolition derby in the sky–

"Tony?"

The voice shocked him out of his self-pity. "Tasha," he replied. "Give me some good news?"

"I'm back on the quinjet," she said. "Auxiliary engine stack is at half power. That should be enough for a quick burst – probably wrench us free."

"Leaving the Guardians' ship where, exactly... ?"

"I guess that's your job."

That figured. He checked power: forty-seven percent. "Tasha, I think I've got a drain somewhere–"

"I don't mean to cut you off, boss, but my engine charge is fading fast. If we're gonna do this, it's got to be now."

He hissed in a breath. Up ahead, that low metal building was coming up fast; he could just make out the small figures of Captain America and Ms Marvel, surrounded by a group of Kree workers. The figures were alarmingly close, and the ships' altitude was still dropping.

"Countdown from five, Tasha."

He grimaced, braced himself, and let go of the quinjet. For a moment he was in freefall, and then his boot-jets kicked in, angling him toward the Guardians' vessel. He reached out and grabbed hold of its nearest vertical stabilizer, pulling himself onto the outer hull of the ship.

"I'm in position," he said. "Fire when–"

Flame burst from the quinjet's engines, sending it shooting

forward. The Guardians' ship bucked, rocked, and snapped free. Tony almost flew off into the air, but he activated auxiliary magnets and clamped his gloves and knee-joints tight to the hull.

He caught a quick glimpse of the quinjet, arcing toward the water. It was dropping fast, and the fire in its rocket-tubes had faded, replaced by thick black smoke. *That doesn't look good*, he thought–

–and then the Guardians' ship dropped sharply, taking him with it. Employee Services, the low metal building, lay dead ahead. At this rate of descent, they would crash straight into the wall.

Tony clamped both gauntlets around a sensor array, a studded protrusion on the Guardian ship's roof. He planted his feet, reared back, and pulled. Slowly, agonizingly, the ship began to rise. Below, the faded flag design on the building dropped lower – lower, lower...

He grimaced, straining human muscle and metal servos. *Come on*, he thought, ignoring a raft of power-level alarms. *Come on, Quill! Little help, maybe?* What was going on inside that blasted ship?

The lip of the roof came into view. Tony let out a sigh of relief – just as the loudest alarm of all went off inside his helmet:

POWER FAILURE

His jets went dead; his arm-servos locked up. A single, dread word appeared before his eyes:

REBOOTING

And the ship began to fall.

On the ground, Kamala watched in horror. The Guardians' ship was headed straight for the building, and it didn't look like it would clear the roof.

She turned to say something to Captain America. But he was staring in a different direction – toward the water, at the fading trail of the quinjet's engines. "Tasha?" he yelled into his earpiece. "Natasha, come in?"

Natasha Romanoff shook her head, dazed. She'd managed to pull the quinjet free of the Guardians' ship, but she'd almost lost consciousness from the burst of acceleration.

She checked the readouts on the quinjet's pilot console: all red. That burst had burned out the auxiliary engine stack, depleting the charge she'd injected from the Guardians' power core. The quinjet was a dead hulk, gliding down toward a hard landing.

She strapped in and braced herself, hoping she'd make it to the water.

Gamora and Drax stood together on the ground, watching their ship drop. Rocket circled in the air, keeping his distance.

Drax turned to Gamora, a stern look on his face. "In my absence," he said, "you have allowed our vessel to fall into disrepair."

She couldn't argue the point.

Inside the Guardians' ship, all eyes were glued to the view ahead. The front viewport, which had been blocked for so long, now showed the roof of that metal building looming closer... closer...

"I've got a weird feeling," Jennifer Walters whispered, "that we're about to enter the discovery phase."

Quill ignored her. The ship was dropping fast; at this rate they'd slam right into the lip of the roof. The engines weren't responding, which left him no choice.

He reached out and stabbed a button marked "KNOCK THREE TIMES."

A beam of red light sliced out of the ship, melting the edge of the roof to slag. Tony released his grip on the hull and leaped away, jetting up into the air. Another beam followed, hotter and brighter. The third was almost pure yellow, like the sun itself.

The roof sizzled, rolled up, and melted. In less than thirty seconds, half of it was gone. The ship dipped down, then rose back up as its engines coughed out a final, unexpected burst of power. It bounced off the still-intact back half of the roof, skidded briefly, then wobbled off into the air toward the water.

Good riddance, Tony thought. His armor had rebooted to minimal power, with priority allotted to flight control and air circulation. Weapons, communications, fine servo movement – those would come later.

He wafted over toward the building. It was exposed to the elements now, its insides visible to anyone hovering above. He moved slowly, hesitantly, a deep sense of dread stealing over him.

I don't want to know, he realized. I don't want to see what's inside. But for him, as for Peter Quill, there was no choice. He turned in midair, fired up his coughing boot-jets, and looked down.

"Oh no," he whispered.

Inside his cold shell of metal, there was no one to hear.

# PART FOUR

## AFTER THE FALL

# CHAPTER 27

Tony Stark hung in the air like a god, staring down. His movements were dronelike, inhuman. He was in shock.

The building's roof had been burned halfway off in a surprisingly clean break. Inside those thin metal walls, dozens – no, hundreds of Kree sat, stood, milled around, or slept curled up in crowded, dirty spaces. One side of the building consisted of living quarters, a large area subdivided by temporary metal walls, curtains, and in a few cases chicken wire. Some of the rooms had as many as eight bunks crammed into them. They had doors made of plywood or just curtains, no windows, and most of the bedclothes looked threadbare and unwashed.

In one room, an argument was raging between two men. In another, a woman tried to corral six screaming children. In a third, three young women struggled to move a chunk of the steaming roof that had fallen in on them. A few more Kree stared up at the sky; one of them pointed at Tony and shook his head in disgust.

Tony wafted up a bit; he couldn't force himself to meet the man's gaze. He jetted sideways to gain a three-quarters view of the living area, which was actually three stories high, with ladders down the side providing access to the higher levels. Each storey couldn't have been more than six feet high, from floor to temporary ceiling.

No windows. No privacy. From the look of it, barely any ventilation – until now, at least. It looked like an anthill, a beehive.

How? he thought. How could this happen? Here, in my father's house?

He wanted to look away, to pretend this horror didn't exist. But he couldn't. The lenses built into his helmet spared him no detail.

Ladders led down from the living quarters into a large open area. One corner held a few CRT-screen computers; a ring of young people circled around, waiting their turns. But most of the space served as a sort of communal dining room, with long picnic tables arrayed in rows along the bare floor. Kree of all ages sat hunched over bowls of food, eating rapidly, furtively. Occasionally they glanced briefly up at the now-exposed sky, then turned quickly back to their food.

A small kitchen stood adjacent to the dining room. Rusted gas stoves, a loud whirring freezer. A few men and women rushed around, struggling to prepare food in a space that was clearly inadequate to the demand.

There was more. A room full of screaming children, guarded by a single ancient Kree woman. An infirmary with a mere three beds, all occupied; two more men laid out on mattresses on the floor. A trio of jumpsuited Kree moving from room to room carting away fallen chunks of fallen metal and plaster on a large, wheeled dolly.

Where the roof gap ended, Tony caught a glimpse of a large industrial area with steam leaking up and out. Beyond that, he couldn't know.

I brought them here, he thought. I offered them work, housing, a new life. And all I brought them was… despair. Filth. Living conditions even worse than those they'd known before, as serfs of the ruthless Kree Empire.

He had to clean this up. He *would* clean this up. What had he told the Kree woman? *Whatever is happening here, I swear it ends today.*

But it was so big. So much to deal with. And so terrible. "Look on my Works, ye Mighty," he whispered, "and despair."

There was plenty of despair to go around.

"These are my friends," said Drax the Destroyer. "They saved my life. I have very little, but they have less. I need very little, so I give what I have. Their arms are strong, but mine are stronger. They work hard in the factory, but I can work harder. That makes me no better than them, but it gives me a duty to help them when I can. I am proud of my work. I am proud of my friends."

Gamora paused on the ladder, halfway between the Kree's open common area and the exposed sky above. Just below, Rocket and Drax continued climbing downward, chattering away.

"OK, but let me get this straight," Rocket said. "There's a freakin' nuclear accelerator on the other side of this research complex, and these friends of yours live like *this*?"

"I did not create this situation," Drax replied.

After the ship sliced off the roof of the metal building, Captain America had run off to help the Black Widow. Drax had led Rocket and Gamora inside the building, through a large hidden door. The Kree had hurried to join them, murmuring fearfully about friends and relatives. Once inside, Drax had offered a tour of this grim place that had weirdly become almost a new home to him.

Drax! Gamora could still hardly believe he was alive. She hadn't really processed that, she realized. Too much going on.

The ladder led down past levels of living quarters, separated from open air only by a thin curtain of chicken wire. In a room no bigger than a walk-in closet, two men sat on a low bed, their heads slumped. One man reached out and threw a rubber ball to a little girl sitting on the floor. She missed the catch; the ball thumped into the chicken wire, lodging itself in the netting. The little girl ran to retrieve it. then froze as she saw Gamora outside, on the ladder, just inches away.

For a moment, Gamora's heart caught. Was it her? The girl she'd met back on Praeterus?

No. This girl was older, with a tinge of blue to her complexion. She gave Gamora a blank look, then reached for the ball. She tore it loose, ripping its skin, and tossed it lazily back to her parents.

"... still don't get it," Rocket was saying. "How in the name of Xandar did you manage to escape an exploding planet?"

"There was another ship hidden inside the spaceport hangar!" Drax laughed. "Did you see that coming? I did not. I did not see that coming."

Drax's friend, the Kree with a Mohawk, called up to them from the floor. "It was a pretty old ship," he said. "We didn't think it worked."

"You guys," Rocket replied. "You, uh, do a lotta drugs back there on Praeterus?"

Mohawk gave a crooked smile.

Rocket turned back to Drax. "So you just stayed with the Kree?"

"Their struggles were prodigious," Drax replied, "assuming I understand the meaning of that word. I am stronger than the mightiest among them, and I saw that I could help them. How could I fail to do this?"

"Yeah, yeah, that's all admirable and stuff. But you never thought to tell us you were alive?"

"I did not." Drax hesitated. "Would that have been appropriate?"

Gamora found herself smiling. Finding Drax had taken some of the edge off her anger; that was a relief, but also a potential danger. There was still a killer here, she reminded herself. The scent of evil underlay this place, like mold that had been sprayed over with perfume.

She had to stay alert; she had to retain her edge. She owed that to the dead of Praeterus, and to the survivors too.

"Don't take this wrong, Drax," Rocket said, "but you don't sound much like a Destroyer no more."

"Horse…" The Kree man paused. "I mean, Drax kept us together during some pretty tough times. Out in space."

"I get that," Rocket said, "but why didn't you show yourself sooner, buddy?"

"When you attacked this installation," Drax replied, "the Kree immediately sought shelter. I was the only one who stayed at my post, on the assembly line."

"Because…?"

Drax stepped down off the ladder, gesturing around. "If this frankly baffling capitalist enterprise must be maintained," he said, "let it be on my back, rather than those gifted with inferior strength and stamina."

"OK, that's the Drax I know," Rocket said. "Unflinchingly self-sacrificing, yet vaguely insulting to all around him."

Gamora reached the bottom of the ladder. This area served as the Kree's dining room and general meeting space; it was vast but busy. Long picnic tables hosted families and other assorted Kree gatherings. Some of the groups talked loudly, with animated gestures, in dialects Gamora didn't understand. Other Kree slumped low, glaring or staring straight ahead. No one seemed to care about the newcomers.

She gazed back at the three levels of living quarters. Inside, that area was a maze of tight corridors. From the side, it looked like a cage divided up into levels. And from down here, anyone could see into the side rooms. A few of the families had hung curtains, but even those couldn't cover the chicken wire from floor to ceiling. These people had virtually no privacy.

*And now*, she thought, *they have even less*. She craned her neck, peering up past the top level, through the open space that had been the roof. Tony Stark floated high above, bright and imperious in that full-body armor of his.

She looked away. She didn't want to meet those glowing, all-seeing eyes.

A grinding noise, from the far wall. Four muscular Kree were in the process of sliding shut a high garage-style door, which Drax had forced open earlier to let them inside. Judging from their grunts and groans, it was a difficult, laborious process.

"Why are they bothering?" Gamora asked. "The roof is…" She gestured up.

"Habit, I guess," Mohawk Kree replied. "We been warned not to be seen outside. Go straight from here to the factory and back again, they said. Break those rules, you could lose your job."

"Who warned you?" she persisted. "Whose rules are they? Stark's?"

"Stark!" Drax glanced up at Tony and let out a short laugh. "He is a mere 'suit', as we say here on Earth."

"We don't know who makes the rules," Mohawk said. "The

assembly line's completely automated. All our assignments come in on computer screens."

Gamora's eyes narrowed. This place was evil, without a doubt, and yet, it was starting to sound as if someone other than Tony Stark was to blame. She felt a strange claustrophobic sensation, as if a deliberate plot – some strange cosmic web – were closing in around her.

"We never even seen Stark before today," Mohawk continued. "In fact, the human workers pretty much stay away from this side of the plant."

"Not that they work weekends anyway!" Drax slapped his friend on the back. "Am I right, My-ronn?"

Rocket blinked. "Your name is Myron?"

The Kree nodded. "My-ronn."

"I named him." Drax puffed out his chest with pride. "I am excellent with names."

"I didn't like my old name." My-ronn shrugged. "I named him Horse, in return."

"Which I despise," Drax said calmly.

"Oh! Sorry, dude. You should have said something."

"Why?" Drax turned and started off. "Come. I have errands to perform."

Drax led them on a winding path in and around the picnic tables, stopping frequently to exchange a few words with the Kree families. My-ronn split off, joining a group of his friends who were taking apart an Earth laptop computer.

A few of the Kree ate from bare plastic plates; some were engrossed in their phones. Most of them looked up when Drax approached, flashing small smiles. They all seemed to accept him, but not quite as one of them. More like a friendly outsider who'd earned their trust.

He *has* changed, Gamora realized. He seemed calmer, less angry, more centered – as if he'd found his purpose here, in this grim place. She found herself envying him. Her own anger, her craving for vengeance, still burned.

A hollow feeling inside made her wonder: *do* I still have a purpose?

A young Kree man in a jumpsuit sat alone, staring straight ahead. When he didn't respond to Drax's greeting, the Destroyer thumped him on the back, hard. The man looked up, blinked, and smiled.

That was when Gamora realized there were a lot more men here than women.

Drax steered the group around a shard of metal that had fallen in the collapse of the roof. It was embedded in the floor, jutting up at a dangerous angle, and still smoking slightly. The Kree ignored it, detouring around it with their trays and their phones. Just one more speed bump in the obstacle course of their lives.

Drax paused at a pair of doors inset into a temporary, corrugated-metal wall. "I must gather some supplies from the kitchen," he said. "But first..."

When he threw open the left-hand door, a burst of giggles and screams greeted him. Gamora followed the group inside, where a dozen or more young children scrambled and chased each other across the floor. A single old Kree woman with tired eyes sat on a folding chair off to the side, playing a game on her phone.

The children turned to look, and all at once they froze. They stared up at Drax with wide eyes.

"Horse!" they yelled.

Then they were all over him, tugging and screaming and laughing. A girl climbed up his side, giggling. Drax laughed in return and flexed his bicep. A little blue boy perched on his shoulder, grinning, and flexed his own tiny arm.

The caretaker looked up from her phone, shrugged, and turned away again.

"Ride!" the kids yelled, one and two and three at a time. "Give us a ride!"

"Later, little Kree-tures," Drax said. That sent them off into giggles again. "They enjoy my wordplay," he added.

"Yeah, it's legendary," Rocket said.

"Come. We must – no, Val-ar, you may *not* have one of my knives – we must move on."

He brushed off the last of the children and led the group through another swinging door. All at once, the laughter stopped.

They stepped into a kitchen no bigger than a large bathroom, lined with grimy, yellowed tiles. Three old ovens had been crammed into one half of the room; they were caked with old food, and one of the doors hung askew, hold on with coat hanger wire. Two women and a man, all in their forties, looked up from their work at a low table.

"I require a few ration packs," Drax said. "For my rounds."

One of the women nodded and rose, grabbing for a crutch. She limped over to a giant freezer and pulled hard at the door. A large rat scurried out from behind the freezer and into the corner.

"This tiny kitchen," Gamora said, "feeds the entire facility?"

The woman paused in her labor and gave Gamora an annoyed look. "It's all we got," she said.

The other two Kree turned to watch. The table in front of them was strewn with half-peeled vegetables: turnips, carrots, celery. None of it looked very fresh.

Rocket sidled up to Gamora. "This Stark dude sure knows how to run a sweatshop," he muttered.

She turned away, studying a ragged bulletin board hanging above the nearest stove. Handwritten notes and circled newspaper clippings promised better housing, deals on bulk foodstuffs, and assorted goods for sale.

"Thank you," Drax said, accepting a large paper bag. "Oh, I almost forgot! I must also pick up some fresh linens."

As he started toward the far door, the Kree exchanged alarmed glances. The man and woman rose from the table and moved quickly to block his way. The woman couldn't have been more than five feet tall.

"You can't go in there," she said.

Drax paused for a moment, considering. Then he nodded and grimaced. "Of course. I forgot."

Gamora frowned, looking up. The edge of the exposed roof hung over the kitchen; the room beyond was still covered, hidden from view – even from above. "Why can't we go in there?" she asked. "What's in that room?"

The small woman turned toward her. "The laundry room is a safe space for women."

"Horse," the man said. "Chir-na will fetch your linens for you."

Drax nodded. The small woman grimaced at him and started toward the door. Then she stopped and turned around slowly. Her hard eyes locked on Gamora's.

"You can come if you like," she said.

Gamora hesitated. Some instinct warned her of danger, but that made no sense. Did the Kree mean her harm? Were they still angry about the incident out on the pier? If they were, surely they wouldn't lure her into a kitchen and ambush her in the laundromat!

She gestured for the woman, Chir-na, to go first. When they stepped inside, the hum and grinding of large industrial washer/

dryers filled the air – and something else: the whistle of blades. Gamora reached for her sword–

–and froze. Four women stood in the cramped space, all young, muscular, and sweating in the thick air. And all holding up knives. They'd turned away from their work, folding clothes and stuffing oversized loads into creaky washers, in order to guard against possible attackers. Their unblinking eyes locked onto Gamora as she followed Chir-na to a table of folded blankets.

Chir-na barely acknowledged the workers. She picked up a single gray blanket, nodded to the woman at the end of the line, and started back toward the kitchen.

The air hung heavy with steam; the tumbling of dryers, the rushing of water formed an oppressive din. Like the kitchen, this room bore witness to a badly overstressed support system. Even with the machines running night and day, it could never keep up with the needs of the several hundred Kree in this facility.

Gamora walked slowly to the door, keeping her hands in view and her movements steady. She bore no kinship, shared no blood with these women, these silent wary refugees from a dead world. But she understood their plight. All too well, she understood.

# CHAPTER 28

Kamala Khan sat alone on the factory loading dock, squeezing her eyes shut. Her head still ached. In fact, her whole body ached. If this was a typical day in the life of an Avenger, she didn't know if she'd live to graduate high school.

She craned her neck, peering at the low metal building. That faded flag pattern covered the side wall. She could just see the big door, down at the far end, that Horse – Drax? – had opened in order to let his friends inside. But she couldn't make out what was inside it, and from this angle, she couldn't see over the wall, either.

She could see one thing, though. Tony Stark, in full Iron Man costume, floating in the sky above. He was barely moving, the lights of his eye-lenses glowing against the midday clouds.

She jumped down from the dock and stumbled over to the flag-building, shaking her head. When she reached the building, she leaned her hands against the cold metal wall. This was a bad idea, she knew. She needed to give herself time to heal. If she used her powers now, she could really injure herself.

But she had to know.

Bracing herself, she willed her legs to grow, to extend,

stretching herself up along the wall. It wasn't very high – maybe twenty feet or so. When she reached the top, she grabbed hold of the exposed edge of the wall, which was still warm from the Guardian ship's ray-blast. To her left, the intact part of the roof ended in a jagged line of molten metal.

She hoisted herself up and looked down. Directly below, inside the building, was a hospital or sick bay of some kind. All three beds and two makeshift cot-mattresses were full; a single medic in dirty scrubs hustled among the patients, administering pills and taking temperatures. One patient, hooked up to a feeding tube with tape on it, was coughing uncontrollably.

Kamala frowned. The equipment looked dated, worn out. She cast a quick glance across the exposed part of the building. Dining room, kitchen, and what looked like a daycare setup of some kind, filled with children. All of them crowded, all filled with rusty, dangerous fixtures.

She remembered Jennifer Walters's words about the Kree's plight. *it's real. And it's a problem.*

Two men entered the infirmary with blood on their faces. The medic shrugged and gestured for them to stand in the corner. The coughing man began to vomit helplessly, all over the floor. Two women in aprons rushed in to assist.

Kamala tensed, preparing to jump down inside. But the women seemed to have the situation under control. So she turned to look up at the gleaming metallic form of Iron Man, still hovering over it all.

Let's see if we can solve the bigger problem, she thought.

She let go of the roof and stretched her legs, rising even higher. Stars exploded before her eyes; she felt briefly lightheaded. But she ignored the pain and kept growing, leaning forward to brace her knees against the lip of the roof.

"Mister Stark," she said.

He didn't reply. His eye-lenses scanned the building below, as if he were cataloguing insects. He looked like an emotionless robot, or maybe a metallic god hovering over its dominion.

"Tony." The edge in her voice made him look up. "Whatcha doing?"

"Hey, kid. You look like crap."

"I'm doing better than them, I think." She waved an elongated hand down.

"Yeeeeah." He reached up to scratch his armored neck. "That's the thing, isn't it?"

He retracted his helmet, allowing her to see his face. The effect was startling. He looked like a person now, not some god or automaton. His brow was lined, his expression filled with worry. Guilt, too.

"Are you OK?" she asked.

He cocked his head, listening to something coming from his earpiece. "Kid," he said, "I gotta go."

"Go?" She frowned, wobbling a little on eighteen-foot legs. "You said you'd get to the bottom of this."

"I am. That's where I'm going." He smiled, reached out to touch her shoulder. "I'm sorry, Kamala. This isn't the way I wanted to spend my Saturday, either."

She stared, aghast. "Are you actually making this about *yourself*?"

"No. No, of course not. I'm just…" He turned away. "Do me a favor? Get together with the Guardians. I know, I know. Just… help these people, any way you can. OK?"

She nodded, wincing at the pain in her head.

"Uh-huh," Tony said to the air. "Thanks, F.R.I.D.A.Y." He turned back to Kamala. "One other thing. Keep keeping me honest, OK?"

*Keep me honest.* She knew he meant it as a compliment, but somehow it just made her angry. "That's not what I'm here for," she snapped. "I'm not your conscience. I'm a person."

"I'm sorry, again. I didn't mean ...." He tilted in midair, staring at the grim beehive below. "I'm sorry."

Then he turned upward, willed his helmet down, and shot off into the clouds.

Kamala stood for a moment, watching him go. Fists clenched, shaking with anger. Had Halla-ar been right, she wondered? Was Stark just a tyrant, a manipulative billionaire who used people up and washed his hands of them? Was that what he was doing, right now – running away from the mess he'd made?

Or was he really trying to clean it up?

She looked down into the building, at the maze-like sleeping quarters stacked three levels high. The plight of those people, trudging up and down the ladders and through the common areas, made her sick to watch. She took a step back and began to shrink down, hoping she could reach the ground before she passed out.

"Here is the clean blanket you requested, Zi-lah," Drax said. "I intimidated the launderers into using extra Snuggle for you."

If the Kree woman realized that was a joke, she gave no sign. She just took the blanket, threw it on the bed, and turned back to the seven children clamoring for her attention. All of them were toddlers except for one preteen boy, who sat on a wooden chair in the corner of the small room, tapping at a phone.

Drax turned and headed for the door. Rocket and Gamora followed.

"Hell of a brood," Rocket said as they stepped into the corridor. "They all hers?"

"Why in the world would I ask that?" Drax replied.

"Yeah. Yeah, you're right." The raccoonoid turned away, ashamed. "We ain't any closer to findin' this planet-killer, you know. Gam, you still think they're here?"

"I'm not sure." Gamora frowned. "Would a planet-killer live in a place like this?"

"They would not," Drax said firmly. "Or at least, they do not. I am certain of it."

He led them down a long windowless corridor, into the still-intact portion of the building. The roof closed in over them, giving the space an even more oppressive atmosphere. It felt, Gamora thought, like a trap.

"Only one more stop," Drax said. "My bag is almost empty."

The corridor grew darker; the sound of Kree activity faded. Drax walked up to a plywood door at the very end of the hall and, without knocking, pushed it open. A smell of decay washed over them; Rocket held a hand up to his nose. Gamora had to force herself inside.

In a tiny room, a single blue Kree sat shivering in an armchair. He was naked, wrapped only in a filthy blanket. He stared straight ahead; his eyes didn't even register the newcomers.

"Sha-karr," Drax said. *"Sha-Karr."*

The man's eyes flickered briefly to Drax. A look of panic crossed his face, then he looked away again.

"I have food for you, Sha-karr." Drax held out the last of the rations. "You must eat something."

The ration fell limply into the man's lap. Drax frowned, dropped to his knees, and took the man's hands in his own. Sha-karr looked up, startled.

"You must eat," Drax repeated.

Sha-karr stared for a moment. His chest was dirty; a few

strands of deep blue hair were matted to his scalp. A small insect crawled up the blanket and onto his head.

"Will you do this?" Drax shook his hands, gently. "Will you eat for me?"

Sha-karr nodded.

"Good."

Drax stood up and turned away. Without another word, he led Rocket and Gamora out of the room. Just before the door closed, she saw the blue Kree peeling open a sandwich, staring at it with something that might have been dread.

"Whew," Rocket said. "What happened to him?"

"I do not know exactly," Drax replied. "But his entire extended family, all that he knew, was lost in the explosion of Praeterus. The others say that, back there, he was a leading member of the community."

Gamora glanced back at the door. What was it that Thanos had taught her, growing up? *Tragedy forges us into fine steel.*

"No," she said aloud. "Tragedy breaks people."

Drax nodded as if he understood. As if he'd followed every word of the conversation in her mind.

"Some people, at any rate," he said. "And those people must be treated with sympathy and kindness. Not simply discarded like trash."

He started back down the hallway. Rocket turned to Gamora, and for a moment she thought he was about to make a sarcastic comment. But he just shrugged and loped off after Drax.

She followed, feeling oddly lost.

# CHAPTER 29

"I hate you," Halla-ar said.

"Hate you too," Kir-ra replied.

The words came automatically to her lips. This had been their customary greeting to each other, ever since he was four years old. They crouched down on the pier behind Stark Enterprises, half hidden behind a pile of rubble – all that remained of Tony Stark's shack. The pier was a wreck: holes in the wooden floor, pieces of concrete strewn all around.

Kir-ra stared up at the sky, watching the figures looming over the barracks. From this distance the Avenger girl, in her blue and red circus costume, looked like a stick figure with comically long legs.

"What's she doing?" Halla-ar asked.

"She's talking to Stark. He's hovering there, like a Sentry or something... oh, wait."

"What?"

"He just flew away." She clenched her fists, shaking. Stark's words still echoed in her mind: *Whatever is happening, I swear it ends today.*

So much for Earthmen's promises.

She glanced back at Halla-ar, the brother she'd protected ever since their parents died. He sat facing away from her, staring out over the water. He's so angry, she thought. He wasn't always like that.

"What's she doing now?" he asked. "Tell me."

She turned to look back up at the barracks. "She's kind of wobbling a little. Oh, she's shrinking back down now."

In a flash he was on his knees next to her, searching the sky. "Sorry," she said. "She's gone."

He shot her a quick glare and sat back down. "I hate you."

"Hate you t– "

"I mean it." He turned toward her with fire in his eyes. "Why did you pull me out of that fight?"

"I was trying to protect you!"

"I can take care of myself. A Kree warrior doesn't need protection."

"You're not a warrior. Yet."

He turned away again.

"That's not what this is about, is it?" She gestured back toward the barracks. "It's about your little *girlfriend*."

"She's a friend. You wouldn't know about that – you've never had one."

The words stung. Her brother always knew how to hurt her. *You've never had a friend.* She thought of the man in the bar, the man in the hood. Was he a friend? He certainly seemed sympathetic, interested in her problems. At least he hadn't made her any false promises.

"You can't trust them," she said. "Any of them. That assassin with the sword is probably still hunting for us. She tried to kill me, before she attacked you. I thought Stark was better than... but he just ran off, as soon as his evil was exposed."

"Is that what they were talking about?" Halla-ar asked. "The Iron Man and… and Ms Marvel? What did you pick up with those stupid enhanced senses of yours?"

"Nothing," she said. "I couldn't hear them. That's not how the training works."

"So you don't know what you're talking about," he grumbled.

A helpless despair washed over her. She loved her brother, this kid on the cusp of becoming a man – and she felt so terribly worried for him. As a young boy, he'd made beautiful pictures. He used to shut himself away in a closet and draw for hours, until she or Grandma came to find him for supper. Artwork wasn't valued much on Praeterus, even before… what happened. Halla-ar had thrown himself into combat training, even receiving acceptance to the Officer Academy. He'd stopped talking about art, as if he wanted to banish the very concept from his mind.

But even then, in the quiet hours of the morning, she would spy on him and find him in the closet with his pad and colored pencils. Until the destruction of Praeterus. Since that day, he hadn't drawn a line.

And now he was so angry…

"Did she look sick?" he asked. "Ms Marvel, I mean."

"She didn't look great."

He leaped to his feet. "I've got to go."

"To find her."

"Yes."

"Why?" Suddenly all the frustration, the helplessness, seemed to bubble up in her. "What is this girl to you? Some sort of teenage crush?"

"She took my side. She stood up for me."

"*I* stand up for you!"

It was too much. She rose to her feet and strode to the end of the pier, circling around a gaping hole in the wood. She stared out over the ocean, watching the fog burn off.

"What are you doing?" he asked.

She turned around. Halla-ar stood by the shack, watching her. For a moment, she could almost see the whole sweep of his life: the sensitive, artistic boy he had been, the proud man he would grow to become, if given the chance. And Halla-ar himself, today, caught on the cusp of an uncertain future.

"I'm getting out of here," she said. "You coming?"

A pained look crossed his face. He shook his head, turned, and bolted toward the mainland.

"I hate you," she said softly. Then, sighing, she turned to face the water again. She raised a hand, shading her eyes from the blazing sun.

"Still can't see it," she murmured.

She reached out with all her senses: heard the rush of tides, felt the crisscross of boats on its surface. Then, closing her eyes, she raised both hands above her head and dove into the water.

# CHAPTER 30

Rocket sat alone, whistling Emerson Lake & Palmer off-key. The laser-wrench in his hand glowed bright, its thin red beam playing against the rust-caked rifle on the table before him. When the gun clicked open, he grinned from ear to furry ear.

"Oh baby," he said, reaching inside. "Aren't you a beauty."

He pulled out a thin sliver of metal and held it up. The sun had come out, shining down into the exposed dining room area of the barracks. The metal gleamed in the light, its surface smooth and flawless.

"Kree Stormranger firing pin," he breathed. "Thousands of years old, and not a scratch on you. How'd a beautiful thing like you wind up in a cheap Kree-Skrull gat like this?"

"Where did you get that?"

Rocket looked up sharply. A short, crewcutted Kree stood across from him, leaning over the picnic table with both arms. Rocket had been introduced to the man – Jer-ra, that was his name. A few more Kree stood behind him, watching.

"I, uh, found it." Rocket pulled the rifle closer. "In an empty room."

"Empty?"

"Well, it was almost empty."

The other Kree drew closer, fanning out to flank Jer-ra. Rocket tensed. He looked at the firing pin in his hand, then at the disassembled weapon in front of him. If a firefight broke out, this thing sure wouldn't be of any help.

Drax approached, pushing through the group. He strode past Jer-ra and clamped a hand on Rocket's shoulder.

"Ow," Rocket said.

"I told Chi-lah you borrowed that," Drax said, pointing at the rifle. "She expects it back when you're done."

Rocket looked at his friend, whose meaty hand still held his shoulder in a painful grip. The Kree looked confident now, even amused.

"Fair enough," Rocket said.

The Kree dispersed, satisfied. All around, in small groups, they were settling down at tables. More people entered the dining area, climbing down the ladders and pouring in from the adjacent rooms. It must be mealtime, Rocket realized.

Drax released his hold on Rocket. "Where is Gamora?" he asked.

"She, uh, wandered off." Rocket rubbed his shoulder. "I wasn't gonna argue with her."

"That is wise." Drax frowned. "But it could be a problem."

"Why? The, uh, planet-killer?"

"No, the killer is not in this facility. As I told Gamora, I have come to know every Kree in these barracks. If the entity you seek is indeed on Earth, it resides elsewhere."

"Then what's the problem? With her goin' off by herself, I mean?"

Drax looked at him, astonished. "She may miss my world-famous samosas."

Before Rocket could concoct a reply – and there were several juicy possibilities to choose from – a burning smell filled the air. Drax stiffened in alarm, turned, and ran to the kitchen.

Rocket picked up the firing pin again, smiling. "Alone at last," he said, "you saucy little–"

He looked up at a scrabbling noise, high up on the outside wall. Several of the Kree rose to their feet, coming to alert. A half dozen of them converged from different tables, scrambling toward the wall. Only a few carried weapons, but a lot of them, he remembered, had served as soldiers.

Captain America leaped over the wall, bounding in through the open roof. He bent his legs and landed in a perfect crouch. The Black Widow followed, executing a showy flip in the air before lighting gracefully on top of an empty table. The Kree watched them in silence.

Rocket couldn't help it. He burst out laughing.

Cap and the Widow turned in his direction. "What?" she asked.

"Sorry," Rocket said. "It's just… you're both so flarking WET!"

Cap stared at him with hard eyes. Next moment, the two Avengers were marching toward him, their sodden boots squishing against the bare concrete. The Kree stepped aside, clearing a path.

"Ulp," Rocket said. He picked up the Kree rifle, which cracked in half at his touch and clattered in pieces to the floor.

Captain America leaned down to glare straight at the raccoonoid. "See how dry *you* are after swimming the Long Island Sound to rescue a teammate."

"I, uh…" Rocket swallowed. "I hear it's a remarkably clean waterway."

"Very low toxicity," a Kree woman added.

Before Rocket realized what was happening, the two Avengers were seated on either side of him, staring him down from both directions. The shoulders of their uniforms were damp against his fur. Even Captain America's wounded arm was hard as a rock.

"Let's talk," the Widow said. "What is going on here?"

"These conditions are appalling," Cap said. "That infirmary alone is a breeding ground for–"

"I know! I know, I've seen it!" Rocket threw up his arms. "Look, I just got here myself. I don't know nothing about this place except its people have exquisite taste in antique weaponry. You should talk to my buddy – or better yet, talk to *your* buddy. You know, the guy whose name is on the building next door?"

Cap frowned, looking up as a Kree deposited a tray of smoking meat on the table. It smelled good. Rocket hoped it wasn't that big rat they'd seen in the kitchen earlier.

"Hey hey," a familiar, very human voice cried. "It's chow time!"

"Quill!" Rocket said, rising to his feet. "For once, I'm actually glad to see you."

Peter Quill seated himself at the table, his eyes on the meat tray. Behind him, Groot and Jennifer Walters approached, talking casually.

"I know exactly what you're saying," Jen said. "It's so easy to get caught in a mid-career rut."

"I am Groot," Groot said.

"Oh yeah, it really sneaks up on you. One day you're sitting there at your desk, eyes propped open by caffeine, practically on autopilot. And the next day it's all you can do to get out of bed."

"I am–"

"Right, of course," Jen acknowledged. "That's assuming you sleep in a bed. And drink caffeine. And…"

Rocket shook his head, thinking: these two are best friends now?! Then he realized: she probably doesn't understand a word he's saying.

"Groot," Rocket said. "Bring it in, big guy."

He immediately regretted the hug. Groot's branches and leaves were as wet as the Avengers, and up close that salt water really didn't smell very good. "OK," Rocket said, disengaging himself. "OK, that's enough bringin' it in."

Jennifer Walters edged away, frowning at the living quarters visible behind bare wire. She was as wet as the rest of them, dark hair matted against her emerald skin. She whipped out her phone, shook water off it, and began stalking through the room, dictating notes in a low voice. Huh. Must have been waterproof and Groot-proof.

A sizzling noise made Rocket jump. He looked around to see the Black Widow on her feet, arm outstretched toward Quill. The stinger on her wrist crackled with electricity.

"I haven't forgot that you crashed into my quinjet," she snarled.

Quill jumped to his feet, still holding the food tray, bits of meat flaking from his too-full mouth. "I divvn't do it! I wavvn't even vere!"

Natasha didn't back down. She circled the table, keeping that electric stinger aimed at Quill. Captain America stood up, raising his shield. Oh great, Rocket thought. More of this flarking crap?

Thankfully Drax appeared, carrying a gigantic steam tray in one hand full of new food. "Good news, everyone," he announced. "I have made tacos, too!"

Everyone froze. One of the Kree rose to his feet and said, "Vegetarian?"

Drax rolled his eyes. "*Yes,* Kah-no."

"Shut up, Kah-no," someone said. A murmur of agreement ran through the room.

Quill's tray slipped from his hand, shattering on the floor. Groot stood next to him, eyes wide and staring. It took Quill a moment to find his voice.

"Drax?" he gasped.

# CHAPTER 31

Several explanations later, lunch began in earnest. Quill kept his face buried in the food. He barely spoke a word. Cap ate sparely, asking pointed questions of the Guardians.

And Groot just stared at his food. Trees ain't much for tacos, Rocket realized.

"So the person who…" Cap hesitated "…who destroyed this planet…"

"I am Groot."

"He's right," Rocket said. "We ain't sure it's a person."

A burst of laughter from the next table. Natasha, the Black Widow, had migrated there to talk to the locals. She seemed to be making friends fast. One of the Kree handed her a towel, then watched with interest as she dried the seawater from her long red hair.

Jennifer Walters paced back and forth, speaking loudly into her phone.

"OK," Cap said, "so this person, creature, entity… whatever it was that caused the destruction of the Kree's homeworld… you're convinced it's here on Earth."

"That's what everybody says." Rocket reached into his bag.

"I thought we were on the right track when my Kree detector, here, started goin' nuts over this place. But so far, we ain't found squat."

"No," Captain America agreed. "But you did manage to terrorize a population of innocent people. Women and men who, from the looks of it, are already barely surviving."

Rocket looked away, watching the Kree mill about, eating the simple food the kitchen had produced. Cap was an idiot – the guy wore a flarking flag on his chest! But his words stung.

"Those poor bastards," Rocket whispered. "It sucks not to be wanted."

"What?" Cap asked.

"Nothing." He swept a hand across his face, wiping away tears.

Drax arrived with another plate of steaming food. "Drax!" Quill said. "Buddy! Sit down, eat with us! God, it's good to see you."

Drax paused, frowned at the food in his hand, and then seated himself at the table. The tray, which was at least three feet around, became his personal plate. He dug in hungrily.

"So," Quill said, leaning into him, "there was another spaceship! I did not see that coming."

"Right?" Drax said.

"I, uh, I really hate to even ask this," Rocket said. "But how's *our* ship?"

"Oh man." Quill gave a boyish grin. "It's gonna need a *lot* of work."

"I am Groot."

"Right. We aren't goin' back to space for a *while*."

"I am Groot."

"Yeah! That's even assuming we manage to drag it out of the bottom of the river."

Still smiling, Quill turned to Drax. Rocket followed his lead, and then Groot. Even Captain America gave "Horse" a curious look.

Drax paused in mid-bite. "I assume you want me to salvage the ship."

Quill shrugged. "Well– "

"Do you have a giant pair of chains?"

"Hell yeah!"

"Very well." Drax turned back to his plate. "Just let me finish this pierogi."

Rocket blinked. "How many kinds of food you got there, anyway?"

Drax looked up, startled, as a green hand snatched a pair of tacos off his plate. Jennifer Walters breezed by, clicked her phone off, and swallowed a taco in one bite.

"Just talked to the Division of Housing and Community Renewal," she said, planting herself down next to Groot. "They'll have a squadron of inspectors out here, first thing Monday. But this stuff takes time."

A rat scurried by, running toward the kitchen.

"Your boy Stark could fix things fast," Rocket said.

"I've been trying to reach him," Cap replied. "No response."

"So he ran away," Quill said, "like the rich kid he is. You know, a real man takes responsibility. A real man cleans up his messes."

"Says the guy with taco sauce all over his fancy spacesuit," Rocket muttered.

"Well, I'm off," Jen said. "Got to make sure my paperwork's in order for Monday. This lawsuit just heated up big time." She paused, turned to Cap. "You sure the kid's OK?"

"Ms Marvel? I left her outside, resting up – she said she was fine. You don't need a ride?"

"I drove here, Steve." She smiled. "You know, in a car?"

More laughter from Natasha's table. They looked over to see her speaking in a low voice, mimicking a stone-faced man. The Kree men at the table doubled over with laughter, clutching their stomachs.

"I think she's teaching them to swear in Russian," Cap said.

Jennifer raised an eyebrow at Natasha. "Good luck with that one," she said to Cap, then turned on her heel and left.

Everyone was quiet for a while. Rocket picked at his food. It wasn't very tasty, but he'd never been particularly choosy in that area.

"May I have your attention?" Drax said.

His voice was grave; they all turned to look. "I have learned much from the people here," he continued. "They were dealt a terrible hand by the universe. Before they came to Earth, they were nothing: useful servants of the Kree Empire, worked to death and discarded by those they served. Now, astoundingly, they have even less."

Rocket found himself nodding.

"They have become my friends," Drax continued. "And I have found that they hesitate to speak of the destruction of their world. As if such a monumental trauma, such unimaginable carnage, is too much for them to bear."

"On Earth," Captain America said, "we call that PTSD."

"But after speaking with my erstwhile teammates, I ventured to broach the subject with a few of my kitchen coworkers. They were appalled by your attack on this facility..."

"Sorry about that," Quill muttered.

"...but they agree with the reason you have come. They, too, believe there is a person or force among them that caused the destruction of World Whose Name I Cannot Pronounce."

"Praeterus," Rocket said.

"That does not sound right."

"It's definitely Praeterus."

"Regardless," Drax continued, "this unnamed world–"

"Again. Praeterus."

"I remain convinced that its destroyer does not reside at this facility. However, we must continue our search for him, or her, or them. Maybe for it. How many pronouns does Earth have?"

"A lot," Quill said.

"If there's a killer," the Black Widow said, "we'll find them." Rocket looked up, startled; he hadn't heard her approach.

"I think you and I better find the elusive Anthony Stark first." Cap rose, nodded at his fellow Avenger, and then turned to Drax. "Thank you for the meal."

As Cap and the Widow started off, Quill said, "Well. If we're gonna be stuck here for a while, I suppose we could help look for the– "

"I was not finished," Drax said.

Rocket, Quill, and Groot all looked sharply at him. Drax's voice had been grim before; now it cut through the air like steel.

"I have become certain of something, these past months," he continued. "The entity behind this killer, this destroyer of worlds – I believe I have deduced its identity."

"What?" Quill stared at him. "Who is it?"

"And why didn't you *lead* with that?" Rocket added.

Drax gestured for them to huddle in. He lowered his voice, speaking in a stage whisper. "It is too dangerous," he said. "Only through my quick wits, with the help of my new friends, have I managed to escape his machinations. The web that tightens around us, this skein of evil spreading out to blanket the cosmos, can only be the work of…"

Oh no, Rocket thought. Oh, no, no, no.

"...of *Thanos.*"

Quill blinked. Once, twice. Then he just shook his head. "Dude. Oh, dude."

"I am Groot. I *am* Groot."

"Seriously," Rocket added. "Seek help, buddy."

Drax looked from one of them to the other. "My friends," he whispered. "One day you will see. One day you will know."

Then he shrugged, picked up another pierogi, and resumed his lunch.

# CHAPTER 32

Kamala saw raccoons. Raccoons with guns. Six of them – no, eight – hovering in front of the sun, pointing their fat-barreled cannons straight at her.

"You know," the raccoons said, their voices converging and overlapping. "You know you know nobody loves loves intimidating children more than."

"Shut up," she said, shaking her head. She knew it was a dream, or maybe a hallucination. Stupid concussion....

"Are you sure," the raccoons sang. "Are you sure you sure this kid is kid is kid kid is is."

"Ms Marvel? Earth girl?"

She blinked. The raccoons were fading, replaced by a single blue face. Great, she thought, I'm really dreaming now. There is no such thing as blue people–

Oh. Wait. "Halla-ar," she said.

She looked around, remembering where she was: the loading dock, built into the outside wall of the factory. She and Halla-ar sat alone under the bright sunlight. The Kree had all fled, gone back to the barracks.

He smiled down at her. "Don't try to move too much. We should get you to a doctor."

"No." She struggled to focus on him. "My healing factor… it'll take care of this. Just need some time."

Kamala raised herself up on her elbows. Stars swam before her eyes; she immediately slumped back down again. "Maybe a lot of time," she said. "What are you doing here, Halla-ar? Why did you come back?"

"I was worried about you." He paused. "I owe you."

With his help, she managed to prop herself up against the stone wall of the factory.

"My sister believes no one on this world cares about us," he said. "She is wrong."

"Well, you know. As an Avenger, I'm obligated to… owww. Oh, my head."

"I really think you should see a doctor." He glanced at the barracks, frowning. "Though the infirmary here is not very sanitary. Perhaps there is a facility for Earth people elsewhere in this compound."

"Halla-ar, listen. Just listen to me." She took his hands and smiled. "It's super sweet that you're worried, but I really will be fine. I've been hurt worse than this. All I need is… well, no more fighting while I heal up. I need to be normal for a while and eat something."

"Normal?" He smiled. "In that mask?"

She smiled back.

He studied her for a moment, then seemed to come to a decision. "Come meet my family," he said. "Be normal with me. We'll grab you something to eat on the way."

"I'm… I'd like that," she replied. "But I'm supposed to meet up with the Guardians. Tony… he told me to…"

She trailed off, thinking. Tony had indeed urged her – maybe even ordered her, as an Avenger – to work with the Guardians. But the green woman, Gamora…she really seemed to think Halla-ar was the planet-killer. What if she came after him again, while Kamala was off… Avenging?

In the end, it came down to a simple choice. What was she, first and foremost? A friend or an Avenger?

"Tony Stark," Halla-ar said. "He wants to find the killer. The one who destroyed my world."

"Yeah."

"Perhaps I can help with that. My people… a few of them live in our housing project now. We could talk to them, you and me. See what we can find out."

She winced. "I don't think I'm up for any more fighting."

"Just…" He smiled. "Detective work, do you call it?"

She nodded. A friend or an Avenger? Maybe she could be both.

With considerable effort, she dragged herself to the edge of the loading dock, dangled her feet over, and tested her legs. "I think I can walk," she said.

He helped her down. When she stumbled in the grass, he wrapped an arm around her waist. That felt nice.

"No fighting," he said, leading her off. "I promise."

She shook her head, then leaned into his shoulder. "Don't make promises you can't keep," she said.

Gamora stood in the daycare room, staring at the mess on the floor. A pair of plastic dollhouses; a toy steamshovel with a missing wheel. Crayons, markers, whiteboards, construction paper. All of it crumpled, dirty, used and reused and taped together to be used again.

The children had all gone now, back to their dirty rooms. To take naps, if they could. If someone else wasn't using the room to talk on the phone, or to trade goods for food, or have a screaming match.

The caretaker sat in her chair, in the corner, dozing off. Phone clutched in her wrinkled hand.

Gamora had walked the entire complex, peered into every possible room. Every time she heard a high-pitched voice, she ran to look, hoping it was the little girl from Praeterus. The girl whose planet she'd promised to save; the girl she'd let down. She searched the dining area, knocked on doors, even ventured again into the laundry room. But each time, her hopes were dashed.

Other Kree haunted her too: the workers in the munitions plant. The wheelchair-bound woman, the blue man with prosthetic limbs. The young woman wired up to her station, almost a part of the machine she served.

One by one those faces came to mind, and one by one they faded. Replaced by the young Kree boy, Halla-ar – the kid she'd fought outside this building. The boy she'd almost killed by mistake, in her misplaced rage and guilt.

It didn't matter, she told herself. One way or another, either way, the killer was still at large. Still out there, still scheming. Maybe even plotting the death of another world.

That was Gamora's purpose. That was what she had to stop.

Rocket and the others wanted that too, she knew. But finding Drax alive had taken the edge off their quest. They were too concerned with repairing the ship, with taking things one step at a time. Even Peter, who she knew would crawl through an exploding nova for her, didn't really understand the urgency she felt.

A wind-up robot paced against the daycare room wall, walking in place, bashing its painted face into the corrugated metal over and over again. She crossed over to it, picked it up, and turned it around. When she left the room, it was bumping its way around like a rubber ball, moving slowly but steadily across the room.

Outside, the sky was clear and bright. The Avengers' quinjet soared overhead, shedding a few last drops of water into the air. Its underside was dented, hastily patched with sealant and metal plates.

Shielding her eyes against the sun, Gamora waved to the quinjet. The jet circled, as if hesitating, then wafted down. It bumped once and settled onto the grass between the factory and the bus station.

A hatch opened and Natasha Romanoff stuck her head out. Gamora ran over, keeping her distance, holding up her hands in a gesture of peace. The quinjet's engines sounded rough; the craft had sustained some damage.

"You're hunting the planet-killer?" Gamora asked.

"Maybe," Romanoff replied.

"I want in."

Romanoff frowned, then ducked back into the jet. Through the transparent cockpit bubble, Gamora could see her conferring with Captain America. Then Romanoff's hand reappeared in the hatchway, beckoning.

Gamora ran to the quinjet and climbed inside.

# PART FIVE

## SKULL CANDLES, WAR STORIES, WHISKY-73

# CHAPTER 33

"Talk to me, F.R.I.D.A.Y. Where am I headed?"

"Stark Tower, Manhattan. Fifth Avenue between–"

"Uh, thanks, I know it. I know the address."

Tony soared in over Manhattan, his thoughts swirling. He barely noticed the green expanse of Central Park spread out below.

"Run down the trail for me again," he continued. "Pepper assigned the Kree project to Harrison..."

"Yes, boss. Who died shortly thereafter in–"

"In a plane crash, over the Andes. I remember. That was suspicious as hell. What next?"

"Oversight of the project passed to a Ms Li-Cooper, who, as best I can tell, does not actually exist. She, or whatever entity created her, delegated responsibility to a mid-level executive with... well, with an odd title. To say the least."

"F.R.I.D.A.Y., you know I hate it when you pause dramatically."

"The gentleman's title is Director of Diabolism and Parapsychology. His name is Jericho."

"First or last name?"

"Nothing else. Just Mister Jericho."

"Well, *that's* not suspicious or anything."

The park passed by underneath, giving way to the dense sprawl of Midtown Manhattan. Stark Tower gleamed dead ahead, its spire jutting up above the older surrounding skyscrapers.

"What about this so-called planet-killer? Any progress on that?"

"All dead ends so far. However, I am pleased to report that S.H.I.E.L.D. has recaptured the Melter."

"Where'd they find him? Sabotaging an off-season ski slope? Never mind, I'm not actually interested."

He touched down on the outer deck, just outside his penthouse office. The armor, following an automatic protocol, began to unlock and disengage from his body. He overrode the process with a quick mental command.

"Let's keep the suit on," he muttered. "Something tells me this might not be a simple human resources issue."

The glass door irised open at his approach. *That's more like it,* he thought. Compared to this place, the Long Island complex really was stuck in the past. He strode inside and through the office, passing an array of papers, displays, and softly spinning holo-schematics. So many projects, he thought. So many balls to juggle.

He came to a private elevator and keyed it open with one armored finger. "Floor?" he asked.

"Sixty-six," F.R.I.D.A.Y. said.

"Pretty high. Diabolism must be booming."

"Sir, I'm not actually certain that–"

"Silent mode, F.R.I.D.A.Y. I'll take it from here."

Floor 66 seemed deserted. He clanked across the carpet to the office marked MR JERICHO, feeling vaguely foolish in the Iron Man armor. He opened his helmet and knocked twice, sharply.

No answer. "Hello?" he called and pushed the door open.

For a moment, he stood speechless. Well, he thought, I don't know what I expected to find. But this wasn't it.

A tall, muscular Black man sat at a wooden executive desk. He wore a jet-black costume with white sigils smeared across it, and a deep violet cape fastened at the neck with a gold clasp. His eyes glowed red; a short chain of shrunken skulls hung from the sash at his waist. One hand rested on a rough-carved staff, leaning up against the desk.

Tony knew this man; he'd fought alongside him. "Jericho," he said. "Jericho Drumm. Brother Voodoo?"

The man didn't look up. "It's Doctor," he said, a faint echo haunting his voice.

"Right, sorry. Doctor Voodoo." Tony stepped inside. "Do you, uh, *work* for me?"

A faint smile. "Doesn't everyone?"

Tony frowned, stepped inside. Something was wrong here. Voodoo's tone was hostile, almost angry. And what was he *doing* here?

A radiation-style shield sat on Voodoo's desk, hiding something from view. Tony edged around until he could see behind the shield where a large human skull glowed softly, the top cut open to reveal a dark red candle. At the base of the skull, several dozen microchips had been wired together in an unfamiliar configuration.

"What you got there, Doc?" he asked. "Model for some new kind of tourist souvenir? It's a little off-brand for Stark Enterprises."

Voodoo still didn't turn to look. He touched a screwdriver to the microchip assembly, raising a brief spark. "It is for the Kree," he said. Another brief echo: *For the Kree.*

"OK, yeah," Tony said. "That's actually why I'm here. What do you know about the Kree situation, anyway?"

"I know they are lucky to have found employment with us."

"The conditions they're living in are... well, shameful at the least. Dangerous and illegal, at the most."

With thick, steady hands, Voodoo lit the candle. A thin, odorless trail of smoke twisted up from it; the microchip assembly began to hum. He watched the tiny flame for a moment, then turned, at last, away from the device. His eyes blazed bright, with a fire that made Tony shiver.

"Would you prefer them to live on the street?" Voodoo asked.

"I would *prefer* we treat them like human beings."

"The accommodations are temporary." (Echo: *Temporary.*) "If the Kree work hard and make something of themselves, they will improve their lot."

Tony shook his head, trying to clear it. He felt caught up in something, some force beyond his comprehension. This was... all wrong...

"Have you not always encouraged frugal business practices?" Voodoo continued. "Among your employees? Those who toil in your vineyards?"

"Not... always..."

He staggered, clutching for the desk. The smoke, he realized – the smoke from the candle. It's affecting me, making it hard to think! He snapped his helmet shut, knowing it was too late; the smoke had already gotten into his system. He stumbled back a step, raised his hand to fire a repulsor ray–

–but Voodoo was faster. He rose to his feet and lifted the staff, chanting something under his breath. Fire shot forth, an eerie blue flame that struck Tony in the chest, spreading out to cover his armor.

"F.R.I.D.A.Y.?"

"Heat shields holding," the female voice said.

Tony activated fire suppressors, sending out jets of foam to quell the supernatural flame. He raised both arms, willing his repulsors to point five power – enough to knock a human enemy into the wall, but not strong enough to burn through flesh.

"Jericho?" he asked. "What's going on? What's wrong with you?"

Voodoo lunged toward him. Tony aimed and fired, just as Voodoo swung his staff in the air. In its wake, a trail of thick black smoke swept across the room.

Tony swore as his repulsor shots went wild. He couldn't see the results, but the sound of breaking glass suggested one of them had hit a lamp. "Switch to radar targeting," he told F.R.I.D.A.Y.

He stumbled around the room, momentarily blind, as a green-outlined grid faded up on his HUD display. Window, desk, and yes – shattered floor lamp. But where was Voodoo?

"Here," Voodoo said, his thick hand clamping around Tony's metal-sheathed throat.

Tony paused, mesmerized, staring into Voodoo's eerily glowing eyes. His armor was at full charge now, his weapons ready to fire. Yet somehow he couldn't move.

"You did this," Voodoo said. (Echo: *Did this*). "Your company, your empire... it rules the poor serfs of this island Earth." Voodoo slammed him into the wall. "Whatever becomes of the Kree – of all of them – let it be on your head."

This time, the echo was different. Tony distinctly heard: *Help me.*

Suddenly he remembered the curse of Jericho Drumm: the soul of Drumm's dead brother, doomed to coexist alongside him in the body of Doctor Voodoo. Was this the brother speaking? Had he somehow gained control of their shared body? What was the brother's name…?

"D- Daniel?" Tony croaked.

Voodoo smiled. "Half right," he said, and squeezed harder.

Tony stared into those eyes, watching as eldritch flames filled Voodoo's pupils. There's something else here, he realized. Another entity – something dark and otherworldly. Something that hungers…

"How?" He gasped. "How many people you got in there, Doc?"

The flames rose higher, and all at once the room was filled with rage. An anger that burned through the veils, that could snuff out whole stars. It sent tendrils into his mind, seeking and probing for weak spots. He recognized it as an invasion, an attack from some vast, unseen enemy. Yet he was powerless to resist.

*Another time*, he realized, *I could have fought this*. But he was too worn down. By work, by exhaustion, and most of all by guilt. Guilt for what he'd allowed to happen, the offenses against the Kree. Guilt for all that had been done, and was yet to be done, in his name.

The fire burned him to ash, and he was lost.

Daniel/Doctor Voodoo held the armored man up against the wall for a long time. His free hand roamed across the man's face, sealing the incantation with a low, whispered chant.

The hooded man stepped out of the shadows, watching with satisfaction. The room was almost silent now; Stark's armor had fallen into inactivity. The only sound came from the skull-device on the desk, humming softly.

He gestured at Stark. "Is he ours?"

Voodoo released the Avenger. Tony Stark tottered for a moment, staring straight ahead.

"Yes," Voodoo said.

"Good."

The hooded man gazed at the slowly smoking skull-device. It had been built at this very facility, using Stark's own money and resources. Just like this cold office, the expensive furniture, the glass windows. Stark, he thought, this is all your fault. You deserve every ounce of pain that's coming.

For a moment, he shivered. Relishing the Master's power, anticipating the chaos that would drown this world in blood. When it's all done, he thought, there will be no rich men. All the Starks – the arrogant, privileged ones who had kicked him around, all his life – would die screaming.

He pulled the hood up over his head, then reached over and snuffed out the candle. The device's hum continued, slightly louder than before. Good, he thought. Building up its charge.

"Box this thing up for me, huh, Danny?" he said. "And make it quick."

"Do not speak to me like that." Voodoo turned to him with a slow, dangerous gaze. "I am not your doll."

The man rolled his eyes. "Please?"

Voodoo glared, then turned to pack up the device on his desk. "You're not coming with us?"

"I'll meet you at the rendezvous. But first…" The hooded man grinned. "I've got a date to keep."

# CHAPTER 34

"So, there we were," the old man said, "two hundred soldiers, all in standard green-and-whites – no skinsuits, no enviro-belts. The heavy cruisers dropped us down on this abandoned Skrull orbital platform and then they just bolted, back into hyperspace before you could say Gods Bless Hala. This was in the early days, mind you, before war was officially declared."

Kamala glanced over at Halla-ar, who sat with her on a lumpy sofa. Across the living room, his grandfather paused to lean back in his armchair, staring into empty air. Grandpa – he'd insisted Kamala call him that – was tall and thick, dressed in a formal beige-and-green uniform that seemed out of place in the shabby, cramped apartment.

"So then we're all alone," Grandpa continued, "and we're all looking at each other, right? We knew the Skrulls could change their shape, could look like anything or anybody. So we're all, every one of us, we're thinking: is this really my buddy? Is this my LT? Or is it a Skrull in disguise?"

Halla-ar flashed Kamala an apologetic smile. She smiled back, feeling a little awkward, but she knew that understanding people was part of what made Avengers business worthwhile. She wanted Halla-ar and his family to know that she'd do everything she could to help them.

"We're all tense, amped up, proton rifles cocked and ready. And then... while we're all thinking the attack is about to come from inside the platform..."

"...the Skrulls attack from *outside*," Halla-ar's grandmother said, entering the room with a tray of drinks.

"I guess you've heard this story before," Kamala said, smiling tentatively.

The old woman, whose name was Ann-ya, handed her a glass of steaming liquid. Ann-ya was very small, with high cheekbones. She wore a pale, functional bodysuit.

"They crash right in through the plasteel window port," Grandpa continued, "and all the air goes WHOOSH, straight out into the void, all at once. I see my buddies, the officers and enlisted men, all shooting past me. Even our resident Accuser goes flying out into space. That's just for a second, mind you, before the cold hits me. Your eyes freeze up first, and then you can't stop watching. They don't warn you about that."

Kamala felt a twinge of discomfort. *Come meet my family,* Halla-ar had said; *be normal with me.* Was this normal? Old people in her family didn't tell strangers about their painful near-death experiences.

"How did you survive?" she asked hesitantly.

"What?" Grandpa shook his head, seeming to notice her for the first time. "Oh! Well, you see, that comes down to the dirty Skrulls again. They fished me out of space with a microtrac, and then they..."

"...they took him prisoner," Ann-ya said, settling herself on a small folding chair. "That's a whole other excruciating story."

"It was more excruciating to live through," the old man grumbled.

"I'm not sure about that," she grumbled back.

Halla-ar looked like he was about to die of humiliation. That made Kamala smile. Old people always embarrass their relatives, she thought. And even though Grandpa's stories were unrelentingly grim, it was still sort of cute the way the old folks finished each other's sentences.

She took a sip of the drink. It felt warm, fizzy bubbles burning their way pleasantly down her throat. The apartment, located on the sixth floor of an old Jersey City housing complex, was small and rundown, with only a single window located behind the old man's armchair. But at least it was quiet. After all their trials, the traumas of war and the literal end of their world, this family seemed to have built themselves a safe little nest.

"Dear." Ann-ya smiled at Kamala. "My grandson says you have powers."

"Uh, yeah," Kamala replied.

"She's called Ms Marvel," Halla-ar said, with a note of pride in his voice.

"Show me." Grandpa's eyes narrowed. "Show me some powers."

"I can't right now. I can't use my powers while I'm healing, or I might hurt myself worse."

"Ha! Earth people." Grandpa turned away, shaking his head. "Always full of excuses."

"Where is your sister, dear?" Ann-ya asked Halla-ar. "She didn't come home tonight."

"I don't know," Halla-ar replied. "Last I saw her was back at the plant."

"The Stark plant?" Grandpa leaned forward, frowning. "When were you there?"

"I told you, Grandpa. Ms Marvel took me there to talk to Mister Stark."

Ann-ya raised an eyebrow. "How did *that* go?"

"Not well," Kamala admitted.

"She moved us out of that place," Grandpa said to Kamala. "Kir-ra, our granddaughter. This apartment, it isn't much. But at least the rats are smaller."

"It is *much* better," Ann-ya said, chiding him. "The children have their own rooms."

"I saw the conditions at the barracks," Kamala said. "I spoke to Mister Stark about it. He says he's looking into it."

"I told you," Halla-ar said, with a fury that surprised her. "He doesn't care."

"They never do," Grandpa agreed. "Earth people... they're as bad as the Kree ruling caste. They don't give a *vata's* tooth about us on Hala, either. We're just trash to them."

"Oh, shut up," Ann-ya said to him. "You're always complaining. So full of hate. I wish you'd stop talking for once."

All three Kree looked away then. Kamala sipped her drink, feeling like an intruder. The wounds this family had suffered clearly ran deep.

"How is she?" Grandpa asked. "Your sister?"

"We hardly see her anymore," Ann-ya said.

"She seemed..." Halla-ar paused. "I don't know."

"Intense?" Ann-ya suggested. "Driven? Obsessed? Over-serious?"

"Hopeless," Halla-ar replied. "Without hope. I'm worried about her."

Another awkward moment. Grandpa sat back, staring idly at a switched-off wall TV. He seemed to have turned himself off too, as if the memories had transported him back to some other, disturbing time and place.

"Whole universe is doomed, you know," he said. "The threat...
you think you're prepped, think you're ready for it. But there's
always something bigger coming. Something hiding in the dark,
something you can barely see."

Ann-ya covered her ears, scrunched up her eyes. "I said shut
up!"

Kamala tensed. Something in the old woman's voice reminded
her of Halla-ar's outburst in the gym, back at school, when he'd
attacked Russell. If there was anger inside Halla-ar – and she
knew there was – then this was where it came from.

All at once the Kree apartment seemed stuffy, oppressive.
The worn sofa, the tiny kitchen... it felt like a dead end, a place
devoid of any possible future. A place to die.

She shot Halla-ar a look, and he nodded quickly in response.
"Uh, Grandma? I think we're going out."

"I've got something to do," Kamala added.

Ann-ya looked up slowly. "For Mister Stark?"

"For the Avengers," Halla-ar said, standing up. "Ms Marvel is
a hero."

The old woman turned those sharp eyes on him, a strange smile
playing at her lips. Grandpa stared blankly ahead. His lips moved
rapidly, silently, as if some old drama was playing itself in his head.

Halla-ar ushered her out through the kitchen, followed by
Ann-ya's steely eyes. Then they were in the building's narrow
hallway, surrounded by thick apartment doors and peeling
plaster walls.

"There are other Kree living here?" she asked.

He nodded. "A half dozen or so. In this building, and the
adjoining ones."

Kamala hesitated, looking back at the number on Halla-ar's
door: 6-66. "Not a great omen," she muttered.

He gave her a blank look.

"Your grandparents... they've been through a lot." She touched his hand, then pulled it away, remembering his aversion to contact. "It can't be easy living here."

He shrugged. "They're my family."

She nodded, feeling out of place.

"Come on, hero." He turned away and started down the corridor. "Let's go find a planet-killer."

# CHAPTER 35

Dave Williard was having the best day of his life. Sure, his boss Kramer had given him a string of crappy assignments. And his Stark keycard had been turned off a day early, so he had to keep asking to be buzzed in everywhere. And yeah, when the guys took him out for lunch, he had the weird feeling they were laughing at him.

But none of that mattered, because this was his last day. His last day listening to Kramer; his last day in crowded, expensive New York; his last day dealing with super heroes. Most important, his last day working security at Stark Tower.

And then the stupid perimeter-breach alert went off, on Floor 66. The creepy floor, the deserted one marked Level One/ Restricted. So of course Kramer had told Williard to take the call. It was the last chance for Kramer to make him eat dirt, and nothing was gonna stop Kramer from doing that.

But Williard didn't care. He was whistling as he waltzed off the elevator, taser in hand. He'd already accepted a job down in Miami, starting next week. His wife Tisa was there now, setting up the new place. Sure, he'd be working for her father, and the old man had never liked him all that much. But at least he'd be in Florida, where the beach was warm and the drinks were ice cold…

"…Tony's transponder signal cut off here – at this location. He's off the grid."

"Can you access the security feed?"

Williard froze, clicked his taser on. The voices were coming from a locked door marked MR JERICHO. He whipped out his keycard, swiped it across the door. Nothing happened. Oh yeah. Fortunately, he still had an old master key in his pocket. They'd miss him when he was gone, that's for sure; they'd miss his accumulated wisdom, his knowledge of how things worked. Ever since Ms Potts left, the whole place had gone to hell. The old ways were being forgotten–

The door swung open and a slim, strong arm grabbed him by the jacket, yanking him inside and slamming him up against the wall. He opened his mouth to protest, then went silent as a sharp, jagged sword pressed against his throat. He found himself staring at a woman with bright green skin.

"Wh- Wh- Whaaah?" he said.

"Drop the weapon," she hissed.

Williard gulped, nodded, and let the taser slip from his limp fingers. He touched his badge and managed, "S- Security."

He stared past the green woman into the room. Natasha Romanoff, the Black Widow, sat at a disheveled desk, tapping at a keyboard. Captain America was there too, watching over her shoulder. The office was a mess: papers and broken glass everywhere, with a distinct burning smell in the air.

"Should I kill him?" the green woman asked.

"Let him go," Cap said, not looking up.

"Do I have to?" the green woman asked.

"Does she have to?" Romanoff repeated.

Shrugging, the woman released him. Williard rubbed his neck, eyeing her nervously. The Avengers, he thought. Whatever they were doing, he was pretty sure they weren't supposed to be doing it. Why did these things always happen to him?

"The footage has been erased," Romanoff said. "There's nothing here for this entire floor."

"What about the rest of the building?"

Her fingers flashed over the keyboard. She looked up at the screen and shook her head.

"Can't get into the system?" Cap asked.

She glared at him. "I'm *in*," she said. "I'm into everything. But there's too many cameras, and I don't know the file system. It'll take time to scroll through them all."

"We may not have time. Tony…"

One by one, their eyes turned to Williard. Romanoff lasered in on him first, like a cat with a bird. Cap looked at him next, and then the green woman.

"No," Williard said. "Oh no. No way. Three more hours and I am out of this creepy place forever."

The Widow's stinger-blast seared into the wall an inch from his head.

"Hey. Hey now." Cap walked up and wrapped an arm around Williard's shoulders. The other arm, Williard noticed, was slung in a cast. "This isn't your fault, soldier – but I think everyone in this room has had more than enough of Stark bureaucracy for one day. Besides, I don't think I can keep these two off you." He smiled and held up his cast. "Not with a bum wing."

Williard turned to the two women. They stood together, eyes glaring at hm.

"Wh- Which camera do you want?" he asked.

"Let's try street level," Cap said.

The green woman watched, amused, as Williard seated himself at the desk. She clamped a hand on his shoulder and kept it there. He brushed aside singed, smoke-damaged papers and pulled up the outside feed on the monitor. A grainy downshot of the sidewalk appeared, with the Stark Enterprises awning hanging in the foreground. People scurried by, all different kinds of New Yorkers: women in suits, men in jeans, nannies with strollers. He wouldn't miss them, he thought. He wouldn't miss any of them–

"Fast forward it," Natasha ordered. Then: "There."

He froze the playback. A tall man in a deep violet cape had just exited the building with a human-sized bundle slung over his shoulder.

Cap squinted at the screen. "Is that … Doctor Voodoo?"

"Never mind that," Natasha said. "Look who's behind him."

It took five minutes to enhance the image, swiveling the angle and filling in details virtually. But when it was done, they found themselves looking at a young man in a dark hooded sweatshirt, with a cruel expression on his face.

"The Hood," Cap hissed.

"Who's the Hood?" the green woman asked.

"Parker Robbins," Natasha said. "Small-time crook who lucked into some big-time magic. He's got a whole bag of tricks, including air-walking and invisibility. Almost took over the entire New York gang system at one point."

"He's sharp and brutal. Very nasty." Cap reached across and zoomed the image out. "He's carrying some sort of bag…"

"Yeah." Natasha pointed at the wrapped-up bundle on Doctor Voodoo's shoulders. "And that's gotta be our missing billionaire."

Cap's eyes narrowed. "Why would Doctor Voodoo be working with the Hood?"

"More to the point," the green woman said, "what are they doing with your Mister Stark?"

"I heard something just the other day," Natasha mused. "Shady dude in a hoodie hanging around Russian bars. Let me make a couple calls."

She stood up and walked to the window, pulling out her cell phone. Captain America just stared at the image on the screen. Williard looked up at the green woman, who still held his shoulder in an iron grip.

"Can I, uh, go now, She-Hulk?" he asked.

The woman stared at him in surprise. She turned to Cap, who shrugged. Natasha Romanoff looked up from her phone and raised an eyebrow.

"I were you, Gamora," the Widow said, "I'd kill him for that."

Two minutes later they were gone. Williard staggered over to the desk and sat down, alone. He was shaking.

His phone buzzed; it was Kramer. Bloody Kramer. He shook his head, imagining the debrief to come. The office was a disaster; all the perpetrators had fled, probably with classified data. If he understood what Captain America had been saying, it looked like Tony Stark himself had been abducted.

Slowly Williard stood up, letting the phone ring. He fumbled with his badge, unpinned it from his shirt, and laid it on the desk. Then he walked back out to the elevator, leaving the door open, and pressed the button marked LOBBY.

With luck, he'd be in Miami by nightfall.

# CHAPTER 36

Tonight the vodka was working. Maybe a little too well. Kir-ra couldn't quite remember deciding to come to the dusty little Russian establishment, after swimming back to Manhattan and toweling the East River filth out of her hair. She shook her head, remembering the shock of cold, the icy impact when she'd first hit that water. Her only thought had been to escape, to leave behind that horrible Stark plant forever.

Now she found herself back at the bar, awash in dark thoughts. She didn't remember seeing the hooded man sit down beside her, either. Like every Earthman, he had an arrogant streak to him. But at least he was a good listener.

"...what I'm fighting for," she said, "my world is gone, the war is over. My brother... I thought I could protect him, at least. But he doesn't want my help."

"You have other people who need you," the man said. "Right?"

"Halla-ar... he should have been an artist. But you know what's funny? All I ever wanted to be was a warrior."

"You are a warrior," he said, his eyes glowing slightly. "But you're an arrow, not a bludgeon."

"I don't know what that means."

He reached out a finger toward her face. She flinched away, then shook her head and allowed him to touch her cheek.

"You've got a little scrape there," he said.

"A man with a cast on his arm and a flag on his chest gave it to me." She gave a dry laugh. "After I had my butt handed to me by a pair of outer-space mercenaries."

The bar swam before her. The vodka, no doubt – in her exhausted state, it was hitting her hard. But something else was wrong, too. Was that smoke she smelled?

"They all make promises," she mused. "'I don't want to hurt you.' 'I will make this right.' All lies…" She shook her head angrily and took a long drink. "The Kree have no friends on this world. *I* have no friends. You, you said that. You said that to me."

"I did."

"My parents were heroes." She turned away, tears forming in her eyes. "They had allies, comrades-in-arms… they gave their lives for the Kree Empire. What am I? What do I have? What's left to believe in?"

He stared at her, his eyes hard now. She reached for him, clamping a hand over his.

"When I dove off that pier," she said, "the water closed in all around me. Then the tide took hold, whisking me away… stronger, faster than I expected. I thought about letting go. Just letting the current pull me down, all the way to the bottom, and never coming up again. Welcoming it into my lungs, inside me, letting it wash all through me and… and destroy me."

He stared at her, a strange fire burning in his eyes. He nodded, and she realized: On some level, he understands.

"What…" She shook her head. "What is that smell?"

"Look." The hooded man leaned in close, staring at her with

those bewitching eyes. "Everyone else lies to you, but I won't. You're right; you have no purpose. You have no friends."

She looked down, into her drink.

"I'm just being honest," he continued. "People like you and me, nobody cares about us. That's why we're in a hole like this on a Saturday night, drinking the worst swill on Earth. No offense, Feliks."

Over in the corner, the bartender shrugged.

"No one cares about you," he repeated.

"You don't have to keep saying that."

"I mean, I don't have much to offer. But maybe I can do something... put a Band-Aid on what's wrong with you. It's a big, cold world – nobody makes it alone. You need a friend, right?" He took her hand and pressed it to his cheek. "Let me be that friend."

She cocked her head sideways, feeling the liquor war with her despair. This was wrong, this was not the answer. But she couldn't even remember the question anymore.

"'Be my friend,'" she repeated. "Another promise?"

"I'll make you one promise, and only one." He leaned in close, and she smelled smoke on his breath. *"No promises."*

Time froze for a moment. She knew this was hollow, she knew it was a pickup. Beyond that, she knew nothing about this Earthman; she shouldn't trust him, any more than the others who had lied and cheated and treated her people like trash. He had set out bait, lured her in, and now he was toying with her emotions. Probing, painfully, at her most vulnerable points.

But he was here, now. And he burned.

"Do you have someplace we could go?" she whispered.

"Ah." He grimaced. "That's a little complicated."

"Come on, then."

She stood up and turned toward the door. He pulled up his hood, reached down to pick up a small travel bag, and followed.

"What's in the bag, anyway?"

He didn't answer, just nodded to the bartender. Feliks didn't even look up this time.

"Wait." She stopped, turned, and pressed a hand to his chest. "You, uh, might have to meet my grandparents."

He smiled, a wide, dangerous smile. Once again, she saw the fire in his eyes, those unearthly flames. They seemed to burn through some unseen dimensional veil, seething with power.

"I love old people," he said.

# CHAPTER 37

Kamala sat with Halla-ar on a low stone wall at the edge of the housing complex, facing the street. Night had fallen. A few cars crept by, speeding up slightly when the projects came into view.

"Well," Kamala said, "that was a bust."

Halla-ar looked at her, puzzled.

"I mean we didn't turn up anything," she explained. "Like, that old lady in 2-43? I do not think she's a planet-killer. She couldn't even find her teeth."

He grunted in agreement. "The Kal-tan couple seem no likelier."

"Or that guy with the eighteen cats!"

"Nineteen." He shook his head. "Cats are not native to Praeterus. I do not understand how he managed to adopt so many, so fast."

"Are you the only... I mean, I didn't see any other kids here."

"There are small children, but no one else my age."

"Sounds lonely."

They fell into a contemplative silence. Across the street, an old strip mall sat abandoned; the roof of the grocery store at the far end had partially collapsed. The only light came from a pizza place fronting on a circular outdoor seating area.

"They're gonna tear all that down," Kamala said, "if the pizza place ever closes."

"This piz-za," he said. "Is it good?"

"Not the way they make it! But I still hope they don't close down."

"This place…" He frowned. "This Jersey City. It is…"

"Like a big city, but not?" She smiled. "Yeah, that's JC."

A breeze blew up; Kamala shivered. Halla-ar frowned at her and asked, "How is your head?"

"It's fine, better. I'm just cold."

"We should get back." He hopped down off the wall. "I do not like to leave my grandparents alone for long. Grandpa in particular has some…"

"…issues," she said, taking his hand and jumping down. "We call them issues."

He smiled. "I like it when you finish my sentences."

"Whoa, whoa, alien boy. Let's take this slow."

They walked toward the apartment. The project buildings stretched up around them, dark brick monuments with few windows. Exterior-mounted floodlights cast occasional pools of light down on the walkway.

A few young people lounged on outside benches, laughing or smoking or just watching the passers-by. They eyed Kamala's costume with a mixture of interest and suspicion. Ms Marvel was a known public figure in Jersey City, but this wasn't the kind of place where super heroes hung out.

A family caught her eye: a young couple with two squirming toddlers. Were they human, or Kree? It didn't matter, she thought. People were people.

"They've been trying to tear this place down too," Kamala said.

"What?" Halla-ar asked. "Why?"

"Well, it hasn't been kept up very well. They say this is a high crime area."

"But so many people live here. Where would they go?"

She gave him a sad smile. "Earth folks don't always think that stuff through."

They came to the central courtyard. The three project buildings all faced inward here, fanning out from the center. The pattern reminded Kamala of something, but she wasn't sure what.

"That woman with the birthmark," she said. "She *might* have been a planet-killer."

"Ki-san? She was my sister's friend, growing up. She is utterly harmless. She flunked her warrior trials because she refused to fight back when attacked."

Kamala shrugged. "Guess we struck out, then." He looked at her again. "Uh, that means—"

"I know what it means." He gestured toward the wall, past an overflowing dumpster, where a floodlight cast a patch of light down on the bare ground. "Would you stand over there for a minute?"

She nodded, puzzled, and walked to the wall. Feeling vaguely silly, she clenched her hand into a fist and struck a dramatic pose. Halla-ar smiled, whipped a small notepad out of his pocket, and started scratching on it with a pencil.

"What are you—"

"One minute. Just a minute."

He frowned, pencil flashing: *sktch sktch, sktch sktch*. She remained perfectly still, feeling vaguely silly. When he finished, he stared at the paper, smiled, walked over to her, and held up the notepad. "What do you think?"

She blinked. He'd drawn a quick sketch of her in the pose she'd adopted, with her fist outstretched, an exaggerated scarf flaring back from her throat.

"It's great!" she said. "I look very... I don't know. Heroic?"

"You are always a hero. To me." He gave her a small smile. "You came to my rescue. You defied Mister Stark."

"You don't need much rescuing," she replied, looking away. "You're a heck of a fighter. And you helped me, too..."

A flash of movement caught her eye. Over by the dumpster, just out of the light. Something gliding along in the air, at eye level... a red blanket, or maybe a cloak?

"What is it?" he asked.

She pointed. "Over there."

She checked the area, but there was no one around; this corner of the courtyard was deserted. She took a long stride, extending and embiggening her legs. Halla-ar followed, stashing the notepad away.

Then, again, in front of the wall: a quick flash of crimson. "There!" she said. "Did you see it?"

"I'm not sure."

She stretched her body upward, searching the area along the wall. Nothing. At least her head didn't hurt anymore; that meant it was safe to use her powers.

"What is this?" Halla-ar called.

She shrank back down to look. He crouched behind the dumpster, holding a softly glowing object in both hands. It looked like a giant eye set inside a frame of metal.

"It was just lying here," he said.

"Bring it into the light."

They walked back to the floodlight. The eye seemed to follow them, turning to meet their gaze. In the light, Kamala could see it was made of some sort of liquid held within a transparent bubble. A delicate, tarnished web of gold held the whole thing in place.

"What is it?" he asked. "Is this some instrument that Earth people use?"

"Not any Earth people I know."

She frowned, glancing back at the dumpster. She remembered that strange red cloak, floating through the darkness...

"Someone was here," she said. "Someone left this for us."

"But why?" He frowned. "Is it some sort of trap? Something left by one of the Avengers' enemies?"

"I don't know. I don't think the Avengers have ever faced off against an evil ophthalmologist." She studied the object. "Maybe it's the opposite. Maybe somebody's trying to help us. In our hunt?"

At the word *hunt*, the eye seemed to brighten. A deep buzz pulsed from it, and then it went silent again.

"Yes." Halla-ar nodded. "To help track the killer."

The eye buzzed again, more insistently this time. The metal around it vibrated, tugging Halla-ar's hands to the left.

"It's pulling me," he said. "Leading me toward something... Hey, what if it *is* a trap? What if it turns me evil?"

"If you turn evil, I promise I'll take you down." She frowned. "Seriously, just go with it. I'm right here."

She concentrated, thinking of the killer. Of all the poor Kree exiled to Earth, forced to live in poverty and work themselves to death just to survive. And those were the lucky ones. So many had already died...

The eye hummed, louder than ever. Halla-ar held it tight, letting it pull his arms one way, then the other. It pointed up toward one of the three buildings, then swung back around toward another one.

"That's your building," Kamala said.

Halla-ar nodded, eyes wide as his arms rose up. The eye swiveled in his grip, staring up at an angle toward a single window. A window that opened onto the back of an armchair, with an old man's head visible inside.

"And that," Halla-ar said, "is my family's apartment."

# CHAPTER 38

Captain America descended the short staircase off the street and froze. Before him, where a subway entrance had once been, a wall of concrete blocked the way. Next to it was a slim, unassuming door.

"Captain?" Gamora called.

He motioned her back. His mind raced, replaying the events, just days ago, of his battle in Pittsburgh. Climbing the fire escape outside the refinery, coming to a window reinforced with concrete. Thin wooden panel next to it...

That's where he'd been ambushed, by the Red Skull's nano-powered goons. Where the Skull had come close to wiping out his arch-enemy, for good this time. Where Cap had sustained the wound to his arm that, even now, ached when he moved too fast.

"Steve?" Natasha recognized his alarm immediately. "What is it?"

"Nothing," he said, forcing himself to smile. "Guess I've got some battle jitters left over from Pittsburgh."

He stared at the wooden door, pulling in quick breaths to oxygenate his system. Pumping himself up, preparing for whatever lay within. Kree warriors? Planet-killers? The Hood? Doctor Voodoo, mysteriously turned evil...?

"Stand aside," Gamora said, drawing her sword. "I will–"

Cap raised his shield and slammed it into the door. As the hinges swung inward, he realized he felt no pain in his injured arm. Had it healed up already? He flexed his fingers. No pain–

"Cap?" Natasha said.

He looked around at the cramped, windowless bar. In the gloom, he registered a few empty tables, an odd-shaped concrete wall, and a small TV. No one in the place except a wiry middle-aged bartender, sharing an open bottle with...

...with ...

"FLAG GUY!" Rocket yelled, raising a shot glass and spilling half his drink on the floor. "Black Window! And my besht pal *Gamora*, the deadliest something in all of someplace! Get in here, you *flarking losers!*"

Cap stood very still, stunned, while Natasha and Gamora squeezed around him into the establishment. Rocket's Kree detector, the gadget he'd displayed back at the barracks, sat next to him on the bar. His aero-rig lay discarded on the floor.

"You are very drunk," Gamora said, shaking her head.

Natasha crossed to the bar and picked up the bottle. "*Whisky-73*," she read. "No wonder."

The bartender shrugged and turned away, pretending to wash a glass.

"Rocket," Gamora continued, "what are you doing here?"

"I followed a woman! Except I didn't know it was a woman." Rocket pointed a thumb at the bartender. "Feliks says it was a woman."

Feliks nodded. He placed a fresh round of shot glasses down on the bar.

"What woman?" Gamora slammed her fist down on the bar. "What are you babbling about?"

"OK. OK, thish a good story." Rocket poured himself another glass. "We was draggin' the ship out of the water. Well, Drax was draggin'. I was just flying around on my aero-rig, you know, supervizhing. Round and around in the air... round and round and round and–"

"Get on with it!"

"OK! Yes sir, Madame Star-Lord. Ow! OK, OK... all of a sudden, my Kree dingus–" he slapped a hand down on the detector "–it started beepin' like crazy. Something moving fast, in the water or maybe underneath, maybe. I figured some Kree was makin' a break for it in a planet-killin' speedboat or something."

"Yes," Natasha observed dryly. "Planet-killers are known for their interest in aquatic sports."

"So I just took off in the air, started following the signal. It took a sharp veer toward Manhattan and started pullin' ahead of me. I was able to stay in range, but barely. Finally tracked it here." Rocket grinned and gestured at the bar. "And here I am!"

Natasha held up the bottle, which was nearly empty. "This stuff was made by the Soviet Union decades ago," she said. "It was rapidly discontinued."

"Yes," the bartender said proudly. "Is hard to get."

"It was discontinued because it caused skin disease, redness of the eyes, and uncontrollable tremors."

"Oh yeah." Rocket grinned. "I got all of that!"

"Nineteen seventy-three," Gamora said, reading the label. "That was some time ago. Did your planet understand the concept of bacterial infections?"

"Rocket," Cap said, pitching his voice deliberately low. The raccoonoid paused in mid-sip, as if he'd been caught stealing. "Where is she now?"

"What? Who now?"

"The woman. The Kree you were chasing!"

"Oh? I dunno."

Gamora frowned. "You lost her?"

"No, no, I think I can still…" He fiddled with the detector, squinting at its controls. It flashed green – just once. "Got it locked to her signal."

"I don't understand," Gamora said. "Why didn't you go after her?"

"I was gonna! But…"

Rocket indicated the litter of shot glasses next to the bottle.

"He is distractable little raccoon," the bartender said.

"I'm gonna ignore that insult, because you're my besht buddy in the world. Or you will be, once you show me another disastrous liquor from your frankly terrifying homeland."

The bartender raised an eyebrow, reached under the bar, and pulled out a bottle labelled *Kapitansky Dzhin*. Rocket reached for it like a baby seeking its mother's arms.

Natasha slammed her elbow down on the bar, startling Cap. She snatched up the bottle, poured a shot glass to overflowing, and slammed it down in one gulp. Feliks, the bartender, watched her closely. She smiled and wiped the "dzhin" from her lips, then leaned forward and started peppering him with questions in Russian.

The bartender gave her an uncertain smile. Keeping his locked on hers, he poured himself a matching shot and downed it with a visible shiver. Then he began talking back in the same rapid-fire dialect.

Cap struggled to follow the conversation. He knew some

Russian, but Feliks and Natasha were speaking too fast. He caught a few words: "alien" and "refugee" and something that might have been "major threat".

Natasha turned to Cap. "According to my beloved countryman, the woman was a tall, wiry type with blue skin."

"Ah," Cap said. "I believe I've met her."

"He says she left here in the company of a man in blue jeans and a dark hood," Natasha continued. "The man is a regular of sorts, but Feliks doesn't know his name. He's not Russian, but he reminds Feliks of some of the criminal gang leaders back home."

"That's got to be Parker Robbins," Cap nodded. "This is all coming together."

The bartender leaned over the bar and spoke to Natasha again. He touched the skin of his cheek to illustrate something.

"He says the woman had a scar of some kind."

"That's good to know," Cap said, "but I think 'blue skin' would have been enough to go on."

"I think *Kree* would have been enough," Rocket said.

Cap frowned. "This Kir-ra... the Kree woman. I don't think she trusts me, or Tony either. But if she's with Robbins, she's definitely in danger."

"Or else she's working with him," Natasha said. "Either way, if we find her, we'll find the Hood. And maybe Tony." She turned to Rocket, then frowned. "Hey, where's your detector thingy?"

"More to the point," Cap said, looking around, "where's your teammate?"

Rocket turned to the bar, where the detector had been, and did a classic double-take. He whipped his head one way, then the other, and then he burst out laughing.

"She took it!" he cried. "Gam... she stole my... AH HA HA HA HA!"

"She's gone, all right," Natasha said.

"She stole my detector! Well, stole it back." Rocket laughed again. "The little thief. I've taught her well."

Cap turned to Natasha. "What's her game?"

"I suspect she got impatient with the floor show." Natasha turned to the inebriated raccoonoid. "Without that thing, you have no idea where this Kree woman went?"

"Ah no, I remember." He tapped his forehead. "I got a mind like a steel net."

"We better move," Cap said. "Oh, no. Do you think Gamora knows how to fly the quinjet?"

Natasha sighed. "She was asking me a lot of questions on the way over."

Cap turned to Rocket, pointing at the aero-rig. "Can you carry someone on that thing?"

"Like you? No way!" Rocket shrugged. "Someone little, maybe."

"Looks like we're stranded," sighed Cap.

"Then I'd better get myself a ride." As he reached for his phone, Natasha pulled out hers as well. "Who are you calling?" he asked.

"The Hood is trouble, and we don't know what he's done with Tony – or how Doc Voodoo fits into this. So I'm calling in the guns." She raised an eyebrow. "Well, one gun. The big one."

Cap nodded. He spoke a few quiet words, then clicked his phone off and started toward the door. Natasha followed, pausing to grab Rocket's arm and drag him along.

"*Podozhdite!*" the bartender yelled.

Everyone stopped. Natasha turned, lowering her phone, and barked out a quick question in Russian. The bartender listened, sweating, and nodded. His cool demeanor was utterly gone now; he seemed terrified. He replied with a couple of unfamiliar words.

Natasha just watched, brow furrowed, and nodded. "*Spasibo,*" she said.

"I couldn't make out all of that," Cap said as they emerged on the dark street. "What did he say?"

"He said beware," Natasha said, her voice grave. "Beware the devil."

In the dark empty tavern, Feliks Andreyevich Litwin stood alone, trembling. He didn't have to wonder what was coming, because it was already here. It was always here.

The TV lit up with an image of fire. "JUST CURIOUS," said a staticky voice. "WHY DID YOU HELP THEM?"

"She was pretty," Feliks said, "and strong. And..."

He swallowed, shrugged, and spread his arms wide at the overturned bottles, the dozen-plus shot glasses littering the bar. A final trickle of *Whisky-73* dripped out onto the floor.

"...and I miss my country."

The TV said nothing more. He could feel the Master's rage burning within him, flames licking at the walls and foundations of his world. But it wasn't mad at him, he knew. He was beneath its notice. All he was, now, was a worker to be dismissed, a ledger item to be erased.

The heat began in his chest and quickly fanned outward. Fire spread through his veins, burned his soft tissues, set his eyes and mouth aflame. Feliks stood still, accepting his fate. With his last breath, before the hot ash of his body crumpled inward and fell to the floor, he gasped out two words:

"*Narushitel' mira.*"

# PART SIX

## THE FRAGILE GRIP

# CHAPTER 39

Gamora stalked down the hall, past door after door. She didn't notice the cracks on the walls, the badly plastered ceiling, or the occasional furtive glances from humans peering out of their apartments. Her attention was focused on the Kree detector, which flashed in a steady rhythm: green-green-green-green-green

Almost there, she thought. Soon. Soon.

She thought of the Kree woman, Kir-ra. Gamora had felt the evil on her, and now the detector had trailed her here, to this housing project. Was she the planet-killer after all? Had Gamora let her go too quickly?

Either way, Gamora knew, this was her quest to follow. In the end, the Avengers had proved as slow, as easily distracted, as her own teammates. She couldn't afford to wait for any of them – not while this evil still roamed free.

Twice now, the detector had burst into fits of activity. There must be other Kree, she realized, living in this same housing complex. But Rocket's modifications had locked the detector onto Kir-ra's signature. Now the device led her to a door labelled 6-66, chipped paint framing tarnished bronze numbers.

She tried the knob; locked, of course. Humans and Kree alike kept their guard up in a place like this. She pulled back and jabbed the doorknob with her elbow. The lock snapped, the knob turned–

"Assassin!"

Gamora whirled to meet the attacker, charging toward her down the hallway. She tossed the detector away, zigzagged from side to side, and grabbed his shoulders – then swiveled to the right, using his momentum to throw him off balance. He slammed to the floor, face-up, with an impact that shook the entire level.

"Mercenary!" he spat.

Gamora sighed. It was the kid, Halla-ar – the Kree woman's brother. "I don't want to fight you again, boy," she said, pressing her boot on his chest to hold him down.

"You hurt my friend," he hissed. "You tried to kill my sister!"

She hesitated, seeing the rage in his eyes. Was it *him*? Was he the killer?

"Guys! Stop it!"

She turned to look down the corridor. The costumed Terran, Ms Marvel, approached, eyes wide. She held a mystic implement of some kind, an orb of tarnished metal with a pulsing, glowing eye inside it.

"What is that thing?" Gamora asked.

Ms Marvel held out the eye for Gamora to see. It strobed and hummed, shining bright. "We don't know."

"It looks like..." Gamora turned away from the eye's gaze. "Like it's *hunting* for something."

"Yeah," Ms Marvel replied. "Same thing you are, I think."

Gamora raised her foot, releasing Halla-ar. He scrambled to his feet and glared at her. Ms Marvel handed him the eye, and he held it up to the door. It glowed brighter.

Again, Gamora hesitated. She thought of a little girl, lost in the destruction of her planet. Of an assembly line where war casualties worked themselves to death. And, finally, of a kitchen full of wary women, forced to band together for protection.

My purpose, she thought, is as urgent as ever. But maybe I don't have to pursue it alone.

"Follow my lead," she whispered, placing a hand on the door.

They stepped into a small kitchen filled with grimy, outdated appliances. Voices came from the next room, around the corner of an open doorway.

"Sometimes," a man's voice said. "Sometimes you can sleep."

"That's my Grandpa," Halla-ar whispered.

Gamora beckoned the kids forward, creeping along the tiled floor. They took up position at the edges of the doorway, so they could see inside the next room. An old Kree man sat in his armchair by the window. Kir-ra perched on a sofa across from him, leaning forward to listen.

"You tell yourself it was a dream," Grandpa continued. "Something that happened to somebody else."

"I know," Kir-ra said. "Grandpa, I know." She frowned, casting a nervous glance down at a travel bag on the floor next to the sofa.

"You think, that's not me. That couldn't be me." Grandpa's voice was oddly monotone, as if he were reading from an old script. "And then it all comes rushing back..."

He turned, eyes suddenly wide and sharp, toward the kitchen.

"...and you know."

Blast it, Gamora thought, he heard us! She jerked her head out of the doorway, hoping to gain a second to think. But the boy, Halla-ar, stepped past her – straight into the living room. She followed reluctantly, with the young Avenger right behind them.

"Brother." Kir-ra stood up. "Where have you ..." She trailed off, peering at the object in the boy's hands. She looked confused, almost disoriented.

Gamora frowned. Nothing here, she sensed, was quite what it seemed. Everything felt off balance, askew. Dreamlike.

The eye surged, glowing brighter than ever. Halla-ar held it up to his sister, and its glow subsided. Gamora gritted her teeth; did that mean Kir-ra was innocent? What *was* this eye talisman, anyway? Was it guiding these two children, or had it placed them under some sort of spell?

The eye let out a loud hum. It seemed to jerk Halla-ar's arms upward, pulling him away from the sofa. He followed its lead, raising it higher as it tugged him across the room. Its light grew brighter, more intense.

The old man watched them, staring blankly. The eye flared, became impossible to stare at directly. Halla-ar stopped short, lowering the object in astonishment.

"You know," Grandpa repeated.

"Grandpa?" Halla-ar whispered.

"It was me," Grandpa said, still staring. "I did those things..."

The bedroom door opened and an old woman walked in. "...I did them all," she said.

A bolt of lightning ran up Gamora's spine. Staring at the old woman – Halla-ar's grandmother – she knew. All at once, she knew.

"You," she hissed, reaching for her sword. *"It was you."*

# CHAPTER 40

They came in over the Hudson River, veering south at the Jersey City waterfront and soaring over the green triangle of Liberty State Park. Captain America hung from the strong, metal-sheathed arms of James Rhodes, the US government's very own super hero: War Machine. Rhodey's silver and white armor had been designed by Tony Stark himself.

As they flew inland, Cap squirmed slightly. "You OK, Steve?" Rhodey asked, his voice filtered through the War Machine armor.

"Yeah," Cap replied. "Just testing this bad arm."

"Sorry. I'll try to make the ride a little smoother."

"No, it's not a problem. In fact, I'm fine. Just get us to the target."

Cap smiled, thinking back to the S.H.I.E.L.D. doctor who'd examined the arm. *A hairline fracture,* the woman had said; *try not to move it.* Don't move the arm? Did she know who she was talking to?

"You got it." Rhodey's voice was tense. "Sooner we find Tony, the better."

Cap turned to look behind them. In the night sky, he could

just make out Natasha clinging to the back of Rocket's aero-rig and attempting to help steer the controls. They seemed to be having trouble keeping up.

"When I said I could carry a *small* person," Rocket grumbled, "I meant, like one of those little symbiotic beings that hitch a ride on somebody else. Or a baby. A baby person, maybe."

Natasha rolled her eyes. "Maybe I should drive–"

"Hey!" Rocket pointed down. "Is that the low-income housing unit we're looking for?"

Cap looked down. Just ahead, a trio of buildings stood out above the surrounding three- and four-story townhouses. They were arrayed in a circle, fanning outward from a central courtyard. "It looks..." He hesitated. "It's designed almost like a radiation symbol."

"Or a pentagram," Natasha said.

"All right, let's land on one of the roofs." Cap frowned, surveying the buildings. "Nearest one, I guess–"

"Uh, Cap?" War Machine's lenses glowed. "Take a look out *past* the buildings."

Cap squinted. In the dark, all he could make out was a wide street and what looked like an outdoor strip mall beyond. "I don't have your night-vision scopes, Jim."

"In the parking lot. It's him." Rhodey's voice rose in excitement. "It's Tony."

Rhodes swung upward, towing Cap along with him. Rocket and Natasha followed, arcing up and over the housing complex, then across the street. The shopping center stood dark, nearly abandoned, and partially collapsed. The parking lot was empty except for a garbage hauler and a large tanker truck.

In a corner of the mall, a lone pizza parlor's windows glowed, opening onto an outdoor seating area with fixed stone tables and benches under dim lamps. Tony Stark stood alone among the tables in full Iron Man armor, face hidden behind his helmet.

"Tony!" Rhodey called.

Cap touched his earpiece. "How'd you escape, Tony? Is the Hood in custody?"

Tony Stark turned to look, his eye-lenses swiveling toward the sky. He watched as Rhodey and Cap descended, with Rocket and Natasha close behind. Slowly he began to lean back, his feet planted in place, body bending at an unnatural angle.

A chill of alarm went up Cap's spine. "Wait, wait," he called. "He's not–"

The uni-beam blasted out from Tony's chestplate, flashing like a comet into the night sky. Cap ducked, then realized the beam wasn't aimed at him. It seared into Rocket, raising sparks on the raccoonoid's aero-rig; he cried out and began spiraling down. Natasha hung on, her legs swinging wildly in the air.

Cap rose back up to face Tony, shield raised. Had he been taken over somehow? Or had someone else overridden Stark's protocols and stolen the armor? Either way, the strategy didn't make sense. Why take out the raccoon first, when a man in a military-grade weapon suit was hurtling straight toward you? A man literally called War Machine?

"Uh, Steve?"

Rhodes had barely spoken the words when a rush of air whizzed past Cap's face. "We're falling?"

"He's in my system," Rhodes said. "I'm fighting him, but he's... Ah, no, he's deactivated my jets! We're gonna..."

The ground rushed up with dizzying speed. Gritting his teeth, Cap thrust his body sideways and leaped free. He spread his feet and tossed his shield in the air, then braced himself. Not on the bad arm, he thought. Not on the arm. Not on the–

He landed gracefully, but his relief didn't last long. Tony was already stalking toward him – lenses glowing, still not speaking. The silence, Cap realized, was the most eerie thing. Tony never went into battle without firing off a few annoying quips.

Rhodey crashed to the ground.

Tony raised a hand and fired. Cap snatched his shield out of the air and flipped it forward, just in time to repel a repulsor beam. The energy rebounded harmlessly – sizzling back onto Tony's armor, knocking him off balance.

Natasha was suddenly, silently at Cap's shoulder. "Rocket's OK, but stunned," she said.

"I'm out for now too," Rhodes said, over the comm. "At least till I can purge Tony from my system. What's wrong with him, anyway?"

Tony staggered, his palms beginning to glow again. "Something's controlling him," Natasha said.

"Or someone." Cap grimaced at her. "Well, we've taken down Tony before. It won't be easy, but–"

"Uh, Steve?"

He followed her pointing finger. The door of the pizza parlor opened, and out walked a figure in black tights with an eerie white glyph painted along them. He held a jagged wooden staff, half-hidden beneath a violet cloak.

"Doctor Voodoo," Cap hissed. "Is he being controlled too?"

"Also," Natasha said, "is he eating a slice?"

Voodoo bit off a chunk of pizza and tossed away the crust. Then he stepped out between two stone benches, several yards away from Tony. He raised his hands and began to conjure, forming an eerie glowing disk in the air.

This is bad, Cap thought. We've been ambushed. Two of our own turned against us, two more taken out right away. And in terms of raw power, Natasha and I can't compare to what we're facing.

"That 'big gun' of yours?" he asked.

She shook her head. "Still twenty minutes out."

Tony raised his hands again, palms and chest plate glowing. Voodoo cocked his head at an odd angle and spread his arms, expanding the mystic energy into a living, glowing shield.

"OK then." Cap slammed a fist into his palm. "You and me."

He gestured forward. She nodded, flashed him a tight smile, and together they charged.

# CHAPTER 41

"Your grandfather had a lot of stories," the old woman said. "He killed people, you know."

Gamora drew her sword. There was no mistake: this was her prey. The face she'd seen in the fire, the burning eyes and high cheekbones. At last her path was clear. The vengeance of Praeterus was at hand.

Halla-ar's grandmother, Ann-ya, stood with her husband in front of the armchair, the two of them sporting the same dull-eyed stare. Halla-ar shifted back and forth next to Ms Marvel, holding the eye-talisman slack at his side. Kir-ra sat on the sofa, blinking in confusion.

"That was his job, killing people," Ann-ya continued. "His patriotic duty. But sometimes he wasn't too picky about his targets."

Gamora lunged, but before she could reach the old woman, Kir-ra leaped up to block her path. She grabbed the Guardian's sword arm in a strong but shaky grip.

"Stay..." The Kree woman shook her head as if trying to clear it. "Stay away from my family!"

Gamora wrenched her arm free and fell into a defensive posture, bracing herself against the wall of the cramped room. "You're unarmed," she said, feeling a sudden pang of sympathy. "And you don't exactly look battle-ready."

"I might surprise you."

"Stop it! Both of you!" Ms Marvel stepped between them, literally pushing the two women apart. "Have you forgotten why we're here?"

"Oh, I remember." Gamora pointed her sword at Ann-ya. "This is her... the destroyer of Praeterus. I remember now."

"Halla-ar?" Ms Marvel called.

The boy approached, holding up the eye. It glowed brighter as he came near to his grandparents. He held it up to Grandpa, and it hummed. When he moved it closer to Ann-ya, it gave off an identical hum.

"I don't know." He stared at his grandfather, whose expressionless eyes were fixed on a point behind him on the wall. Then he turned to Ann-ya. "Grandma?"

Ann-ya blinked and looked up, as if she'd suddenly come out of a trance. She glanced at Gamora's sword and let out a short, humorless laugh. Then she turned solemnly to Halla-ar and Kir-ra.

"He escaped from the Skrulls," Ann-ya said, as if nothing had interrupted her story. "He came home broken, barely alive. Six months I nursed him, took care of him, bathed him and changed his dressings. And then he died in my arms."

Gamora felt the shock run through everyone in the room.

"Wh- What?" Kamala gasped.

"Grandma?" Halla-ar said. "Wh- What are you saying? Grandpa's not dead. He's here. He's right here."

The old man stared straight ahead. He didn't even blink.

"Sometimes…" Ann-ya walked to the center of the room, eyeing each of them in turn. "Sometimes you convince yourself it was a dream. Something that happened to someone else. And then it all comes rushing back, bleak and terrible. And you know: it was me."

She turned, despair in her eyes, to face Gamora.

"I did that thing."

"Well, I guess that's enough war stories."

Gamora whirled toward the sofa, searching for the source of the voice. The air seemed to shimmer, clearing to reveal a man in jeans and a hooded sweatshirt, with dark, staring eyes.

"*There* you are," Kir-ra said to the man. She seemed confused, disoriented. "I… I thought you'd gone out–"

The hooded man reached out, cobra-like, and grabbed Kir-ra in a headlock, pulling her down onto the sofa. Gamora tensed, prepared to strike – then froze as she saw the Glock in his hand, its barrel jammed up against Kir-ra's temple.

"Stay back," the man said. The gun's hammer was cocked back, ready to fire. "Just stay back, now."

"Let her go!" Halla-ar cried. "Who are you?"

"I'm a friend of your sister's," the man said. "She brought me here to meet the family. I was enjoying the stories – nice and bloody. But then the party started to get crowded, and I thought it might be better to… cloak myself."

That sweatshirt… Gamora remembered Captain America's description, back at Stark Tower. "The Hood," she said.

"Right! They call me that, because…" He tried to gesture at his hood and wound up pressing his arm harder against Kir-ra's throat. "Ah, sorry, doll."

"Kill – you," Kir-ra gasped.

"You might, under some circumstances. But you had a lot

to drink back at the bar, while Feliks poured me glass after glass of colored water. And the device in my bag here was busy too, secreting a sort of dulling herb into the air." He shrugged. "Voodoo? I don't understand it."

Gamora glanced at the old woman. Ann-ya had retreated to stand beside her husband, at the armchair across from the sofa. Her expression showed nothing but dull resignation; she seemed not to care at all that a strange man was menacing her granddaughter at gunpoint.

"Why – me?" Kir-ra asked.

The Hood gave her a creepy smile. "I needed to be here, in this charming little hovel, for what's coming. Oh, I could have just broken in, but it's so nice, so *civilized* to be invited inside. And, well…" He shrugged. "I enjoy spending time with lonely, desperate women."

Kir-ra struggled, but the Hood just kept smiling. "I was right," he said, "you're no fighter."

Ms Marvel exchanged glances with Halla-ar. They started toward the sofa – then stopped as the Hood turned to face them.

"Look, I'm not stupid," he said, pressing the gun against Kir-ra's head. "There's four of you and one of me; ultimately I am not going to win this showdown. I just need the green Amazon over there to *not* murder an old lady for a few more minutes." He paused. "You know, when I say that out loud, it sure sounds like I'm the good guy here."

Gamora watched him, eyes narrowing. She could take down a normal human before he could blink; probably the Earth girl or the Kree boy could manage it in a few seconds more. But could any of them get to him before he pulled that trigger?

"Just listen to the old bat's story. That's all I'm asking." He looked from Gamora to Ms Marvel, and then finally to Halla-ar.

"That's reasonable, right? I'm being reasonable. You want to hear the end, don't you?"

The boy, Halla-ar, watched with teeth gritted, clenching and unclenching his fists. Grandpa stood still as a statue, one hand resting on the back of his armchair.

Ann-ya let out a long sigh and hung her head. She crossed past her husband and half-fell into his armchair. Then she began to cry.

"When he died," she sobbed. "When he was gone, I had nothing. All three of my children taken by that war, and now him."

Gamora glanced at the Hood and Kir-ra. He was hunched forward; she listened anxiously, unable to move. His gun hadn't moved from her temple.

"I kept his death from the young ones. From my poor, innocent grandchildren." Ann-ya let out a dry laugh. "I told them he'd gone away, back to Hala to receive some honor. Little Halla-ar... you were so proud of your Grandpa."

Halla-ar trembled, staring as he listened. He wiped a tear from his cheek.

"But I... I was so alone," Ann-ya continued. "I went a little mad. I started looking into the dark arts. Not much of that on Praeterus! But I managed to craft a few idols, cast a few spells."

Gamora frowned. This was not what she'd expected. How could this frail, grief-stricken woman be the creature that had destroyed a planet?

"Eventually I broke through... well, through something. A veil, a curtain between worlds. Found myself face to face with–"

"The devil," the Hood said. Something flashed in his eyes.

"I don't know," Ann-ya said. "I don't... All I know is, I'd had enough. All my life I toiled for the Empire, sent my children and my husband off to fight and die. And the Kree rulers never gave me anything in return. No one had ever done anything for me, until that moment.

"This, this devil... he asked me to do something. And in return..." She glanced up, almost wincing. "He gave my husband back to me."

Ms Marvel glanced at the stunned Halla-ar, then said, "You're saying this entity actually resurrected him? Brought him back from the dead?"

"No, he wasn't the same. He only said things... things that I already..." Her voice faltered. "But I could pretend. Sometimes I almost believed it was him."

Gamora studied Grandpa. He seemed even more still now, as if he were made of stone. His eyes were closed.

"A poor reward," Gamora hissed, "for genocide."

"You don't know... you don't understand. The loneliness." A flash of rage crossed Ann-ya's face. "The neglect."

"So you agreed to destroy your world. To murder tens of thousands of people, all your friends and neighbors."

"I didn't understand," Ann-ya said. "He didn't fully explain the price, and I didn't ask. When the day came, he just sort of... took me over." An unearthly fire rose up, just for a moment, in her eyes. "It was like a dream."

"Oh, come on, *Grandma*." The Hood smirked. "Be honest."

"Honest?" She laughed again. "Yes. To tell the truth, I knew."

"Grandma," Halla-ar croaked. "Grandma, no."

"'Grandma, no,'" the Hood mocked. "Oh, this was worth it. Such drama! So much pain, so many feels."

Halla-ar moved toward him. "I will kill you–"

"I knew," Ann-ya and her husband said, in unison. "I knew, and still I killed them."

Gamora winced. The two voices – one dead, one alive – sounded eerie, discordant. She could feel the fire behind Ann-ya's eyes, the still unseen enemy.

"I knew," Ann-ya whispered, and bowed her head.

Halla-ar stared in horror.

The Hood burst out laughing. "Now that!" he cried. "That's what I call an ending–"

Kir-ra jabbed out, thrusting a rigid hand into his neck. He let out a strangled noise and released her; she tumbled to the floor, gasping. The gun slipped in his hand, but he managed to keep hold of it.

Gamora, Halla-ar, and Ms Marvel all charged at once. The Hood watched them come and laughed. He raised the gun to his eye, sighted carefully–

–and fired *past* them, emptying the chamber into Grandpa.

Gamora skidded to a halt, ducked low, and turned to look. Across the room, Grandpa's figure seemed to shake and waver as the bullets struck him. His eyes opened once, and the look of surprise on them seemed very real. Very human.

As the final bullet sliced past him to shatter the window, his eyes rolled up into his head and he crumbled to dust.

"No." Ann-ya stared in horror at the pile of ash that had been her husband. "Not again."

Ms Marvel and Halla-ar grabbed the Hood roughly, but he just laughed. "The big climax," he said. "A shock ending!"

Ann-ya sifted her husband's remains through limp fingers. "No. No no no." She looked up to the ceiling, opened her mouth in a silent scream, and began to glow.

"No," Gamora whispered, staring at the old woman. "It's happening again."

"He promised." Ann-ya turned, shining, to glare at the Hood. "You promised!"

The Hood's eyes flared bright. He threw off Halla-ar and Ms Marvel, and reached down for his bag.

Ann-ya began to stalk toward him. Her face, her features, were lost in the fire. The same cosmic fire that had consumed the planet Praeterus; the failure that had haunted Gamora, all these long months.

There was no choice, no conscious decision. Gamora threw herself at the glowing figure, slashing out with her sword. The heat, the radiation, washed over her in an agonizing wave. She cried out, feeling the sword slip from her hand.

She caught a quick glimpse of Ms Marvel struggling to her feet. Kir-ra clawing her way across the floor, clutching her head. Halla-ar raising a hand to shield his eyes from the blazing radiance that filled the room.

The Hood ignored them all. He reached into his bag and pulled out a strange skull-shaped device. His eyes were wide, hungry, filled with the power that possessed both him and that poor, anguished old woman.

"Sometimes," Ann-ya said, "you tell yourself it was a dream…"
As Gamora's arms closed around that raging form, bolts of agony rippled across her skin. Once again, as in the dome on Praeterus, the stored energy of a dying world shot through her – burning her flesh, shattering her senses. And once again, inevitably, she failed to hold it, and was lost to pain and darkness.

# CHAPTER 42

Outside in the parking lot, Captain America led the charge, shield held before him. The Black Widow followed, her wrist-stingers crackling with energy.

From a prison made of bones, Jericho Drumm watched in frustration and helpless, mounting horror. The image filled the air, huge and inescapable. Cap with his wounded arm and boundless determination; Natasha with teeth gritted, figuring the angles as always. Tony Stark standing like a stone, waiting to meet them with weapons charged.

And the fourth figure: Jericho himself, in the full ceremonial garb of Doctor Voodoo. Except it wasn't Jericho who controlled his body – not anymore. He had been both possessed and dispossessed by his dead brother, Daniel, mere days ago. Now Daniel wielded the Shield of the Seraphim, the Rings of Raggadorr, and a thousand other mystical implements, in addition to the innate powers of Doctor Voodoo. He even held the Staff of Legba, the compass-rod that had guided Jericho whenever he found himself at a crossroads in life.

Under other circumstances, Jericho might have appreciated

the irony. He, who had used his power to take possession of others' bodies many times in the past, had fallen victim to the same fate. But as he watched the two Avengers run to their doom, he felt only desperation.

*Brother!* he cried, in a voice that made no sound. *You must stop this!*

He ran to the wall of his cage, a thin lattice of bones held together by strands of mystic energy. Spotting a small opening, he dove for it – but the bones clattered and shifted, filling the hole in the wall, and he rattled up against them. He cursed and turned back to the images in the air–

–just in time to see his own body raise the Shield of the Seraphim, a shimmering gold disk. Captain America and the Black Widow struck the shield and flew backward, repelled by the mystic barrier.

Jericho let out a howl of frustration. He could see every detail of the battle, but he was powerless to act! He reached out and rattled the bones of his cage.

Then Daniel's voice was all around, mocking and malevolent. *YOU KNOW THIS PRISON IS ONLY IN YOUR MIND, RIGHT?* He laughed. *SORRY. MY MIND, NOW.*

*Break off your attack,* Jericho demanded. *The Avengers are our allies!*

*THEY ARE THE MASTER'S ENEMIES,* Daniel said. *THEY MUST BE PUT DOWN.*

*Brother, we have always worked together. As Doctor Voodoo, we have fought as one. Why... How can you turn against me this way?*

Daniel hesitated. When he spoke again, Jericho could hear the anger in his voice.

*PERHAPS I NO LONGER WISH TO RIDE IN THE BACK SEAT.*

Jericho watched as Natasha and Cap climbed to their feet, preparing for another assault. But it was hopeless. Their power was no match for Daniel's – let alone for the weapon-suit of Tony Stark.

He decided to take another tack. *Brother*, he began, *you still follow the ways of voodoo, do you not?*

Daniel did not reply. Outside, Iron Man began to raise his glowing repulsor-hand.

*This "Master" of yours… he is not Bondye, the good god. He is no god of ours, not even a loa. He is unworthy of your fealty!*

*HE IS A PLAYER IN THE GAME. ONE OF MANY.*

*You know he has hold of your mind, don't you?*

In the parking lot, Stark let loose a bolt of energy. His targets leaped away, Cap in one direction and Natasha in the other. The repulsor beam struck a bench, blasting it to rubble.

*Your puppet's moves are sluggish*, Jericho observed. *Your grip is fragile.*

*SO IT IS WITH DOLLS. BUT YOU KNOW THAT BETTER THAN MOST, EH? HOW MANY BODIES HAVE YOU DONNED LIKE FRESHLY LAUNDERED SHIRTS, ONLY TO DISCARD THEM WHEN THEY OUTLIVED THEIR USEFULNESS?*

A short distance from the combat, James Rhodes lay still on the pavement. He was trying, Jericho knew, to activate a government protocol that would override Iron Man's control of his armor. But that would take time.

*I WISH I STILL HAD THAT PIZZA*, Daniel said. *WOULD YOU GET ME ANOTHER SLICE, BROTHER? OH, WAIT, YOU CAN'T.*

Jericho clenched his fists. Ever since childhood, Daniel had known exactly how to anger him. But this was no time for games.

He had to use every argument, every tool at his disposal, to stop this madness.

Stark took to the air, repulsors glowing.

*What has your Master promised you?* Jericho asked. *A kingdom?*

A long moment passed. Then, finally, Daniel spoke: *HE HAS PROMISED TO END MY EXISTENCE.*

The words struck Jericho like an arrow. He knew Daniel had died once, and been resurrected in spirit form. Now, for the first time, he realized how miserable his brother was in that half-life. Daniel's pain, his misery, had given the Master an opening to worm his way into their shared mind and take possession.

*YOU CANNOT UNDERSTAND*, Daniel continued. *YOU LIVE IN THE CURRENT OF LIFE, BORNE FORWARD ON A TIDE OF MOTION. FOR ME THERE IS NO MOTION, NO FUTURE OR PAST. I DO NOT LIVE, BECAUSE I CANNOT DIE.*

*Daniel*, he said. *I'm sorry. I never thought—*

*NO. YOU DID NOT.*

Tony Stark took to the air in a shaky, uneven flight. Captain America reached up, grabbed hold of his ankle, and swung hard, slamming Stark against a stone table. Stark rolled, dropped to the ground, and fired off a volley of repulsors.

*But there is still an order to the world,* Jericho said. *A system of currents and energies that cannot be violated, even by adepts like ourselves.*

Natasha let loose a bolt of electricity, which sizzled off the Shield of the Seraphim. *SORRY, BROTHER, THAT TICKLED A LITTLE. WHAT WERE YOU SAYING?*

*Only that you risk violating the unspoken law of the universe. Remember what the Greeks called it? "The labyrinth that is a straight line." The order that grants us power, that gives us life.*

*"THAT GIVES US LIFE"? DO YOU HEAR YOURSELF? I HAVE NO LIFE.*

Natasha whirled back, somersaulted once, and landed next to Captain America. They conferred for a second, then turned to face Tony Stark.

*HMM,* Daniel said. *I THINK OUR TIN FRIEND COULD USE A POWER BOOST.*

Stark stiffened. Mystic flames rose up to fill his eye-lenses. The glow of his palm-repulsors deepened, darkened, and took on a distinctly magical quality.

*Brother!* Jericho rattled the bones of his cage. *You must stop this! Your so-called Master – he has warped your mind!*

For a moment, Jericho thought he sensed anger. Am I getting through? he wondered. Or is Daniel's attention merely elsewhere, focused on charging up his puppet of meat and steel?

*PERHAPS YOU'RE RIGHT,* Daniel said. *BUT REALLY, BROTHER…*

Iron Man raised his repulsors, eyes glowing bright. Jericho raged, his ectoplasmic hands clutching at the ivory bones of his prison. The prison, he now knew, that Daniel had built to escape a cage of his own.

*… DOES IT MATTER?*

# CHAPTER 43

"Come on, Tony," Natasha said. "Remember all those training sessions? How many times have I kicked your ass?"

Tony Stark didn't answer. He just stepped forward, weapons hot, flames burning in those eerie eye-slits. Then he fired both repulsors – a chaotic, living beam of energy, fueled by the demon inside him. Natasha leaped and tumbled, catching part of a shot on the arm.

Cap heard her swear, but he couldn't spare the time to check on her; he had his hands full with Doctor Voodoo. The caped man advanced toward him, firing bolts of eldritch energy straight through that one-way mystic barrier. Cap held up his own shield, wincing at the unnatural vibrations.

"Jericho," Cap called, "Jericho Drumm! You know me, right? We've fought together before."

*JERICHO?* The voice seemed to echo in Cap's brain. *JERICHO'S NOT HOME RIGHT NOW.*

"Who are you, then? Why are you doing this?" Cap circled around, searching for a way past Voodoo's shield. "Am I speaking to the Hood? Have you taken control of Doctor Voodoo?"

Anger flashed in Voodoo's eyes. *NO MAN CONTROLS ME.*

Cap braced himself for the next attack – but Voodoo just stood rigid and raised his staff. As mystic energy flared, Cap felt a strange tickling in his brain.

*WHY DO YOU RESIST?* the voice asked. *ALL THIS FIGHTING… IT MEANS NOTHING. JUST ANOTHER SET OF RITUALS, IMPARTING THE ILLUSION OF CONTROL. ALL THEY HAVE EVER BROUGHT YOU IS PAIN.*

At the word pain, Cap felt a twinge in his injured arm. A sliver of doubt ran through him.

*GIVE UP YOUR ILLUSIONS…*

Then he felt them: tendrils of energy, probing and prodding. Searching for weakness, for a way inside his mind. This, he remembered, was one of Doctor Voodoo's powers: to possess other people's bodies.

*…YOUR FUTILE DREAMS OF FREEDOM.*

He raised his head, forcing himself to stare Voodoo straight in the eye. Summoning all the will, all the strength of mind that had seen him through a thousand harrowing battles, from World War II to the present day.

"Sorry, Doc," he said. "No one pulls Captain America's strings, either."

Doctor Voodoo glared back through the shield. Then, slowly, he began to smile. He turned his gaze up and to the side – where Natasha clung to the top of a lamppost, trading blasts with Iron Man.

"Natasha," Cap called. "Tasha, watch out!"

She stiffened. *He's doing it*, Cap thought – trying to take control of her!

Cap braced himself, raised his shield before him, and charged Voodoo head-on. The two shields met in an explosion of sparks, raising tendrils of dark energy into the air. Doctor Voodoo stepped back, holding his mystic barrier steady. Cap twisted his body, favoring his good arm, and tilted his shield at an angle.

Cap had seen the Shield of the Seraphim wielded before, by Doctor Strange; he didn't understand its origins, but its power was undeniable. Cap's own shield was forged of a nearly unbreakable Vibranium alloy. Slowly its edge began to pierce the mystic energy, slicing a sparkling gash in the shimmering barrier. Sweat beaded on Voodoo's brow, betraying the strain on his system.

But Cap knew he was outgunned. Voodoo outpowered him by a huge margin. All he could hope to do was hold out until–

Natasha tumbled through the air, limbs spinning, and kicked both legs into Doctor Voodoo's head. He cried out and fell backward, losing his balance. Before he could recover, she jabbed a stinger-powered fist into his chest, sending an electrical charge sizzling through his body.

"Word of advice," she hissed. "You don't want to be in my head."

Voodoo's mystic shield flickered and winked out. Cap lunged forward, jabbing his shield into the sorcerer's chest, knocking him to the ground.

"Cap!" Natasha called.

He spied a flash of red and gold a second too late. Tony Stark blasted him point-blank with a repulsor; Cap managed to raise his shield, but not quickly enough to block the full impact. He flew back, twisted as he fell, and landed – painfully – on his bad arm.

He looked up through a haze of pain to see Tony advancing, repulsors glowing hot. Iron Man was a formidable opponent under any circumstances, and the agony shooting through Cap's arm put him at a further disadvantage. But Tony's movements seemed stiff, uncertain. The possession, Cap thought – is he fighting it?

"Hey, Tony," he said. "Rough day at work, huh?"

He struggled to rise.

"We've had our differences," he continued. "Hell, that's an understatement. Remember Geffen-Meyers?"

At the reference to the super hero Civil War, Tony stopped. He looked down to study Cap, head cocked at an unnatural angle. But his weapons still glowed bright.

"You're an arrogant child, sometimes," Cap said, "but you're nobody's fool. I know how strong you are, Tony, and I know this isn't you. Whoever… Whatever's inside your head, you've gotta fight it!"

Tony's lenses blinked on and off. When they came back on again, flames rose within them. He raised his repulsors and fired.

Cap ducked, raised his shield – then scurried backward, fleeing from a burst of machine-gun fire. He backed up into a corner where two intact benches met, with the stump of a stone table before them. He peered up, over the shield, and gasped.

Tony danced jaggedly side to side, bullets bouncing off him in all directions. He dropped to one knee, aimed himself at the sky, and took off shakily into the air.

James Rhodes, War Machine, stood revealed on the pavement, the machine gun mounted on his arm still smoking. He turned, aimed upward, and fired off another volley at Tony's low-flying, wobbling figure.

"You heard the man, Tony!" Rhodey yelled. "This is not you. Now get down here and stand down, so I can stop denting that pretty armor of yours!"

Tony cocked his head, as if listening to instructions.

"And don't try to get back into my system," Rhodey said. "I got that covered."

Tony pivoted in midair, dove straight into the stream of bullets, and reached for Rhodey's arm. With a hideous crunch, he ripped the machine gun clean off Rhodey's armor and tossed it aside.

"Hey!" Rhodey yelled, staring at his own exposed arm. "You know you're the one's gonna have to fix that, right?"

Natasha stumbled toward the benches, dropping down to wedge herself in next to Cap. "How you doing?" he asked.

"Still me," she replied. "But whoever's inside those guys really did a number on me."

"Me too," Cap said, wincing at the pain in his arm.

"OK," she said, pulling him back into the crook between the stone benches. "What we need to do is, we draw on our 'inner determination' and 'dogged resolve' to–"

"Will you *please* lay off the tabletop gaming?"

Rhodes limped toward them, his armor sparking. Rocket was nowhere to be seen.

"Voodoo's back on his feet," Natasha said. "Whatever's got hold of these guys, it's not going to go down easily."

They watched together as Tony dropped down to a shaky landing next to Doctor Voodoo. The two men turned toward each other, heads bobbing up and down. As if they were conferring, Cap thought, without words.

"You know," he said to Natasha, "this'd be a real good time for your 'big gun' to…"

A grinding clatter pierced the New Jersey night. They looked up to see a dark birdlike shape, soaring into view over the housing project.

"Huh," Natasha said. "Not the gun I was expecting."

James Rhodes crouched down next to them, eyeing the sky. "Is that…?"

"Yep," Cap said. "The Guardians of the Galaxy."

Tony Stark and Doctor Voodoo turned to watch as the Guardians' ship drew closer, clattering and wobbling in the sky. Its surface was covered with patches; something that looked like a huge Band-Aid had been pasted over the cockpit. As it dropped down toward the parking lot, one wing dipped too low and sliced the top off an abandoned shopping-cart station.

"Yikes," Rhodey said.

The ship righted itself, bounced, and came to rest. Its exterior lights briefly illuminated the neglected parking lot, the toppled shopping carts, the bullet-riddled pavements. Then the lights winked off as the ship's hatch began to slide open.

"Well," Natasha said, "this should tip the odds in our favor."

"Yeah," Cap said, eyeing Stark and Voodoo. "So why don't I feel better about this?"

# CHAPTER 44

Kir-ra shrank back against the wall, shielding her eyes. Her grandmother, Ann-ya – or whatever was left of the old woman – knelt down in the center of the room, mouth wide open, energy flaring from every pore in her body. The Hood braced himself against the sofa, holding up a bizarre device shaped like a skull with a maze of circuitry at its neck. He reached inside the skull, wrenched free a candle, and tossed it aside.

The blank socket-eyes of the skull began to glow. Lights flashed across the base. All around the room, the swirling energy redirected itself toward the Hood. It narrowed to a thin, intense stream, flowing from Ann ya's shrunken form into the skull-thing's gaping, hungry mouth.

The Hood. Staring at him now, Kir-ra wondered how she'd been so taken in by a man she barely knew. She could feel the alcohol buzz, along with … whatever else had been affecting her, back in Staryymir. But that was no excuse. Was I that lonely? she thought. So tired of carrying all the weight, so desperate to make a connection on this sad, hostile world?

Whatever the reason, she'd brought him here of her own free will. Here, to this apartment she'd sought out with great effort, the safe space she'd struggled to carve out for her family.

And even here, she'd acted like a fool. When he vanished on the sofa, she'd just thought he'd stepped out to the bathroom or something. Stupid, stupid!

She thrust those thoughts aside; this was no time for guilt, or self-pity either. She'd been trained in Sen-Zha techniques, but she'd never had a war to fight in, never had a time or place to use those skills. Maybe this was the time. Maybe she could still make things right.

The unearthly radiance made it hard to see, so she cast her awareness outward. The assassin, Gamora, lay on the other side of the room, unconscious but alive. A moment of panic: where was Halla-ar? Ah, there – on the far side of the sofa, moving slowly. His heartbeat was strong, his blood pressure elevated. And behind the sofa, the costumed Terran– Ms Marvel – was creeping toward Halla-ar, stretching those unnaturally long legs to cover the distance quickly.

Oh no, Kir-ra realized. They're trying to sneak up on–

Grinning, the Hood reached out with his free hand and backhanded Halla-ar across the face. Then he tossed the skull-device up in the air, slapped Ms Marvel away, and caught it with his other hand. The girl bounced off the wall and dropped down behind the sofa.

Halla-ar was down too. Kir-ra reached out again, feeling his heartbeat – and something else, too. A residue of eldritch energy, in his and Ms Marvel's bodies. The same energy that filled the room, flowing in a steady stream from Ann-ya into that eerie skull-thing.

"Oh," the Hood said. His eyes burned bright, his hands trembled as he clutched the skull. "Oh my."

Once again, despair washed over Kir-ra like a deadly tide – just like that time, mere hours ago, when she'd felt the pull of the deep ocean waters. She shook her head, forced herself to confront the stew of emotions roiling within her. Guilt: how could she have trusted the Hood? Self-loathing: she'd allowed him to hold her hostage, to intimidate her family. Finally, shock and grief for her grandfather. Grandpa who was dead and gone, whose death she hadn't even had time to mourn.

It all added up to one dark, overwhelming feeling: rage. The same rage, she realized with a shock, that her grandmother had felt when the love of her life was taken from her by the winds of war.

Now Ann-ya raised glowing hands to her eyes, as if trying to block the blazing energy flowing out of her. "I'm sorry," she sobbed. "Oh, I'm so sorry."

Grandpa might be dead, Kir-ra realized. But her grandmother was still alive – for now, anyway. And so was Halla-ar. Her brother, the boy she'd vowed to protect.

The tide of despair receded. Kir-ra reached behind the sofa, her hand brushing against Ms Marvel's unconscious form before settling on a thin metal object. The spare rod-weapon she'd stashed there, in case of… well, an attack on her family.

This definitely qualified.

She whipped the rod around, thumbing it to full power. Current crackled across its surface; the Hood turned, surprised – a moment too late. The rod slashed across his face, burning into his cheek. He cried out and shrank away.

"Stop this," she said. "Stop it now!"

He edged sideways along the sofa, keeping hold of the skull. Energy still pouring into it, filling it with power.

"So fierce," the Hood said, grinning. "Oh, you were worth the chase."

Enraged, she swung the rod again. Still smiling, he lifted the skull higher, shifting the energy stream toward her–

–into the path of the rod. Kir-ra cried out as the flaring energies, the stored power of a world-shattering gamma reaction, sliced her weapon neatly in half. She let go and scrambled away, watching as the two halves of the rod sparked, went dark, and clattered to the floor.

The Hood staggered and fell back onto the sofa. He shifted his grip, keeping hold of the skull with one hand while he wiped blood from his face with his sleeve.

Kir-ra frowned. He clearly had some supernatural power, either inborn or acquired through unknown means. But as more and more energy flowed into his device, he seemed diminished, even weakened. Was the Hood the real threat here? Or was there something larger behind him, something not of this world at all?

"Why?" she shouted into the fiery maelstrom. "Why are you doing this?"

"I told you! I've had to fight for everything in my life." He grimaced. "This is no different."

Ann-ya let out a plaintive wail. Kir-ra turned to see her on the floor, her figure almost lost in the blinding glow. Her hands trembled, sifting almost tenderly through the ashes of her long-dead husband.

"I killed them," she said. "I killed them all."

Kir-ra tensed. The kids, Ms Marvel and Halla-ar, were still unconscious. Gamora too – not that she'd trust that woman. And Ann-ya was deep in her trauma, lost in a pit of sorrow and regret.

It's up to me, Kir-ra realized. I'm the one who brought the Hood here; I've got to take him out, even if it kills me. She tensed herself, prepared to leap. If she could just knock that skull out of his hands–

Ann-ya let out a piercing scream. Energy flared, brighter than ever, a tidal wave of power slamming, burning, flooding into the skull. Its eyes flared bright, its circuitry glowed and sparked. The Hood struggled to keep hold of it, his body arching in pain.

Then, all at once, the glow faded. Ann-ya slumped to the floor as the radiance left her body.

Only the skull still shone with power. Blinding, pulsing, throbbing white-hot. Like a sun captured inside a child's snow globe.

The Hood stared at it, eyes wide… and in those eyes, flames rose up in response. "It burns," he whispered. Then he rose, stumbled once, and turned to Kir-ra.

"Well," he said. "I guess the chase is over."

*He's going to kill me,* she thought. *He got what he wanted, and now I'm going to die.* She'd failed again. Failed to save her grandmother, her brother, and the Earth girl too. Even Gamora, the assassin-for-hire, shouldn't have to die this way.

The Hood grinned. She had the strange feeling he was feeding off her hopelessness–sucking it in, allowing it to fuel his hatred and evil. Just as his device, whatever it was, had absorbed the death-energy of her world.

Then his face fell, and for an instant he looked human again. "Don't come after me," he said. "You'll regret it."

He took off at a run and sped past her, using his powers to literally sprint up into the air. He stepped over Ann-ya's fallen form and soared over the armchair, clutching the skull-device tight to his body. Then he crashed shoulder-first into the broken window, shattering it, and leaped out into the night.

Kir-ra fell to her knees, exhausted and traumatized. Ann-ya lay perfectly still; Halla-ar and Ms Marvel were also down. A minute, Kir-ra thought. I just need a minute to catch my breath.

But in the corner of the room, the assassin was stirring...

# CHAPTER 45

Natasha edged closer to Rhodey and Captain America, tucking herself in between the two stone benches. "The Guardians," she said. "I thought there'd be more of them."

Cap nodded grimly. The Guardians' ship trembled slightly in the open parking area. Peter Quill had emerged from the gangplank, but when he motioned inside the ship, only Groot followed him out.

"No Drax," Cap said. "I was hoping for Drax."

"Is he the big guy?" Rhodey held up his damaged machine-gun arm. "We could use some muscle out here."

Cap lifted his head up briefly, making a quick survey of the area. Tony Stark and Doctor Voodoo stood several stone benches away, lit by irregularly spaced lampposts. They seemed dazed, their movements stiff. Were they fighting the entity that controlled them? Or just waiting for new instructions?

Most of the stores were abandoned: diner, convenience store, liquor store. The pizza parlor, off to the right, was the only thing open, next to a hardware store with signs reading FINAL WEEK! Across the lot, two trucks stood in front of an abandoned grocery store. One was labelled OSCORP CHEMICAL.

And on the other side of the wide street, the housing project rose up like a dark leviathan. Whatever happened, Cap knew, the battle had to be kept away from those houses. Too many innocents, too many potential casualties.

"Stark!" Peter Quill marched across the parking lot, arms wide. "What's the matter, huntin' planet-killers too much for you? Decided to call in the big boys?"

"I am Groot," Groot warned.

"Quill, you idiot!" Rocket flew up behind them on his aero-rig. "I didn't call you here to *help* Stark. I called you to *whoooaa what now?*"

Tony Stark's head twitched. His eyes flashed red. Rocket's rig sparked, sputtered, and veered up out of control. He bailed out, leaping off with all four limbs flailing. Groot stretched out a pair of branches and caught him.

The aero-rig swooped up, riderless, and lurched in a jagged course through the air. Cap leaped up, afraid it would hit the pizza parlor; there could be civilians in there. But the rig jerked right at the last minute and crashed through the window of the hardware store.

"Hey!" Rocket wriggled free of Groot's grasp. "My ride!"

Tony turned toward them, raising one glowing palm. Voodoo watched him, but made no other move.

"Stop!" Cap yelled.

Steeling himself, he started across the battlefield toward Tony and Voodoo. Natasha let out a sigh and followed, with Rhodey just behind.

"Hope you've got a plan, Steve," Natasha muttered.

"Working on it," he whispered.

The Avengers and Guardians converged in a cleared area, between the tables. Voodoo watched them advance, but made no move. Tony's head twitched back and forth, turning toward one group, then the other. It was impossible to read his expression through that helmet, but Cap knew he'd got his attention.

"I don't know what this is all about," Cap said, forcing himself to face Tony and Voodoo directly. "But I know one thing: something is controlling you."

Again, anger flashed in Voodoo's eyes.

"You're wastin' your time, Cap," Rocket said. "Stark never listens to nobody."

"Yeah, I don't think he's being controlled," Quill said. "Nothing could get through that tree-stump of a head. No offense, Groot."

"I am Groot," Groot allowed.

"Hey Stark!" Rocket called. "Just curious. When you ruthlessly exploited several hundred immigrant workers, was that *you* doin' it or was someone 'controlling' you?"

Tony's eyes glowed again; he took a step back. Again, Cap wondered: is he listening? Is any of this getting through to him?

"Steve," Natasha hissed. "The plan?"

"It's a waiting game," he replied. "Until your backup gets here …"

A streak of light appeared above the housing project, shooting through the sky over the street. Cap frowned; was it a comet? No – the motion was irregular, unnatural. And within the glow… a human form…

"The Hood," Cap said.

Parker Robbins strode through the air, stepping his way down as if he were descending an invisible staircase in the sky. He leaped over Cap's head and came to rest on the pavement, between Stark and Doctor Voodoo. They made no move to acknowledge his arrival.

"Well. Here we all are." The Hood held a skull rigged up with odd circuitry, glowing with power.

"Where's the woman?" Cap demanded. "The Kree you brought here?"

"Brought her? She brought *me*." The Hood wiped blood from a fresh wound on his cheek. "Didn't work out, though."

"What do you want, Robbins?" Natasha demanded. "And what is that head-shop gizmo in your hand?"

"This?" The Hood held up the brightly glowing skull. "This little marvel is possibly the greatest fusion of science and magic ever constructed on Earth. I don't understand a single microcircuit of it myself, but that's why god gave us IT people. And wizards."

Rhodey held up his remaining weapon-hand. "Shall I take it out?"

"Too risky." Cap held up a hand. "We have no idea how much power is contained in that thing."

"Oh, a lot. A lot of power." The Hood smiled. "All the stored power of that sadly departed world, Prakitus."

"Praeterus." Quill stepped forward, fists clenched. "The planet's name was Praeterus."

The Hood shrugged. "Whatever."

Cap struggled to assess the situation. The skull's glow was too bright to stare at directly. Tony was clearly possessed – or mesmerized, or something. Doctor Voodoo stood very still; every once in a while his face twitched. What was going on with him?

"Listen, creepazoid," Rocket said. "You know we ain't gonna let you just leave with that skull-thing."

"I am Groot. *I am Groot.*"

"Oh, my friends will keep you busy," the Hood replied. "Not forever, but long enough for me to find the tool I need."

"And then?" Cap asked.

The Hood stiffened for a moment. Flames rose up in his eyes, then settled down again. "And then," he said, "the Earth will die."

The air seemed colder, suddenly.

"Huh," Rocket said.

"Yeah, that's a conversation stopper," Quill added.

"Robbins," Cap said, "you're not some galactic warlord or godlike entity. Earth is your home."

The Hood's eyes turned dark. "Earth never did anything for me."

"All the same," Natasha said, "if the world goes splat, won't you die with it?"

"The Master will take care of me."

"You sure about that?"

"No." He shot her a hard glare. "But if not, that's just one less white trash kid from the Bronx."

"That would almost be sad," Rocket observed, "if it wasn't comin' from a sociopath with a mystic weapon burnin' a hole in his hand."

A quinjet roared past overhead, moving at full speed. It braked, executed a sudden turn, and dropped down to land behind the shopping center, out of sight.

"Last chance, boys." Natasha smiled. "If I were you, I'd surrender now."

All eyes turned to a walkway between two abandoned stores, leading to the back parking lot. A slim figure in a light jacket strode out and stopped short, staring at the assemblage of superpowered people.

"Hi, Bruce," Natasha said.

"Hey, I know that dude. That dude's the Hulk!" Quill turned to shake his head at Hood and Voodoo. "Oh, you guys are in for it. You are in for it now."

"You really are," Rocket agreed. "When the Hulk throws down? It's a world of hurt."

Bruce Banner stepped forward. He flashed Natasha a quick glance, then turned to face the Hood. He raised both hands and, slowly, clenched them into fists.

"Backup's here," he said, a dangerous look crossing his face.

Cap took a step back, instinctively, as Banner began to transform. The scientist's fists trembled and his muscles began to swell. An emerald tinge began to creep across his skin.

"A world of hurt," Quill repeated, grinning. "A *world*? Try a whole solar system."

"Yeah! A flarkin' solar system!" Rocket thought for a second. "Maybe a whole Hurt Galaxy?"

"Oh, that's a *whole lot* of hurt right there!"

Then Cap noticed something. The Hood's eyes were wide – but not with fear. He seemed hungry, delighted. Almost giddy with anticipation.

"Oh," the Hood said. "Oh, this is perfect." He raised the glowing skull. "I thought I'd have to find you, but here you are!"

Again, flames filled the Hood's eyes. When he continued, his voice sounded louder, echoing through the night. "ALL MY PLANS FALL INTO PLACE. SOON THIS WORLD WILL FOLLOW PRAETERUS INTO OBLIVION."

That's not Parker Robbins speaking, Cap realized. That's his Master… the unseen force behind all this!

"Let's skip to the fun part," the Hood said. He raised the skull into the air and fired off a burst of energy from its mouth.

Power arced through the night air, lighting up the sky. It struck Banner in mid-transformation, spreading out to cover him in a corona of energy. He shook his head and let out a puzzled growl – half Banner, half Hulk. Then he arched his back and screamed.

Peter Quill snapped his faceplate closed and drew his gun. "What the hell?"

The power continued to flow, blazing from the skull-device into Banner. The Hood cried out in pain and fell to his knees but held on tight to the device. Cap tensed and cast a quick glance at Natasha. Her eyes were wide.

"I am Groot!" Groot cried.

"Yup, just like the psycho said," Rocket stared. "'That's Praeterus, all right. What's left of it, anyway. That's the power the dome-machine was tapping, from the core of the planet."

Banner's scream ranged up and down in pitch, settling into a deep growl. He began to change, to grow larger. Soon he was fully Hulk-sized, the living weapon the Avengers knew so well.

Then he *kept* growing.

"Gamma power," Rocket continued. "Gamma... oh. Oh, flark."

"Come on," Cap said. "Move!"

He ushered Natasha and War Machine away. The Guardians followed, looking back warily. Together they sought shelter against the Guardians' ship, ducking down under one wing.

Stark and Voodoo stood perfectly still, watching the Hood. "Oh," Hood said, grimacing. "Oh, this *does* hurt."

The Hulk's growl became deafening. A thick green aura surged around him, radiating outward. As it passed through the group, one by one the assembled heroes clutched their heads and cried out in pain. Cap felt himself thrown backward; Rhodey struck the hull of the ship with a loud clang. Groot sprouted new shoots to hold his teammates in place.

The power flared brighter. The figure that had been Banner became larger, thicker, more menacing. A metallic gleam sprouted from his shoulder.

The aura struck the shopping center, shattering every window this side of the pizza parlor. Trees flew through the air; lampposts snapped in half and took flight. Fierce winds blew; giant cracks appeared in the pavement.

The Hood let out a cry as the skull in his hands went abruptly dark. He fell to the ground, stunned.

Then the Hood, like everything else, was lost in the green glare. The creature, the thing that had been Banner, was now at least eight feet tall. Spiked armor on his shoulders and legs reflected the blinding energies all around. He held a huge, deadly axe in one hand.

"Oh no," Cap said.

"Uh…" Quill gestured at the figure. "I, um, I don't remember the Hulk looking quite so… metal."

"That's not the Hulk," Natasha said. "Not the one you know, anyway."

"I, uh… I am Groot?"

The green man turned his eyes to the heavens, and let out a roar that shook the Earth.

"That is *Narushitel' mira*," Natasha explained. "The World-Breaker."

# PART SEVEN

## WORLD-BREAKER

# CHAPTER 46

The World-Breaker stood once more on Earth. The planet of his birth; the planet that had felt his most terrible wrath, seen his greatest displays of power and his deepest outpourings of grief. The world, most of all, where he had experienced utter, humiliating defeat at the hands of his enemies.

Some of those enemies had gathered beneath him. The Iron Man; the woman with stinging arms. The man with disk and wings, the Machine of War. Other puny beings stood with them: Space Cowboy, Rat with Hands, Moving Shrub. A pale man with a skull in his hand, and a purple-cloaked Black man who reeked of magic.

The World-Breaker growled, hefting his immense axe. Power surged through him, power tinged with a flavor he'd never tasted before. It fueled his rage, fed his fire like pure oxygen. This, he knew, was his time. His control over this body, over the monster that lived within the human Banner, was now complete.

And at last, his enemies would perish. Even now they skittered and chattered on the ground, glancing up at him with fear. The World-Breaker smiled. Good, he thought. Be afraid. Soon, in your last minutes, you will know what real fear is.

He lifted one foot, relishing the sight of his enemies scattering. Then, for just a moment, he hesitated. Remembered a call for help, the sweet voice of the stinger-woman. A hasty flight in a metal bird, bringing him here for some desperate, forgotten purpose.

He snarled, banishing those thoughts to the graveyard of the past. Then he brought down that massive foot as hard as he could, cracking tar and soil with an impact that shook the world.

In the royal laboratory of Wakanda, alarms blared. Voices crackled over handheld comms; reams of data scrolled down screens. Lights strobed red, signaling the kingdom's highest level of alert.

"Brother," Shuri said, "please silence that alarm? I'm trying to analyze this."

T'Challa, son of T'Chaka, smiled at the request. His sister was the only citizen of Wakanda who thought nothing of issuing orders to the king – even when he wore the ceremonial uniform of the Black Panther, guardian of their people.

He moved to comply, but Okoye, his personal guard, was quicker. "I have it, my king," she said, punching in a code on a wall panel.

T'Challa nodded and crossed the room to join Shuri. She stood over a table with a full-sized monitor built in, her small hands swiping at a hundred overlapping windows.

"Is it a seismic disturbance?" he asked.

"In part," Shuri replied. "ESMC readings are off the charts. But that isn't what bothers me."

He followed her pointing finger to a readout showing a rising red bar.

"Radiation," he said. "Gamma, if I'm not mistaken."

She nodded. "I have seen this pattern before."

T'Challa, too, recognized the arc of the radiation curve. He turned away, shaken. "The World War Hulk incident," he said. "Two years ago. The planet barely survived that attack."

"My king." Okoye stiffened to attention. "Is Wakanda safe? Should I activate the perimeter defenses?"

"If these readings are correct," Shuri said, "I doubt anywhere on Earth is safe."

"And I doubt that sealing off our perimeter will prove effective." T'Challa turned back to the display. "Where is this centered? Is that New York City?"

"I... think so? If not, it's right next door." Shuri shook her head, puzzled. "American geography..."

T'Challa paced away, troubled. Under normal circumstances, his priority was clear: protect Wakanda at all costs. The highly advanced nation, hidden in the depths of Africa, needed its king – and ever since his father's death, T'Challa had borne that burden as best he could.

But if the entire Earth were endangered, that complicated things. T'Challa was also an Avenger, and in that capacity he had fought world-threatening menaces before. Sometimes that required him to leave Wakanda, for the greater good of humanity. In either case, the Avengers might have information he could use.

"Calls are coming in, my king," Okoye said, holding her phone away from her ear. "The United Nations, S.H.I.E.L.D. Something called Starcore Station as well."

"Ignore them," he said. "Please contact Captain America."

She nodded and called up a menu on the phone. T'Challa studied the big monitor, frowned, and changed his mind.

"Belay that," he said. "Get me another number instead."

"Location?"

He reached down to the table and spread two black-gloved fingers apart. The map of New York zoomed out, labels appearing on the various neighborhoods. Shuri gave him a curious glance.

"Greenwich Village," he said.

# CHAPTER 47

Captain America landed in a crouch, his every instinct on high alert. The jarring impact still echoed in his bones, the memory of once-solid earth flinging him up into the air. He took in the state of the pavement first: smashed, torn up, ravaged. A long crack ran under the Guardians' parked ship, tilting it at a dangerous angle.

War Machine groaned, pulling himself upright. Groot wrapped protective branches around Quill and Rocket, who'd taken a nasty bump on his head. Natasha was already up and perched on the ship's wing, studying the emerald monster that had caused this chaos.

The Hulk. The World-Breaker. He stood in the night before an abandoned convenience store, glowing with power like a newly born star. He growled softly, eyes filled with a dull but familiar rage.

Rhodey frowned at the Hulk. "The World-Breaker," he said. "I remember. But he seems different this time... less..."

Natasha leaped off the ship's wing. "Focused?"

"What is this World-Breaker jazz, anyway?" Quill asked. "Sounds like an excuse to sell action figures."

"It's the most dangerous version of the Hulk," Cap explained. "When he first appeared, his adopted world, Sakaar, had just been destroyed. The World-Breaker drew strength from the rage and grief of that event."

Quill furrowed his brow. "So he's still the Hulk... still Bruce Banger..."

"Banner," Natasha growled. *"Ban-ner."*

"...but he's powered by the death of whole planets?"

"I am Groot."

"Yeah." Rocket eyed the Hulk nervously. "He says whatever destroyed Praeterus had plenty of rage to spare."

"That rage comes from Parker Robbins's master." Natasha shook her head. "And it's inside Bruce now."

"He does seem angry," Rhodey observed.

"Anger's pretty much on-brand for the Hulk," Cap said. "Any version."

He scanned the area, searching for other enemies, and spotted the Hood in a far corner of the shopping center. Robbins stood in front of the pizza parlor, holding up the skull-device. Iron Man and Doctor Voodoo stood with him, laying their hands upon the device – which had gone dark, apparently drained of power.

Tony's gauntlets glowed, and a halo of eldritch energy rose from Voodoo's fingers. Cap frowned. What were they doing? Were they charging that skull-thing up again, using the power of that unseen Master? The entity that had engineered the destruction of Praeterus, and now threatened the Earth as well?

The Hulk growled again, lifting his head to glare at the assembled heroes. Cap could feel their eyes on him – Natasha, Rhodey, and the Guardians too, all waiting for him to decide on a course of action. He made a snap decision: the Hood could wait. The Hulk, the immediate threat, must be dealt with first.

Cap gritted his teeth, hissed in a breath, and turned to face the monster. "Bruce!"

The Hulk's eyes narrowed. He lowered the axe and peered at Cap. His lips turned down into a suspicious frown.

"Bruce Banner," Cap said. "You in there, man?"

Then those green lips twisted into a snarl. The Hulk took a single step toward Cap, shaking the ground. He whipped his head up, staring at the street and the housing project beyond.

"Uh-oh," Rhodey said.

The Hulk turned away and spat on the ground. Then he stomped off, moving steadily toward the far end of the mall, where two trucks were parked in front of an abandoned grocery store. With each huge footfall, the tar cracked and the ground shook.

"Uh, what's he doin'?" Rocket asked.

"He's heading for the street. Trying to get around us." Cap raised his shield and moved to intercept. "We've got to stop him – contain him here. The devastation he could cause, in this state, is…"

Natasha fell in next to Cap, wrist-stingers crackling. Rocket followed, staying – Cap noticed – just a bit further back. Quill and Rhodey took to the air, with Groot backing them all up.

Natasha stepped in front of the group. "Easy, big guy," she said, holding up a hand to the Hulk. "You're one of us, remember?"

The Hulk stared down at her. He seemed even larger than before – nine feet tall, at least. Waves of green energy sizzled off him.

"Where did that *axe* come from?" Rocket asked.

"In this form," Cap explained, "the Hulk can grow armaments directly out of his own bones."

"That's just gross," Quill muttered.

Hulk growled at Natasha, then straightened up. He lurched to the side, and Cap moved to block him. The others followed.

"Bruce," Cap said, "this doesn't have to turn into a fight. You know these guys backing us up – War Machine and Star-Lord? They've got a lot of firepower between them."

"That's right, baby." Quill bobbed in the air, spinning his element gun on his finger. "Star-Lord and War Machine!"

"He said 'War Machine and Star-Lord'," Rhodey observed.

"We'll let the agents sort it out."

The Hulk's brow furrowed. He took another step, toward the Oscorp Chemical truck parked in front of the store. Once again, the heroes blocked his path.

With a roar, the Hulk pivoted on his heels, raised the World-Breaker axe, and brought it down on the tank of the chemical truck. The tank exploded, sending a gout of flame shooting skyward. Thick smoke poured up, dark and toxic.

The Hulk turned, crouched down, and let out a hideous scream. The green aura blasted out from him in waves, and again Captain America felt himself lifted up and swept through the air. He reached out and grabbed hold of a lamppost.

The Hulk raised his axe to the heavens and roared again. Quill and Rhodey flailed in the air, blown by the savage winds. The chemical truck burned, filling the air with a foul, charred stench.

"That truck," Cap gasped. "It's deadly. It could poison the whole area. You, Guardians – can you get rid of it? With your spaceship?"

Quill grimaced, watching the truck burn. "Maybe."

"I am Groot," Groot said hesitantly.

"Yeah," Rocket said, touching Groot's nearest branch. "Groot – he can't get near it. The toxic chemicals would kill him."

"Then it's up to you two. Groot, you're with us."

Quill shrugged, swung down, and snatched up Rocket off

the ground. "You think we can do this?"

"I dunno," Rocket replied. "Ship's still a mess. I ain't had time to fix the… what's your name for it?"

"The LET'S GET IT ON circuit?"

"We are so doomed," the raccoonoid muttered. Then they were gone, flying through the dark toward their ship.

"All right," Cap said. "Everybody else, on the Hulk–"

"Steve," Natasha said, pointing off in the distance. "What about them?"

Over by the pizza parlor, the Hood held up the skull-device, which glowed with renewed power. Robbins started back toward the Avengers, with Iron Man and Doctor Voodoo following right behind.

The ground shook again as the Hulk stomped in rage. He stood with fists clenched, a dark silhouette against the smoke rising from the burning truck.

"I think it's gonna take everything we've got to bring Green Giant down," Rhodey said.

"There's no choice," Cap said. "The Hood is still a threat; we'll have to split our forces."

"Maybe not," Natasha said.

She gestured toward the road. Squinting, Cap saw Kir-ra, the blue Kree woman, sprinting toward them, her electric power-rod crackling in the night. And alongside her, emerald legs pumping, was… Gamora?

Kir-ra skidded to a halt, narrowly avoiding a human-sized crack in the pavement. Her face bore a small scar and several bruises. "Are you going to zap me with that stick again?" Cap asked.

"You going to hit me with that?" She gestured at his shield.

"Fair enough." Cap glanced towards the Hood. "Look, I can tell you're a fighter. But the Hood is our responsibility."

"You're wrong," she said. "He's mine."

"You can't take on three powered beings alone," Natasha said.

"She's not alone," Gamora said.

The two women stood together, their faces flickering in the light of the burning truck. Kir-ra held her power-rod high; Gamora's hand rested lightly on her holstered sword. The Guardian's face and arms were blistered with fresh burns, but the determination in her eyes was undeniable.

Natasha eyed them suspiciously. "You two BFFs now?"

Kir-ra glanced at the green woman. "We've, uh…"

"We've come to an understanding," Gamora said.

The ground trembled. The Hulk let out another roar and started their way.

"No more time," Cap said. "Groot, Tasha, Rhodey, we're on Hulk duty. Gamora, if you get in trouble, yell for help."

"From you?" Gamora gestured at his injured arm. Then, before he could take offense, she said, "Come on," and led Kir-ra away, across the parking lot.

Rhodey hovered in the air, watching the Hulk approach. He flexed his exposed hand, where the machine gun had been; then he powered up his weapons. His remaining arm-cannon glowed hot.

"This is gonna hurt," he said. "Isn't it?"

Cap raised his shield. Once again, he remembered the attack of the Red Skull, the reek of oil in the Pittsburgh refinery. The pain of bones cracking under the assault.

The Hulk opened his mouth wide and roared.

"Yeah," Cap said. "It's gonna hurt a lot."

# CHAPTER 48

Rocket stared at the truck. It had been reduced to a seared chassis, but the fire showed no sign of going out. Blue flames formed a halo around the cracked open chemical tank, rising up into a column of thick black smoke.

"Hey," Quill called. "Little help here?"

Rocket turned to see him stumbling down the gangplank from the Guardians' ship. A long, thick metal chain hung around his shoulder, weighing him down.

"Just a sec, buddy," Rocket smirked. "I mean, Captain."

Across the parking lot, Captain America's team had engaged the Hulk. A thick green fist punched somebody down into the tar – Rocket couldn't make out who it was.

He met Quill at the end of the gangplank and took hold of one link of the chain. "You're not liftin' very much," Quill grumbled.

"Hey, I weigh like sixty pounds! Why are these chains wet?"

"That's from when Drax used 'em to drag the ship out of the river." Quill sniffed. "They smell like Long Island."

As they approached the truck, the stench became almost unbearable. Rocket turned to Quill, shrugged, and together they tossed the chain over the flaming vehicle. The links sizzled, the waters of Long Island Sound evaporating with a quick hiss.

"That was pathetic," Quill said. "You've got no arm at all."

"Yeah? Well, you got no brains."

"Oh, great comeback."

"I know, it was weak." He reeled a little. "This smoke is makin' me dizzy."

The fire surged. "What now?" Quill asked, shrinking back from the heat. "How are we gonna tie the chains onto the thing? We can't just stick our hands in there."

"Don't have to. They're smart chains."

"What?"

"Smart chains!" Rocket gestured at the truck. "They tie themselves. See?"

They peered into the fire. As the flames surged again, the chains began to contract against the cylindrical oil tank. They twitched once, then clamped tight with a sharp click.

"Huh," Quill said. "Smart chains."

Rocket took hold of the farthest link and tugged. "Feels solid," he said. "OK, I'll just climb on board and tow 'er into orbit–"

"What?" Quill glared down at him. "What do you mean, you'll tow it? I'm the pilot here."

"You?" Rocket laughed. "You're a terrible pilot. Your night vision bites, and you'll prob'ly die from the fumes before you even get above the–"

"If you say *Kármán Line* I will murder you where you stand."

Rocket paused a moment, then raised both hands in surrender. Quill nodded, said "That's right!" and headed back to the ship. Rocket watched, struggling to keep a straight face, as the Earthman fastened the chain to the ship's aft hook, climbed inside, and bolted the hatch.

He waited until the engines thrummed to life before he burst out laughing.

"Oh," he gasped, "'Oh, please let me tow a toxic chemical mess into orbit!' Hahaha! 'Hey, I'm the pilot around here!' 'Please, please let *me* risk my flarking life trying to keep this red-hot mess from spilling radioactive sewage all over New Jersey!'"

The ship rumbled, tottered, and lifted off. The chain followed it upward, uncoiling slowly as it rose off the pavement. Rocket eyed the ascent, still smirking, and gave Quill a big wave. "Knock yourself out, sucker."

When the chain snapped taut, he scrambled away. The truck groaned, flared, and began to tip on its side as the ship pulled it upward. Suddenly things didn't look too safe down here either.

The sounds of combat reached him from the Hulk-ward side of the parking lot. Something was going on over by the pizza parlor, too. Was the Hood fighting somebody? That looked like... Gamora. Where had she been, anyway?

"Maybe," Rocket mused aloud, "just perhaps, I could be of more use if I was to find and repair my aero-rig. Yeah. That would allow me to, uh, fly! While assisting the others in taking down a group of super-powered lunatics and a possibly hypnotized Avenger with flarking *cannons* built into his hands."

Yes, he thought. Yes, that was both the prudent and the practical course of action, even if it took a little while to accomplish. *Especially* if it took a while.

He set out across the parking lot, giving the Hood's posse a wide berth, wincing at the sight of the flaming truck lurching cabin-first into the sky. He kept to the shadows, moving slowly, carefully – in not a very great hurry at all – toward the hardware store where his rig had crashed.

•••

"Earthman!" Gamora cried, drawing her sword. "Your plan is finished, your evil Master doomed to fail—"

The Hood raised the skull-device and fired off a blast of eldritch energy. Gamora cried out in surprise as the bolt struck her in the stomach, propelling her up into the air. Kir-ra watched as the Guardian sailed across the parking lot, past the spot where Captain America and the others were battling the Hulk, and slammed hard into the side of a garbage truck.

The Hood shook his head, dazed, and studied the skull. It was dark, burned out, its circuitry fused and smoking. He tossed it to the pavement, where it shattered with a crack.

"Magic!" he said. "Powerful stuff."

Kir-ra drew her power-rod, hoping Gamora was still alive. The Guardian had appealed to her back in the apartment, making a strong case for them to work together. *You and I,* Gamora had said, *we both know what it's like to lose everything.*

So they'd agreed to an alliance – and already, with one blow, the Hood had removed Gamora from the equation. Now, shaking his head, he turned to Kir-ra. "I told you not to follow me."

She glanced past him at Stark – who stood upright, stiff and unreadable in the Iron Man armor. The other man, Doctor Voodoo, just stared straight ahead, his face twitching.

That left the Hood. He had powers of his own, she knew, even without the skull-device. But he seemed exhausted, used up, his hands dark with burns from the power he'd absorbed. The wound on his cheek dripped red in the harsh lamplight.

"You know," she said, "you really don't look like much."

He turned sharp eyes to her. They were human now, with no trace of those unearthly flames. But they burned all the same.

"My father used to say that," he hissed. "Before he dragged me into the cellar for a beating."

"Am I supposed to feel sorry for you?" She stared at him, aghast. "You murdered my friends, used me against my family. You destroyed my world!"

"Me? I've never been off this planet. It was your beloved grandmother who trashed the old Kree homestead."

"There's no difference." She glared at him, thumbed her power-rod to life. "You've all got that thing inside you."

"Yeah, but it works in different ways. Grandma and me, we made a willing deal with the Master. The industrialist here didn't have that choice…though he's a card-carrying member of the gang now. And our expert in Haitian mysticism – well, he's complicated."

A deafening roar filled the air: the Hulk, raging again. Kir-ra flinched, but didn't turn to look. She didn't dare take her eyes off the Hood.

"And now our work is done," he continued. "The Hulk will crack this world in half, just as dear old Grandma lit the fuse that ignited hers. The Master prefers to use locals to do his dirty work… the irony is almost as sweet as the pain, he says."

"And then what?" she asked. "More worlds, more death, more destruction? Planet after planet, one after another, across the universe?"

"OH NO, CHILD."

She started, took a step back. The flames filled his eyes now, and the voice was not his own.

"THEN COMES THE INVASION."

Flame spat from his mouth, dark and magical. She flinched away as it engulfed her, burning her skin. She staggered backward and fell to the pavement, her power-rod rolling away.

When she looked up, the Hood was staring down at her. The flame was gone, as if purged from his system. His eyes looked almost sad.

"So long, dancer," he said.

Then he turned to Iron Man. "Kill her, OK?" And before she could climb to her feet, he was walking up into the air, mounting that invisible stairway to vanish in the darkness.

She struggled to rise, desperate to pursue him. But she'd barely pushed herself up to her knees when Iron Man appeared to block her way. He moved awkwardly, his servos whining in protest. Both the man and the suit, she knew, were damaged.

"Stark," she said.

His eye-lenses pulsed, glowing bright. He raised an arm and fired; she rolled aside, wincing as his repulsor-beam blasted a hole in the pavement. She glanced across the pavement at her power-rod: too far away.

"Stop it!" she cried, tumbling to her feet.

He fired again – once, twice. She danced aside, easily dodging the blasts.

"Sloppy aim, Stark," she said. "You're not really trying to kill me, are you?"

The next blast came much closer.

"Well, maybe part of you is." She shook her hand in the air, feeling the heat of the near-miss on her fingers. "But I think you're fighting the influence of this… this Master. Whatever it is."

She shifted side to side like a boxer, waiting for an opening. When it came, she dropped to a crouch, rolled past an uprooted stone table, and snatched up her power-rod in both hands. Stark's head jerked, his eye-lenses following her movements.

"OK. OK, listen to me." She backed away, holding up the rod. "I don't know what's going on inside that helmet. I don't know what *usually* goes on in your head! But…"

He raised a hand, glowing with power – then lowered it again. His body went stiff again, the glow fading from his eye-lenses.

Hands trembling, she lowered the power-rod. This was crazy, she knew. In that armor, he could vaporize her with a single blast. And she had no reason, no rational basis for trusting this man. At best, he'd been criminally negligent in his treatment of her people; at worst, he had systematically victimized and preyed on them.

But she'd spoken with Stark, looked into his eyes. And if the Kree were to survive here on Earth – assuming there was an Earth left after this! – then maybe someone had to take a chance. A first tentative step onto a new path.

"Stark," she said. "Do you remember what you said to me? Out on the dock?"

She dropped the rod, let it clatter again to the ground. His blank lenses followed it as it bounced once, twice.

"Whatever is happening," she said, "it ends today. I swear it."

# CHAPTER 49

Gamora landed hard against the garbage truck, bashing a two-foot dent in the door. She struggled, sprang free, and landed on her feet, then reeled briefly.

She'd been hit on the head a lot lately. That, she vowed, was over.

She looked around, getting her bearings. The truck stood parked in front of the abandoned grocery store with the caved-in roof. Straight ahead, the Hulk stood ten feet tall, glowing with radiant power.

Captain America and Natasha faced off against the Hulk, standing at different levels on top of... something. Gamora squinted and made out a network of wooden trunks and vines, forming a multileveled platform. She smiled; Groot had pulled this trick before. At the siege of Fortus Prime, he'd formed himself into an entire organic fortress for the Guardians' grueling, two-day assault. Now he was providing the same support for the Avengers.

War Machine swooped around in the air, squeezing off shots like a biplane buzzing King Kong. He swung in close and managed to land a bullet on the Hulk's face, just below that massive eye. The Hulk raged, growled, and swept a hand through the air. Rhodey jetted upward just in time, but the air current knocked him off balance, sending him tumbling off through the night sky.

The Hulk roared in frustration, raising both fists. The green aura, the blazing power, fanned out from his gigantic armored form, blasting the outer wall of the grocery store. In that power, that rage, Gamora saw the same energies that had destroyed Praeterus. She saw the face of the little girl, lost in the fire, and she knew her quest was not over. Not as long as that rage remained loose in the universe.

She had to stop it from consuming another world.

Natasha called out a few words to Groot. He stretched out a thick plank of a branch; she leaped onto it and took off, sprinting toward the Hulk. Cap yelled out a warning, gesturing for her to stay back. She ignored him and charged, both stingers firing.

The Hulk barely turned to look. He let out a roar and reached out, grabbing the Groot-plank in both hands. Then, planting his legs firmly on the pavement, he thrust his arms out to either side, ripping the entire platform apart.

Groot screamed. Natasha flew into the air. Cap tumbled in the opposite direction, landing on the ground with a hard thud.

The Hulk raised his head, eyes glowing, and stared at the housing project across the street. Oh no, Gamora thought. He's going to flatten that place, kill hundreds of people. Then he'll move on to the next building, and the next, and...

A figure caught her eye, moving along the row of stores. A kid, no more than fourteen, had emerged from the pizza parlor and stopped short, watching with terrified eyes. He wore an apron stained with tomato sauce and a hat with a picture of a stylized chef throwing a pizza pie up into the air.

He works there, Gamora realized. Poor kid's probably been hiding out inside while we turned his parking lot into a battle zone!

The Hulk turned slowly, leaned down to stare at the kid, and let out a fearsome growl. Gamora watched with mounting horror. She had no idea what this version of the Hulk was capable of. Would he actually murder a teenager in cold blood? She couldn't afford to find out.

She drew her sword and ran, screaming and howling like a madwoman. At first the Hulk just furrowed his brow, as if an insect were buzzing in his ear. Then he turned toward her.

The boy blinked, dropped his fries, and ran off.

Mission accomplished, she thought, as a huge shadow moved to cover her.

The Hulk picked her up in both hands, squeezing her tight. He brought her up to his face and roared again, a foul wind that buffeted her like a hurricane. She struggled for something to say – something soothing that might calm him, make him loosen his grip–

"I will toast your rotting carcass!" she gasped.

Oh, well.

The Hulk growled in fury, clenching his fists tighter. His grip was like a vise; the power radiating out from him was almost inconceivable. He seemed overwhelmed by that power, lost in its fire, as much its victim as its master.

Gamora scanned the area, searching for help. Groot lay sprawled on the ground, gathering his remaining branches back into himself. Natasha was crawling away from the battle site, dragging Cap's limp form along with her. War Machine lay stunned, shaking his head.

Across the parking lot, Tony Stark's repulsor rays flashed once, twice. Kir-ra! she thought, her heart sinking. Another person she'd failed–

The Hulk squeezed again. One more would finish her. She squirmed, wriggled her hand. Her sword arm was pressed against her leg, but if she could work it free–

Then she heard the wheeze and clatter of an engine. She looked up, turning along with the Hulk to peer over the roof of the shopping center. This wasn't just any engine, she realized. A modified long-range hyperspace converter... probably an old one, from the sound of it, and in bad need of tachyon calibration...

A starship soared into view – a Denebian luxury yacht, garish with its sleek lines and ornamental fins. With a shock, Gamora recognized it: one of the Praeteran evacuation vessels, the ships that had brought the Kree to Earth.

The Hulk shook his fist, roaring.

The ship swooped down and paused in midair to hover above the grocery store. My-ronn, the Kree worker, stuck his head out of a hatch. A phalanx of Kree workers, in full battle armor, appeared alongside him. They braced themselves, poised to leap.

"You called it, Horse!" My-ronn cried. "It's him!"

Drax the Destroyer pushed past them and jumped into the air. "HULK!" he cried, pointing his knives down. "SMASH!"

The Kree let out a battle cry and followed him down. They landed on the Hulk's shoulders, his head, his arms, slashing with knives and firing proton guns. He screamed and flexed, throwing them off as fast as they arrived.

Gamora wriggled free of the Hulk's grip; Drax leaped down to meet her. She gasped for breath, nodding in gratitude. As the Hulk set her down on the pavement, she said, "Hulk smash?"

He smiled and crouched low, preparing to leap up and join the battle.

"I have always wanted to say that," he said.

Jericho Drumm watched the raging conflict play out in the air above his brittle cage. The Hulk's power lit up the night, glowing like the herald of some unearthly invader.

Which, Jericho knew, was exactly what it was.

*Brother,* he pleaded. *Even you must see this has gone too far!*

Daniel did not reply. He'd been silent for several minutes, during which time their shared body had not moved a muscle in the outside world. The Hood had fled the scene, and Tony Stark stood sparring with the Kree woman.

Jericho clenched his fists in frustration, rattling the bones of his cage. Outside, the newly arrived Kree descended on the Hulk like a swarm of insects. The Hulk swept both arms around, scattering them across the pavement.

Jericho rose to his feet. *Brother!*

The Hulk howled again. But this time, something was different; the aura around him surged again, then flickered and faded away. Jericho peered at the image – and all at once he knew.

*You're doing something,* he said, *aren't you? You've erected some sort of mystic barrier around the Hulk. You're containing one aspect of his power – the gamma radiation – so it doesn't kill anyone.*

Still Daniel said nothing. But as Jericho stood within his prison, a shimmering appeared around his outstretched hand. A rough-hewn wooden staff formed, firm and warm in his grip.

The Staff of Legba. Or, at least, its mental equivalent. That meant he was on the right path, that the powers of voodoo had not forsaken him.

It meant something else, too: he was right about his brother.

Daniel hadn't fully abandoned all the principles by which he'd lived. Even when that life was long over, and the prospect of ending his half-life had proved too tempting a prize to resist.

But Daniel hadn't abandoned his Master, either. Not yet. And until he did, this battle – this atrocity, this rampage of planetary destruction – would not end.

Jericho paused, marshaling his strength. *Listen, brother,* he began. *Please listen. For both our sakes... for the future of our souls. For the gros bon ange we share, and the ti bon ange that is unique to every man and woman.*

*There is an order to the world...*

Kir-ra was so startled by the arrival of the evacuation ship, she almost missed the red-and-gold fist flying toward her. She ducked, avoiding Stark's blow by less than an inch.

He paused, quivering, and stared at his hand. *He's still not really trying,* she thought. That gave her an opening – one that wouldn't last forever.

"You said you'd help them!" she cried.

He froze. Turned glowing eyes to stare at her.

"My people," she explained. "You made me a promise, remember?" She gestured at the Hulk and at the dozen or more Kree swarming over him. "Are you going to keep that promise? Or are you just *lost* inside that shell?"

He flexed his metallic joints. For a moment, she thought he was going to attack her again. Then the helmet retracted to reveal his blank-eyed, staring face.

"Lost," he said, so quietly she almost missed it.

"I know," she said. "Whatever that thing is, inside you... it feeds on your own despair, doesn't it? It preyed on my grandmother, on her grief and resentment. Made her do terrible things."

"Can't fight it," he gasped. "Can't keep it all together."

"I know. It's hard. I've made mistakes too." She blinked, turned away. "I brought a killer into my house, let him use me against my family. I endangered the people I love most."

Green energy flared in the night. In the distance, she could see the battle raging against the Hulk. Her own people, fighting a last desperate stand alongside the heroes of Earth.

"My world is gone. My Grandpa is dead. My war was over before I ever got to fight it." She forced herself to face Stark directly. "But I'm trying. I'm trying to make things better. That's what we do, right? That's what people do."

His cheek twitched. He staggered back against a stone table. Now she could see the pain, the struggle in his eyes.

This is it, she thought. The final appeal.

"Help me fix this," she said. "Please."

# CHAPTER 50

Rocket whizzed out of the hardware store on his aero-rig, heading straight for the Hulk. Drax clung to the monster's back, pummeling him with blow after blow. And approaching from the other direction—

"That's it, big guy," Rhodey called, guns blasting. "Hold him still!"

The Hulk lurched to the side, hurling Drax into the air, and pointed his metal shoulder-guard at the approaching War Machine. Bullets spanged off the World-Breaker armor, bouncing back toward Rhodey. He twisted in midair, but a few shots struck his steel-plated torso.

Rocket waited for the fire to die down, then boosted the aero-rig to full power. "Heads up," he cried. "Comin' in hot!"

The Hulk turned to look, growling in surprise at the furry creature flying toward him. He took a giant step backward, crashing into the battered wall of the grocery store. He coughed and staggered into the store, reaching up to sweep the last shards of ceiling aside.

That's it, dumbass, Rocket thought. Just stay off balance for one more minute…

He reached down, fumbled with a hastily rigged catapult harness, and fired off a dozen Insta-Light Logs. The Hulk watched, baffled, as logs landed all around him inside the store, settling down onto chunks of collapsed ceiling and deserted grocery aisles. He caught a log out of the air and held it up, staring at it like a child with a strange toy.

Rocket thumbed a switch on: a stripped-down lawnmower engine, strapped to the bottom of his rig. The engine rattled to life. When he reached the store, he kicked in the leaf blowers, letting loose a rainfall of lighter fluid straight down on the Hulk.

Then he dropped a single match and waited. Such a well-equipped hardware store, he thought. Too bad they're closing down! Well, that's late capitalism for you–

The logs went up all at once, surrounding the Hulk with fire.

"Like I said," Rocket said, smirking. "Hot!"

Drax charged the store, laughing, and leaped on the Hulk's back again, ignoring the flames. Rhodey swooped down and fired off another volley of shots.

The Kree starship had retreated upward. The Kree themselves formed a perimeter on the wall of the neighboring store, lying on their stomachs and squeezing off shots at the Hulk. When Natasha joined them, My-ronn gave her a welcoming high-five. She picked up a proton rifle and joined the firing line.

Groot stayed at a distance from the fire, generating hard fruits and flinging them at the Hulk. Gamora circled the battle, swords drawn. Waiting for her chance.

When the lighter fluid ran dry, Rocket boosted his aero-rig to full power again. As he swooped around the Hulk, for just a moment he saw hurt and confusion in those emerald eyes. It's not his fault, Rocket realized. He didn't ask for any of this. Not the Kree, not the power of Praeterus, not the platoon of heroes arrayed against him. He didn't even ask to become the *Hulk*…

In an instant, hurt turned to rage. The Hulk reached back, grabbed Drax, and pounded him – a terrible blow at close range. The Destroyer gasped as he hurtled over the wall of the grocery store. The Hulk stomped out of the store, batting out flames with his massive hands. He looked up at Rocket, then at War Machine, and he growled.

Then he seized hold of the garbage truck with both hands, hefted it, and flung it into the air. Rocket veered aside, but it caught his rig a glancing blow, sending him spinning out of control. Rhodey took the full impact. The truck slammed into him with a sickening crunch.

Rocket clattered down to a shaky landing. Groot hurried up to him, concerned. "I'm OK, I'm OK," he said.

"I am Groot…"

"Yeah, the lawnmower's totaled."

On the roof, the Kree continued firing. The Hulk turned toward them and roared again, green energy flaring. The Kree cried out, clutching their heads.

"I am Groot?"

"I dunno," Rocket replied, grimacing. "But it's gonna take a lot more than a home improvement spree to stop that guy."

Jericho forced himself to ignore the cries, the impacts, the flaring energy of the World-Breaker. The true battle was inside this cage of bones. The battle for Daniel's soul, for his good angel.

*… an order to the world,* Jericho repeated, *one that cannot be violated. Not by you or I, no matter how powerful we may dream*

ourselves to be. Certainly not by your Master, who is not of this world at all.

Still Daniel was silent. But the walls of the prison seemed to waver, the bones shimmering from milk-white to clear and back again.

*That order… that balance… we are strongest in it when we work together. Then we are our best selves, our finest angels. Then may all sins be redeemed, all bad works made good.*

*Join me, brother. Walk the path that leads you home. Let us wield the gris-gris in concert, as we were trained to do. As we were meant to do.*

Again, the bones shimmered. Jericho heard a sob and whirled around. In the center of the cage, Daniel crouched down, head in his hands.

*Forgive me, brother.* Daniel looked up, his eyes full of anguish. *I had to see it. Had to see the monster before I understood…*

Jericho frowned. He was not free to leave; the cage had not vanished. Images of battle still filled the air: Black Widow dazed on the ground, Groot making a fierce assault against the raging Hulk. Jericho studied his brother, sobbing on the floor. Was this some sort of trick?

No matter. Nothing in the world mattered more than Daniel. If saving him meant falling into another trap, Jericho would gladly brave the danger.

*Brother,* he said. *Take my hand…*

The air turned thick; the bones flared scarlet. The images all around vanished, replaced by a dozen views of the same visage: a head on fire, with eyes as white as chalk. A demonic vision from beyond this plane of existence.

The Master.

Daniel let out a cry of terror. Jericho held up his staff and, with his other hand, reached out to grasp his brother's shoulder. He did not have his equipment, his thread and candles and graveyard soil, here in this inner space. All he had was his will.

*Papa Legba*, he chanted. *Open the gate, open the gate. Protect this place from all intruders. Banish the evil from this house—*

LITTLE MAN OF HERBS AND WAX. The Master laughed, his white eyes focusing on Jericho. I AM NOT HERE FOR YOU. NOT YET.

Then those eyes turned to his brother. *No*, Daniel said. *No, please!*

*Stand away*, Jericho warned. *Papa Legba, Papa Legba—*

HE OFFERED HIS SOUL, the flaming vision said. NO GOD OF YOURS MAY KEEP ME FROM HIM.

Daniel let out a plaintive cry, his eyes wide in their sockets. Then he crumbled inward, dissolved into mist, and vanished.

Jericho winced, disoriented, as the outside world flooded in. The Master was gone too, and so was his cage; Jericho sat on a cold stone bench, alone in the New Jersey night. Half a football field away, the Hulk flared bright, battling the combined forces of the Kree, the Guardians, and the Avengers.

He was free again, in his own body – the body of Doctor Voodoo. A body he now occupied alone. There was no trace of Daniel, his thoughts or his spirit-form.

*Brother*, he vowed, *I will find you. Whatever you've done, wherever it takes me. I will find you and lead you home.*

He felt a moment of loneliness, a cold shiver of self-pity. Then he gathered his cloak around him and strode off toward the light.

Captain America lay on the hard pavement, bracing himself with his good arm. Stars swam before his eyes. Come on, soldier, he thought. Get it together. Get up!

The sounds of fighting, of gunfire, surrounded him. His shield lay discarded on the ground; without thinking, he reached out for it with his injured arm. He unbent the arm slowly, stretching the cast. The arm didn't hurt at all – not even a twinge.

I'm healed, he thought. Finally!

Rolling on his side, he closed his fingers into a fist and flexed his bicep. The cast ripped open, falling aside. He paused for a moment, gathering his strength–

"Want a hand?"

Tony Stark stood in the light of a streetlamp still wearing his armor, but with his face exposed. Cap scuttled away, unsure.

"It's OK, I'm me again. For better or worse." Tony pointed a thumb behind him. "Had a little help."

The Kree woman, Kir-ra, stood watching warily. She held her combat rod, poised and ready for action.

"I'm only as good as my employees," Tony continued. "What am I saying? I'm nowhere near as good as my employees."

Cap grimaced and held out his hand – the one that had been in a cast, just seconds ago. Tony grasped it firmly and pulled him to his feet.

"Back in action," Tony said. "You and me."

"Looks that way," Cap said.

"You ready to do this? Do some Avenging?"

"I think so. Yeah." Cap smiled. "I think I'm whole again."

"Not me. But I'm getting there."

Cap turned to stare at the battle raging in front of the grocery store. The Guardians and the Kree were keeping the Hulk at bay, with a little airborne help from War Machine. But it was a stalemate at best.

"Sooner or later," Cap said, "he's gonna get away from us."

"Yeah." Tony shook his head. "We really made a mess of things this time."

Cap frowned at him. "'We'?"

Kir-ra raised an eyebrow at Tony. "You *are* the one who brought a planet-killer here."

"Hey, Tasha called for the Hulk! OK, OK, beside the point." Tony paused, thinking. "My armor's barely at half charge. I can raise a few green bruises, maybe draw some blood here and there, but I'm never gonna bring him down. We need something else."

A violet cloak seemed to waft out of the darkness. "Perhaps," Doctor Voodoo said, "this 'something else' is already within us."

Cap took up his shield. "Jericho Drumm," he said. "You been deprogrammed too?"

"Or are you just the spooky side of our giant-sized gamma-ray problem?" Tony asked.

"I was never programmed," Voodoo said, "merely held captive. But I have escaped my prison, and I believe I can help."

"He's telling the truth," Kir-ra frowned. "I think."

"I'm not sure who to trust anymore," Cap said, keeping his shield raised. "But if you've got an idea, Jericho, well, bring it on."

"It will require considerable sacrifice from myself and Mister Stark," Voodoo replied. "We must confront the evil behind this, head-on. The experience will not be pleasant."

Tony laughed.

Cap lowered his shield, staring at him in shock. "You think this is funny?"

That elicited a fresh burst of laughter from Tony. Kir-ra and Voodoo exchanged worried glances. "I'm sorry," Tony said, letting out a last giggle. "It's just... 'not pleasant'?"

He looked up just as the Hulk let out an earth-shaking roar. An enormous green fist slammed into Drax the Destroyer, sending him flying across the parking lot.

"What could be worse than this?" Tony asked.

# CHAPTER 51

A trio of police cars screamed up, lights flashing blue and red in the night. They veered into the shopping center, fanning out around the parking lot. Six doors opened at once, officers dropping low as they drew their guns.

"I got this," Captain America said.

"Keep them away," Tony said.

Cap trotted off toward the cops. One arm clutched his shield tight, the other was raised high to greet them. He's back, Tony thought. Healed, whole, and ready to save the day.

I hope I am, too.

He watched in alarm as the remaining façade of the grocery store collapsed with a thunderous crash. The Hulk swept the rubble aside, growling, and started toward the street. The Guardians had already reunited, in the parking lot, to form a barricade against him. Drax stood in front, fists clenched, with Groot and Gamora just behind. Rocket circled in the air, backing them up.

On the adjoining roof, Drax's Kree friends had blockaded themselves behind a pile of rubble. They popped their heads up in an irregular rhythm, squeezing off shot after shot. Tony caught sight of Natasha among them, firing her electrical blasts.

But nothing stopped the Hulk. His green-glowing eyes lit briefly on the cluster of police cars, and a snarl rose from his lips. Then he turned his attention to the housing project across the street and began to stomp toward it.

"Have you made the necessary adjustments?" Doctor Voodoo asked, startling Tony.

"Oh! I think so." He looked down at his chestplate, which was exposed to reveal a maze of circuits. He fitted a last connection into place and closed the cover. "Assuming I know what I'm doing. Mixing tech and magic always makes me reach for the anxiety meds."

"Papa Legba will guide us," Voodoo said, holding up his staff. "Assuming *I* know what I'm doing."

"Is that supposed to be reassuring?"

"Well," Voodoo replied, "I am your Director of Diabolism and Parapsychology."

Tony smiled.

"Remember," Voodoo added, "the process will involve great pain, on both a physical and spiritual level. We must not waver, not stop for a moment, if we wish to accomplish our task."

"Let's do it." He took a deep breath. "Let's make this right."

Kir-ra ran up, out of breath. "The… piz-za parlor?… has been evacuated." She turned to Tony. "What else can I do?"

"Just get to a safe distance and wait. In case I, you know, explode or something."

She nodded, eyes wide, and touched his shoulder for a moment. Then she backed away.

The Hulk took a gigantic step. The ground shook, pavement crumbling to powder under his foot. The World-Breaker raised his axe and roared to the world.

"It must be now," Voodoo said.

"Spaceman," Tony hissed into his suit-radio. "You in position?"

"Oh yeah."

With a shaky, rattling roar, the Guardians' ship came screaming down out of the sky. Its front-mounted cannon began to glow, strobing from yellow to orange to red-hot.

"Heads up," Peter Quill cried. "Here comes the BIG BUTT BEAM!"

The ship swung low, executing a wrenching turn in midair. The beam lanced out, striking the Hulk straight in the chest. He cried out in rage and pain.

"Yeah, OK," Rocket said, his voice filtered over the comms. "That *is* a better name."

With a mental command, Tony closed his helmet. He blinked in a precise pattern, issuing a complex series of orders to his armor. Gamma rays, radiating outward from the Hulk, appeared in a schematic before his eyes. He flinched at the levels: eight megaelectronvolts... nine, and climbing...

"Do not be distracted by the science," Doctor Voodoo said. "You must reach deep inside. Recall the feel of his evil, the stench of his presence. Part of it is still with you; part of it will always be with you."

He's right, Tony realized. The extradimensional entity that had worked its will through the Hood, that had given Doctor Voodoo's brother such power – a chunk of it still lingered. A terrible, squirming creature in the corner of his mind, a mewling thing that he could not bring himself to look upon.

"Yet you must," Voodoo said, as if reading his mind. "Just as I must confront it. The devil that stole my brother from me and perverted the arts to which I have devoted my life."

Grimacing inwardly, Tony forced himself to look. The creature was not a creature; it was a stench, a stain, a hole chipped into the armor of his mind. A void that had already existed, filled now with the remnant of this almost viral invader.

The thing's presence, its foul nature, reminded him of his recent failures. The ambush in the Manhattan office; the trashing of the Long Island facility. His employees, hypnotized and murdered. His own lack of leadership, which had allowed the Kree to be mistreated and abused.

Pepper.

As despair washed over him, he caught a quick glimpse of Jericho Drumm's thoughts. An image of bones, of children playing. A man crumbling to dust.

"Do not look away," Drumm's voice quavered. "Know it for what it is."

The not-creature, the cancer in his mind, began to burn. Harsh flames, black and terrible, strobing up and down like curtains. He forced himself to watch, renewing the commands to his armor. Searching for the right frequency...

Outside, the Hulk took another step. He swatted Rocket out of the sky, then let out a roar that shook the air itself.

"There," Voodoo said. "Do you see it?"

All at once, he did. It was the fire that had consumed Praeterus, the otherworldly spark that had ignited the planet's core. The trigger that could unleash near-infinite energies.

"Now," Voodoo said, holding out the Staff of Legba. "Take hold."

Grimacing, Tony closed his hand over the wooden staff. An irresistible pull took hold of him, a hypermagnetic attraction. He raised his arm and aimed the receptors in his glove at the source of that power, at the techno-mystic energies that threatened to destroy the Earth.

At the Hulk.

Power surged into Tony's armor, flowing through his receptors, filling his batteries. Radiation, infused with eerie mystical energies – pouring in, hot and fast, overloading and spilling over into his reserve cells. Ten megaelectronvolts. Eleven. Thirteen…

A chorus of alarms sounded in his ears. The armor began to heat up; sparks broke out along the servos, in the reactor conduits and air circulation pipes. He dropped to his knees, sweat rising within his helmet.

"Can't… hold it," he gasped.

The Hulk turned in surprise, watching the fiery energy flow from his own chest down to the gleaming man on the ground. He raised an enormous hand, trying to stop the flow, then howled in pain as the energy scorched his tough skin.

"Keep going," Voodoo said. His voice sounded distant.

Tony issued mental commands, venting heat manually, tamping out microfires as fast as they broke out. But it was too much. "I can't do it," he gasped.

"You must."

"This one suit of armor…" The repulsor on his left hand burst into flame. "It wasn't built to hold the stored energy of a planet!"

"How 'bout two suits of armor?"

Through his pain, he registered James Rhodes's presence beside him. "You sure you're up for this?"

"Well…" Rhodey held up his damaged weapon-arm. "I'd feel better if I had my machine gun."

"Yeah, that one's on me." Tony blinked out a rapid-fire series of technical commands. "Most of the radiation is gamma," he said. "Your receptors open?"

Rhodey nodded.

They clasped hands, repulsor barrels touching in a spark of

eldritch energy. Immediately Tony felt the power ease – flowing into Rhodey's suit, into the War Machine armor. Twelve MeV... eleven...

"Tony," Rhodey said. "I don't... don't think I can..."

"Just hold on," Tony replied.

He slumped down against a lamppost, running a quick survey of his own armor's systems. The radiation levels had dropped, but they were still hovering way above critical. He could barely see. A dozen tiny fires still raged across his suit. Reluctantly he snapped open his helmet, gasping for air.

"Armor's already damaged," Rhodey said. "Containment circuits failing..."

"Doc?" Tony called. "Doc, are we doing it?"

Voodoo's voice was faint. "Yes," he said, "but you must continue. At least two-thirds of the energy still resides within the World-Breaker."

The Hulk stared down at the stream of power draining out of him – the shimmering energy that threatened to light up the two Iron Men like candles. He seemed baffled, puzzled by it all. By the power that could destroy this world.

"Tony," Rhodey said. "Tony, I'm overloading!"

Two-thirds of the energy, Tony thought. That means twice as much yet to come. Numbers danced before his eyes. The radiation was rising again. Rhodey's armor was already sparking, overheating.

I've failed again, he thought. Failed the entire world, this time. We can't handle this much power. We're not going to make it....

# CHAPTER 52

The Hulk stood, power surging from every pore of his emerald body, staring down at the metal men drawing that power slowly out of him. He raised his head to the sky and howled.

Kir-ra crouched on top of a lamppost, watching from a distance. With her Sen-Zha training, she *felt* that howl. She sensed the Hulk's confusion, his rage – and in that rage, she felt her world die all over again.

He's in agony, she realized, somewhere deep inside. He came here to help his friends, and now it's all gone wrong. The savior has become the destroyer.

She cast her awareness wide, piercing the darkness. She saw the police cars waiting silently along the edge of the parking lot. Captain America and the Black Widow sprinting toward the road, working with Groot and Gamora to block the Hulk's escape.

Drax had doubled back toward the grocery store and was leading his Kree friends in a wide circle around the monster, planning some sort of sneak attack. Rocket crouched down against a stone bench, reloading a contraption on his flying device. Up above, the Guardians' ship was beginning another descent toward the battle scene, with Peter Quill at the helm.

Kir-ra turned to look down. On the pavement, not far away, Iron Man and War Machine writhed and sparked. Stark's eyes gaped wide, his armor glowing bright as energy from the Hulk surged into it. Rhodey's suit was charred and dented, little fires breaking out in the joints and along the jagged edges where his machine gun had been. Doctor Voodoo sat cross-legged on the ground, his staff held horizontally to touch both men's armor. He was glowing too, his mouth open in a soundless scream.

They're doomed, she knew. All that power will light them up like a torch.

She gripped her power-rod tight, feeling it crackle to life. Was this finally her chance? The war for which she'd been trained – the battle that had eluded her, all her life?

The Hulk took a half step away, then stopped. He seemed trapped, held in place, as if leashed by the energy stream flowing out of him. His metal shoulder-plate clanked as he leaned down to glare at a familiar suit of armor.

"STARRRK," he growled.

In a single motion, he reached down, grabbed hold of a lamppost, and yanked it out of the ground. Wires sparked, shards of metal snapped free. Snarling, he grabbed up another lamppost, and another.

Then he tossed them at Tony Stark.

Kir-ra leaped, acting purely on instinct. She swung the rod, intercepting the first of the lampposts with a sizzling impact. The post flew aside just as her shoulder slammed into the second one. She gasped and tumbled to the ground.

The third lamppost slashed past her. No! she thought. Not fast enough–

A thin repulsor beam lanced out from Stark's upturned palm. The lamppost sizzled, melted in half, and clattered to the ground.

She whipped her head around, astonished. Stark was still staring straight up, his face twitching. She crept in close, squinting through the glow of energy. His eyes flickered over to her, the vaguest hint of a smile teasing at his lips.

"M- Multitasking," he said.

A deafening roar filled the air. She turned to see the Hulk glowing, brighter than ever. Clenching his fist, rearing back to bring that axe down on his tormentors. And on her.

"Attack!" Captain America screamed.

The Hulk whirled to face the renewed onslaught. Cap led the charge, leaping up to smash his shield into the Hulk's face – taking care, Kir-ra noticed, to avoid the blazing energy flow. Gamora followed, jumping and slashing, her sheer ferocity startling the Hulk, forcing him back. Groot grabbed hold of the monster's limbs in thick corded vines; Natasha jabbed out with her stingers, one after the other, in rapid succession.

Quill's spaceship shot down out of the clouds, veering around hard to meet the Hulk head-on. Cap ducked away as Quill fired off that red-hot energy beam again. The Hulk cried out and stumbled back, away from Stark and the others.

"Be careful!" Cap called. "Don't let the power stream touch you!"

Drax yelled a few words in Kree, and his friends leaped onto the Hulk, guns blazing. The Hulk reared and roared, throwing them off. Rocket whizzed around in circles above the monster, pelting him with something that looked like patio tiling. Even the cops got in a few shots, but their bullets couldn't penetrate the Hulk's tough hide.

Kir-ra thumbed her power-rod to life again. This is it, she thought. This is why I'm here. All her instincts screamed at her to leap into the fray – to join the fight–

–but her intellect told her something different. The Hulk faced a massive, powerful attack force: Avengers, Guardians of the Galaxy, Kree warriors, and Terran law officers. Among them, those heroes had defeated everything from common purse-snatchers to galactic-scale threats. Now all that power, all their combined might, had come together to fight a single enemy, a gamma-charged monster powered by the energies of a destroyed world.

And the monster was winning.

She took a step back, flinching as the Hulk tossed Captain America aside like a doll. What more could a single warrior add to that fighting force? Especially one like herself, trained primarily in passive fighting arts?

Rocket dipped a little too close to the power stream, and let out a yowl as it singed his fur. The stream continued to flow from the Hulk down to Stark and War Machine, who lay in a single, blinding pool of energy. Smoke rose from the two suits of armor. Doctor Voodoo lay next to them on the pavement, eyes closed, his hands twitching around his staff.

OK, she thought. Maybe one more fighter couldn't make a difference. But her training had other uses.

She closed her eyes, casting her senses outward once again. Blocked out the bone-thudding impacts, the cries of pain, the searing energies that threatened to tear this world apart. Blocked out, too, the rage and anguish of the Hulk, the desperate fear and courage of Earth's defenders as they made their last stand.

And all at once she knew: there's something else. Some*one* else. Someone who might still turn the tide.

The Hulk roared to the heavens. He reached out, tossing Groot and Natasha away, and scooped up the back half of the broken garbage truck. When he swung it into the path of the energy flow, the truck burst into flame.

Again, her instincts screamed: fight! But she knew that wasn't the answer. She knew, now, what she had to do.

She took one last look at Stark and the others, lying bathed in the power that would soon kill them. Then she leaped over them and ran, sprinting across the road toward the houses beyond.

# CHAPTER 53

Just as Tony was about to pass out, the Hulk's roar shocked him awake. Scathing energy surrounded him; his skin was baking inside his armor. He could feel joints melting, smell circuits frying, both in his own armor and in Rhodey's. Voodoo lay behind them, his eyes and mouth overflowing with power. Tony couldn't tell whether he was conscious or not.

The source of that power glared down at them, mouth twisted in a snarl. The Hulk shrugged his huge shoulders, sending My-ronn the Kree and a few of his friends flying.

Gamora, Rocket, and Groot had pulled back to guard the edge of the parking lot. The cops had retreated too, to take care of their wounded. Cap and Natasha were still picking themselves up, eyeing the Hulk grimly.

The monster glared down at the energy flowing out of his chest. He dipped a finger into it and howled in pain. He flexed a bicep, showing off the World-Breaker armor, and raised his axe in the air.

Tony raised his head to look over the energy stream, staring the Hulk straight in the eye. "Hey, big green," he said, gesturing at the axe. "Everything's a weapon to you, right? The whole world is... war."

A low growl.

"You would have liked my dad," Tony said.

The Hulk hesitated, snorted, and tossed his axe aside. The weapon struck Drax on the head, stunning him, just as he was moving in for another assault. The Kree caught him and hustled him away from the battle.

Then the Hulk staggered closer, growling at the energy linking him to the two metal men, and raised both hands in the air. Tony stared up at those gigantic fingers, watching as they curled into deadly fists. Which, he wondered, will kill me first? The Hulk's two-fisted punch, or the stored energies of a murdered world?

A bright blue boot streaked into view, slamming down onto the pavement between Tony and the Hulk. Tony caught a glimpse of a familiar red and blue costume, with a jagged gold stripe running down the center...

"Heads up, Mister Stark! I mean, Tony!"

Kamala, he realized. It's Kamala!

With a whiff of burning solder, his optical receptors shorted out. All at once he was blind, helpless as he lay on the cracked pavement. The Avengers had retreated, and the Guardians were still playing defense. All that stood between him and the raging monster was one teenage girl, a novice Avenger who'd had her powers for less than a year.

And yet, Tony found himself smiling.

The Hulk roared, stomping both feet. The energy stream linking him to Tony jolted to one side, tugged like a shimmering rope by his heavy, lurching movements.

"Watch out, kid," Tony gasped, twitching as he lay on the ground. "The energy... Don't get in the way of the flow..."

"I know all about the energy," Kamala said.

She danced sideways to avoid the deadly power flow. She'd taken stock of the battlefield on her way in; all the other heroes were either injured, reinforcing the perimeter of the shopping center, or still catching their breath from the last attack. That left a lone girl from Jersey as the last Avenger standing.

"No problem," she muttered out loud. "We got this. I got this! Yes, we're obviously trying to convince *ourselves* of this fact..."

The Hulk turned his attention back to Tony, who had gone still. He seemed to have lost consciousness. But that flow of energy continued, from the Hulk into the two armored Avengers.

The monster roared and raised his fists again. Grimacing, Kamala willed her body to expand, to thin, spreading out through the night air. Then she charged, wrapping herself around the Hulk's massive fists, pinning them together.

The Hulk growled in anger, shaking his bound hands in the air. Kamala flailed, dizzy, struggling to hold on. No use, she realized – he's just too strong! When those fists drew dangerously close to the energy stream, she sprang free, her sheetlike body retreating off into the wind.

She dropped to the ground, willing herself back to her usual shape. The Hulk shook his head in confusion. At least, she thought, I distracted him from Tony. For the moment, anyway.

She glanced over at the street. Rocket, Groot, and Gamora stood guarding the sidewalk, but no one else had arrived yet. No one coming across from the housing project. Where are they? she thought.

The Hulk reached out and grabbed her around the waist. She cried out, twisting to avoid the energy pouring forth from his chest. She willed her body to thin out, contracting enough to slip free, coiling down to land in a pile on the ground. The monster's hands closed on air, and again he screamed in frustration.

As she reverted her body to normal, a heavy hand came down on her shoulder. Captain America had crept up behind her. His cast, she noticed, was gone. Natasha stood just behind him, grimacing.

"Brave work," Cap said. "But you can't take that creature on by yourself."

"I have to," she said, glancing again at the street. "For just a minute or two more."

"Steve." Natasha stepped forward, eyeing the Hulk. "He's gonna go after Tony again."

The Hulk let out another ear-piercing roar.

"Can we distract him?" Natasha asked.

"Love to," Cap replied. "But with what?"

Kamala's eyes went wide. "I know," she said.

Before Cap and the Widow could protest, she turned back to face the Hulk. His armor gleamed in the light from the streetlamps. His flexed muscles were as thick as cables. The energy flaring from him lit the night like a jade beacon.

Furrowing her brow, Kamala concentrated as hard as she could. Her body began to expand in all directions. As her mass increased, her costume shifted along with the molecules of her organic form. The strain of this, she knew, would wear her out, maybe even nullify the power that was still healing her concussion. But there was no time to worry about that, not now. Only one thing mattered.

She had to grow.

When her head was level with the World-Breaker's, she turned to him and screamed, as loud as she could. He whirled around to look, tethered only by that relentless energy stream holding him fixed to Tony Stark. The monster let out a strange, puzzled noise.

Kamala knew she couldn't match the Hulk's strength. She

didn't have his muscle mass, and she wasn't powered by the same extraterrestrial energy. She couldn't mimic that strange armor he wore, either. And she sure couldn't match him for sheer, savage power.

But maybe, she thought, I can be bigger.

As she rose up to tower over him, the Hulk's expression turned to sheer, unstoppable rage. All at once, Kamala realized her mistake. A Hulk-sized opponent was a novelty for the monster, a potential sparring partner. A curiosity.

But an opponent *larger* than himself… that was something the Hulk couldn't bear.

Howling, he turned his armored shoulder toward her and charged. Metal, backed by the strongest muscles on Earth, slammed into her, knocking her off her feet. As she fell, she shrank her body down, knowing that a landing at giant-size might seriously injure her. Even at normal proportions, the impact sent a painful jolt up her shoulder. She shook her head, dazed, looked up…

…and smiled.

Captain America and Natasha had turned to greet three newcomers. Kir-ra and Halla-ar staggered across the parking lot, supporting an old woman between them: their grandmother, Ann-ya. The old woman looked tired, haggard from the ordeal back in the apartment. But determination shone in her eyes.

Kamala smiled. I did it, she thought. I distracted the Hulk… just long enough.

She ran over to help her Kree friends.

# CHAPTER 54

Tony struggled to rise. His armor held him down, half the servos were shorted out, and he was still blind. With considerable effort, he swiveled his armor's half-fused neck joints to survey the scene. Rhodey lay beside him, unmoving. The blazing energy flow still linked the two of them to the looming Hulk. Doctor Voodoo lay on the pavement too, his staff still resting across the two armored men's legs.

The Hulk glared down, a low steady growl issuing from his lips. He seemed confused.

A crunching noise made Tony turn. Ms Marvel and the two Kree, Kir-ra and Halla-ar, moved toward them, along with an old woman who seemed radically out of place in this devastated battleground. The Guardians had begun to gather behind them, along with Drax's Kree friends.

"Ann-ya?" Ms Marvel asked. "Are you–"

"That's far enough." Ann-ya, the old woman, struggled free of her grip. "Let me go!"

As Ann-ya approached the energy flow, a flash of fear crossed her eyes. Then she turned toward the Hulk and took a step forward.

"Stop her," Tony gasped.

"No," Ms Marvel said. "Captain America! Keep everybody back!"

The Guardians, Natasha, the Kree – everyone stopped in their tracks. One by one, they turned to look at Captain America. He paused, shield raised, and shrugged. "You heard her."

Ann-ya picked her way around the energy stream, stepping over the unmoving form of Doctor Voodoo. Her movements were slow but sure, her expression determined and purposeful. She positioned herself in front of the Hulk, just to one side of the gleaming, searing energy flow.

"That power," she said, "the pain. It doesn't belong to you."

The Hulk peered at her, let out a strange, puzzled noise.

"It's *mine.*"

She reached out a hand and, with surprising speed, jabbed it into the Hulk's stomach. He arched, bellowing in pain. The energy flow from the Hulk shifted, whipping and sparking in the air. Tony felt his own pain ease, his armor's temperature dropping as the flow reversed itself. Flowing out of him, out of Rhodey and Doctor Voodoo…

…into Ann-ya. All of it, every ion of mystically charged gamma radiation, surged into the old woman – from Tony and the others, and from the Hulk as well. She gritted her teeth, shrieked, and began to glow.

Natasha swore and started running to rescue the old woman. But Kir-ra and Halla-ar blocked her way.

"No!" Halla-ar said.

Tony's armor began to reboot. He heard a sigh of relief from Rhodey. Groot and Rocket reached out and helped them to their feet.

"Is Earth always like this?" Rocket asked.

"I am Groot…"

"No, no, I kind of like it."

The Hulk's emerald halo, too, was weakening. The World-Breaker armor – on his shoulders, across his chest – began to waver. As they watched, it softened and retracted back into his body.

"Quill was right," Natasha said, stepping back to watch. "That is kind of gross."

Ann-ya cried out again – a high, human noise – as all the rage, the pain of a lost world flowed into and through her.

"No," Halla-ar said, "I can't…" He started toward his grandmother, but Kir-ra held him back.

"She has to do this," Kir-ra said. "You know she does."

Ms Marvel strode up on extended legs and touched Halla-ar's shoulder. He grabbed her hand, almost hungrily, and together they stared at the blinding-white form of his grandmother. Tears welled up in his eyes.

The Hulk seemed to recede, shrinking down to his normal seven feet in height. The World-Breaker axe shimmered and vanished. His howls grew quieter, like the cries of a dying animal.

The Guardians' ship came swooping down out of the darkness. Tony squinted. Was that a *man* on its wing…?

"Get me lower, Quill," Drax the Destroyer yelled. "Lower!"

A chime told Tony his armor was fully mobile again. He realized something else, too: a weight seemed to have lifted, a burden of rage and guilt. The rage of the Master, gone along with the death-power of Praeterus. He watched the last of the energy sputter out of his chestplate, wafting almost casually into the old Kree woman's body. All he could see within the glow was the outline of her face, sharp high cheekbones topped by hollow eyes.

Gamora joined them, staring into the glow. "Here we go again," she whispered, so quietly Tony could barely hear it.

As the ship soared by overhead, Drax leaped off the wing.

Ann-ya howled again, louder than ever. The energy flared, threatening to burst free of her. "Um," Rhodey said. "Is, uh, is that supposed to happen?"

Drax landed on the Hulk's shoulders and brought down both fists on his head.

Tony sat up in alarm, but Doctor Voodoo was already on his feet, lunging forward with his Legba staff raised. The staff jabbed into Ann-ya's form, and for a moment, unimaginable energies danced on its surface. Voodoo grimaced and held firm. The energies of Praeterus, the last remnants of the dead world, surged through the staff.

Then, all at once, the energy was gone.

The Hulk cried out and fell.

Ann-ya collapsed next to him.

The shopping center was suddenly, shockingly quiet. Smoke rose from the shattered garbage truck, the grocery store, from the sparking stumps of uprooted lampposts. Cops moved in cautiously, shining flashlights into corners, whispering baffled questions to each other.

Rocket, Groot, and the Kree workers gathered around Drax, staring at the fallen Hulk. Captain America, Natasha, and War Machine soon joined them. Quill brought the Guardians' ship around to yet another shaky landing.

By the time he arrived, the Hulk was no more. Bruce Banner lay on the pavement, face down.

"Captain," Drax said, "should we help your oddly pale friend?"

Cap and Natasha exchanged quick glances. "Thank you," Cap said to Drax, and together they took hold of Banner's arms.

A few feet away, Halla-ar knelt over the body of his grandmother. Ms Marvel stood with him, resting a hand casually on his back. Tony and Kir-ra watched, with Voodoo and Gamora behind them in the shadows.

"She's gone," Halla-ar said.

"She paid," Kir-ra said, squeezing Tony's hand. "She paid for what she did."

"I'm sorry." Tony turned to face her. "I'm sorry, Kir-ra. I didn't know – didn't understand what you'd been through." He flashed a sympathetic smile at Gamora. "You too, I think."

Gamora nodded and turned away.

Tony turned to Voodoo. "What did you... Uh, where did all the energy go?"

"To *his* realm. The devil who set all this in motion." Voodoo held up his staff. "I hope it will keep him busy for a while."

"*I* hope it hurts," Gamora said quietly. Kir-ra gave her a quick, knowing glance.

Rhodey staggered up, wearing a civilian jumpsuit. He carried his armor's smoking remains in both hands. "Tony," he said. "Let's never do this again, huh?"

Tony smiled.

As the first rays of dawn rose over the housing project, he cast a long gaze around at the assembled heroes. Some were of Earth, some hailed from far-off worlds; some practiced magic, while others, like himself, wielded the power of technology to perform miracles. Some had asked for their abilities, others had had strange powers thrust upon them. And still others – including Kir-ra, Halla-ar, and the terrestrial police – had no special powers at all.

But they'd all come together today, to stop a tragedy from repeating itself. To avenge the death of an innocent world.

Today they were all Avengers.

"Come on, people. It's a new day." He started off toward the Guardians' ship, waving for the others to follow. "Let's see if we can get this one right."

The Hood darted through the courtyard of the housing project, keeping to the shadows. The sun was just rising; floodlamps were winking off. With luck, he'd be gone before full light.

The plan had failed. Somehow the Avengers, with their assorted extraterrestrial allies, had managed to bring down the World-Breaker. Jericho Drumm had broken the Master's hold on his brother, while that stupid Kree woman had snapped Tony Stark free of Daniel's conditioning.

Even more disturbing, to the Hood, was the fact that he could no longer feel the Master's presence. Did that mean the Master had no further need of him? Or had something gone catastrophically wrong in that other realm, beyond the dimensional veil?

No matter. The Master was near-omnipotent; he had conquered his own realm, and could draw on all its stored energy. That made him stronger than any entity in *this* dimension. He would be back, soon enough, and the Hood would once again–

"Well, well. Parker Robbins, right?"

He rounded a corner. Jennifer Walters, the She-Hulk, stood before him in a crisp burgundy business suit and sensible heels, carrying a briefcase in one hand.

"Easy, Robbins." She smiled. "I just came to serve some papers."

He eyed the briefcase. It was a nice case, he noted, made of real leather with jeweled clasps. The sort of briefcase a person with money would carry.

"Yeah?" he sneered, putting on his best tough-guy attitude.

"Yeah." She cocked her head, still smirking. "But since we're here…"

The last thing he saw was her emerald-green fist flying toward his face.

# CHAPTER 55

The daycare room was almost bare. Most of the toys had been packed up and moved out of the Kree barracks, leaving only a couple of mats on the concrete floor. Gamora and Halla-ar circled the room, holding up wooden practice swords, each eyeing the other for an advantage.

"Be the aggressor," Gamora said. "Don't let your enemy think he's better than you, even for a moment."

"Like this?" Halla-ar launched himself across the room.

Gamora took a half step back, raised an eyebrow, and grabbed him out of the air. Using his own weight against him, she twisted him sideways and down, pressing the flat of her sword against his chest. His sword clattered away, and he landed on the mat, barely raising his arms in time to protect his head.

"Like that," she agreed. "But it helps to have the skills, too."

"I hope we'll have lots of time to practice," he said.

Gamora didn't answer. She was staring at the corner of the room, where a single toy had been left behind: a familiar wind-up robot with a worn, painted smile. Its legs moved slowly, head bumping again and again against the wall.

A rumble of voices from outside. "I think the speech is starting," Halla-ar said.

Gamora ignored him. She picked up the robot and examined it. Its stubby legs pumped in the air.

"What are you doing?" he asked.

She wound the robot with a few rapid strokes and set it back down, facing the center of the room. It whirred and began to march, steady and firm on its feet.

"Learning to live with failure," she whispered.

She couldn't tell if he'd heard her. He eyed the door anxiously. "We should, uh, probably go join– "

"You're going to have my back, right? That's the idea?"

His eyes went wide. He nodded vigorously. She tossed the practice sword to him, and he snatched it easily out of the air.

"Again," she said.

"Gentlemen, ladies, and non-binary sentients! Earth people and Kree, Guardians, Destroyers, and oh, all right, my fellow Avengers too…"

Tony paused, standing on top of the table, surveying the crowd that had gathered in the dining area. Captain America and the Black Widow sat in folding chairs near the back – one arm each around Bruce Banner, who looked badly shaken. James Rhodes was with them, his armor newly repaired; at the word "Avengers", he cocked his hand into a gun and mock-fired it at Tony.

"…I'd like to welcome you to the last-ever gathering in the so-called Stark Long Island Employee Services building."

A cheer went up from the Kree, who formed most of the audience. My-ronn led the applause, raising his fist. Drax watched his friend for a moment, frowning, then howled out a cheer that drowned out all the other voices.

"This structure was originally built to house munitions," Tony continued. "As many of you know, I swore off that business some years ago. I can't tell you how sad and angry it made me to learn that this facility had been repurposed, by rogue forces within my company, into something equally vile."

Jennifer Walters sat alone, jotting notes on her phone. She looked up once, then returned to her work.

"I was negligent," Tony acknowledged, "and many of you here paid the price. I'm sorry for that. I want you to know I've redoubled my efforts–"

"DOOO YOUR WORRRK!" Peter Quill yelled, cupping his hands like a megaphone. Next to him, in the front row, Rocket burst out laughing. Groot covered his eyes in embarrassment.

"That's… Thank you, Quill. That's what I'm trying to do. Just, uh, on an unrelated note, when are you going back to space again?"

"SOOOOOOON!"

Even Groot smiled at that one.

"Well, buddy, I can honestly say planet Earth will be a lot quieter in your absence. As for this facility… well, it's seen better days." He gestured up at the roof – or, rather, where the roof had been. "In a mere forty-eight hours – sooner, if the movers get finished – this old eyesore will be torn down. In its place, we'll be building a brand-new modern facility that will truly provide Employee Support. This will include cutting-edge health services, true daycare with adequate staffing, and unlimited… cronuts? I'm reliably informed that those are the favorite Earth food of the Kree. Is that correct?"

"Yeah!" My-ronn yelled, shaking his fist again.

"Good. Yeah. As for your living accommodations: the movers have already packed up most of your gear. All of you, the Kree

I mean, will be housed in Stark Manhattan hotels for the time being, or in the location of your choice."

Murmurs of approval. Natasha smiled at him. Jennifer gave him a cautious nod. Groot said, "I am Groot," which Tony chose to take as an expression of support.

"As for the costumed among us… I'd like to thank every one of you, Avenger and Guardian alike, who stood together with us last night. A special shout-out to our very newest Avenger, who not only went toe-to-toe with the World-Breaker Hulk, but did it in the most bone-chilling way conceivable: by imitating his horrific face…"

He searched the crowd and finally located Ms Marvel, sitting in a back corner with Kir-ra. They were whispering urgently, engaged in some intense conversation – not listening to his speech at all. He felt unreasonably annoyed.

He took a deep breath and moved on. "As for me, I've made a lot of mistakes in my time. This place, this situation, was one of the worst. And, well… this is probably the theme of my life, but I just want to thank you all for giving me a second chance." He paused. "For what it's worth, I promise that the Kree will be treated fairly and equitably by Stark Enterprises from this day forward. And to that end…"

He glanced at the women again. Still talking.

"…I'll be counting on my new Employee Liaison, Kir-ra of the Kree, to keep me honest."

All eyes turned to Kir-ra. She stopped in mid-sentence, startled.

"Whah?" she said.

After Tony finished his talk, the crowd went its own ways. Kamala stayed with Kir-ra. She was really starting to like the Kree woman.

"...really sprang that on me," Kir-ra said. "What do I know about being a lee... liaze–"

"Liaison," Kamala said. "Well, Tony likes to do things like that. But he usually knows what he's talking about."

"He's very arrogant," Kir-ra grumbled. "Oh, look out."

They veered aside as a group of movers crossed the floor, pushing a hand truck covered with packed boxes. Other groups bustled around, stacking up folding chairs and breaking down the picnic-style tables that filled the dining room.

"I think there's two kinds of rich people," Kamala began, "on this planet, anyway. There's the pampered, isolated ones that don't have to listen to anyone else. And then there's the pampered, isolated ones that don't have to listen to anyone else, but sometimes they can be shamed. Tony's definitely the second kind."

"That's... wow. That's profound." Kir-ra shot her a look. "How old are you again?"

They walked outside. Construction vehicles prowled around, removing bits of rubble. At this rate the area would be cleared ahead of schedule, and the rebuilding could begin.

They came to the Guardians' ship, where Peter Quill was hauling a box of extremely used cassette tapes up the gangplank. He looked as happy as any man Kamala had ever seen. Drax followed, lugging a comically large suitcase with a big sticker on it that read EARTH. Groot emerged from the ship and stretched out his limbs to help them.

"So," Rocket said, following Groot over to Drax. "You're back on the team?"

"Yes," Drax said.

"What about your new family? The purpose you found, the debt you owed to the people that saved your life?"

Drax shrugged. "I have done enough. Debt paid."

"Drax?" Gamora walked up to join them, with Halla-ar just behind. "You believe you've fulfilled your purpose?"

"In this place, yes," Drax said. "And you?"

"No. Not yet."

"Nor I." Halla-ar frowned. "We have not found the true killer of Praeterus. My grandmother was merely its pawn."

"There's somethin' suspicious about that reward the Kree are offering," Rocket said. "I think we ought to look into that." He followed Groot and Drax into the ship.

Halla-ar stepped up onto the gangplank, then stopped. He turned to look back down at his sister.

"So you've decided?" Kir-ra asked.

"Yes," he said. "I'm going with them."

Kamala had known this was coming, but still, her heart sank a little. She realized she'd been hoping Halla-ar would change his mind, decide to stay on Earth. Was that stupid? she wondered.

"The gods have played tricks on us, brother." Kir-ra stared off, a distant look in her eyes. "I always wanted to be a warrior. You were an artist. Now you're going off to fight, maybe, and I'm going to be a lie… a lee-eyez—"

"Liaison," Kamala said.

Kir-ra sighed. "But you must live your own life."

"I hate you," Halla-ar said.

"Hate you too," Kir-ra said softly. Then she turned away and started to walk off.

"Hey!" Halla-ar called, running down onto the ground.

Kir-ra stopped and turned.

"I really do hate you," he said, tears forming in his eyes. "I mean, a whole lot."

She smiled. "I know." Then she turned to Gamora and said "Take care of him. I mean it. Or that sword won't save you next time."

Gamora raised an eyebrow, nodding.

The ship began to rumble, shaking the ground. Kamala stumbled, grabbing at the gangplank railing for support. When she looked up, Kir-ra was gone.

Gamora started up the plank. "Peter's warming up the engines," she said, pausing inside the hatch. "Be quick."

Then they were alone, just the two of them. Suddenly, Kamala couldn't think of a thing to say to this boy, this stranger she'd grown so close to, so quickly.

"I'm sorry," Halla-ar said, taking a step up the plank. "I have to do this."

"Don't apologize." She stretched up to face him. "You did good, you know? You helped save... well, the Earth."

"I had a good teacher. Speaking of which, I won't miss that school." They both laughed. "But I will miss you."

"Oh! I almost forgot." She reached into her pocket and pulled out the talisman – the mystic eye they'd used to locate the planet-killer. "I still don't know what this thing is. But it's yours."

"Keep it," he said. "I've got a weird feeling you're the one that's gonna need it."

She nodded, frowning.

"I think..." He paused, gathering his thoughts. "I think I can be both, you know? A warrior and an artist."

She forced herself to smile. "I think you can be anything you want."

"Will you tell my sister that? She might need to hear it."

"Of course."

"That reminds me..."

He reached into his pocket and handed her a crumpled sheet of paper. She took it, frowned, and unfolded it. It was the sketch of her as Ms Marvel, the one he'd drawn in the courtyard the night before.

She smiled, wiping a tear from her eye. "Thank you," she said. She leaned up to give him a goodbye hug–

–just as Peter Quill appeared in the hatchway. "Time to go, spaceboy!"

The ship's engines grew louder. Halla-ar gave Kamala a quick, apologetic smile. She touched his hand briefly, then sprinted down off the gangplank. When she reached a safe distance, she stopped and turned, suddenly eager for a last look at this boy. A strange sadness came over her, as if she were losing something she'd never really had to begin with.

"So you're an artist!" Peter Quill wrapped his arm around Halla-ar's shoulders, leading him inside. "I got creative urges too, you know. I always wanted to be a songwriter."

"Yeah?" Halla-ar asked.

"Yeah. Hey, maybe we could work together! You know – you know how people love those greeting cards with songs in 'em? Like with dogs, and babies and bunnies and crap? Oh, that's it. That is IT. You can draw the cards and I'll write the songs! This is gonna be great…"

Kamala shook her head, stifling a laugh. Five minutes later, when the ship finally vanished into the sky, she was still smiling.

Kir-ra found Tony on the pier, near the Avengers' quinjet, saying goodbye to his teammates. In his crisp three-piece suit, he looked like a different man than the armored zombie she'd battled just hours before.

The Hulk looked even more different. Bruce Banner grimaced,

adjusting his glasses. "Sorry again, about all the…" He flexed his lean muscles and mimed a roar.

"My fault," Natasha said. "It was my call."

"Bruce. *Doctor Banner.*" Tony waited for him to look up. "When we bring you in, we know the risks. We just didn't count on some old bat with the stored power of a dead planet, this time."

"That *was* a long shot," Banner acknowledged.

"Things took a bad bounce," Captain America said. "Next time'll be different."

"Next time?" Rhodey asked. "Next time maybe you can give me a little more advance warning."

"Promise," Tony replied. "Assuming I'm not under the influence of voodoo."

Rhodey smiled, snapped his helmet shut, and took off into the sky. Natasha crossed to Tony, gave him a quick hug, and said "We're off too." She beckoned to Banner. Together, they started toward the quinjet.

Cap lingered. "Speaking of Voodoo…"

"The doc's vanished." Tony frowned. "Think he's gone looking for his dead brother. I'm a little worried what he might find."

"And the Hood?"

"In custody, but he's not talking."

Cap grimaced. "This isn't over, is it?"

"It is for now." Tony held out his hand. "Thanks, Cap."

Cap nodded, then turned to Kir-ra. "Ma'am," he said, tipping an imaginary hat in her direction. Then he turned and sprinted across the pier, to the quinjet.

Kir-ra stood with Tony, watching as the jet lifted up into the sky. "You know," he said, "I really think this is going to be a new beginning."

She said nothing.

"I mean it," he continued. "I feel much more in control of things now, ready to move forward. My god, I'm a lucky– "

"Liaison?" she said.

He turned to her, blinked.

"I am not going to be your lapdog," she said. "Your… rubber stamp? A friendly face on a bad situation."

"I wouldn't dream of it," he said. "I want you to solve these problems. The resources of Stark International are at your disposal."

"OK, then. What about where my people are going to live? Those hotel vouchers are only good for a month."

"I – well – they're going to be making considerably more money now, so–"

"They still need help. You can't just expect people to build themselves new lives in a foreign place, with no assistance whatsoever."

He turned to face her directly, a smile playing at his lips. "You did."

"I did. But I'm one person, not three hundred and eighty-four. That's not the way immigration works."

"Point taken. F.R.I.D.A.Y.?" He cocked his head, listening to a voice in his earpiece. "Add a couple decimal points to the Kree redevelopment fund. Scratch that; no limit." He turned back to Kir-ra. "Happy?"

"I'm getting there."

He did smile, then. A charming smile, she thought; one that had probably melted a lot of hearts.

"You may only be one person," he said, "but you're a very impressive one. Maybe we could have dinner tonight? Discuss your salary and perks over a fine Bordeaux?"

"That's a generous offer." She took a step back. "But my attorney will be handling those negotiations."

"That's right," Jennifer Walters said, striding out onto the pier. "And my client does not come cheap."

"Attorney," Tony repeated. "Ah. Of course."

"Just looking out for my clients, Tony." Jen raised an eyebrow. "Get me a deal memo ay-sap on the liaison thing, and we'll hash out the deets. In the meantime, let's keep this on a professional level, OK?"

"Yes, counselor." He stepped back, raising his hands in surrender. "Message received."

"Dinner's at your discretion," Jen said, leaning in to Kir-ra. "But if he makes the smallest move out of line, you let me know."

"I'm not worried," Kir-ra replied. "He's the kind that can be shamed."

Jen shrugged, patted Kir-ra on the shoulder, and turned on her heel to leave. "And don't sign anything!"

When she was gone, Tony flashed Kir-ra a quick, embarrassed smile. Then he turned and walked slowly to the end of the pier. She followed, avoiding the rubble left from yesterday's battle. That seemed like a long time ago.

"What do you see now?" he asked, staring out over the water.

"I'm not sure," she frowned. "I'm glad you caught the Hood, but my brother says we haven't found the true killer. The power that destroyed my planet, took over your mind and infiltrated your company, and tried to devastate your world as well."

"Yeah. We got the hitman, but not the mob boss."

All at once, her training kicked in. She detected a sudden rise in his heartrate, a fear-scent filling the air.

"You know something," she said.

"Maybe."

When he turned to face her, the look in his eyes chilled her to the bone.

"I hope I'm wrong," he said.

# SIX DAYS LATER

# EPILOGUE

This time it wasn't a yeti; it was a sludge monster. By the time Kamala fought it off, chased it back into the sewers, and sealed all the surrounding manholes, the sun was setting over Grove Street. She had a layer of slime on her that a half-dozen towels couldn't manage to wipe off.

If she went straight home, she could take a nice, long shower. But that would involve making up a story for her parents, who didn't know about her Ms Marvel identity. She couldn't handle that right now, so she cleaned up her costume as well as she could and did one last sweep to ensure she hadn't missed anything.

She found herself wondering about Halla-ar. Where was he right now? Living a life of swashbuckling adventure, fighting off hostile aliens alongside the Guardians? Or just holed up in a cramped spaceship cabin, drawing pictures of greeting-card bunnies?

Eventually she realized she'd wandered all the way to the abandoned shopping center across the street from the housing complex. The place where the Avengers and the Guardians, along with the Kree, had battled World-Breaker Hulk for the future of the planet.

"I think my subconscious is playing tricks on me," she muttered to herself.

She picked her way across the cracked pavement, under the flickering streetlamps. The stores were completely roped off, the half-collapsed buildings surrounded by sawhorses and police tape. Even the pizza parlor was dark, she noted sadly.

She perched on one of the few intact stone benches, still thinking of Halla-ar. And of Bruno, too. That kiss seemed less important than before; they were getting back to being friends again.

*That's all I'm ready for right now*, she realized. *With anyone.*

"Oh, man," a voice said. "The brooding costumed hero, preoccupied with some deep personal drama?"

Kamala leaped to her feet, stretching her neck all the way around. A lean red and blue figure dropped down from the streetlamp on a line of thick gooey cord.

"I *invented* that jam!" Spider-Man said.

Kamala blinked "Spi… Spi…" she said. "Spider-Man?"

"The one and only. Well, except for the one who hangs out in Brooklyn. You're a friend of his, right?"

"Yeah," Kamala said. She and Miles had worked together a few times.

She tried to keep her voice casual. But she'd never met O.G. Spider-Man before, and while she hated to admit it, it was kind of a thrill. Like getting to meet some old rock star – Mick Jagger, maybe, or Madonna.

"Real talk, kid," Spidey said. "This is no coincidence. We came here to find you."

She frowned. "We?"

He turned and gestured off into the distance, toward the police barricades. In the shadows, she could just barely make out a shifting red cloak moving against the darkness.

"What is that thing?" she asked. "I've seen it before. Across the street from here – in the projects–"

The cloak turned toward her. A human figure emerged slowly from the darkness, clad in the red and blue robes of Doctor Strange. She let out a little surprised noise.

Spider-Man sighed. "He does that to people."

"Ms Marvel," Strange said. "I have need of you."

"You…" She frowned, reached into her back pocket. "You're the one that left this for me," she said, holding up the eye talisman. "You helped us track the World-Breaker energy back to Halla-ar's grandmother."

"I did."

"Wait a minute." Her eyes grew wide. "Is this the Eye of Agamotto?"

A gentle smile crossed Strange's lips. "*This* is the Eye of Agamotto," he said, touching a talisman at his throat. "What you hold is a lesser charm: the Eye of Vouk. A sort of cousin to my own."

"And… and you– "

"I'd hoped that Stark and the Guardians could defeat our enemy's plans. With your help, they did manage to prevent the World-Breaker from wreaking havoc – and, in the process, they dealt the enemy a serious setback. But he will recover; this I know from long experience. Which means I must take more direct action." He paused. "I must gather a team of champions. A sort of Shadow Avengers–"

"He says that like he *hasn't* been practicing the name for weeks," Spidey said.

"–to battle this would-be devil on his own playing field: the murk, the ether. The crawlspaces of reality; the shadows between the worlds."

"Whoa. Hold on." Kamala's head was spinning. "What does this thing *want*? Why did it set up the Hulk, the World-Breaker guy, to turn the planet into mashed potatoes?"

"Earth has unique defenses," Strange explained. "All that you experienced, beginning with the destruction of Praeterus, was designed to lead to this. Cripple our world, and the invasion would become easier."

"Invasion? Of what? What's left after you get rid of the Earth?"

"Why, our entire realm. All that we know of as reality."

She sat down on the bench, stunned.

"I don't think you want me on *that* team," she said.

"That's what I told him!" Spider-Man said. "About myself, I mean."

"I'm serious," she said. "I'm more of a local-hero type. I've hardly ever been out of this city."

"You stood up to the Hulk," Strange said. "Only a handful of people can make that claim."

Spider-Man nodded. He pointed both index fingers at Strange, then at himself. Then, slowly, he turned and pointed at her.

"What..." She shook her head. "What is this 'enemy,' anyway? The Hood, Halla-ar's grandma, Doctor Voodoo – they all made deals with it. Is it, I don't know, the Devil? Is there really such a thing?"

"He is not the Devil of myth," Strange said, "though it pleases him to present himself as such. It allows him to spread fear, to crush rebellions and extend his rule over conquered peoples."

"OK." She felt a bit of relief. "So he isn't the Devil. What is he, then? What's his name?"

Spider-Man straightened up, eyeing Strange. The sorcerer stood tall, backlit by the streetlamp; at his chest, the Eye of Agamotto pulsed once. He's the guardian of our realm, Kamala thought. She could almost see the threats, the monsters, the creatures of scales and flame waiting to squirm in through the shadows, blocked only by this one man.

"His name," Doctor Strange said, "is Dormammu."

# ACKNOWLEDGMENTS

This book was written during a particularly strange and trying time – not for me in particular, but for the entire planet. Hopefully you're reading this in some near-future utopia of jetpacks, flying cars, and ubiquitous vaccinations, and have no idea what I'm talking about. But because these things matter, here are the people who contributed to – and helped keep me sane during – the writing of *Target: Kree*.

My family: Mom, Jeff, Kathy, Robyn, and Rosemary. Honorable mention. FaceTime, which kept us all together.

The helpful, accommodating people of Aconyte – especially Marc, who asked me to play with all these wonderful toys and then cleared the path; and Gwen, who shaped the manuscript and pushed me to flesh out the characters, especially Ms Marvel. I also want to note Anjuli and the ever-helpful Ness who, as I write this, is still struggling to deal with my silly American bank.

The Marvel gang! Jeff and Caitlin, you're just a few miles away, but it might as well be a continent. Hope to see you soon.

A quick blanket thank you to *21st Century Technology,*

including the Marvel Unlimited app and Disney+, both of which supplied quick, invaluable reference for this book.

The amazing crew at AHOY, who provide emotional support while they eat up so much of my freelance time: Tom, Hart, Frank, David, Deron, Sarah, Kit, Lillian, Hanna, Cory, and Rob.

All the friends who offered advice on writing and business – or just emotional support – at a time when reaching out was harder than usual. In no particular order: Marie, Alex, Shawna, Axel, Keith, Lauren, Bob G, Alisa, and a few dozen others I'm blanking on right this second. Sorry! I'll catch you next time!

The local breweries: Folksbier, Svendale, and Threes. Look them up when you're in Brooklyn! They are the best!

Our stupid cats, Rocko and Bebe. The only creatures I know who actually enjoyed the lockdown, because they had us all to themselves.

And of course my partner, Liz Sonneborn. I can't imagine a better quarantine buddy, in this or any other galaxy. Love you always.

*Stuart Moore*
*Brooklyn, New York*
*April 2021*

# ABOUT THE AUTHOR

STUART MOORE is a writer, fiction editor, and a multiple award-winning comics editor. His many novels include *X-Men: The Dark Phoenix Saga*, *The Zodiac Legacy* (created and cowritten by Stan Lee), and *Thanos: Death Sentence*. He has recently written comics such as Deadpool the Duck, Batman, and EGOs. Stuart is the former editor of the Marvel prose novel line, founding editor of Vertigo, and of several other comic imprints

*stuartmoorewriter.com*
*twitter.com/stuartmoore1*

# MARVEL XAVIER'S INSTITUTE

*The next generation of the X-Men strive to master
their mutant powers and defend the world from evil.*

# MARVEL HEROINES

*Showcasing Marvel's incredible female Super
Heroes in their own action-packed adventures.*

# MARVEL LEGENDS OF ASGARD

*Mighty heroes do battle with monsters of myth to defend the honor of Asgard and the Ten Realms.*

# MARVEL UNTOLD

*Discover the untold tales and hidden sides of Marvel's greatest heroes and most notorious villains.*

# WORLD EXPANDING FICTION

## *Do you have them all?*